A WOMAN WITH A *Voice*

ISBN: 978-1-7356327-0-4 (Paperback)
ISBN: 978-1-7356327-1-1 (Ebook)

Printed in the United States of America.
First printed edition 2020.

Worlds Unknown Publishers
2515 E Thomas Rd,
Ste 16 -1061
Phoenix, AZ 85016-7946

www.wupubs.com

A WOMAN WITH A
Voice

Joan Cheboswony

Worlds Unknown Publishers

Love is sweet, sour, bitter, hot, and salty;
an excellent balance of everything.

To Family

Tom, Linda, Joy, Asenath and Renee. It was because of your inspiration and encouragement that this book was written.

For culture

When I travelled out of my village in Kenya, I was exposed to new tastes and experiences which has expanded my worldview. I have learned and appreciate so much about other cultures, different from that of my own.

CHAPTER 1

The Letter

"MEGGIE, I KNOW YOU'RE UPSET," Linda began.

"Upset?" Meggie raised her voice with an ironic smirk on her face.

"Whatever Meggie wants, she gets regardless of all obstacles. Remember? What happened to your rules of life—living unafraid and confident? You manage your life like a billion- dollar corporation with sophisticated risk-management strategies. You're not going through a fatal surgery. My friend, you'll survive." Linda raised her voice with a stern reprimand as she reminded Meggie of her own principles. She stood so close to her friend that she could smell her breath and hear the rhythm of her breathing. "When did you become a doormat pygmy? Eh! Now is the time to be creative." She gave Meggie a tight hug. They stayed still for a while, crying silently.

The two clinical officers, Linda and Meggie, were in Meggie's office at the Rift Valley Provincial Hospital in Nakuru, Kenya. Meggie handed her best friend and work colleague a rejection letter from the U.S.–Kenya academic exchange program—Meggie's final hope for post-graduate medical training.

Meggie and Linda began work at the hospital about the same time, two and a half years earlier. Meggie also pursued a public health path with an epidemiological emphasis. "I know your approach to life is atypical," Linda told her friend. "You're a bold risk-taker. I've seen you stand up to challenges in a decisive manner." Smiling at Meggie, Linda said, "I respect the fact that you're not afraid of making mistakes. You often leave your comfort zone to explore new adventures."

Meggie listened, but her slouched posture showed her attitude to be one of defeat. Meggie's father encouraged her to pursue medicine. After a career in general medicine, he transitioned to a leadership role as the chief executive officer at the hospital where both women worked. He helped the institution look to the future by providing cost-effective, exceptional medical care.

When Linda looked at Meggie, she saw tears streaming down her face. "Hey," Linda said gently, "something will turn up. You're a fighter. You've come this far!"

"I put everything into my applications. The horse was right by the water, but I couldn't make him drink," Meggie said, sighing heavily.

"You're a tough cookie. You've overcome worse disasters. The universe is not done with you," Linda insisted. "Many people assume that guiding principles are only for institutions, businesses, and organizations, but not you, Meggie. You live by your principles. I've known you long enough to recite them," she said. "The first is a focus on family. Second is integrity. The third is a positive, hopeful, and growth-minded mindset. Fourth is self-leadership, the propelling factor. Fifth, you believe in community and collaboration to expand your horizons to your local community and beyond. You identify those who were also champions for the same cause. Sixth, you take a wholistic approach that helps you understand how things fit into a broader context. And most importantly, you get things done. Nothing comes out of doing nothing. Do I have that right?"

Meggie looked at her friend with weary eyes and nodded.

"Get a grip," Linda said, handing Meggie some tissues as they settled in their chairs.

"You don't understand. I spent countless hours completing the admission and grant applications to the United States, Canada, and Australia–Kenya Education Exchange programs and another three Kenya government grant programs. Then, I completed all the essays, and interviews, over many sleepless nights. The rejection hurt so badly. My dreams are dashed." She covered her eyes with her hands and bawled.

Linda listened attentively and looked directly at Meggie. "You left out the one you really wanted from China, only that Mandarin was an outright disqualifier," Linda responded, empathetically, and Meggie smiled through the tears. "Ever since I met the two American epidemiological researchers, Cheryl and Willy, I felt compelled to move into the public health field—working with nongovernmental organizations focusing on infectious diseases."

"I know," Linda acknowledged.

"But I never told you what fascinated me. I learned from them that in America, the National Malaria Education Program, which began in 1947, became a success within four years. Can you imagine? Why is malaria still a major killer here in Kenya, more than sixty years later? Eh! I want to be part of the solution to this problem. Several people told me that I could advance in the public health field. So, I did my research, and applied to programs and grants within Kenya and abroad."

"Hey, I know how hard you worked at this. I'm sorry that for once in your life, you were not successful. There will be other opportunities. Remember, a 'no' is not the end of the road, rather a corner that requires some rethinking and re-calibration to get to your destination. You've done it before. Do you recall that incident in high school? The principal placed you in a music class but you wanted to be in the textile-design class?" Linda asked.

"Of course, I remember," Meggie responded, miffed that Linda was trying to steer the conversation in a new direction.

"You stood your ground, literally, outside the principal's office for two days. She gave in eventually. Remember? More opportunities are out there, but you might not be able to see them now," Linda reminded her. "Your current situation is simply an opportunity to explore other avenues. And, of course, you would be telling me this if I were in your shoes right now."

Meggie took a breath, shrugged her shoulders, and straightened in her chair. "You're right. This isn't the end of the world, after all," Meggie said, fiddling with the tissues in her lap as she tried to pull herself together.

"Let's get cleaned up, before someone accuses me of instigating trouble for you," Linda said, joking. Meggie had a strong personality. Her father had taught her that it is weak to show emotions. It was unlike her to cry even in very tough situations.

"Forget about me, what's going on with you and Willy?" Meggie asked to change the subject.

"It's nothing serious. Why are you interested?" Linda laughed sheepishly to lighten the mood.

"Hell, no! I will remain among those people in their thirties wondering why they're still single," Meggie said. Her chin jutted out defiantly.

"Let me guess. You're a hyper-risk manager of love. Your risk-management plan is love-proof. Instead of a plan to reduce risk to a certain level, you have eliminated love altogether." Linda was teasing, but Meggie bristled.

"Are you saying that I'm not capable of love?" Meggie asked.

"No. No. Love will find a way when you don't expect it, and you have to be ready to enjoy the ride. Don't be afraid," she said.

Meggie's ringing phone interrupted their conversation.

"I need to take this. See you later," Meggie said as Linda nodded and walked out of her office.

"Thank you for calling Rift Valley General Provincial Hospital. Dr. Meggie Jepchumba; speaking. How may I help you?"

"How are you doing today, Meggie?" her mom, Libby, asked.

Meggie's shoulders began to droop. "Not good. I just received a rejection letter from Harvard. All of my applications were rejected. I'm discouraged," she said downheartedly.

"I know how disappointed you are, dear. Things will get better. Let's keep working on it. I'll organize additional options to explore."

Because Meggie was an only child born to career parents, her mother was indulgent in providing love and varied experiences for her. She sometimes was overprotective, trying to solve all of Meggie's problems, and was disappointed when things didn't go well for her daughter. Too often, she invaded Meggie's space.

"I know that I should stop feeling sorry for myself and develop a plan of action, but I'm not quite ready to do that. I need more time to think through my options and sulk a bit. What about you, mom?" Meggie asked.

"Your dad and all the others are doing well. This Saturday everyone is coming for dinner at six o'clock."

"Yes, I know. I'll be there at ten o'clock in the morning to help with the cooking—our usual routine when we have dinner guests."

"Perfect. Remember, it's not the dinner that counts but the memory of the meal and the people."

I know this mantra, mom. And, I agree. The people are the focus, but we still have to prepare a welcoming feast."

Meggie's parents lived in a villa nestled in the leafy gated community of Milimani Nakuru, a suburb in Nakuru, was built on a hill. It was a ten-minute drive from the hospital offering its affluent residents panoramic valley views of the city center and Lake Nakuru National Park. Their house with five bedrooms, seven bathrooms, and a housekeeper's residence had a well-manicured garden and an Olympic-sized swimming pool. The lower level of the house contained the housekeeper's residence, a small kitchen, and a wine cellar. The second level featured a cloakroom, a family room with a fireplace, and a dining room. All the bedrooms were on the third floor. The open floorplan on the ground floor led to a spacious covered patio, where the family entertained relatives and friends.

Meggie's mom had designed this, their Monday through Friday workday residence. She wanted her home to be a testimony to her work. As a work-from-home architectural consultant, her clients were impressed with the magic she brought to her creations.

Meggie's parents spent most of their weekends and holidays in their rural home. On this continuous 105 acres of land in the Eldama Ravine, they had thirty acres of exquisite flat tillable cropland, and forty acres of pasture land. A natural spring ran through the valley, that had fifteen wooded acres filled with quality timber. Her mom also designed this country home with four bedrooms, three baths, a detached two-car garage, and a large storage building.

Despite the beauty of the two homes, Meggie loved her independence and moved out on her own as soon as she could afford to do so. However, one of Meggie's core principles was that family came first. She spent a lot of time with her parents in their home during the weekends and dinners during the week—if time allowed. Meggie lived in a gated two-bedroom apartment in Nakuru, five minutes from the hospital. Young professionals lived in this area of the city, particularly those who worked at the hospital. It offered an urban feel with many bars, restaurants, fitness centers, and coffee shops—perfect for entertainment and with many conveniences.

When she arrived at her parents' country home at Eldama Ravine on Saturday, her mother noticed that her usual brisk gait was slower than usual. "You're still taking the rejections too hard," her mom told her.

"Yea, Linda told me that the rejections offer me another opportunity to go down a different path, but I still feel hurt," she admitted.

While walking through the kitchen, she noticed a stack of mail on the countertop. "Wow, are you going back to school or something?" Meggie asked her mother with curiosity.

"Absolutely not. I was done with school a long time ago. Have a seat," Libby said pointing to one of the high chairs.

"Your father is busy. He works nonstop," Libby lamented with a deep sigh.

"I understand. His job is demanding. With computers and cellphones, there's no separation between work and home. I get it," Meggie said.

"I made breakfast," Libby said as she poured coffee into Meggie's favorite mug. Her mother had given her as a present in her 18th birthday. It was encrypted, be slow to trust. She looked at it and smiled thinking, good advice but not easy to implement.

Meggie took the coffee, shrugging. "Breakfast in my world usually consists of a bowl of Weetabix, if I remember to sit down and eat"

"Breakfast is the most important meal of the day," Libby said as she handed Meggie coffee, a glass of fresh orange juice, two scrambled eggs, Weetabix, and toast with jam and butter.

Meggie smiled to herself. "Here I am an adult, but you can't help being endearingly maternal, even about breakfast," she said smiling at her mom.

"I did it again. Didn't I? You are a twenty-eight-year-old woman, and I still tell you how to eat properly," Libby responded, ashamed.

"Yes, mom. Just know that children of overprotective parents can grow up to lack confidence," Meggie said, smiling. She appreciated her mother's self-awareness and acknowledgment of the issue.

Meggie's mother sat next to the paperwork. "These are other great universities I researched after our conversations. You meet every requirement, and I chose them according to the amount of grants they offer," Libby said as she shuffled through the papers.

Meggie looked at her mother as she talked, but her heart was not in the conversation. "Mom, I appreciate all the work you've done, but I'm not ready to begin this process again. I need to focus on other things for a while." However, Meggie looked through the stack of papers and the mail.

"Did you even hear a word I said?" Libby asked with a raised voice. "You are the most stubborn human being on earth. We can afford to send you to Harvard, but you want to do it your way. We are doing all this because we want you to get whatever you want. The only reason you are sad is that you want to work for everything. No handouts. No favoritism. No nothing. You want to earn everything with your sweat," her mother lamented.

Meggie looked at her, astonished. "Mom, others would die to see their kids stand on their two feet. They would be proud to see them earn their way to success, just the way you and dad did," Meggie said.

Libby was horrified to hear that from her daughter. "Oh baby, am I doing that?" she asked gazing at her daughter.

"Without a doubt. Are you that scared that I might fail?" Meggie asked.

Meggie's challenge made Libby reflect. Wouldn't every parent who acquired some wealth, particularly if they worked their way up, always want their kids to never live the way they did. My aspirations are for my daughter to have more and to live a better life than I did at her age. At the same time, I hope she's humble and hardworking to earn her own success. Libby thought that she was doing that all along.

"I love you anyway, no matter what. Relax, everything will be alright," Meggie assured her and sighed much as her mother had when she discussed her father's workaholic tendencies. "I appreciate that you went to this trouble, but I'm sorry. I've moved on. Can we focus on other things?" Meggie asked as she sorted the letters, putting aside those addressed to her.

Meggie suddenly fell off the high chair on which she was sitting. She screamed.

"Meggie! Are you hurt?" Her mother rushed to her daughter with panic. "What happened?" She kneeled next to Meggie, trying to see what was causing her daughter's pain. Meggie shook her head indicating that she wasn't hurt. Then, she extended a letter in her right hand to her mother.

Her mother started screaming as she read the letter. The commotion caused Meggie's father, Eddy, to rush to the kitchen in a panic, alarmed by the screaming. "What's going on in here?" he demanded..

Libby gestured for him to come closer and handed him the letter.

"It's an acceptance letter from Saguaro State University's (SSU) College of Public Health." He read, "The leadership and faculty of the college are impressed by your unique academic achievements and experiences, which prepared you to join scholars in the field. We recognize your experiential wealth." The letter continued, "You will be valuable to the university." He saw the lavish financial aid package that they offered.

"I know all your other applications were unsuccessful, but this university is offering you a grant, including a small stipend, tuition, student health insurance, and resident tuition. Great news," he said, catching the excitement.

"Yes. So, my stubbornness paid off," Meggie said as her parents laughed with her at the good news.

"We always are proud of you," her father said. "Now, we can be thankful for this good news. Your determination has won out." He laughed and cried at the same time as he pointed to Meggie. "That's my girl right there. Bravo, Meggie, I am proud of you."

Meggie rose from the floor and ran to her father. Her mother joined them for a warm group hug.

"It's time to celebrate. We'll have a few more for dinner. I'm calling my friends to join us at dinner tonight. Not a word to any of them. Not even to my grandparents." Meggie demanded secrecy from her parents as she rushed to call Linda.

Her parents nodded with beaming grins on their faces.

"Hi Meggie. This must be something serious. You never call me this early," Linda responded.

"Not really, I just wanted to talk to my friend. That's all."

"Okay, what's up? Linda asked, curious but speaking in an undertone.

"Oh, he's there, isn't he?" Meggie asked, curious too.

"Who?" Linda asked.

"Willy, silly. You talked to me almost in a whisper as though you were avoiding waking someone up," Meggie responded.

"What? Are you serious?" Linda asked. "What in the world gave you that impression? How do I even know if he likes me and is truly interested? Actually, he is interested in you—not me."

Meggie realized that Linda was either scared or in denial. "I think the question is, why do you think that he's not interested in you?" Meggie asked.

"I wouldn't ask if I had an answer?" Linda raised her voice to disapprove of Meggie's undermining her line of questioning.

"Are you sure?" Meggie asked with genuine curiosity.

"I'm scared, Meggie. I've been burned so many times," Linda lamented.

"I know. Just remember, it is not up to you to find people to love you. You are already loved. Willy should enrich what you already have. So, you've got nothing to lose." Meggie said.

"Thanks, Meggie. You're a good friend," Linda said.

"You're welcome! I'm always here for you. By the way, do you have plans for tonight? Why don't you come along with Cheryl and Willy for dinner this evening? I'm at Eldama Ravine with my parents," she explained. "Join us for dinner at six o'clock this evening," Meggie said.

"I've no plans. I'll check with Cheryl and Willy," Linda said.

"Thanks. Now, wake up, enjoy the day," Meggie said, smiling as she hung up.

That evening, the first ones to arrive were Meggie's paternal grandparents, George and Ester, two feisty, loving individuals. Then, Linda arrived with their two American friends. Meggie's maternal grandparents Kiptarbei and Talai were the last to arrive.

Meggie's mother was a modern woman. At fifty-two years old, she stood five feet four inches tall with twinkling brown eyes and short black hair. Her arms were pumped up, and she unapologetically showed off her biceps by wearing a sleeveless dress. With her designer's eye, she frequently went overboard in organizing the dinner table and seating plan with place cards making it clear where everyone should sit at the dinner table. She believed that a successful dinner gathering of family and friends was for the enjoyment of each other's company with good food. As queen of the family and the hostess, her job was to encourage socialization, and much like her daughter, she thought planning out all the details would achieve the result she wanted.

She positioned herself at one end of the table with Meggie on the other. They always seated her paternal and maternal grandparents as far apart as possible to keep the peace. Meggie's paternal grandparents sat next to Libby. Grandpa George was a large man, more than six-feet-five inches and still imposing even in his early eighties. He had dark brown eyes and salt and pepper hair. He was a deeply religious retired minister, and served as a senior advisor to the local church. His wife, Meggie's grandma, Ester, was seventy-eight- years-old and a foot shorter than her husband. She had a pleasant smile and a firm jaw. Ester served as the local church women's senior group advisor.

At the opposite side of the table were her maternal grandparents. Grandpa Kiptarbei was among the leadership who initiated the annual Tugen cultural festival. He also was in his mid-eighties and stood six-foot one inch tall. His gray hair was still abundant, and his posture was steely. His deep, husky voice was so unique that everyone in the village described him by it.

His wife, Grandma Talai, was an entrepreneur who maintained a store that supplied fresh foods to the local community. She, too, had gray hair and brown eyes. Grandma Talai was still a firebrand. She realized early in her life that education, which the British brought to Kenya, was valuable although she did not agree with everything that the Brits brought with them. She used her influence to encourage girls to attend school. As an elder in her community, she earned respect and was highly trusted.

Linda, Willy, and Cheryl were the buffers between the grandparents.

When everyone was seated, an empty seat remained next to Meggie. "Seriously!" She muttered as she ran to call her father from the study. He had a slim-build and was a well-toned fifty-four-year-old workaholic and exercise junkie. Meggie understood why her father never paid attention to time. He was so attuned to his projects.

She introduced her father to the visitors. Her mother thanked everyone for coming, and announced the buffet setup. A pleasant conversational flow animated the guests. Then, Libby noticed her father eating with his hands.

"Dad, let me get you some silverware," Libby said.

"I love eating with my hands. It's not a crime, is it?" Kiptarbei teased with a smile.

"Not a crime, but it makes a certain impression while dining in public," Libby replied

"Ah! Sorry but I'm not going to change. Eating with my hands makes me feel good," Kiptarbei said.

Willy looked at Meggie. Their eyes met, and he asked, "Is it okay if I join you?" He turned to look at Kiptarbei and then at Libby. "If it's okay with you, ma'am," he asked for approval.

Their laughter ushered in a more relaxed mood. Willy stood up and returned his silverware and joined Meggie's father's in eating with his hands.

Meggie's paternal grandpa, George, intently watched the incident.

"Oh boy, here we go again, what now?" Eddy looked at George.

"I bet he thinks I'm primitive and uncivilized," Kiptarbei said.

"I didn't say that. Did you hear me say a word?" George asked. The battle began between the grandparents. There was always a conflict with them as a result of the clash of the traditional Tugen practices of Meggie's maternal family with the profoundly Christian beliefs from the other side. Each grandparent had strong, often conflicting convictions based on his perspective, which brought an electric tension to any gathering.

As the dinner ended, Meggie stood up, and everyone turned to her. "Three things warrant today's celebration," she said as she held her champagne glass ready for a toast. "One, the pleasure of meeting these two wonderful colleagues from America. They opened a world out there for me that I might never have thought about if it weren't for them. Second, here's to my partners in crime; my family and my dear friend, Linda. You all have supported me and encouraged me to push myself to the limit to achieve my goals. Third, I've been accepted to and am going to Saguaro State University in Arizona with a full scholarship," she said with tears welling in her eyes.

Linda covered her mouth with her hand in shock. "But— I thought you had received all regret letters?"

"Yes, I thought so, too, but Saguaro State University offered me a scholarship. I was reluctant to apply to this university because they had clearly specified medical doctors and I am a clinical officer. I got the letter this morning," Meggie said. "Thanks to my overbearing mother, this is one of the universities I overlooked, but she insisted that I apply anyway. I remember we did it together, but I left before the form was mailed. She completed the form and used our Ravine home address, and here we are."

"Welcome to America!" Cheryl led the toast, and everyone cheered.

"Congratulations, Meggie. My friend Ryan attends the same university. I'll let him know about you," Willy said.

"When do you leave?" Linda asked, elated for her friend.

"I should be there by August 26th," Meggie responded.

Considering how devastated Meggie was about her rejected applications, everyone was excited for her.

"Let's catch up some time, so we can tell you all about America—going beyond the myths," Cheryl suggested. They agreed on a happy hour that Friday.

It was late when the celebration finally came to an end.

After the guests left, Libby handed her husband and her daughter a printed post-cleaning task checklist.

"Smart woman," her husband commended her as he dutifully accepted the list. They both understood the routine. Package the leftovers and store them in the fridge, clean the dishes, put away the trash, and on and on. She used the same checklist after every event. They followed it, then, they all went to bed exhausted but very proud of their daughter.

CHAPTER 2

Liam Meets Meggie

ALWAYS THE METICULOUS PLANNER, LIKE her mother, Meggie plotted every step of her move to the United States. Under her student visa, she could enter the United States no earlier than thirty days before the last week of August when her program started. However, she could get her visa twenty days in advance, allowing her some cushion in case any unforeseen problems arose. She had received a signed F 1-20 form allowing her to get a student visa, and her information was already in the U.S immigration database, but she needed to pass an interview.

Looking at the calendar, Meggie began to freak out. She hoped her interview for a student visa would go well the first time, but that was not her only concern. A U.S. consular officer had to determine if she met the requirements to travel, and even if she passed the interview and got the visa that did not guarantee entry into the United States. She logged onto the Nairobi embassy consulate and started the application but stopped because it required other documentation. Panicked and frustrated, she laid her laptop down on the bed and strode into the kitchen. She opened the fridge and removed a chilled bottle of water.

Meggie, she told herself: visualize what you want to happen. Keep positive, she thought out loud as she rushed back to the things on her task list. She needed a passport-size photo, the detailed requirements of the image were quite lengthy but not hard to fulfill.

Meggie's weekly work schedule was packed. Every shift began with reviewing reports from other doctors. Then, she studied the charts of patients she expected from the emergency room who needed her care. She followed up with other patients. At the end of the week, she felt relieved when she could leave all the problems behind her when a new shift took over and Meggie got ready for her happy hour meetup at six.

At a local bar, Meggie's friends Linda, Cheryl, and Willy were already settled. She ordered Amarula cream liqueur, her favorite drink, as she sat next to Cheryl.

"How is your planning going, Meggie?" Willy asked.

"Apart from anxiety about unknowns, things are going well," Meggie replied.

"This trip will be my first time on a plane," Meggie confessed, surprising Cheryl and Willy.

"What do you normally take with you when you fly?" Meggie asked.

"I try to pack light when traveling within the United States," Cheryl replied. "But when I told my friends and work colleagues about coming here to Africa, they recited everything they had seen in the news and social media, and told me what they thought I'd need to bring with me, from water to medicine, gloves, tasers, stun guns, you name it. They explained that Africa was extremely dangerous," Cheryl said with a hearty laugh.

"Yeah, I got the same message. One of my colleagues cited rampant robberies in Nairobi. He didn't know if I'd come back alive," Willy added with a sardonic chuckle.

"Are there any other American misconceptions about Africa that I should learn about?" Meggie asked, curious. Awareness of these myths became important to Meggie. She felt horrified by the extent to which the world saw the African continent as a dangerous, frightening place.

"Many people in America don't even realize that Africa is a continent; they think it's a large country ravaged with violence and invested with horrible disease," Willy explained.

"Yes, HIV/AIDS and Ebola in particular scare the heck out of everyone. I think many people think that every bad disease originates out of Africa," Cheryl reflected on some things her friends told her.

Linda and Meggie listened silently, absorbing all the myths about their country.

"I was told that African hotels are not up to American standards. So, I came with my own cleaning supplies and disinfectants, medicines, clean sheets, and toiletries. They were definitely wrong. Some hotels here are way better than some I've stayed in in the States," Willy said. That sentiment lightened the mood of the discussion.

After listening to these misconceptions, Meggie swore she would be an ambassador for Africa. What she heard from her colleagues was not the true story of Africa. She realized that she had set a big role for herself. Of course, many people from Africa were out there in the world; she was just a small fish in the big sea. She wondered if she could make any difference in promoting and representing an accurate picture of Africa in United States as she completed her studies.

"We probably have misconceptions about America, too," Linda said. "We hear that everyone in America is rich, that poverty is only in other parts of the world but not in America."

Willy drew in a deep breath and said, "Although many people are affluent, many families can't afford to buy food. They live on donations from others. Many children depend on their schools for the only real nourishment they get during the day."

"Do you sleep with your doors open at night?" Meggie asked.

"Hell no," Willy said. "Although we don't use bars on our windows and doors, in some communities people do. We lock our doors and protect our homes with security systems."

"So, it's not as safe as here. Are there burglars over there?" Meggie asked, fascinated by what she was hearing.

"Oh, yeah. Probably no different from what happens here," Willy said.

"Good to know. Now, tell us about Ryan, your friend?" Linda asked "Is he single?" Everyone laughed at the directness of her question.

"What do you want to know about him?" Willy asked.

"You've known Meggie for a while now, is he a good match for her?" Linda asked, chuckling.

"Stop it, Linda. I'm going to study, not to hook up," Meggie responded.

"He's about six feet five inches tall, and he's African-American," Willy said as Linda grinned.

"Oh, Meggie, that sounds sexy. Did you hear that?" Linda teased.

Willy laughed. "He's very athletic. You'll notice him; he has broad shoulders." Linda was leaning closer as Willy talked about Ryan, and she couldn't resist having some fun.

"...and a hard muscled six-pack with sharp lines that narrow down toward his waistline, just the way you like it,

Meggie," Linda concluded the description while everyone laughed.

Meggie laughed the loudest as she stood. "Enough already. I'm going to the restroom," she said and escaped the amusing, though uncomfortable intimate discussion. When she returned, everyone was ready to leave. Willy paid the bill for everyone. Meggie felt some of her tension dissipate after a pleasant evening with great friends who made her happy.

Finally, Meggie's last night in Kenya arrived. She put her computer aside and did some deep breathing exercises to calm her nerves. Not only was she a woman traveling solo, but she was beginning what she hoped would be a marvelous adventure. She laughed out loud. Meggie always considered herself a strong woman. She couldn't understand how her thoughts had allowed her to drift deep into her hidden vulnerabilities. That was unlike her. Meggie was not one to show weakness, but now, she felt thrilled and excited while feeling scared and overwhelmed simultaneously as she organized herself for her next chapter of her life in Phoenix, Arizona.

Even without travel, the world always came to Meggie through books and technology. Through her reading she traveled the world and met many people through the eyes of her favorite authors. Most journeys were mind-opening and magical. Meggie engaged all her senses—she smelled the river dolphins in the Sundarbans in Amitav Ghosh's *Hungry Tides;* saw the kite runners of Khaled Hosseini, and felt touched by the female friendships in Lisa See's *Snow Flower and the Secret Fan.*, and felt with them. It did not matter whether she was reading fiction, history, or memoirs, as long as she learned something new. Now, she was traveling not to neighbors but to the United States of America.

Meggie's journey began aboard a Kenya Airways flight from Nairobi. From there, she flew to Charles-De Gaulle Airport in Paris. She was excited, but her stomach was doing cartwheels. Meggie fidgeted nervously with her fingers, and her seatmate noticed her anxiety and commented, "I'm no fan of plane travel either."

Meggie said, "It's funny, when I was small girl, about seven, this is what I wanted," Meggie said.

"To be a pilot?" her seatmate asked for clarification.

"Oh, no. To grow wings and fly up in the sky, just like a plane," Meggie said.

Her seatmate chuckled. "Now, you have it," she said and turned back to her paper.

After more than sixteen hours, Meggie looked out the window and enjoyed the view of Atlanta. This is the beginning of wonderful things, she thought. From what she could see from the window of the plane, unlike Nakuru, Atlanta was a huge city with many tall buildings, residential communities of different sizes, parks, sports stadiums, and roads with high capacity vehicle lanes crisscrossing each other. Everything was many times bigger than what she had seen before.

In Atlanta, since she was on an international flight connecting to a domestic one, she had to clear customs. Since Atlanta is among the most significant international airports in the world, the checkout line was extremely long. Meggie was surprised that the clearance proceeded swiftly without any issues.

Finally, she boarded the flight from Atlanta to Phoenix. She wondered if Phoenix would live up to the image described in the travel magazines she read: "A breathtaking city that comes alive at night, surrounded by a range of mountains. Its main streets run on a meticulously planned, precise grid with clean and well-marked roadways. The iconic architecture in wide-ranging shapes and elevations streams a yellow-orange glow of glitter everywhere."

Yes. Now, I am going to see the world! Dreams surely come true; Meggie whispered to herself as she settled in the window seat. About three and a half-hours later, Meggie exited the plane at Harbor International Airport, in Phoenix. Shortly after she exited, she heard a broadcast announcement about where her bags would be. She was pleased that she didn't need to go through uncomfortable checks again.

Meggie arrived to a boisterous welcome from a team of six students from the university waving signs with her name. They received her with handshakes and hugs, making her feel instantly welcome.

"Thank you! Thank you!" Meggie exclaimed while executing a mock bow.

A male student stepped out from the group and led Meggie to the side as the rest of the team went on to welcome the next student. This tall, casually dressed sexy guy greeted her. "I'm Liam," he said, extending his hand. She discreetly looked him up and down. Meggie was mostly drawn to well-dressed men, a sign that he cared about looking good. However, he passed the test. He wore Italian imported shoes, a sign that he cared about looking good. Then, she met his eyes. Meggie stared straight into the most beautiful eyes she ever saw, like the coastal beach—clear refreshing blue water. It felt as though she might sink into them.

"Meggie," she said, extending her hand to meet his, "but you already know that."

"Yes, Meggie, I do. Some American colleagues of yours in Kenya alerted Ryan, a fellow student, that you would be joining us. They thought very highly of you. Ryan had a prior commitment and asked me to come and meet you on his behalf," Liam said.

"Thank you," Meggie replied.

"Meggie is a great name, by the way. You're as exquisite as your name," Liam replied, smiling. He kept the handshake short while maintaining eye contact.

"Thank you, but I doubt that my parents or my grandparents knew what the name stood for. I bet they were thinking about Mary Magdalene," she responded, laughing out loud.

"Are they Catholic?" Liam asked.

"No, African Inland Church," she replied.

"Which denomination is that? Protestant?"

"Not sure, Baptist maybe?"

"Interesting. Your grandparents were not mistaken, by the way. Meggie is a Creek saint's name. It also means *pearl*, something special and of great value," he said.

"How did you know the derivation of my name?" Meggie asked, curious that a stranger would know about her unusual name.

He evaded her question. "So, what's the story behind your name?" Liam asked taking hold of her luggage. "But, before you tell me, do you have other bags to claim?"

"Oh yes," she said.

He directed her toward the baggage claim area where they waited until her luggage spun around on the carousel.

Meanwhile, she told him about her heritage. "Way back when most of East Africa was colonized by the British, the Brits could not pronounce Tugen tribal names. The Brits mandated that people in the area use a Christian name as the first name for their children," Meggie explained. "What about your name?" she asked.

"Liam, the protector, he replied," leaning toward her with a smile.

"Do you know the meaning of every name?" Meggie asked never content to let her questions go unanswered.

"Absolutely not," he shook his head. "But I know the origin of many names. A name is a significant expression of who that person is. When I know a person's name, I can start a conversation with some context."

"I see," Meggie said. Meggie thought it's strange for people to choose first names that meant something. Her parents named her Meggie to ensure that everyone pronounced it correctly and she fit in well with the beliefs of the British colonial powers. She thought that Liam was an entertaining player with a native wit.

"Anyway, Meggie, we appreciate your coming to join the Saguaro State University family," Liam said, reverting back to his official university duties.

"Thank you. I'm humbled by your hospitality," Meggie replied.

"I'm glad you feel that way," he responded as he put a quarter into a slot to choose a carryall with wheels to help her with all the other suitcases she brought.

Meggie was tough to impress—especially by members of the opposite sex. Liam created an impression on her of a polite, friendly, and very likable person. Such a feeling was unchartered territory for her.

"Do you have everything with you?" Liam asked, wanting to confirm she was ready for the trip to the university.

"Yes, I'm ready," Meggie responded with a twinkle in her eyes.

"Follow me. We'll head to campus," Liam instructed.

Phoenix was hot, Meggie thought as she walked out into the desert heat behind Liam.

"It's warm here in Phoenix right now," Liam said, as if reading Meggie's mind.

"That's an understatement," she replied.

Meggie learned a lot about Phoenix from tourism marketing materials. She knew that its nickname was "The Valley of the Sun." Meggie thought that was a bit of a misnomer. It should have been The Sandbox of Hell. "The Almighty must have been in a hurry and forgot to turn up the air conditioner. Oh Jesus, what does this place do to you?" she muttered to herself. "I've never experienced such heat. I come from a region with temperatures ranging from 77 degrees during cold months to 86 degrees in the hotter months.

"Come on," Liam nudged her gently. "You'll get used to it. Currently, in August, the temperature's already dropped to about 103 degrees. Before you know it, it'll be November, and the temperatures will be down to 75. Surprisingly, the big reason visitors come to Phoenix is the year-round sunshine and warm temperatures. You'll learn to like it," he assured her with a warm smile.

Meggie shot him a skeptical look.

"Yes, really. You'll get used to it," he assured her. Liam scanned the sea of cars for their Uber cab.

"This is us," Liam said as he turned toward the driver and gestured. The driver stepped out of the car and loaded Meggie's three suitcases into the trunk.

"The road we're on serves as the east-west dividing line of Phoenix," Liam explained.

Meggie looked out her window: She was not disappointed with the sights. Just as the phoenix bird arises from the dead in mythology, the city of Phoenix was quite alive and even better than she imagined. Phoenix was flat compared to the hilly topography of Nakuru. The main streets ran on grids, and seemed well-planned. In the distance she could see the low mountain ranges that surrounded the city.

"Does Kenya look anything like this?" Liam asked.

"Not even close. I live in Nakuru. A town with temperate climate all year round. There are many trees everywhere," Meggie said, noting the lack of trees in Phoenix.

"We live in a desert. Here's the desert giant saguaro cactus," he said, pointing out some cactus plants they passed.

Liam turned to see if Meggie was seeing what he was talking about. He met her eyes close up for the first time. He stopped and just stared for a moment. The silence felt awkward. For a moment, he was lost. He couldn't explain what he saw. He felt something that he couldn't put his finger on.

"Have you been to Kenya?" Meggie asked. She, too, felt awkward and asked the first thing that came to her mind to break the awkwardness.

"No, but I'd love to one day," he said.

"I'll take you there, one day," she replied as they approached the campus.

Somehow, the idea of going to Kenya with her seemed quite reasonable to him. Finally, the Uber driver arrived at the university and her apartment on campus.

"Liam, is everything new here?"

"Yes, the majority of the designs throughout the property are modern. To the left of this pathway are the residence halls. We're heading there first. After you," Liam said, then turned, attempting to point while struggling with two heavy suitcases. He put one down and stretched his right hand and pointed. "This campus is huge. Let's get you settled and then do a thorough tour tomorrow. You look tired, and there's plenty of time to get to know Saguaro State University."

"Agreed. I am tired after thirty-six hours of traveling," Meggie admitted, finally feeling the wear of her long journey.

Meggie followed him to the Sonora Residence Hall, a dorm exclusively for the graduate and non-resident student community. Liam was lugging two of her three suitcases.

Liam ushered her to the Student Affairs office where she picked up her apartment keys. She handed them to Liam who led them out of the office and to the apartment. He opened the door and asked her in before him. Meggie's apartment was a roomy one-bedroom with a walk-in closet, a fully-equipped kitchen, and a bathroom.

"This is great," she said, looking around her new home. "Do you stay far from here?"

"Actually, the floor just above you," Liam said. "For now, try to settle in. I'll be back at six to take you to dinner."

Meggie looked at her watch. "Mine still reads Kenyan time. 3:00 in the morning," she said, amused.

"That would be an inappropriate time for dinner," he said. "I'll see you later. It's now, 8 a.m. so, set your watch for Arizona time." Liam walked out and closed the door gently behind him.

CHAPTER 3

Barsy

As soon as Liam left, Meggie smelled the funk of two days traveling without a bath. She looked around her pleased that the apartment was spacious. Meggie opened one of her suitcases and took out a towel and toiletries that she had carried from home and hurried to the bathroom. She took a long bath.

She unpacked and put on her loosely fitting bathrobe to allow her body to breathe easy as she made up her bed and organized her apartment. When everything was in place, she picked up her purse from the coffee table and searched. She couldn't find what she was looking for until she realized she was looking for her phone. Like a zombie, she realized that she was mindlessly looking for a phone that was not there. She didn't come with one. Unlike drugs, cigarettes, and alcohol, technology can unintentionally become an addiction. Kenyan technological gadgets don't necessarily work internationally. Meggie needed to settle first before she could address her lack of connection. However, anxiety gripped her mind and triggered a fear of missing out due to lack of immediate access to the outside world. Like her father, Meggie was a technology junkie.

Meggie opened one of her suitcases and selected an outfit for the evening dinner, then she got dressed, brushed her teeth and felt ready to conquer Phoenix.

Meggie was fidgeting and pacing around her living room when she heard a knock at the front door. She glanced at her watch, now set to American time, and guessed it was Liam. If so, he was exactly on time, something she appreciated—especially since her father was so unconcerned about time.

Liam greeted her warmly, giving her a discrete glance and noticing her good looks and well-defined features. She had changed into skinny blue jeans that defined her long athletic legs, a top, a jacket and platform shoes that made her tall, toned figure even more striking. Liam looked up at her delicate beautiful chocolate face.

"You look great," he complimented her. Her dark brown eyes met his. He looked away to avoid any awkwardness as Meggie rushed back to the living room and picked up her handbag from the coffee table.

However, he told her, "You don't need that jacket. Remember, it's very hot here."

"I know, but I'm more comfortable this way."

They walked side by side in the growing darkness along the lighted pathway to the main dining hall. Unlike the standard cafeteria style that Meggie was accustomed to from her previous college. The dining hall featured a collection of restaurants with specialized choices and distinctly unique and interesting dining concepts. Additional fast food stations and a common area with endless rows of self-service dining options lined the perimeter.

"I'd like a tour to see what our options are before we order, if that's alright with you?"

"Absolutely." Liam was happy to show Meggie around and to spend more time with her.

"Other places to eat are all around campus." Liam explained the campus dining structure. "This dining hall is reserved for graduate students associated with professional health care schools. We could access another dining area, such as the dining hall primarily for undergraduate students, but our choices there would be limited to meal plans. Also, food trucks with different food choices are scattered throughout the campus on specified schedules."

Liam led a tour of their current area through Mongolian style food, pizza with a dizzying array of toppings, special sandwiches, a salad bar, and a dessert station.

Meggie turned to Liam with her decision. "Would you mind if we went back to the Mongolian food?" she asked.

"Not at all. Why Mongolian?"

"It's close to what I am used to; white rice, beef, and veggies," she said.

"Why not try something different?" Liam suggested.

"I love trying new things, but not today. I'm starved, and I need to fuel up for the challenges of tomorrow. What would you like to eat, Liam?" she asked, smiling.

"I'll eat your choice today. Tomorrow we'll go with mine," he said, craftily inserting himself into her life.

"Where did tomorrow come from?" Meggie asked, teasingly.

"Wishful thinking on my part. I'm hopeful for another tomorrow," Liam said, chuckling. Soon after, they received their food.

"What do you think?" Liam asked.

"It's delicious. The crunchy, sweet, and spicy tastes are heavenly. I love it."

They ate in silence for a little while. "We just met, but you seem to be a nice guy," Meggie said thoughtfully, breaking the silence.

"Don't be fooled by first impressions," he said, smiling mischievously. "I'm pretty opinionated sometimes."

"Really?" she asked.

"My friends tell me so. They say I'm too vocal, and too eager to share my straight shots of controversial views," he replied, shrugging nonchalantly.

"Ah! Simply smartass, they think. We shall see. I'm worse than that," Meggie added.

"How so?" Meggie's demeanor seemed so calm. Liam was intrigued.

"I'm unapologetic in my opinions, but I like to think I'm open-minded," she said.

"Some people think my views are outrageous. However, just like you, I recognize another side, and I'm willing to listen," he explained.

"You have met your match, then," Meggie said, laughing loudly. By the way, you're the only person I know here right now. And, I don't even know your full name," she looked him straight in the eye.

"Liam Grant Barsy," he replied.

"Barsy? Did you say Barsy?" she asked, genuinely surprised and with eyes widening. "I heard such a name back home. I don't think it has anything to do with you," she said.

"Yes, I know. I often get the same reaction when people hear my last name," he said.

"Interesting, it sounds different and familiar at the same time," she said, smiling and gazing at him.

"Yeah, I want to learn more about my roots. I've been trying to learn about my heritage for the past five years without much success. Maybe you can help me?" Liam replied impulsively.

"I just met you, Liam?" she responded with a laugh.

"Yes, indeed," he said, cringing at his overenthusiasm.

"So, what's your story?" she asked. Being around Liam made her want to know more about him. Their conversation flowed easily, as if they had known each other for years.

"My story? It's as atypical as my last name." He tilted his head back as he chuckled.

"Not aliens from Neptune," she responded.

He turned back to meet her polished chocolate face and gazed into her big brown eyes. "Ah! No," he said. "Perhaps Jupiter but definitely not Neptune," he teased back. After more banter, he began an explanation.

"The name Barsy began with my grandfather. His father, Harper Stevens, was a firefighter, and his mother, Naomi Stevens, retired from the Army.

"So, your great grandparents were not Barsy?" she inquired.

"No, my grandfather never mentioned any other relatives from that Barsy family lineage. It was as if Barsy appeared from nowhere and suddenly moved forward. I wondered why for a long time."

Meggie was intensely present, never removing her gaze from him. "What about your father?" she asked.

"He knew as much as my grandfather told him. My father is quite a reserved man. He moved to Arizona for professional development, and decided he liked the area enough to stay. He never left. His father grew up in suburban Westwood, Massachusetts."

"And?" she quizzed him further.

"My grandfather knew he was adopted but didn't give it much thought, since the Stevens treated him as their own. He was their only child."

"Wasn't your father curious to know about his extended family? To me, family is vitally important. Family includes parents and siblings as well as clan and kinship that constitute a village. At some point, I'll tell you more, if you're interested," she said.

"Yes, I am. I'll hold you to that promise," he said. "My grandfather's adoption was a closed adoption, which meant that no one knew about the parents of the adopted child. No identifying information was in the adoption records."

"Wow, a dead end," she responded sympathetically with a heavy sigh.

"Everyone was willing to let it go and accept not knowing—except me. I persisted, always asking questions about Barsy. I would ask, 'Where are other Barsys?' 'No other Barsy is in my school?' My teacher asked me where I came from because of my name. I asked my dad, 'where do I come from?'"

"One day, when I was about twelve, I was home sick. My father came to my room to cheer me up. I was miserable with stomach flu. I asked him about the Barsy name. He must have been tired of hearing the same questions over and over again. He left the room without a word. I thought he was angry with me."

"I'm so sorry," she said softly. Meggie unconsciously held Liam's hand but withdrew it immediately. She was stunned by her actions.

Liam responded immediately. He powered on his phone to divert the awkwardness that had just resulted and added, "My dad came back into my room. He brought some laminated pages from a newspaper and sat down next to my bed and allowed me to read the story in the newspaper." Liam handed Meggie his phone, displaying an image of the newspaper story.

Meggie repositioned herself next to Liam and read the following story as he held the phone. She was afraid of her reactions from close contact with him. She read the story, "Westwood Best Basket Christmas Gift."

"Harper Stevens was a firefighter, and his wife, Naomi Stevens, was a retired Army captain. Both were active volunteers in Topsfield community events. Harper held highly regarded leadership positions in many local committees and associations. They were well-known and celebrated people in the community. They didn't have children."

Liam interrupted Meggie's reading to tell her the next part of the story. "What the newspaper didn't print, but I later learned, was that after many years of trying to conceive a child, Harper and his wife sought help for their infertility. Both were tested. Harper felt devastated to learn that he had a problem that couldn't be corrected. He couldn't have children. He knew how badly Naomi wanted a family. Harper loved his wife too much to put her through the pain and agony of not being able to have a family. But Naomi took it in stride. She knew all wasn't lost.

"I think grandpa knew he was adopted. His parents were much older than those of his classmates. But they constantly reassured him that they loved him very much. His parents didn't often discuss personal issues. So, he didn't know much about the details of his adoption, but he grew up in a loving environment and my grandfather never bothered to ask questions."

"At that time, resources to help him satisfy his curiosity were limited," Meggie said.

"You're right. Anyway, my dad continued to read me the article, and I learned something about my grandpa's roots in the detailed account of events."

Meggie continued to read from his phone.

"On a cold December night, Harper dressed warmly for his morning shift at the fire department. He held a mug of hot coffee in his left hand while pulling the door open with the right. As the door opened, Harper saw something just outside the door. He switched on the outside security lights, and opened the door wider. Next to the door was a large handmade basket with leather handles. He took a few steps closer to the basket marveling at its craftsmanship.

Harper picked up the basket, covered with a soft gray blanket. He carried it to the breakfast table. Suddenly, he heard crying from inside the basket. Harper almost dropped the basket in shock, but quickly placed the basket on the dining room table. Without looking further, he ran upstairs to get his wife.

"Wake up. Wake up, Naomi! You have to see this," he yelled.

"What are you talking about?" she said, dazedly hauled out of sleep.

Harper practically pulled his wife out of bed and dragged her downstairs. By now, the noise from the basket was a distinct scream. Naomi slowly opened the folds of the blanket to reveal a newborn baby wrapped in a bloody white towel, crying hysterically. Its tiny eyes were shut and looked swollen. Tears streamed down its cheeks. Its hair was a sprinkle of fuzz. She immediately noticed the umbilical cord lying on the baby's chest and a piece of paper wrapped around it. Naomi removed the paper as gently as she could. She was shaking violently.

Naomi opened the letter next to the baby and read it out loud.

'*You are a generous, loving couple. The child has no home with me. I want you to have him. I know he will be okay with you. I am sad to see him go, but this is the right thing to do. His family name and that of his generation will be Barsy. Do not try to find me. I beg you for the safety of the baby and your family. Naomi and Harper, thank you in advance for your kindness*'

The letter was anonymous and typed without any way to determine or trace its source.

Naomi urged her husband to call the authorities as she gently picked up the baby and pressed him to her breast. Naomi sobbed loudly, but looking down at the newborn baby, she instantly turned into a mother. She felt as though she had carried the child in her womb for the past nine months. She was overwhelmed by the sudden and intense love she felt for the child.

Harper called the authorities and stood dumbfounded by what was unfolding.

He watched Naomi with the baby in her arms. She exemplified pure, unconditional love. He walked toward his wife, embraced her and the baby, and whispered to her, 'You were right. God had planned this for us.'

Law enforcement respected the wishes of the baby's mother in the note and took no further action. They named the child Isaac Barsy.

Meggie was transfixed by his story. She was glad Liam was comfortable enough to share his family's story with her.

"I told you. My grandfather, Isaac Barsy, was adopted in very weird circumstances," he said, smiling. "I hadn't meant to tell you quite so much, but something about you makes me want to share things with you," he explained softly.

"Yes, that's quite a story. This is quite shocking—almost far-fetched," she blurted. "I didn't mean to doubt you," she said, looking momentarily embarrassed.

"That's okay. When I heard the story as a kid, it seemed distant and magical. The realistic perspective wasn't important. I was glad I had something that explained Barsy, that was all that mattered," he said.

Meggie saw the soulful look in his eyes. Just as she always did with people she met, she quickly summed up his character and found him to be kind and authentic although she realized that she didn't much know him yet. However, he fascinated her. She wanted to know more about him. He was a man with confidence yet unafraid of his vulnerabilities.

"I agree that the story seems implausible," he responded with dignity and poise to her reaction to the story.

"I would have thought the same if I were in your shoes. It sounds unreal, but it's true."

"So, did you ever find out more about your great-grandparents?" she asked with curiosity.

"I started investigating father beginning five-years ago, but I haven't been successful," he admitted.

"You're a scientist, I'm guessing. A DNA test should give you what you need, fast," she said.

"That's the next step. Sometimes the unknown is scary, a Pandora's box." Meggie detected the fear of what the genetic test would reveal displayed in his eyes.

"Pandora's boxes are my thing. It's the profound, inexplicable secrecy in its mysteries that intrigue me," Meggie retorted. "You're looking at a master investigator," she laughed.

"You're hired," he said, beaming. Liam was also fascinated by her. It felt easy to trust her. He couldn't stop telling her more than he had shared with anyone else. He was on emotional cruise control.

As Meggie imagined the Pandora's box, she wondered if any of Liam's physical traits revealed clues to his past. He was nothing like the Barsy family she knew in Kenya, for sure, she thought.

In college, Meggie recalled that she met a Kalenjin student from Eldoret, Kenya, whose last name was Barsiran. He shortened his name to Barsy. Barsiran was a well-known family name with a sacred role of the Nandi tribe in Kenya.

But that definitely could not have anything to do with Liam because the student she knew was a black African in Africa. Liam was white. Maggie quickly catalogued Liam's characteristics as though she were to issue a report on him. His chestnut-colored hair had a curl to it, and he had ocean blue eyes, an oval-shaped face, and a slightly hooked, thin nose. His small mouth supported thin lips. His physique was well toned. She guessed he was about 6-feet 3-inches tall. He flashed a crooked smile frequently, and displayed a cocky, charming confidence in his unique walking swagger—like that of a star with Hollywood stature.

"Enough about me," he said with a laugh. "What about you?" he asked.

"What do you want to know?" She once more met Liam's question with a question.

He leaned back in his chair, looking thoughtfully at Meggie. "Whatever you want to talk about? Family, career, anything. I'm intrigued. I want to know more."

"I'm an only child and work as a clinical epidemiologist for the Kenyan government at the Rift Valley General Provincial Hospital. My favorite foods, as you just found out, are rice and beef stew." Their conversation was suddenly interrupted, and neither one of them was pleased.

"Hey, Liam."

Liam pushed back his chair and stood up, shaking a man's outstretched hand.

"Ryan Forester, this is Meggie," Liam said. Ryan said, "So glad Liam's taking care of you. I was supposed to pick you up, but I had prior commitments and Liam agreed to help.

"Meggie Jepchumba," Meggie extended her hand to Ryan as she observed him. He was as her American friends described: African-American with a dark complexion and an athletic build. He stood about six foot three inches, about Liam's height. He had a simple, short haircut that acknowledged Ryan's curly hair's black nature, His dark brown eyes were slightly uneven. He had a broad nose, and full lips. He looked like any other ordinary guy until he smiled, exposing perfect, dazzling white teeth.

"Nice to meet you in person at last, Meggie," Ryan said. "I heard a lot about you from my friends."

"My pleasure," Meggie said standing up stretching to her majestic height. "They have nice things to say about you, too."

"Good to know," Ryan said as he turned to face Lai, then Liam. "I want you to meet Lai Li. Lai is part of our program, too," Ryan said as he put a friendly hand on Lai's shoulder.

"Great to meet you, Lai," said Liam.

"I am sorry, remind me of your name again," Lai asked Meggie.

"Meggie Jepchumba," she replied, smiling.

"The pleasure is mine," Lai replied politely.

Meggie noticed Lai's engaging smile. She felt happy to be among a group of smiling people. Meggie assumed Lai to be from one of the many ethnic groups in Asia. The Kenyan government had many development partners from China. They built half of the new projects in the Rift Valley General Hospital where she worked.

Lai was five-feet six-inches tall with short straight black hair and dark eyes with wide cheekbones.

"Meggie arrived from Kenya earlier today," Liam told them.

"I hope you don't mind us joining you," Ryan said as he motioned to Lai. It was too late to decline the request, Ryan pulled out the empty chair beside Meggie, opposite Liam. Meggie sensed that both she and Liam were annoyed at this intrusion.

"Where in Kenya do you come from, Meggie?" Lai asked.

"The Great Rift Valley," she replied.

Ryan said, "I've never been to Kenya but have friends deployed to the World Epidemiology Network (WEN), a nonprofit organization with a regional office in Nairobi," Ryan said.

"What does the organization do?" Liam asked directing the question to Meggie.

"WEN provides epidemiological and laboratory services to the public health systems at all levels in the country," Meggie responded.

"I worked for the same organization at Siem Reap, in Cambodia. I just completed my project then enrolled at SSU," Ryan explained.

"I've never heard of Siem Reap. Is it a place in Cambodia?" Lai asked?

"Yes. It's a popular resort town with colonial and Chinese-style architecture." Ryan said, not giving anyone an opportunity to get to know Lai, who was taking in all the conversations going on around him.

"Have you been to Kenya?" Liam asked Ryan.

"Not yet. I know a lot about Nairobi from Cheryl and Willy, my friends stationed at WEN."

"What do you do at WEN, Meggie?"

"I'm a clinical epidemiologist and visit WEN occasionally. I work closely with your friends, Ryan," she explained. "They're the only Americans in the Nairobi office," Meggie said.

"When did you last see them?" Ryan asked, grinning with excitement.

"About a month ago. I interact with them at many events for WEN's HIV/AIDS surveillance program through the hospital. They're involved in systematic data collection, analysis, and interpretation of data on new and existing HIV/AIDS cases. Their goal is to disseminate their findings."

After a short, slightly awkward silence and deliberately changing the subject, Meggie asked, "So, where are you from, Lai?"

"Guangdong, on the South China Sea coast," Lai said.

"I've never heard of that place,' she said, intrigued by the sound of its name.

Lai chortled. "I'd love to take you there, if you want to see," he said.

"That must be an expensive adventure," Liam said, jokingly.

"You might be surprised. It's worth it," Lai replied.

Meggie was tired and looking for an escape to return to her apartment. "Liam, my dear brother, it's getting late," Meggie said, blushing slightly. This was the second time that she had addressed Liam gazing into Liam's eyes, and he immediately picked up on her body language cues. She wondered if it were obvious and looked away quickly. That was too late.

"You're kidding, right?" Lai asked squinting as he looked at Meggie and Liam.

"About calling Liam my brother? I don't kid. I'm dead serious," she replied.

Ryan looked at Liam, then Meggie, then back at Liam. He wondered if Meggie were joking and would burst out laughing momentarily. There was silence and anticipation for a while.

"Okay, we've got to get back to the apartment. It was a pleasure meeting you both," Meggie said as she stood.

"We just got here, and you're leaving?" Ryan said, disappointed. He noticed how comfortable Liam was with Meggie. Ryan thought: this cannot be happening. I asked Liam, my friend, to meet a friend of my buddies from Kenya. Within hours, before I even get the chance to know her, he's already making a move on her, Ryan thought to himself.

Instead of saying what he was feeling, he responded, "It was nice to meet you. I didn't mean to take up all your time." He was jealous and irritated and Liam saw through it. His immense desire to present a strong first impression consumed him. He wanted another chance to show his prowess. Ryan thought he needed another opportunity for Meggie and him to get more acquainted.

"Are you guys free for a drink tomorrow after the All-Star Science Award?" Ryan asked. "Meggie and I would be delighted to get together again for lunch. Right Meggie?"

"See you tomorrow," Ryan replied quickly.

Lai watched this competitive behavior unfold in silence and decided to smooth things over. "What the hell is going on?" Lai asked Ryan after Liam and Meggie left.

"What," Ryan asked.

"Man. You seem pissed. Is it with Liam?" Lai inquired.

"Sorry, do I look mad?" he asked, embarrassed.

"Yes. The question is why? You have no relationship with Meggie. You barely know her, so why?" Lai asked.

"I had a perception of her from all the good things my friends told me. And she's a gorgeous woman. I dreamed about being important in her life, and now I feel at a loss. Willy and I, my WEN friend, had it all planned out. I would pick up Meggie when she arrived. Then, my scheduled changed. Liam is a good friend of mine, so I asked him to cover for me. The rest is history."

Lai chuckled. "You don't think they are in love within the last few hours and will go to the altar tomorrow, do you?" Lai asked facetiously.

"It looked so; don't you think?" Ryan asked.

"But don't you have a girlfriend?" Lai asked, confused.

"Yes, but I'm still jealous," he admitted to Lai, with whom he had formed a brotherly bond. He trusted him with his vulnerabilities.

"Secure your heart with daggers. Sponges will let in unauthorized access," Lai advised.

"That sounds wise, but I'm not sure what it means," Ryan said.

"Ryan, you will get it when it happens to you. We should go. I, too, feel tired," They continued their conversations as they headed back to their apartments.

Meanwhile, as Meggie and Liam approached the elevator at the lobby of their apartment building, Meggie stopped and stared at Liam. "What was that about with Ryan?" Meggie asked.

"Just an invite for lunch," he said.

"No," Meggie said. "You answered for me without asking me. I don't know you well enough for you to read my mind. For years, I've paddled my own canoe, directing it, and suddenly, you're giving me directions, but your answer was correct. It has me confused," she said. "I barely know you, Liam," she said.

"I'm your brother, remember?" he responded, his eyes smiling.

"I feel comfortable around you, but I hope not to give any false signals or anything more than that," she said.

"I'm your brother," he said again. "I mean that literally. Count on me," he replied, and opened his arms for a hug.

"It will be an interesting ride with you," she whispered before she pulled herself away. Meggie let out a sigh and pressed the elevator button, relieved. She had observed that Liam was protective of her. She felt some assurance and safety when she was with him.

"I'm sorry to cut this evening short. I'm so tired. I don't want you to have to carry me to my room on your back. I could drop dead asleep any minute now. Let's head back," Meggie said.

"We wouldn't want that to happen," Liam whispered, grinning. The elevator door opened and they quickly went in. Liam pressed the second and third floor buttons. He decided to get out at the second floor with Meggie and walked her to her apartment since this was Meggie's first night on campus.

CHAPTER 4

Coffee

Meggie awoke to the ringing of her bedside alarm. She felt refreshed and energized, ready to start the day. She jumped out of bed and headed straight to the kitchen, a small, attractive area with a light gray ceramic floor, white walls and cabinets, gray granite worktops, and stainless- steel appliances. She spotted a package of Starbucks Kenyan coffee near the coffee maker on the kitchen counter.

How thoughtful, she thought to herself as she smiled. I wonder if this coffee is Liam's doing.

Thinking about this gesture reminded her of her mother's instructions when the family left the house. Her mother always told them: "Be thankful for every thoughtful act of kindness that comes your way."

"Why?" Meggie asked her one day.

"People will mostly remember how they felt about something long after it happened more than anything else," her mother replied.

Seeing the coffee made it feel like a typical day at home. She measured the coffee and water into the pot and let it brew while she prepared for the day.

Meggie finished combing her hair when she heard a knock on her door. She opened the door, and smiled when she saw Liam.

"Good morning, Liam. Come in. Coffee's ready."

She went to the kitchen and poured two cups of coffee. Meggie motioned Liam toward the apartment's private balcony with panoramic views of the campus and the South mountains.

"I love this balcony I can see the campus, colorful and peaceful," Meggie said.

"Agreed. The balcony showcases the campus buildings with neat, clean straight lines. From what you tell me, I'll bet your mother would like this," Liam said.

"Definitely," she replied.

The open, free-flowing design was also reflected in Meggie's apartment. The apartment had few walls but many built-in shelves in bold gray and white accent colors.

"Did you sleep well?" Liam asked.

"I did. I was exhausted after the lengthy plane trip. Now, I feel ready for this beautiful day," she replied with a smile. Liam looked at her anew and was fascinated with the slight dimple on her left cheek.

"How do you like your coffee?" she asked as she pushed some sugar and cream toward Liam's side of the table.

"I like it black and strong," he smiled. "What about you?"

"The opposite, sweet with cream," she responded smiling back. "Please thank whomever provided the Kenyan coffee. It was a thoughtful gesture, and I greatly appreciate it. Having such native coffee makes me feel at home, and that means a lot."

"I brought it" Liam replied. "You're welcome."

They sat quietly, sipping their coffee and taking in the stillness of the morning. "So, what do I need to know about Kenyan coffee?" Liam asked teasingly.

"Actually, Kenya is blessed with climatic conditions conducive for growing the finest high-quality coffee beans. Our coffee is among the top-rated in the world," Meggie proudly explained.

"Seriously?" Liam interjected, laughing.

"Oh yeah, look it up!" she responded and laughed with him. "No kidding, Kenyan coffee is actually a rare Arabusta hybrid coffee bean of arabica and Robusta species found just in Africa. The quality of the beans and natural-processing technique provide its delightful taste. As Kenyans, we take great pride in our coffee and have studied its genetics to improve its quality over the years. Taste it?"

Liam took a sip of the coffee. "Wow. It tastes damn good!" he exclaimed.

"I told you," she replied. "So, what's today's plan?" she asked eager to spend more time in Liam's company.

"I thought we'd take a tour of the campus," he replied.

"You look smart today, by the way," Meggie complimented Liam.

"Are you saying I looked dumb yesterday?" he asked, teasingly.

Meggie laughed. "It came out wrong, didn't it? I meant you look great," she said.

"*Smart* is one of those words that means something different depending on the part of the world you're in. Here, it implies intelligence," he said.

"I figured that out almost immediately from your response," she said.

"You look smart, too," Liam gave Meggie a lingering look.

"Thank you," she replied, bowing her head and chuckling.

Liam was mesmerized by her looks. I'm in trouble already, he thought. Liam was becoming frightened by where his thoughts were taking him. He had just met Meggie, and already his mind was moving fast past the normal acquaintance process. His mother always warned him of fools who were only wise through their eyes.

He had never felt so captivated by a woman's beauty. Meggie's gorgeous African features aroused him. She was about six-foot two-inches tall, with very dark skin. She wore short natural hair. She dared an almost shaven head. Her penetrating dark brown eyes were enhanced by her high arched eyebrows. He followed her mesmerizing fluttering eyelashes, as they effortlessly articulated her emotions. Her full lips seemed to invite and meet his lips. Her smile turned into lovely dimples exposing straight white teeth. Liam felt blown away every time he looked at her.

Meggie wore a light blue blouse with a lacy cutout trim and feminine flounce. The blouse's V-neck design emphasized her long neck. The three-quarter sleeves with lace trimmed double ruffle cuffs exposed her smooth, dark-skinned hands with long slender fingers. Her black knit leggings complemented the blouse. Liam thought she looked exquisite.

As he thought about her, he realized her character exuded strength and balance. She was different from what Liam thought he knew about black women. He knew her less than forty-eight hours, but he already noted her courage and her fiery independent streak. She displayed confidence in her conversations and mannerism, but she also could be funny and quite often witty. Her outgoing nature pleased him.

"Your accent is different," he said, looking intently at her.

"Yours is different, too," Meggie replied.

"Do I have an accent?" he asked, genuinely surprised.

"Oh yeah. You sound different than I do." She looked straight in his eyes, laughing.

"So, who has the accent, you or me?" Liam asked jokingly, and they both laughed.

"An accent is a form of identity, like a name or a place," Meggie commented. "Some people prefer to erase it to fit in well. I'm the opposite, I believe people should be proud of themselves—the whole package of who you are—how you speak, where you come from, what you eat, how you look, all of it. Someone else shouldn't convince you otherwise. As long as you learn how to speak and write well in a language, that should do," she said emphatically.

"I agree with you," Liam replied. He gazed at her for a moment. "Ready for the tour?" Liam asked as he stood and picked up their mugs from the table. "Welcome to the home of the Longhorns, you'll hear a lot about them."

Liam guided Meggie through a paved pathway with well-manicured trees and streetlights on both sides.

"This place looks beautiful. The modern design of the campus' architecture is carried over to the landscaping," Meggie pointed out.

"Absolutely. The color schemes of the buildings complement the plant life and blend in well with the surrounding environment. The gardens have low profiles, hilly vegetation, and beautiful flower gardens designed to stand out," Liam added, unable to keep his inner tour guide from making an appearance.

"As I mentioned, my mother is an architect with interior and exterior design experience. Your descriptions would please her," Meggie commented.

"Mine too," Liam stopped abruptly and turned to her.

"What?" she asked for clarification.

"My mother, also is an exterior and interior designer," he said.

"Small world," Meggie commented. "Mine is obsessed with modern architecture."

"We have much in common," he said as they proceeded on the planned tour.

"In front of us is the New Canyon Administration Block. It's the tallest, most iconic landmark on campus. Both the president and provost have offices on the top floor."

"The governance team are at the top," she said in an ironic tone. "The principal's office," Meggie commented, joking.

"Oh yeah! I was there a lot at a young age in high school. I messed up here and there. Nothing major. What about you?" Liam asked.

"Nothing major. But they knew me by name, for sure," she said.

"What did you do?" he asked, wondering what sort of high school mischief Meggie might have been involved in.

"If I were forced to do something I didn't want, I waited outside the principal's office until my case was resolved two days later," Meggie said.

"What? No classes? You didn't go home at the end of the day?" Liam asked, curious.

"No classes, but I was forced to go home," Meggie explained, laughing.

"You were one determined girl," Liam said in an admiring tone. "Anyhow, most of the leadership team also have offices there," he pointed. "The third floor houses the financial hub of the university—where they plan and control the campus finances. The student financial advisors are here."

"Awesome," Meggie said. "Are banking services in this building?"

"Not in this building," he replied, and described several banking options available within the campus. He appreciated the fact that Meggie was concerned about practical things as well as academic ones.

"The admissions office is on both the first and second floors. The first floor has a photo studio, front desk, and many academic and student advisor stations."

"So, I need to be here first thing tomorrow morning to get my student ID, correct?" Meggie asked.

"Yes," Liam nodded.

"Perfect," she responded.

They passed the McKinley Student Union, where they ate the previous evening. "You already know this building. They walked to the next building, the library. He was not used to a woman keeping up with his long strides, but Meggie, he could tell, was an athlete and in good shape able to match his pace.

"This immaculate, extensive modern glass-walled building is the library. We spend most of our lives in this four-story building here at Saguaro State," Liam chuckled. "It has about three million print volumes, one and half million e-books, two hundred thousand journals, and more than three hundred databases, and, of course, other resources, too."

"You're an amazing tour guide—equipped with detailed knowledge. I'll bet you're like that with most things," she suggested. "Were you a nerd as a kid?

"You've nailed me," Liam responded. "I didn't think it showed. Perhaps that's why I went into the sciences so I could figure out how things worked."

"Research here will be fun," Meggie said.

"Let's go to the basketball court," he said guiding her. "Are you a sports fan?" he asked.

"I am terrific in the 1,500-meter races," she replied. "I ran track for my previous university."

"Somehow, I'm not surprised. You've been able to keep up with me as we walked. Are you still a runner?"

"Sure," she answered. "Some days I like to take a long run especially early in the morning when it's cool or in the evening at twilight. I think that's a magical time."

"We'll run together some morning," he promised. "Next is the SSU arena with a seating capacity of 15,000. Beyond this are the baseball field, the soccer field, the gymnasium, the tennis facility, and the clubhouse," he said pointing out each as they walked along.

"We've only covered a quarter of the campus on this tour, and I'm already tired and starving," Liam lamented jokingly.

"Me too," Meggie responded. "There's a lot to take in. You're a good tour guide."

"Thanks. I appreciate that, but you've told me that already."

"I wanted to see if you were paying attention to what I said," she bantered back.

"Let's head toward the SSU Health Care Complex Center. That huge building houses all of the health care-related colleges," he explained as he guided her toward the building.

"How many colleges are there?" she asked.

"Six: dental, medical, public health, nursing, health care administration, and informatics. Most of your lectures will be here. But let's save the rest of the tour for another time," Liam suggested.

"Agreed. I owe you lunch, and the type of food is your choice. Please take us to the closest restaurant," Meggie suggested.

"I was thinking the same thing," and they both laughed. "I know just the place."

He steered her around the corner to the burger place. "Remember what I said yesterday? Your choice yesterday and mine today. I'm a man of my word," Liam said, beaming. "This is my favorite place for burgers.

"So, you remembered," she said.

"Of course," he reassured her. "You're important. I remember important people and important things."

"I often come with my buddies to kick back and have fun after a long busy week," Liam said, excited.

Some of his friends were in the restaurant, drinks in hand and waiting for their burgers to be served.

"Hey Liam," one of his friends greeted him. He saluted them both and went to wait in line with Meggie, so eager to get back to her that he did not introduce her to his friends who greeted him.

"I have never eaten a burger. What's that yellow thing?" Meggie asked pointing to the advertised burger on the wall.

"That's cheese. Do you like cheese?" he asked.

"I don't think I've tasted cheese," Meggie replied.

"You're about to have the food adventure of your life. The hamburger is the food most coveted by Americans. If someone tells you they miss home, it isn't their house they miss, it's the burger," Liam said and Meggie laughed.

"I'm not sure I even know how to eat it. This will be my first time," Meggie said, looking horrified.

"I'll order you the triple burger like mine, Everything will be fine. Don't worry," Liam said. Meggie looked at him, horrified. Between the three pieces of ground beef was dressing, bacon, and veggies.

They settled at a table for two in a corner with their drinks as they waited for their order to be called. When he heard their order number, Liam retrieved the burgers and headed back to the table.

"Look around. No one cares how people eat. There's no special way of eating a burger. You hold the burger in your hand, bite into it, and get dirty. Then, you wipe your mouth off with the napkin. You see, nothing to worry about, right?" Liam said, reassuringly.

"You don't use a knife and fork?" Meggie wondered.

Liam smiled widely. "Nope."

As they enjoyed their burgers, Meggie assessed how little she knew about Liam. She had intuited that he was a nerd in school, which he confirmed. She knew about his grandfather's adoption, where he lived, that he spent much of his time studying, and guessed he was part of the team at the SSU Health Care Complex Center.

"What exactly do you do, Liam?" she asked.

"I'm a doctor, a graduate of SSU some years back."

"Seriously? I didn't anticipate that answer."

"Why not?" he asked with amusement.

"You don't fit the geeky 'doctor-type' personality," she answered.

"How so?" Liam asked, puzzled.

"Highly intellectual, which you are. Obsessive, introverted, and eccentric, which you are not," Meggie said. "At least, I don't think so."

He shook his head, looking into her eyes.

"Oh, no. No, no! Don't take what I say as wrong. I'm not stereotyping or judging doctors."

He grinned and said, "You just did."

"I have great respect for doctors. After all, I'm a doctor myself. We have a lot on our plates, with twenty-four/seven work schedules—without any vacations. However, if doctors didn't sacrifice, we probably would all die," she said.

"Maybe not, but I get your characterization of doctors. Really, I do," Liam said, laughing loudly. "Of course, I'm making fun of myself as well."

Meggie realized that Liam, like her, was outgoing. As he continued speaking, she realized that his background was similar to hers.

"You have a point. Doctors do tend to be workaholics. In fact, most of us work seven days a week without vacations or weekends off. I'm one of those, and that's why I'm here. The university offered a postgraduate degree in an interdisciplinary, two-year program. This program is especially geared to practicing doctors interested in participating in health care policy," he explained.

"Kind of a doctor mixed with a politician," Meggie interjected.

"Something like that. I love medicine. but I'm not fond of the lifestyle associated with being a doctor, the stress, and the lack of flexibility. My patients are the love of my life. Nothing is more satisfying than saving lives. I'm humbled and grateful for the privilege and opportunity to serve them," he said with misty eyes that showed his feeling of emotional satisfaction.

"Speaking of the love of your life—I presume you're not married."

"Once more, you've right."

"Any girlfriends?" Meggie asked boldly.

"No, not really," Liam said. "And you?"

"I've been too busy. Anyhow, there have been people in my life with unique relationships that have colored my thinking about getting married," Meggie said.

"What do you mean?" Liam asked.

"I need a recipe for a fabulous long-lasting relationship. I've seen it, but I don't know what the people in these relationships do to achieve happiness in their romance over the long haul," Meggie said.

"I have a recipe," Liam said, impishly.

"Has it gone through research and development to perfect it before you call it a recipe ready for mass production?"

"Okay. Okay," he laughed.

Meggie looked seriously at Liam and, turning the conversation away from the very personal said, "You should be thankful, Liam. Very few people in this world enjoy what they do like you do,"

"I know, and I'm incredibly thankful."

"So, why go for another degree, if I may ask?"

"I'm obsessed with news from cable TV and online. Every time I get a chance, I check on health care-related policy discussions, conversations, and debates. It directly affects my work. Oftentimes, politicians have no clue what they're talking about. They don't operate in our world."

"I hear you. I actually scrunch up my face, groan, and kick at anything close to me and sometimes have meltdowns wishing I could be part of the decision-making process when I hear all the misinformation spewed out," Meggie said.

"Oh, yeah, me too. That's why I decided to quit complaining and getting frustrated. From now on, I'll be the change that I want to see in the world, as Mahatma Gandhi said," Liam proclaimed.

Meggie laughed loudly, and he looked at her with astonishment.

"Liam, you should see the intensity on your face. You want it so bad. I truly believe that your dreams will come true. Sooner rather than later, you'll be the Permanent Secretary for the Ministry of Health," she said.

"You mean Secretary of Health and Human Services?" he asked.

"Whatever they call it here," she replied with a laugh.

Liam looked at his watch and announced, "It's late, time flies with such good company."

"And the burger was actually good," Meggie said.

"I told you," he said as he looked at Meggie. She had just taken her last bite and a tiny piece of it was stuck below her lip. He pondered what to do next.

"What is it?" Meggie asked. "Is something on my face?" she asked, embarrassed.

Liam's gaze was beyond the food on her face, his attraction to her was beyond his own will. He came out of the trance quickly and smiled at her, "Oh, no. it's nothing," Liam said. Then, he quickly took a clean napkin from the table and wiped off her chin.

"Thank you," she said softly and stood. "We better get going."

"Yes," Liam said and cleared the table.

They talked all the way to the elevator. Liam pressed the up button and the one on their left opened almost immediately. He ushered her in first. Liam pressed two, then hesitated. Meggie watched and looked at him.

"I'll see you to your door first," he said.

"I'll be okay. You can go home," Meggie said, chuckling.

"My job will be done when you're inside safely," Liam said, seriously. Meggie did not comment but noticed that he was taking his responsibility for her comfort and orientation seriously. No man had spoiled her like he did. She felt flattered.

CHAPTER 5

Awards and Ignorance

THE NEXT DAY, SHE RECALLED her mother's voice as she prepared for the day. "Be the best version you can be for anyone who walks into your life." As confident as she was, anxiety sometimes crept in. No one was immune. Exactly as she had arranged, Meggie went to the Canyon administration building and met with her academic counselor, who advised her to transfer some thirty credits.

"I did not expect this," Meggie said. Yesterday's conversation with Liam about the public policy program crossed her mind. She also liked policymaking, and now with the credit transfer she had extra space for additional credit hours. She felt enthusiastic about adding courses in policymaking. The extra money she had for upkeep together with her savings were enough to add on the extra program emphasis.

"Here is the schedule for your orientation, a map of the campus, and a goodie bag. Welcome to the family," her advisor said warmly.

Meggie thanked her advisor and left the building to return to her apartment to plan the rest of her day. She intended to go to a bank to get her financial life in order here, then purchase a phone, and finally buy groceries and school supplies. Meggie sat at her dining table and made a checklist of the things she needed to accomplish. She thought how well trained she was—definitely her mother's daughter.

At Wells Fargo Bank, she opened an affordable and convenient student checking account. Then, Meggie bought a phone. Her plan included texting and data abroad. Meggie's last project for that morning was a trip to SSU Mall, which had copy services and a game room where students went for fun after their hectic academic schedules. The mall offered a bookstore; an Amazon pick-up station; a post office; a health care service center with a medical, eye, and dental care; and a farmers' market, among other services. Meggie purchased her groceries and school supplies and returned to her apartment. She was wiped out and needed time to rest before her first official orientation event at one o'clock.

At ten minutes to one, Meggie was in the lecture hall and noticed Lai sitting at the far end in her row. She moved to the empty seat next to Lai. "Hello, Lai. Do you mind if I sit here?" Meggie asked.

"Hi Meggie, absolutely not," he said enthusiastically. "Glad to see someone I know."

Meggie looked around and saw a wide array of people in attire from different cultures and ethnicities around the world. The students mingled and chatted.

"Why aren't you dressed up?" Lai asked.

Meggie lifted her hand to expose the Kenyan flag-beaded leather bracelet around her wrist. "What about you?" she asked.

"I missed the memo, next time," Lai said.

The university president gave a welcoming speech, and urged students to sit next to someone from a region they had never visited.

"I am with you. I have never been to Kenya," Lai said.

"And I have never been to…I'm sorry, where was it again?" Meggie asked.

Lai laughed. "I get it, Guandong, tough to pronounce."

"I'll sit with you, too," one of the resident student coordinators joined them.

The speaker instructed them to share within their respective groups their most common mythology, story, belief, or assumption from their different cultures and report back. Meggie thought—this was a variant of the discussion she had with her friends in Kenya at the happy hour when they talked about the myths they had about Africa and America.

Whispering not to be heard, Lai turned and moved close to Meggie. "Seriously? We will be discussing our childhood stories?" Lai did not seem impressed by the idea.

"I love those stories. My grandmother told me many stories when I was a young girl. Here is one story my grandma told. A gentleman from a faraway land visited a village. He met a widow whose family was without food. 'I will help you,' the gentleman assured the widow. In his luggage were dried meat and mushrooms. The gentleman offered the mushrooms to the widow. 'I have no money,' she replied. 'Take it, I beg you. Your family will die. Don't you worry. There is plenty where it came from,' the gentleman said. She fried the dried, dense, meaty chanterelles with butter and salt and gathered her family for the meal. There was a knock on the door, and she opened it to find the stranger at the door. 'What brings you back?' the widow asked.

'I want dinner. I know no one here,' the gentleman said. 'I have just enough for my family,' the widow said.

'What about the mushrooms?' the gentleman asked.

'Come to the table and join us for dinner, I promise to pay you back,' the widow said. 'Take it. Your family will die. Don't you worry, there is still plenty.' The widow toiled away, from sunrise to sunset. Yet, she had no money left to pay the debt.

Once again, there was a knock on the door, and she opened it to the stranger. 'What brings you back again?' the widow asked. 'It is too late in the night, and I want a place to sleep,' the gentleman said. 'I have room just enough for my family,' the widow said.

'What about the mushrooms?' the gentleman asked. 'What happened to the gentleman, the one who wanted to help my family? The one I trusted for help?' the widow asked, crying. 'I trusted you,' bawled the widow. 'You know I have none, but still, you want more, why?'

'Just business, not personal,' the gentleman grinned. 'Woman, you knew damn well that there is nothing for free, but you still took it.'"

The resident student coordinator laughed throughout Meggie's relating of the story.

"What's so funny?" Meggie asked.

"In another version of that same story, in the American political realm, the gentleman is a snake, and the widow is a poor woman," the resident coordinator explained.

"Tell us," Meggie insisted.

"The story is told through a song, 'The Snake' recorded by Al Wilson in 1968. It's about a kind woman who finds a beautiful distressed snake, frozen by the lake on her way to work. The woman gently took it to her house out of pity and generosity. She fed it and kept it cozy and warm. Overtime, the snake recovered and grew stronger. One day, the lady, who had grown fond of the snake, stroked and kissed it. She didn't expect what came next," she said looking at Meggie.

"It bit her, didn't it?" Meggie asked.

"Oh yeah. Brutally," the resident student coordinator said, breaking up with laughter. "It didn't end there. The snake looked her in the eye with disgust and said, 'all along you fricking knew I was a snake and not something else, a snake for God's sake. But you took me in anyway.'

"Instead of showing gratitude, he bit her," Lai interpreted the resident student coordinator's story.

"That's right, just like any many other ghastly ungrateful people out there," Meggie commented. "When I was younger, the story was intended to deter young children from trusting people they didn't know. As I grew older, as a teenager, my family used the same story to warn me about predators who will sweet talk young girls promising the moon and eventually use blackmail and aggressive tactics to solicit sex."

"How does this apply in politics?" Lai directed the question to the resident student coordinator.

"Politicians use the story to illustrate the extent of the threat by some groups of people. These politicians warned that a day will come when groups of dangerous criminals will deliver the fatal poisoned snake, and we will all die," she said. "Of course, this is extreme, but it provides a threat and scare tactics that the politicians can use to rally people against various groups."

"We have a version of it in China, too. The gentleman in our version is a monster. The widow in the story is a hungry man," Lai said.

"This story has a lot of universal truths and concerns inequalities, exploitations, you name it—the powerful who take advantage of the poor," Meggie said.

"I get it. Be careful. Monsters are out there. When the deal is too good, think twice. I presume that was the message. It's basically the same story illustrating that human nature is vulnerable. The story takes many forms but we all have similar wants and fears," Lai summed up the story before they reported back to the group.

"Well put. I agree with you, Lai. A message can promote good or be twisted to propagate evil," Meggie concluded. The resident student added a comment as they focused their attention on the facilitator.

"Interestingly, every story I heard from the groups as I moved around the room was unique. However, the only differences were in the use of diverse names, settings, characters, and varied storylines depending on the region of the world. The messages were of heroism, love, compassion, acts of kindness, forces of good as well as the threat of evil. We are diverse but equal. Wouldn't you agree?" she asked the audience.

Everybody agreed. Then, Meggie commented, "I totally agree with your comments. We already know most of this, but the human genome project ended many myths about diversity. All human beings are 99.9 percent identical in their genetic makeup. The 0.01 percent differences are due to other factors, such as diseases. People across the world have a common thread binding us as human beings. No one race is superior." Meggie explained: "Diversity is the icing on the cake. It adds richness to society."

A young man in the audience queried: "What do you say about those who think otherwise. For instance, someone who believes that they belong to a chosen superior race and others are less as per their religious or cultural believes"

"Meggie, would you like to answer?" the facilitator asked.

"Definitely. Not every piece of information, believe or knowledge is true. The strategic intentional spreading of falsehoods is more dangerous than ignorance. However, too often the ignorant follow along only too willing to learn from the masters of deceit. Ignorance then breeds monsters Such situations cause evil."

"Interesting view." The coordinator then pointed out, "Each of us is unique with a particular genetic blueprint. We have a distinct gender orientation, come from a particular region, ethnicity, or race, are believers or non-believers in a higher power, to list a few ways to think about who we are. Each of us needs to build relationships and understand other cultures to expand our perspectives about the world," he said.

Meggie, never one to be shy, added, "I need to grow in my views about how I think about the world outside my own." Several students sitting near her nodded their agreement. Looking around her at the diversity on display in the room, she thought: this program and the people are a great start toward this objective. By the end of the meeting, Meggie made new friends and felt inspired.

Slightly before four o'clock, Meggie walked into the Longhorns Theater, opposite the SSU Health Care Complex for the final event. Meggie sat in the tenth row next to the center walkway. The master of ceremonies announced the All-Star Science Award, the most prestigious award the university gave, honoring those who made contributions in science, engineering, and technology. The award was designed to motivate creativity and innovation in students to pursue research work--the university's way of assuring high achievers that the university would provide them with opportunities, tools, and the right conditions necessary for their success. The winners received a $50,000 grant funded by sponsors and a golden metal figure with raised hands holding a star mounted on a dark brown marble base—similar to an Oscar.

The university provost, as the chief academic officer, introduced the event. The university leadership team sat on the stage with the provost. Representatives of their sponsors presented awards. After many awards, the emcee announced, "This last award is for an exciting biomedical research project that unraveled the genetic component of rare and deadly gynecological malignancies. A normal human cell is stable, while cancerous ones are not. Their behaviors are observable through the genome-hybridization technique. This year's winner's team identified and determined biomarkers for ovarian cancer."

Since several people worked on projects related to ovarian cancers within the university research community, there was suspense about who the recipient was. The speaker continued, "This year's winner and other collaborative global scientists solved one of the mysteries that ravaged patients." The emcee knew how to keep the suspense going because he started smiling and looking across the room from left to right, panning through the crowd.

"And the winner is," the speaker paused for a second, while there was deadly silence in the room, "Dr. Liam Grant Barsy. We recognize the honoree's love for his patients and convey the community's gratitude for his dedication to their health care needs."

Liam and his team received standing ovations and prolonged applause. Caught off-guard, with her mouth wide open, Meggie stood with the rest and applauded. Doctor, geneticist, researcher, politician? Who is this guy? He never ceases to amaze me, Meggie thought.

Liam saw Meggie within the crowd and looked in her direction as he gave a short speech of thanks.

Oh, brother, you have a lot of explaining to do, she mumbled to herself with amusement and sat down with the rest of the audience as Liam finished his speech. After Liam's speech everyone streamed out of the theatre to the after-party. Ryan surprised Meggie, "Meggie, let's get out of here. The line to congratulate Liam is way too long," he said. "We'll catch up with him later."

Meggie wanted to decline, then hesitated and moved along with Ryan to the Western Tavern. Ryan secured a table and they settled down to wait for everyone else to arrive.

Liam thanked those in the reception line, then noticed Ryan's text: "*Meet me at Western Tavern in 15. I'm with Meggie!*"

Liam replied: "*Be there in 15.*"

Damn! He's with her, Liam thought. Liam was not rushing into a romantic relationship with Meggie and was baffled by the mixed messaging in his brain. He was jealous of Ryan's connection to Meggie. I better get my act together to redeem myself from yesterday's behavior, he convinced himself. Prior to Meggie, he always presented himself courteously and as a strong leader. Many people found him exceptionally valuable. It was important for him to gain and retain people's respect.

Liam wanted to celebrate a great day with his friends. He rushed to the bar where Ryan and Meggie sat at a table. Liam sat at a ninety-degree angle from Meggie, not too close but with enough space for some body language opportunities. He smiled about the thought and brushed it aside for the moment.

"Congratulations, Liam, you deserve it," Meggie said, gazing at the award on the far side of the table.

"Thank you, I was just doing my job," he responded modestly.

"Congrats, man. Great accomplishment," Ryan said.

"You amaze me. When do you do all these things?" Meggie asked.

"Remember, I told you. I'm married to it. All I do is work," Liam admitted.

The bartender approached their table. "What can I get for you, ma'am?" he asked.

"Do you have Amarula?" Meggie asked.

"Amarula? What drink is that?" Ryan asked.

"It's a cream liqueur from South Africa," Meggie replied.

"Coming right up," the bartender replied. Several minutes later, the bartender handed the light coffee-colored drink to Meggie.

Liam commented, "It looks like Bailey's Irish cream."

"Correct, but this one is special," Meggie said. "It's from the African marriage tree," Meggie said.

Liam and Ryan looked at each other and laughed.

"You are scientists. Do some research. The benefits of Amarula will make a profitable research question." Meggie chuckled as the bartender interrupted them.

"What would you like, sirs?" the bartender asked.

"Cognac, double,on the rocks," Ryan responded.

"Same, straight up. I'd also like a glass of water," Liam responded.

Liam was confident and in a great mood. He dressed for the occasion in a tight-fitting navy- blue suit and a different pair of sleek black shoes. He loosened his tie, and he stylishly unbuttoned his light blue shirt. Meggie dressed casually in black jeans and a light yellow short-sleeved T-shirt with a low, round neckline. Meggie wore her signature tribal golden-coiled choker necklace. At the center was an intricately designed sun (*Asis*) pendant. A matching bracelet on her right wrist complemented her outfit.

"Your necklace is unique," Liam remarked.

"Right, this is a modern version of a tribal necklace. It signifies a single woman not interested in marriage," she said, laughing. "In my Tugen cultural heritage, jewelry has symbolic meaning. Necklaces, bracelets, and pendant designs indicate one's position in society. Decorations and color designs show a person's social standing, creativity, beauty, or prosperity. Tribal neckwear symbolizes bachelorettes. Mothers wear elongated earrings and large, stacked-up flat beaded disc neckwear. I never remove my necklace. The pendant is a good luck charm. Then, to make things more complicated, I add my monotheistic Kalenjin tribal beliefs. Our single divinity is *Asis,* the sun, represented on my pendant."

"Any jewelry for bachelors?" Liam asked, laughing.

"Three of us could use bachelor jewelry," Ryan noted wryly.

"Unfortunately, not. No restrictions for men. Absurdly unfair," Meggie said.

"Why do you suppose some cultures and religions still suppress women and treat them unequally?" Ryan asked. "I don't understand because I don't believe such myths."

"From a religious perspective, and taken literally, God made man first and woman next, to be his helper."

"Baloney. You don't believe that, do you?" Ryan asked Liam with a smirk.

"I do...,"

Before he could complete his response, Liam pointed to the ring on Meggie's third finger of her left hand as he diverted their conversation. "That's a little confusing. I mean the ring on your finger. Why the ring?" he asked.

"Deflection," she said, looking serious.

"I see. You almost fooled me," Liam replied, laughing. "Let's get some champagne so we can celebrate. I'm quite pumped up today."

"This is your day," Meggie said. The champagne arrived quickly. They raised their glasses and offered salutations.

"May successes in your life journey give you happiness," Meggie said, beaming at Liam.

"May you find happiness in America and stay happily ever after," Liam smiled broadly.

"In your dreams," she retorted as she sat down. Meggie's goal was to learn and go back home to carry on her duties in the hospital. She had no intention of staying in the United States after her program.

"To your success and accomplishments," Ryan said.

Then, Liam lifted his glass and made a toast, "To all my friends—old and new," he said winking at Meggie.

Meggie felt unnerved by such direct flirtation. As bold as she was, she was accustomed to conservative environment where such discussions occurred in private and with people you are familiar with.

Later, after many of the others wandered off, Liam and Meggie remained at the table. Liam turned to Meggie and said, "On a serious note, let's pick up where we left off last night. You were about to tell me something about yourself when we were interrupted. What do clinical epidemiologists do? I mean, what do you do?" he asked, scooting closer to Meggie.

"I am a doctor at Rift Valley Provincial Hospital in Nakuru. I also assist the infectious disease department head. Clinical officers are doctors, equivalent to a Doctor of Osteopathic Medicine (DO) in the United States. The British colonial government introduced this service in 1928, and it's a critical component of Kenya's health care and a source of doctors since then," Meggie explained.

"What is the difference between that and an MD?" he asked.

"Training and scope of practice," she replied. "I earned straight A's in my Kenya Certificate of Secondary Education

(KCSE), the entrance for Kenyan universities. Since I wanted to earn money quickly, I opted to attend Egerton University, where I graduated with a Diploma in Clinical Medicine—a dual diploma in medicine and surgery, and a license to practice. The training was a 'boot camp' as they call it in the States, a hands-on patient-focused training combined with coursework and intensive residency.

"I provide care and treatment to patients within the hospital, where I trained and did my residency. I diagnose and treat diseases and injuries, order and interpret medical tests, perform routine surgical procedures, and refer patients to specialized practitioners, when needed. I later added epidemiology through an online postgraduate diploma. This training was necessary for my role in Kenya's Center for Disease Control (CDC) HIV surveillance programs."

Liam was genuinely surprised at the scope of what Meggie did. Meggie was a mystery, too.

"I've loved being a doctor since I started my residency. No time to even get to the good extra-curricular stuff," she said laughing, implying parties and sex. Meggie realized how strange it was to even consider talking about sex openly. Doing so was a cultural taboo among her family and friends in Africa. Innuendos about sex were only spoken in coded language.

"Liam admired Meggie's confidence, and freedom in discussing her private life. He was encouraged by her trust on him.

"Anyway, thank you for letting me enjoy this special occasion with you," Meggie said as she turned away to look at her watch. "I think it's time to retire for the night."

CHAPTER 6

The First Class

AFTER DELIBERATION, MEGGIE ADDED AN emphasis on public health administration in international development as an aspect of her training program. The focus of the program was on the economic, social, and political progression of developing and transitioning economies. The new focus fit perfectly with her public health work. Based on her training, she could affect policy changes to bring better living standards to many. She would acquire the skills needed to assess complex development problems and employ analytical tools for effective and efficient solutions. Her job in Kenya equipped her with proficiency in advanced micro- and macroeconomics, and advanced statistics that leaned more toward epidemiology. Meggie believed that with the training from this current program, she could meet the challenges back home.

She gave herself a pep talk to hit her stride for the first day of class. Meggie realized the stakes in her new graduate work. In whatever she did, she exceeded expectations, and aimed to live life unafraid and confident while carrying out her responsibilities.

She strode into the life sciences building. She approached a woman on her left side, walking her way. “I’m Meggie Jepchumba,” she said as she extended her hand to greet her.

“Hello, Meggie. I’m Isabel Adams,” the woman replied. “I know your name from my roster. Welcome to Dr. Odette Dyer’s class. I’m her teaching assistant. It’s a pleasure to meet you.” Isabel was about five-feet five-inches tall and while she looked pleasant and poised, there was nothing outstanding about her. Her blond hair was slicked back in a tight band. She didn’t use much make-up. Her angular face was highlighted by hazel-colored eyes and glasses that looked expensive. Isabel had high cheekbones accentuating her wide smile. A sizable birthmark pervaded her check toward her left ear.

“The pleasure is mine,” Meggie replied, excitedly.

“You’ll be blown away; she’s really good,” Isabel said. “I’ll be there to provide support through this journey. I took Dr. Dyer’s class last year. I wanted to continue working with her as her teaching assistant and working collaboratively with a new group of students.”

“Thank you, that gives me confidence,” Meggie said.

“You’re welcome,” Isabel said graciously. Meggie noted the seating chart posted on the class door and assumed her assigned seat in the middle of the second row. The professor walked in at the top of the hour. Everyone quieted as she stood at the podium. The professor surveyed the new group, rubbing her palms together as if she were in a cold room. “Good morning. Welcome to the first class on economic, social, and political progression of developing and transitioning economies. My name is Dr. Odette Dyer,” she greeted the class.

Odette was African-American, about five-feet four-inches tall. She was slender and wore her short hair in a natural style. She looked young but powerful. She was the epitome of a fashionista of academia in a cream-colored pencil skirt with a brown leather belt. She carried a brown leather computer bag with the classic look of a vintage handbag, and she strode confidently in dark brown stilettos. Her navy-blue shirt was tucked in. It had zip pockets and sleeves buttoned at the cuffs with epaulets at the shoulders.

"I've been working in this field since graduate school—some twelve years ago. My job is to prepare you as leaders of the next generation in developing and advancing economies. I'll guide you to be able to independently and successfully hold influential policy, management, and leadership positions anywhere on the planet. I was born and raised here in Phoenix, Arizona. I'm not married and have no children. I may not understand why the dog ate your homework," she said. The class laughed and started to loosen up. "Now that you know who I am, let me get to know you. We'll start from the first row to my right."

Professor Dyer logged on to the classroom computer and switched on the projector so that students could view her presentation. "Please, briefly respond to the questions outlined. The class has twenty people in assigned groups of five students. Your group's name is on your nametag. The names came from the quarry birds of the west: owls, falcons, eagles, and hawks."

"How did you choose the group names?" a student asked.

"Well, I love birds to the point that my family and friends become judgmental because they don't understand why I spend quite a bit of money to keep some in my house. The groups are named for major birds of prey of the west, which are very competitive and stunningly beautiful," Dr. Dyer said as she pointed to the names of the birds on the PowerPoint slide.

Meggie looked at her nametag. She was a Falcon. She wondered if Liam, Ryan, or Lai were on her team. Liam was seated behind her, but his tag was not visible to her.

Dr. Dyer's slide asked the following questions: "What is your name? Where are you from? In which program are you enrolled? What do you do? What inspired you to enroll in this program?"

The first student said, "I am Lai Li, assigned to the Falcons. I was born and raised in Guangdong, South China, and moved to the big city after high school to pursue college and career. I'm an administrator in an international development program. By training, I'm a software engineer in Shenzhen. I'm looking to be inspired." Everyone laughed.

"You came all this way to be inspired. Lai?"

Lai thought for a minute, then said, "Yes, you've got to get out there and search hard to find your purpose, it doesn't just find you."

"You're in the right place. Welcome to Phoenix, Lai," Professor Dyer said. "Who's next?"

"Ryan Forester, Falcons. I'm from New Mexico. I'm an infectious-disease-surveillance epidemiologist for the state. I'm enrolled in public health policy. I want to translate the epidemiologic language into public health care policies that help people."

"What prevents you from doing that currently? Aren't you the guy presenting the numbers?" a student at the back row asked.

Ryan faced the student, "I'm the workhorse at the backend. I conduct the research, do everything in between then present the findings in consultations with physicians, educators, and government health officials. I don't have the last word, not on policy anyway. My input becomes a non-expert recommendation, which doesn't hold water. This program advances my authority."

"Welcome aboard, Ryan, I hope you enjoy the class," Professor Dyer said. "Next?"

"Meggie Jepchumba, the Falcons. Born a Tugen and raised in Baringo District, Kenya. I enrolled in health care informatics with an emphasis on administration in international development. I'm a doctor and epidemiologist at Nakuru General Hospital. I am, like Lai, looking for inspiration to become something more vital than I am right now. I want to influence change and make life better for a larger group of people."

"Searching for purpose, like Lai?" a student next to Meggie asked.

Meggie slightly tilted her head toward her but was still looking at the podium, "I already have a purpose. To serve others. Not to tell them what to do but to be grounded enough to give them knowledge sufficient for them to make the best-informed decisions," she said.

"You want to walk on water, like Jesus," another student said, jokingly. "I'm not perfect, like Jesus, but I want to place the interest and needs of those I serve ahead of my own-self-interest," she said.

"Those are big dreams, Meggie. Dream and make it happen. I can see the fire is burning bright in you. You can do it. Welcome to the class," Professor Dyer said. "Next."

"Sally Cohen, a Falcon. I was born in California but moved to Arizona fifteen years ago. I'm enrolled in public policy. I'm a cloud economics consultant. As Ryan said, I'd like to be able to translate technical language into policies. I laugh when I see Washington confused because they aren't tech-savvy and don't fully comprehend the issues." Everyone laughed.

"How would you do things differently?" Meggie asked.

"Decode with layperson's language so everyone could understand," Sally responded.

"What difference will that make? Senators can hire IT experts as their assistants. They have the money," another student suggested.

"True. But remember, it doesn't hold water until you have the authority, just like Ryan said. Evidence of expertise is the key. That's why I'm here," Sally said.

"I see. Tech support for a senator. Not bad at all. Welcome aboard," Professor Dyer said. "Next."

"I'm Liam Barsy, on the Eagles' team. I'm Arizona born and raised. I enrolled in public health policy. I'm a doctor. I want to contribute to all aspects of American health care policymaking. I'm tired of watching those with no clue about what we do dictate how we should handle our business."

"You sound matter-of-fact," Professor Dyer said, smiling.

"Damn right!" Liam said.

"Physicians, particularly in Congress, have been on the rise," Ryan noted. "Do you see any changes in access and costs for the rest of us?" he asked. "Rome wasn't built in a day. Health policies may not consider many issues that medical practitioners see every day. With more of us in the arena, we have the ability to contribute to policies that represent realities of the populations we serve," Liam explained.

"With that attitude, I can confidently bet every dime I've got that you'll be what you want, "Professor Dyer said. "The last Falcon."

"My name is Leon Pernere from Great Britain. I was born and raised in Scotland but moved to London when I was a teenager. I'm enrolled in public administration. I'm the head of public engagement strategy and policy at Glasgow city in Scotland. I just want to earn more money. Will you help me do that?"

"You are in the wrong profession, my friend," a student at the end of the row said. "Unless you want to be a politician with very many lobbyists."

"Anything for good money," he responded with a laugh.

Professor Dyer laughed aloud. "We'll see about that. With the level of Mr. Barsy's confidence, let's do it," she said. "Now it's your turn," she pointed toward Isabel.

"I'm Isabel Adams, Dr. Dyer's teaching assistant. Please let me know if you have any questions."

"Isabel always undersells her abilities," Dr. Dyer said. "Please tell them what you do."

She turned to face the class and explained. "I'm a Ph.D. candidate in public policy in my last year of study. My dissertation is in its final review process."

"What's the focus of your study," Lai asked.

I investigate whether health care policymakers use data during the policy making process," Isabel responded.

"I advise each one of you to start thinking about your own research projects to complete the program," Dr. Dyer explained.

"How do you balance life and college?" Meggie asked.

"I work part-time in a public policy advocacy firm. We engage in legislative decision making on matters of insurance and regulatory oversight," Isabel said.

"Do you ever play?" Sally asked, jokingly.

"When I'm not studying, writing papers or working, I like to volunteer at the Department of Veterans Affairs Transport Network in Phoenix. I help vets with disabilities. Many have challenges making it to their doctors' appointments. I also frequently hike the South Mountains to get rid of daily life stresses," she concluded and turned back to face Dr. Dyer.

"You want to look to her as a role model of an exemplary intellectual. She has all the necessary traits; humility, courage, empathy, autonomy, integrity, you name it," Dr. Dyer smiled as Isabel objected.

"How were the groups formed? The Falcons, my team, have diverse expertise. How will this work?" Ryan asked.

Professor Dyer walked back to the podium. She turned to the next slide. "Ryan ushered us to our next item—diversity in the groups. You all are in various facets of health care. So, assume the opposite, conformity and compliance with established rules."

Leon interrupted, "Like in cults and tribes—with cults being religious or other groups with controversial beliefs and strict rules. For tribes, think of primitive savages with bows and arrows and feathers on their heads," he said.

"Odette, is it alright if I call you by your first name?" Meggie asked the professor.

"I don't care," Professor Dyer responded, impressed with Meggie's straightforwardness.

"I don't understand why people who never belonged to tribes provide examples to insinuate that tribes are everything backward, egocentric, and socio-centric. This idea doesn't make sense, particularly if their assumptions are not experiential. Such people have no idea how a tribe works, until they experience it," Meggie said leveling her gaze at the class with increasing ire in her eyes. "Tell me how a tribe conforms and complies?" she asked.

"Ha! Meggie, you hit the nail on the head," Lai explained. "I belong to the Hakka tribe, and I concur with your observations. Would you agree that an individual from a tribe is often stereotyped? Take me, for instance, a Hakka man. I only do as the tribe says. I cannot function as an individual except..."

Meggie interrupted, "…and as a Tugen woman, I only know and believe everything from my tribe and no other."

Silence reigned when Meggie stopped talking. Everyone was intensely curious, shifting their gaze from Meggie to Lai. Liam broke the silence.

"We refer to our political parties as 'tribal' when they are partisan and exclusively aligned to their party's philosophical liberal or conservative ideologies—when they can't compromise. What's the difference?"

"This is getting interesting," the Professor said. "Liam, to whom are you directing your comments," she asked.

Liam looked at Lai, then Meggie, and decided that it was the safest to ask Leon.

"Leon, what's the difference?" he asked. Everyone laughed at who he directed the question to.

Leon gazed at Liam with impish eyes. "How would I know, Liam?" he asked. "In London, we use the term 'tribe,' particularly 'tribalism,' to describe primitive battles." Everyone laughed, including Professor Dyer.

Meggie walked toward Leon. She stood in front of him and smiled, then extended her hand and said, "You're an honest man, Leon. Many indeed assume and believe exactly the way you put it," she said.

"Whoa! Let me educate my fellow Falcons," Lai said. The other teams were quiet, fascinated by the unfolding discussions. "A real tribe, like the one I come from, constitutes a traditional society. Blood ties unite my family, my aunts, uncles, and clan, and my whole community. We have a common culture and dialect. Our tribe's dress code is unique, and our cuisine is delicious.

"What many do not know is that tribes operate as most democratic societies do with a balance of power. They are just different. My people are as intelligent as those in western cultures or other parts of the world. They are nothing close to the assumptions provided by my esteemed colleagues. Look at Meggie, a Tugen woman. She appears flexible and adaptable in this setting. She is curious to know about other places; I am hoping she is fair-minded as you all are, self-motivated, and beautiful as hell," Lai looked at Meggie.

"Damn right," Meggie said and laughed. "It is true that tribal people sometimes may be underprivileged. In some situations, they may not have enough to be as elegant and sophisticated as we all look. I assure you that, just like us, they strive for upward mobility. They are witty and sincere hardworking people, miles and miles away from the dirty, ignorant stereotypes many presume them to fulfill. I will be happy to invite each of you for a visit to see the true Tugen culture," she said genuinely.

Professor Dyer clapped her hands, and the rest of the class joined her. Everyone was on their feet.

"Lai and Meggie have summed up important cultural understandings very well," Professor Dyer said. "What you just experienced here is why I use a multidisciplinary approach in my classes. For the teams, I identified students from different but related professional backgrounds and diverse cultural societies with unique passions. From your observations, why do you think I chose this particular approach?" Professor Dyer asked the class.

"To gain from conversations and experiences of peers," Ryan said.

"Sally, why?" Professor Dyer asked, nodding at Ryan's response.

"Cross-functional collaboration," she replied.

"We all bring expertise and diverse experiences to make policies that meet the needs of the public," Dr. Dyer added.

"Public policy is critical for every aspect of life and affects everybody. Its formulation involves interactions among individuals, societies, institutions, and competing interests, as well as ideas," Sally affirmed.

"Well put, Sally," Professor Dyer said. "I'm hoping that you will be motivated to dig deep into issues. I expect passionate debates and reasoned, defensible decisions. The intent is for the team to work together. Any questions?" she asked.

After a quiet interlude, Professor Dyer took a deep breath. "The real world out there is messy. You just proved that a few minutes ago," she continued. Everyone laughed. "Another aspect of this class involves taking some of these complex real-world problems, engaging in out-of-the-box thinking, and working collaboratively to propose effective and efficient solutions."

"Now, transition to your teams. Get to know each other. I will visit each group to give you additional information on the expectations for this course. Please ensure that your team-meeting-space setup is comfortable to enhance learning and limit distractions."

The Falcons all sat together. The group moved to the northeast corner of the classroom and placed two rectangular tables together and sat on the outer perimeter.

"I like this arrangement," Sally said. "This will work for our current conversations."

"U-shaped may have been better," Meggie said.

"We don't have to present, do we?" Lai asked.

As soon as they settled, Ryan delivered an initial icebreaker. "Who's seen the movie *Bruce Almighty*?" He was surprised that everyone had. "Okay, like Jim Carrey, you're God Almighty with unlimited powers. You can play nice or be a badass; the choice is yours. What would you do with your powers? I know it's a tough hypothetical question now since we're all grownups," he said as he grinned and waited for his teammates' answers.

"If I were God, there would be no pain and suffering," Sally went first. Everyone laughed at her introduction. "Seriously, as an economist, I wish I could get into the heads of people to better comprehend their fears and uncertainties, along with their needs and wants."

"You don't need God to get that now, Sally. I can help you with that through data mining. Let me know what you need. I have access to the largest databases. I can examine them and generate any information you need," Lai said.

"No. That's the point I'm making. I already have that, but we still have economies crashing, inflation, deflation, poor decisions, you name it. We have all the data you can provide. Something's missing," Sally said.

"What?" Meggie asked with curiosity.

"Economics is about people—their minds, and the vision of the future. Individuals and societies have political perceptions. When these combine with the unexpected, the result is a very complex world. Imagine if you had that power to know in advance how to mitigate or eradicate problematic issues before they surfaced?" Sally asked

"The world would be heavenly," Meggie responded.

"Okay. I find technology fascinating and always imagine if unlimited, affordable, readily available internet connectivity were in every corner of the planet, it would ensure everyone can access everything they need to know and every opportunity thinkable," Lai said.

"Wow, that's pretty ambitious," Ryan commented. "Meggie Almighty, what would you do?" he asked.

"If I were the Almighty, I'd make knowledge available and accessible. We must enable and enhance people's capacity to provide for themselves," Meggie said. "Google is not the complete answer." Everyone listened curiously. "Now, if I were God, my number one priority would be family security. Can you imagine if every family were secure?" she asked the team.

"That doesn't make sense. You mean hire guards for every family on the planet?" Sally asked.

"Sally," Meggie called her out by name and fixed her eyes on hers. "Envision a world where you, your husband, and kids are totally secure. I mean you have everything from health, education, peace, safety from any harm, and have prosperity and power. The whole package," Meggie was intense.

"Wow, be my God, Almighty Meggie, please," Sally begged, and everyone burst out laughing. The team felt totally immersed in the conversation.

Leon interrupted, "You all lean toward sorting out global issues mostly caused by humans. What do we do with those who continue to cause problems?" he asked and chortled.

Lai laughed out loud. "Almighty Leon's priority is to alleviate or eradicate this issue," he said.

"How?" Meggie asked.

"It would be simple to shut down every act, thought, or harmful ambitions, but it is more complicated than that. Free will, right or wrong, moral and immoral, can be subjective. Not to play God but defend the God that I know. He gave people free will and guidelines to support their moral and ethical decisions and actions. If I use the same analogy, I will combine all the efforts of Almighties Sally, Lai, and Meggie, and my suggestion to make the world a better place."

"Now, your turn, Ryan. What would be your priority?" Lai asked.

"I didn't think I had to answer since the question came from me," he said with a grin, as Professor Dyer approached their team.

"How's it going for the Falcons?" she asked.

"Great," Ryan spoke first to escape the group's conversation. "We're ready for you, Dr. Dyer. What have you got for us?" he asked.

The Professor handed everyone on the team an eighteen-page comprehensive spiral-bound syllabus. Lai scooted a chair next to her. "Please, have a seat with the Falcons," he said.

Professor Dyer complied. She took the team through the contents of the syllabus. "This syllabus is the living and breathing word of this course. Drastic consequences occur if you don't pay attention to these things. I say this lightly because you're all professionals, and you know why you're here," she said.

Meggie appreciated the comprehensively laid out program alignment linked to the learning objectives and assessment strategies. The rest of the manual contained administrative details.

"Any questions?" she asked the group.

"Can we schedule a session outside class as a group if we have questions?" Ryan asked.

"Absolutely, just a minute," she said and returned to the podium to retrieve some paperwork from her bag. She handed each member of the Falcons her schedule.

"My schedule fills up quickly. I can come to you as long as it's within this building. Never in the residence area." Professor Dyer moved to the podium and said, "If you can hear me, clap once; one," she called out to the class. A few students heard and clapped. "If you can hear me, clap twice; one, two." Three-quarters of the students were following her, and she needed the rest to join. "If you can hear me, give me three; one. two, and three." She raised her voice grinning. "Great! Did you have fun? I did," she beamed.

Professor Dyer was not afraid to show off her prowess and passion in her expertise. She was excited and challenged the students to be brave and vulnerable at the same time. "Don't be afraid to be wrong because mistakes are learning opportunities. I want to turn you into fair-minded, evidence-based individuals who open themselves up to things contrary to your own beliefs. A last word before you leave," she said. "By the end of this class, if you can reason through problems, I mean any personal, family, work, or global issue from peers, cultural, religious, or political, and find appropriate solutions, then I'll be confident that you will serve the public well, and I have done my job well. Thank you everyone. I'll see you later."

As they walked out of the class, Meggie, Liam, Ryan, and Lai congregated outside the building chatting.

"Hey," Ryan said as he talked to his colleagues. "I'm a member of the SSU basketball team. We have to take the Western Athletic Conference by storm, and we need you guys to come cheer us on."

"I have season tickets," Liam said.

Ryan looked at Lai and Meggie, who were expressionless.

"I've never attended a basketball game," Meggie said.

"I play all the time," Lai said.

"You do?" Ryan asked, excitedly.

"On my Android, of course," Lai said mischievously, and everyone laughed.

"Tickets are on me for you two for the first game in three weeks," Ryan volunteered.

"You'll love it," Liam said to Lai and Meggie as they parted ways.

Finally, the day of the game arrived. Ryan had organically evolved to be the organizer of the event and showed up earlier than the rest. He planned a full experience with snacks and drinks before the game.

"Hi Ryan, where are the others?" Meggie asked as she approached Ryan from the back.

"Still early," Ryan said as he admired Meggie who was wearing a SSU tank over a mesh turtleneck, a knit blue hat in the school's team color, bleached cropped tight jeans, and white sneakers.

"You look great." Ryan handed her his colored team hat. "This will complete your ensemble."

"I thought about it, but no thank you, I am so used to my head not being covered, it feels uncomfortable with a hat. Thanks, anyway," Meggie respectfully declined Ryan's offer.

Ryan and Meggie chatted, enjoying their drinks and snacks as they waited for the rest of their group. The quartet agreed to convene at one of the coffee-selling concessions at the upper level of the arena that Ryan suggested. Apart from coffee, there were hot dogs, bratwurst, popcorn, quesadillas, and other items on the menu.

"I like coffee a lot—second only to basketball. I especially enjoy the caffeine. Morning and afternoon double shots are part of my routine. I think I'm addicted. What about you?" Ryan asked to engage in further conversation.

"Iced chai latte," Meggie said.

"Why?" Ryan asked.

"It's my mother's favorite. She made us spiced tea every morning, all from fresh ingredients," Meggie responded.

"You have chai latte in Kenya?" he asked, surprised.

"We had it even before you. *Chai* is an Indian word for tea. Tea originated from India more than 5,000 years ago. We adapted it from the early immigrants from India who helped the British with the construction of the railway," she explained.

"Interesting history, we Americans sometimes think we're the first in everything," Ryan said, chuckling.

The others arrived, and they moved to their seats in the arena. Students wore team colors. Loud music reverberated, and the cheerleading squad and the teams primed for action. It looked like a party, not a game. Regardless of the result of the game, the entertainment was hard to beat.

Ryan was a volunteer coach of the team and regularly sat near the players in the arena, but today, he sat with his friends as part of the audience. However, before the game started, the coach requested that he substitute for a player who was not feeling well, which made the game more interesting because Meggie and Lai had someone playing for whom they could cheer.

The game was lively all through, but nothing topped the tension of the last five seconds. The teams were tied at eighty-three points each. Ryan, defending the ball from the opponent, faked left and in the nick of time moved to the right, hitting a twenty-foot jump shot that gave SSU a two-point lead of eighty-five to eighty-three. That sent fans streaming onto the court, reveling in SSUSSU's dramatic victory. Meggie got off her seat and was one of the first on the court, and jumped into Ryan's arms with exhilaration. She held onto him for a while, their eyes locked.

"Congratulations," she said as she pulled away and rushed to find Liam and Lai.

"Did you see that?" Lai asked Liam.

"Yes, of course," Liam said, irritated.

Lai noticed and kept his thoughts to himself. Liam kept close tabs on Meggie when they were together. During the game, Liam sat next to Lai. Ryan made sure that Meggie was as far away from Liam as possible, on the opposite end of the stands. Liam wondered if this were intentional because they ignored him throughout the game.

"I loved it, I'm going to get season tickets," Meggie said as they exited the arena.

"I told you. I'm glad you liked it. I'll see you at the next game," Ryan said as Liam changed the subject.

CHAPTER 7

The Supreme Majesty of the Grand Canyon

A FEW DAYS LATER, RYAN, LAI, Meggie, Isabel, and Liam were relaxing in the student union.

Liam spoke up, "I have a complimentary gift package to the Grand Canyon, and I'd love it if you all joined me. It's a two-night Grand Canyon tour bundle for five that includes round-trip train travel and two nights at the La Quinta. Meals are also included."

"How did you get it?" Lai asked

"It's a complicated story, but this is a real deal without any strings," Liam assured them.

"Seriously?" Meggie asked with excitement.

"Seriously. I want to use the opportunity to show you one of the seven wonders of the world. At the same time, I'll get to know more about Africa and China. I think there's too much I don't know," Liam said.

"When?" Meggie asked.

"The reservation is in six weeks.," Liam said. "Please come."

"Deal," Meggie accepted and extended her hand to seal the deal. "However, it's only fair if you agree to learn more about my family," Meggie explained.

"That sounds provocative," Liam said.

"It is. You'll learn a lot through the lens of the three generations of family history."

Ryan, jockeying for position in the group after Liam's show of generosity, asked, "So, what do you miss most about Kenya, Meggie?"

"Family and work," Meggie replied as she disengaged herself from the exclusive conversation with Liam.

"What is the next plan for your research, Ryan?" Meggie asked after a short silence.

"Tell me, Meggie. I hear research is easier done in Africa than in the United States?" Liam asked.

"How so?" she asked, startled by his question.

"Consent and access to population are easier, resources are cheaper," Ryan interjected.

Meggie was quiet. Liam talked about the high disease occurrence in Sub-Saharan Africa and the significance of doing research there to help improve the situation. He pointed out the poverty state of Africa. "Millions live on a dollar per day. The latest and greatest of technologies from the United States will advance the standard of living and development in the region." He talked with passion as if he were having a conversation with someone from Australia—not Africa.

"And how do you know about all that, Liam?" Meggie gazed at him with cold, flinty eyes. "You are wrong, you know," she said.

"Of course, Africa has its challenges, just like any other place on the planet. However, I'm extremely disappointed that you do not have a broader understanding of Africa. It feels as though you see me only as a route of access to what you need to get the research done cheaply. I respect you very much, but your ignorance about Africa and the people who live there is abhorrent. As highly-regarded professionals in society, words carry weight. Some people will believe the lies and those insensitive stereotypical assumptions," Meggie said as she stood to signal the end of the conversation and began to walk away from the group.

"I apologize for what I said. It was uncalled for," Liam apologized.

"Let's part before we extend the damage," Meggie said, feeling a rush of disappointment.

"I'm sorry," Ryan said, trying to persuade Meggie to stay.

Meggie walked back to the table and contributed her share of the bill. Then, they quietly parted and left for their respective apartments.

Liam followed her as she walked fast. He caught up with her after a few minutes. "I'm truly sorry, I hope you forgive me," Liam said as he tried to catch up with her long strides.

Meggie listened without interrupting, then she said, "I expected you to know better, Liam. I don't expect empathy but evidence-based discussions other that the standard layman's perspective through the lens of myths. But anyways, I appreciate your effort. It means a lot to hear that. Acknowledging your mistake is the first step, and I'll give you the benefit of doubt."

At the elevator, Liam ushered Meggie in. She reached out to the floor buttons before Liam and pressed the second and third floor. Liam got the message and did not get out on the second floor. "Sleep tight, Meggie. Again. I'm really sorry," he said as the elevator doors closed. She turned back and smiled before the elevator doors completely shut. Liam felt relieved as he got out and walked to his apartment on the third floor.

About a week later, Liam handed everyone a sheet of paper. "This is the itinerary for our Grand Canyon trip."

Liam had outlined the trip from the three-hour shuttle drive to Flagstaff, then to the La Quinta Hotel in Williams and the return trip to campus. The train adventure, rim tour, skywalk, Indian country adventure tour, and more were on Liam's carefully planned itinerary.

"We can't afford all this," Ryan commented.

"No worries. It's all paid. I told you, this is a complimentary gift package," Liam said. "See you next Friday. We can Uber to the shuttle. Be on time."

"What do I need for this trip?" the ever-practical Meggie asked.

"It is a normal weekend trip. It'll be warm up there. Wear light, casual clothes and bring a few warm pieces just in case," Liam said as he exited.

Meggie recalled what her mother said, "The Grand Canyon is the epitome of supreme majesty. No other natural wonders in the world are like it." Meggie wondered if the real thing would meet her built-up expectations. She was beyond excited. Her goal was to make memories to share with her family back home.

Liam was at the apartment driveway with Isabel thirty minutes before the others. Meggie, Lai, and Ryan followed.

"Hi, Isabel," Meggie greeted Isabel with excitement.

"Hi, Meggie," Isabel replied.

"I'm glad you came; this will be great," Meggie said.

Meggie and Liam took over the rear seats of the shuttle. "Do you realize we're all alone here at the back? Are we the only ones who like to sit in the back?" she asked Liam. She hadn't expected to sit beside Liam, all alone for a three-hour journey, and they were both searching for words.

"Do you mind?" Liam asked. He was excited to have Meggie for himself at the back but was not sure if she was okay with that.

"About what?" Meggie asked.

"Sitting by me, all alone," Liam replied teasingly. "By the way, do you like it here in Phoenix?"

"I do. I'm getting accustomed to the heat already. The people are friendly. It's getting to be home. It wasn't easy, but I'm getting there," Meggie explained.

Liam turned to her, "Meggie. I want to understand more about Kenya, your tribe. Would you mind telling me more about you?" he requested. Liam was not sure if he were intruding into her personal life

"It's not all pretty," Meggie said. "However, I don't object." Meggie recognized she felt secure with Liam and was not afraid to talk with him and to share personal things that she wouldn't share with others.

"What do you mean?" Liam asked."

"In my family, we had major conflicts based on ideology versus tradition. Some of the stories of this conflict may seem strange to a person outside of our culture. Our family story is influenced by colonialism and Christianity," she explained.

"I can take it, try me," Liam said.

Meggie reached into her backpack and retrieved her iPad. "Over time, I compiled my family's photos with associated historical accounts from their recollections. My grandparents narrated this three-generational story about British settlers and missionaries coming to Africa. In particular, the missionaries believed that God called them to redeem the African continent, the darkest place on the planet, where the settlers came to bring civilization," she said.

Meggie began her narrative. "I lived with my parents and was very close to my grandparents through my childhood and most of my adolescence in their rural homestead in Baringo district. Each of my parents had a very different perspective on life from each other due to their unique life experiences with their parents. My mother was brought up in the traditional Tugen culture. My father was raised as a Christian. The exposure to these two compelling, competing cultural values forced me to become a critic of my thinking. I had to figure out what made sense for me to believe, Tugen culture or Christian values.

"Committing to either was challenging. I had to figure out where I stood, as I loved both of my parents and wanted to consider their respective viewpoints fairly and respectfully—without bias. Situations for such questioning arose from everyday conversation since I was a little girl.

"My story begins way back—during the times when British settlers ruled, and the Christian missionaries arrived. My grandparents were young when Christians established the Africa Inland Mission (AIM) in East Africa.

"In the early 1900s, Kenya was already a British colony, called the British East Africa Protectorate. The Protectorate included the area now known as Kenya from the Indian Ocean inland, as well as Uganda. The British colony established new laws that outlawed most of the Tugen culture and practices. The AIM in East Africa and in the Kalenjin areas shaped the history of my family, starting from my grandparents' generation. AIM's mission was to evangelize to the darkest spot in Africa's continent,' as the Philadelphia Mission Council put it. AIM's idea of the dark continent still reflects the current mindset of many outside of Africa. Little has changed in many people's views."

"Meggie, excuse my naiveté," Liam said cautiously, wanting to avoid any potential misconceptions that may occur.

Meggie interrupted. "I understand. You don't have to walk on eggshells," she assured him. "I have the strongest shock absorbers. Don't be too cautious with me. Remember, I told you that I can be stubborn. I can take it and won't be offended. I will question, challenge, and oppose with evidence if I disagree with your viewpoint."

"I've never been to Africa," Liam said.

"So, I assume that your African experience comes through pop culture, cable TV, online media outlets, and some perspective in academic forums. You probably think of Africa as a continent of simple, primitive, unsophisticated, war-torn, famine-stricken, disease-infested, lawless, and positively vile individuals."

"Not completely," Liam said.

"From my experience, talking with people here, Africa is often painted with a broad negative stroke. A question for you, Liam. 'What's the first thing that comes to you when you hear about Africa?' Meggie's voice was gentle and calm. She was genuinely curious about how Liam would reply.

"Anything? Positive or negative?" he asked.

"Okay, let's balance. Positive, then negative."

"Well, on the plus side, it's a major tourist destination, a pristine setting for exotic wild animals. On the negative side, the typical American thinking about Africa believes that it's a poverty and disease-ridden continent," he said.

"Fair enough. There is so much misinformation out there; it's mind-boggling. Animals are plentiful, that much is true. They are in conservancies, just as in other parts of the world." Meggie laughed.

"As a young kid, I thought they roamed around everywhere," he said and smiled.

"You mentioned poverty. A high percentage of Sub-Saharan Africans do live in poverty. However, Africa, as a continent, has a third of the world's global mineral reserves, the most diamond reserves, and is a major player in the global oil market. We even lead in platinum production," she said.

"So, what's the problem?" he asked.

"Poverty emanates from complex multidimensional experiences. Specific causes depend on who you ask, or which report you read. I am not sure of the motives of these report writers sometimes," Meggie said.

"Motives?" he asked.

"These reports depend on the method of data collection, the interpretation, and the recommendations that flow from them. The motives could be vested interests or genuine, supportive gestures. There are indisputable issues within the continent. There are also major exploitative aspects at the same time," she said.

"The disease thing though is true; you can't dispute that. Numbers and images don't lie, do they?" Liam asked. We use data from reputable international institutions.

"I agree that they tell a story. However, you also know that disease acquisition is not unidimensional, but multidimensional. There are many socio-cultural and socio-economic factors at play to name a few. So you can't just take numbers at face value. Numbers alone, don't paint a picture of what is happening on the ground"

"True and I agree with you on that," Liam said.

"But in some instances some people have misused even those numbers and images. They have interpreted them to suit their needs. We may have limited access to some health care resources, just as in other regions of the world, but the myths and misinformation get baked in the cake. The narrative ranges from everyone has HIV/AIDs; to Ebola virus is rampant everywhere; there are unacceptable, below-par levels of hygiene; and you will die in the jungle because there are no qualified doctors, to mention a few of the myths," she said.

"Brutal, but that's the impression that every layman get," he said. "Meggie, it's your turn. Tell me something about America that you know," he said.

She laughed. "Okay, but I thought I could get away with not answering," she said.

"Absolutely not. I want to know," Liam responded with interest.

"The one idea that pops into my mind and is common where I come from is the arrogance and the ego problem," she said and laughed out loud.

Liam erupted with laughter. "Do you see that in me?" he asked, hoping she would say no.

"No, you're just confident and cocky," she responded, laughing until tears streamed down her cheeks.

"Oh, come on! We all have flaws. So, sometimes I can be unreceptive to other opinions or ideas, or have a hostile reaction if someone challenges my beliefs. The elephant in the room is out the door. I'm glad we're on the same page," Liam exclaimed with a sigh of relief and a smile.

"Why the sigh? These discussions are interesting," Meggie said.

"You don't understand. Talking about sensitive things such as political views, race, inequality, and other related stuff in America is like walking a tightrope," Liam said.

"Are there sensitive things that you want to say sometimes but don't?" Meggie faced Liam as she posed the question. I am not going to be judgmental.

"We do it without knowing. I just offended you when I talked about diseases in Africa," He said.

"True, but we ague our positions reasonably. Sometimes passionately in order to dig deep into the underlying reasons behind those discussions," she said.

"OK, I do have some," he said. Meggie had a nice way of putting things into perspective, he thought to himself. She could easily be a confidant; someone you could pour your heart out to. He thought he could trust her with those intimate things you wouldn't want anyone to repeat. He felt that Meggie was becoming even more than that to him. He readily acknowledged that around her he felt sensual.

Liam was still trying to define exactly what his feeling was toward Meggie. His eyes were locked on her lips as she spoke. For a moment, he stopped concentrating on what she was saying. Her lips were full, and moved gracefully with every word she spoke. He wanted to kiss them.

Meggie cut-off the gaze and turned to her iPad. "Can you share?" she asked.

"People are afraid of saying the wrong thing or making mistakes," he said. Liam did not share specifics but thought a broad perspective would do.

"Ignorance is worse. Awareness and progress are good things. Things will be better. Historical evidence shows progress. Fighting for rights and other issues will always continue to improve the lives of people over generations.," she said. Meggie read about extreme harsh comments related to sexuality, gender, and race in America and recognized that Liam took a sensitive approach to these topics. For the moment, their conversation was respectful and nonjudgmental—but they were not divulging personal thoughts at this point.

"You were telling me about the dark continent as told by your grandparents," he said, redirecting the conversation back to Meggie's stories.

"I recall how my Grandpa Kiptarbei explained the concept of the 'Dark Continent.' I thought it meant that it was night all the time, and in some parts, it was more pitch-dark than others. It is the way my grandpa expressed the idea in the Tugen tribal language, *'Kilenyjech chumbek kitui ng'anasani wee lakwani, kitui ne bo kwong'ut* (the European people told us the region was very dark, child, it was pitch-dark),'" she said with her eyes tightly closed to demonstrate how dark it was.

"I later understood that 'Dark Continent' was a figurative expression. However, I doubted my grandfather's comprehension of the mission's concept. I asked, 'Grandpa, how did you see Grandma if it was that dark?'

He responded, 'I used the eyes of my heart.' He assured me I would understand that when I was older."

Meggie removed and unrolled the three large maps of the United States, Africa, and Kenya that she had brought with her. She placed the map of Africa on top of the others.

"You have an iPad, why bring the physical map?" Liam asked.

"There's something special about the real thing," Meggie said. "This guy, Peter Scott, from New York, arrived at the coast of Mombasa in November 1895, to start the mission" she explained as she moved her finger along the map and pointed to the city. "He was the initial AIM missionary from America. Grandpa explained that it took them two months to arrive."

Liam lowered his head to get a better look at the map. "Fascinating! He must have been adventurous to be willing to sail all that way on treacherous open waters to the unknown," he said.

She lifted her face from the map to look at Liam. "Understatement," she said as she looked at him. "He bundled up his entire nuclear family for the adventure. His action is the definition of conviction. He was willing to give up everything for what he believed."

Meggie moved the maps to the side, and opened her arms imitating the British accent and said, "*Other sheep I have, which are not of this fold, them I also must bring...*"

Liam laughed. "What was that all about?"

"That quote was from the inscription on David Livingstone's tomb's in England. Livingstone greatly inspired Scott. Scott opened up opportunities that shaped many generations in Africa, but not without controversies and misunderstandings," she said.

Liam smiled at her and said, "You should be an actor."

Meggie smiled back and continued her narrative. "Scott embarked on a safari to the interior of Kenya with other colleagues supporting missionaries from America. They brought their families to join the mission. The male missionaries left the women and children at the coast because of the dangers of such a safari. A caravan of Scott and his team with hundreds of native men on camels ventured toward central Kenya.

"The men traveled for many days, exposed to the elements of the Tsavo region including lions. They also encountered other dangerous animals, such as elephants, leopards, and cheetahs. The men lit bonfires and stood on guard with weapons every night. They were always ready for the lion's swift leaps and stealthy crawling through the nearby trees and bushes. In a month, they arrived in central Kenya where they established their first mission station."

Meggie saw Liam's transfixed gaze, so she continued. "In 1907, Barnett Albert, an Australian married to a Swede, joined the AIM mission in Kenya. The couple met on the sea voyage to Africa and decided to get married. They joined the rest of the mission and had children. Members of their family ended up in the Great Rift Valley to serve the Kalenjin about thirty years later."

Meggie pointed at the map of Africa with her finger. "Kenya is right here in the Eastern part of Africa," she said. "Do you see the Great Rift Valley?" Meggie asked Liam. As she pointed to the map, their hands touched.

Liam felt the jolt of that flesh meeting and got nervous and sweaty. He was conscious of her every move.

"See, the East African rift starts here in Tanzania then goes all the way through the south, and continues northward toward Ethiopia." Meggie guided Liam through the map.

After making her last point, Meggie reverted back to the Kenyan map, "In Kenya, the East African rift runs from Lake Turkana in the north down south," her fingers traced the path on the map. She stopped, looked at him and said, "Different ethnic groups inhabit the Kenya Rift Valley. The most well-known are the Kalenjins and the Maasais. Kalenjins are known internationally for Kenya's legendary top long distant runners while the Maasais serve as Kenya's national symbol," she explained.

"Where in this map do you come from?" Liam asked, curious.

"Right here, the Tugen homeland," she said as she pointed at the Eldama Ravine town in the map.

"You mentioned you're from the Tugen tribe."

"Yes. The Tugen is one of the eight Kalenjin sub-tribes[1]. The Tugen tribe is in the Baringo district within the Great Rift Valley. The tribe is among the southern Nilotic dialect

---

[1] The other Kalenjin sub-tribes are Kipsigis, Nandi, Elgeyo, Maragwet, Pokot, Sabeiny, and Endo.

speaking Kalenjin group." Liam found this to be fascinating, but had trouble understanding everything Meggie told him.

"Among the Kalenjin tribes, can you understand the different language dialects?" Liam asked.

"Not all. As a Tugen, I understand Kisigis, Elgeyo, and Nandi. Marakwet, Sabeiny, and Endo, a bit, but not Pokot," Meggie replied.

"As an American, I only speak English. I'm accustomed to a society where people blended together. America is often referred to as a 'melting pot.'" Liam realized his situation was unlike Meggie's where the different tribes spoke distinctive languages, lived apart, and performed their own unique practices.

"You're amazing. I admire your ability to speak more than one language," he said. "How does your homeland compare to Phoenix?" he asked.

"Tugen land is spectacular, surrounded by two freshwater lakes. Lake Baringo to the north has more than 470 species of birds," Meggie said.

"I've heard that Africa is flamingo paradise," Liam commented.

"Absolutely. Our area is known for its migrating flamingoes. Lake Bogoria is one of those places of paradise, to the south of the valley basin, a little south of the Equator with natural geysers and hot springs. The hypersaline nature of the lake is a bonus for the flamingos. Millions in dense pink packs float on the surface of the lake—a breathtaking sight!"

"How big is Tugen?" Liam asked.

Meggie pointed back to the map. "The Tugen people are spread out, about a hundred miles in each direction," she said, illustrating the area with her finger.

"Some of my relatives were young when the first AIM Christian missionaries came to Kalenjin land. My grandparents had a very close relationship with them. Their perspective of the world was like day and night."

"How so?" he asked, eager to learn more.

"My existence began with four unique individuals; Grandpa George, Ester, Kiptarbei, and Talai."

"Why are your grandparents' names so different?" Liam asked. He suspected it had something to do with British settlers or Christian missionaries.

"I see I'm not the only one with a twisted past," Liam said.

"You'll be surprised. All of us have some twists and turns in our path. While yours is a mystery, and you still have a long way to find all the pieces of the puzzle, mine is about understanding who I am and figuring out what to believe in," she replied.

"I thought I was the only screwed up kid on the block," he said.

"I'm more screwed up than you are," she said, and they both laughed.

The shuttle driver interrupted then with an announcement—"We're ten minutes from a rest stop."

Liam checked his watch and commented, "That was fast. Already an hour since we left Phoenix. You're a nice person to talk to Meggie," he said.

"You too, Liam." She smiled up at him. "Since the time we met at the airport, it's been easy to talk to you," she added.

"Oh, thank you." Liam looked into her eyes and smiled at her.

Ryan interrupted them by calling out from the front, "Are you guys getting out?" he asked.

"Yes. I need to visit the restroom," Liam responded.

As soon as they stepped out, Liam commented, "Great place to stop and stretch out. There are clean restrooms and vending machines."

"Follow me. There's something I want to show you," Liam said as he motioned Meggie behind the facilities.

"Wow. What a stunningly beautiful panoramic view of the valley," she commented.

"It doesn't get old. Every time I stop by, it takes my breath away," he said.

"I bet there's no place like it," she said.

"Not until you see the mother of all wonders, the Grand Canyon," he said with enthusiasm as he stared at her.

"You look beautiful too," Liam said and wondered what was going on with him. He never said things like that. His statement came out of nowhere.

"Thank you," she said. Liam noticed her blush.

They chatted a little and departed to their respective restrooms.

Meggie emerged first and joined Isabel. "It's great to get out of books and just enjoy nature," Meggie said.

"Have you checked out the valley from the viewpoint over there?" Isabel said and pointed behind the facility.

"Yes. It's stunning," Meggie said.

"Arizona is a special place. Apart from the Grand Canyon, there are Native American cliff dwellings, ancient cultures and towns, and many other natural wonders."

"I hope to see as much as I can before I return home," Meggie said.

Lai called everyone back to the bus for the next phase of the journey.

As they resettled in the back of the van, Meggie said, "My family dynamics taught me that you cannot convince yourself you are right all the time. I didn't depend on others in making decisions regarding what to believe or not believe. Members of my family believed what they wanted to, and, most importantly, what made them happy. I dared to explore ideas that were uncomfortable and my exploratory journey continues."

Liam said, "I'm eager to hear more about your family's story."

"Okay, then," Meggie said. Meggie showed Liam a page with black and white photographs of young teenagers. As he pointed to George, Kiptarbei, Ester, and the other woman then known as Jerono, Meggie introduced each one.

In the photograph, George wore a shirt, shorts, and shoes. Kiptarbei was in traditional Tugen attire of shorts and gladiator shoes. His headdress was of beaded jewelry, and his ears had heavy brass coils that weighed down his earlobes. Jerono was in a sleeveless embroidered garment, a beaded headband, earrings, brass bracelets, and piles of beaded necklaces. Ester dressed in a conventional blouse, skirt, and shoes.

Meggie narrated, "George and Ester remembered with nostalgia the arrivals of the missionaries. The AIM agent recruited George, in particular, at a very early age. Their homestead was close to where the mission station was in Kapropita near Kabarnet town. Kabarnet was named after the AIM agent, Ally Barnett. *Ka* (homestead of) and *barnet* (the name of the agent). Pronunciation was quite a challenge for the Tugen people. The name *Kapropita* originated from complications in pronunciation of Corporal Peter, a British settler master, and the rest is history.

"The missionaries frequently visited George's homestead to request assistance because George and his family lived adjacent to the mission station. The missionary's calls ranged from asking for food sources to learning the native language and culture and most importantly gaining access to the rest of the community. The Tugen people lived sparsely with families and neighbors far from each other.

"The Christian lifestyle came with specific rules of engagement. After conversion to Christianity, the missionaries developed living quarters within the mission station. They asked converts then to move away from their families and live close to the missionaries, and referred to them as *Kristianik* (the Christian believers). Outside the Christian-community-quarters were the *kipteng'ekinik* (the non-believers). The missionaries ensured the Kristianiks complete isolation from the rest of society. Converts were to abandon their cultural practices and follow their new adopted way of life.

"George and Ester were Christian converts while Kiptarbei and Talai were non-believers, in case you are wondering about their difference in names and styles of dress," Meggie explained.

"I almost figured that out," he said. "What about their families?" Liam asked.

"George moved away from his family and lived with the missionaries in the mission station. As a Christian convert, George was not allowed to visit with his family or any other relatives; he was forbidden from ever practicing his Tugen culture."

"What would happen if your grandpa disobeyed and moved back to his parents?" Liam asked.

"Public admonishment, shame, humiliation, and scare tactics," Meggie said.

"George had only two choices. There was the needle's eye size narrow path to heaven or the wide road to the ever-blazing kingdom of hell. My grandpa precisely remembered most Sundays; those who strayed from the path by saying hello to their relatives were admonished publicly in front of every other convert in the church. By shame and humiliation, the missionaries managed to keep and grow the Christian community."

"So, why did your grandpa and others accept these demands without any fight?" Liam asked.

"Great question. I asked the same thing," Meggie said and paused for a while.

"And…?" Liam asked.

"According to grandpa Kiptarbei, the Christian missionaries had unmatched power and weaponry," she said. "The British settlers were closely associated with Catholic and Protestant missions in Africa. They had an advanced arsenal, unimaginable savagery, and colossal power. The missionaries, however, were characterized as Godly people of virtue and goodness, with an unwavering commitment to sacrifice their lives to save others from their sins. The missionaries and settler administrators were able to separate their roles from the eyes of the natives tactfully in the eyes of grandpa Kibtarbei. The missionaries were servants of God and the administrative settlers were law-and-order enforcers.

Christian teachings required a lifestyle of pure submission to authorities. Those particular principles were critical for the lifestyle. Roman 13:2 clarified, 'Therefore whoever resists authority has opposed the ordinance of God…' Titus 3 states, '1 remind them to be subject to rulers, to authority to be obedient…' 1 Peter 2:17 said, 'Honor all people, love the brotherhood, fear God, honor the king.' And so on. These are examples of misconstrued and misused teachings that drove many to submission to reinforce law and order as Kiptarbei perceived it. George thought otherwise, but these were significant Christian teachings that enabled many people to be civil and live a godly, respectable life.

"Kiptarbei thought George could not see through the masquerade. They vehemently disagreed on their perceptions on this particular issue. He saw the missionaries as sympathizers with the settler's rules. In my opinion, this was ironic because missionaries and the settler administrators still ate from the same table. I can understand there was some confusion on their part," Meggie said.

"How did the missionaries manage to convert so many people in such a short time?" Liam asked.

"Many were convinced that Christianity was more powerful than *Asis* the sun god. The indigenous Tugen people were extremely scared about the return of the Son of God because of human imperfection. Who is perfect every second of the hour, no one?"

"According to Kiptarbei, missionaries identified and converted specific members of families, then isolated them. The results ranged from ruined family ties, eroded customs, screwed up minds, and cultural systems forever destroyed. The worst was that the people who were now Christian converts or worked for the settler administration and the rest of the community deemed them traitors. If they worked for the missionaries, they became the enemies of the Tugen people. They were still blood relatives and members of the families. One of the Kalenjin sub-groups, known as the Pokot, was not influenced by the missionaries at the beginning."

"How did they manage that?" he asked, gazing at her with intense focus.

"They were no joke," she said. "They went mano-a-mano with the missionaries as well as the settlers and administration, each group trying to outdo the other. Each party understood very well that whichever party won the battle would practice all the customs and cultures of the other."

"How did they do this?" he asked with increased excitement.

Meggie slid and leaned over to Liam's ear. With a whisper, she said, "you know about the Central Intelligence Agency (CIA) waterboarding techniques, right?"

"Yeah, the interrogation technique simulating the experience of drowning. You know it has been banned, yes?"

"I know that the Pokot rituals were child's play compared to waterboarding. Both techniques violate human rights, but those who infringed on their cultural practices were subjected to some painful punishment. I heard that the Pokot's technique was even worse than waterboarding."

"That sounds horrifying. I wouldn't want to play with them." The story you told chills me to the bone.

The British settlers and the administrators and the missionaries eventually signed an agreement. If the British colonial territory wanted to work with the people of Pokot, they were to practice the Pokot customs, rituals, religion, and participate in their ceremonies. More importantly, they were to learn and be fluent in the Pokot language. The reverse was true, too, the British colonial government expected Pokot people to convert to Christianity, obey their laws, and learn to speak fluently in English. The British and the missionaries decided to stay away from the Pokot. Some members of the Kalenjin tribe who did not like the changes made by the British migrated to Pokot territory. Every immigrant regardless was to practice Pokot's customs, rituals, religion, and participate in their ceremonies and speak their language fluently."

"I figured George didn't migrate to Pokot?" Liam turned to Meggie and asked.

"No. He didn't. He was already branded a traitor. George was gifted," she said, smiling. "George could sell you a half-acent torn shoe for the price of a million-dollar gemstone, and you would buy it without thinking. The missionaries loved him," she said.

"George, even at the age of twelve, grew to be a great evangelist. He would visit the villages accompanied by a mission agent to spread the gospel. He also attended a school established within the church. He successfully convinced many parents to convert to Christianity and enroll their children in school to give them better lives. Most of them saw him as a role model and wanted their kids to be like him. He was a great asset to the mission.

"The Europeans settlers were very sophisticated in their expansion of influence through the world and in Africa. In the Tugen community, they established policies that restricted the movement of people and their livestock, which impacted the nomadic way of life that sustained their livestock. In the process, they calculatedly wiped out most of the traditional Tugen society systems and economies.

"The new Christian converts needed to be sustained and trained to carry out evangelical duties in the community—a train-the-trainer concept.

"To accomplish this goal, George needed to complete catechism, a form of preparation for baptism through question-and-answer teaching techniques that covered the major Christian principles. Upon completion, an AIM agent took him to the river, pushed him under the water to signify the burial of his old life. Then, he was reborn as he rose out of the water, a figurative symbol of commitment to a Christian way of life. They gave him the name George after baptism as his first name. He continued to go to a school where the three R's were essential basic knowledge and skills for reading scriptures, a fundamental tool for evangelism.

In Kiptarbei's view, the AIM evangelists focused on the concept of redeeming and healing the body, soul, and spirit. In a nutshell, George surrendered everything; body, soul, and mind as directed by the Christian missionaries," she said. "He no longer had control of any of them."

"I can understand, he made a personal choice to be a Christian," Liam interjected. "Correct me if I'm wrong. From what you're telling me, no one forced anyone to do what they didn't want to do, right?"

"Good question, I wondered the same thing," Meggie said, pausing.

"And...?" he urged, anxiously waiting for her response.

"This is my interpretation from what I gathered from him," she said with a sigh of resignation. "The British settler's rule and missionaries both in their unique ways used external forces such as money, military force, legal status, and physical strength. Simultaneously, internal forces such as vulnerability to disrespect, shame, humiliation, and inhumane treatment rendered him powerless. He also saw benefits in the Christian path. He liked school and evangelism, minus the powerlessness that he vehemently despised."

"I'm more interested in how they pulled off the body, soul, and mind evangelical strategic plan," Liam said, leaning forward toward her persuasively.

"Godliness and cleanliness were associated with the body," she said. "The evangelists made it clear to George from the beginning that the wages of sin were death. The worst part for him was his soul's dreadful eternal turmoil in hell. So, George memorized and lived by 2 Corinthians 5:1, 'Our body is the temple of the Lord in which the spirit lives here on earth. When the house is destroyed, then God will give another house. That house is not made by man's hand, but God made it. It will last forever in heaven.'"

"The evangelists taught that it was paramount for people to keep their body clean, literally. Anything evil outlined in the Ten Commandments of the Bible was an abomination."

"Thou shall not kill, kiss, get laid, or think about killing, kissing, or getting laid," Liam said jokingly.

"Yes, right!" Meggie said, laughing loudly.

"Refrain from indulging in bodily pleasures, tequila, Captain Morgan, Chateau Lafite Rothschild Paulliac," he said with sarcasm, raising his hands high and then dropping them with mock despair.

"Oh yeah, right!" she responded with amusement and raised her right eyebrow.

"That wasn't all, evangelism through medicine was critical to the mission. The first missionary doctors established dispensaries within the mission stations. These were staffed with nurses from the mission as well as trained indigenous Tugen converts as nurse aids. The mission provided services and correlated Western medicine with the healing power of God. Everyone understood that the power of God through their medicine made people better faster. How would one think otherwise if the observable evidence was obvious? People were healed faster when they visited dispensaries compared to using traditional medicine.

"No one told George the backstory of Western medicine, that they too at one time had epidemics because they didn't know better, that they died of diseases because of lack of hygiene, proper methods of sanitation, and waste management, that they have progressed and discovered better ways of treatment instead."

Meggie turned to face Liam. "Christians believe that humans have immortal souls. They considered all things related to the psyche or mind as an integral part of the body. Specifically, this includes feelings, thoughts, desires, beliefs, and all the resulting actions. Kiptarbei thought George's mind was in captivity. He had a Bible verse that guided every aspect of his life. For the mind, Philippians 4:18, 'Finally, brothers and sisters, whichever true, whatever noble, whatever is right, whatever is pure, whatever is lovely, whatever is admirable, if anything is excellent or praiseworthy, think about such things,'" she said.

"The verse is awesome. That's an exceptional standard to live by."

"I agree with you in the context of an unbound, self-directed, self-monitored, and self-corrective mind. A mind that has been dominated by intellectual conquest is a fully suppressed, limited mind. In this case, Kiptarbei was convinced that George had put his Christian beliefs ahead of his own. Even worse, he was thinking of himself, and his Christian beliefs without any regard for his family and his community's feelings," she said. "Liam, what if someone told you that God only expected you to drink from this well. That is, if there is no alternative, and if you think otherwise, you will burn in hell because God says so. If you get thirsty, and you think about a soda as an alternative, that is sin," she illustrated with an analogy.

"Come on, Meggie! That's harsh judgment, don't you think?" he asked.

"Kiptarbei didn't think so. He wondered how anyone could disown his own family because they were sinners," she said. "In his mind, George had done exactly that, and Kiptarbei always wondered how something like that could happen."

"But what choice did George have? What would you have done, Meggie? Put yourself in his shoes and tell me, what could you have done?" he questioned her judgment.

"I don't know." Meggie was feeling frustrated by Liam's view of George's choices.

"I get it, but think about it. You're a doctor, Meggie. How many times have you been faced by situations in which you had to choose between two unfavorable choices? That's what George had to do. Making a choice must have been very hard for him. He was caught by the balls and squeezed so tight he couldn't breathe. Can't you see that?" he said, trying to bring Meggie out of her obvious vexation.

She raised her head and looked at Liam. "Do you practice any religion? How did you come to practice it? You don't have to answer if you don't want to," she said.

"I like the question. I've never thought of it as practice. It's not like the way we practice medicine: However both have a culture, processes, rules, and rituals." Liam contemplated for a while. "Protestant, I suppose I practice Protestantism," he said. "What about you?" he asked.

Meggie considered for a moment. "Protestant, too. I mainly attend the African Inland Church, the one I grew up in. But I consider myself a spiritual person. I go to any church whenever I want to. I worship mostly with the church near where I live. However, I have spent time with all the religions in my town. I am very uncomfortable with the associated rituals and rules in organized religions. I don't want to end up like George," she said.

"Processes, policies, and culture are important for consistency. You should know that better than most, as a doctor," he said.

"Yet, the practice shouldn't be rigid. There needs to be room to evolve and change. Don't you agree?" she asked.

Liam looked quizzically at Meggie.

"The inability to evolve and change greatly affected my family and eventually shaped who I am today," she said.

"What happened?" he asked,

"It's a long historical journey. When George became a Christian, those he left behind believed in their own God. That created conflict," she said.

"The other side of my family was immersed totally in Tugen culture with no influence from the outside world. Kiptarbei's family were also spiritual people. They believed that *Ngony* (earth) and *Kipsenguet* (heaven) were dynamic and permanent. Christianity, which was gaining roots in Tugen land at the time, believed that the world would one day come to an end upon the return of Jesus Christ. Unlike the Christians, indigenous Tugen people believed there was no end to the world. They believed that floods, earthquakes, and lightning were natural phenomena, not a form of punishment by God."

"How do you compare Asis and Christianity?" Liam asked.

"When I look at religions or spirituality, I see how the concept of a higher power is approached differently," Meggie responded.

"Look around the world. Most wars are religious. Each side tries to justify that it is the chosen one. Each side is passionate about its own beliefs—convinced that their religion is the legitimate and superior one," Liam said.

"Sure, the Christians deemed those who believed differently as lost or sinners," Meggie said. "Tugen elders traveled to the highest elevation of Tugen hills to offer sacrifices to the sun god. They would rise at dawn and carry specially prepared wood for the occasion. Up at the top of the hill, they prepared a gazebo and arranged firewood. They would then lay out the sacrifice and watch it burn as they chanted prayers."

"That sounds like Abraham sacrificing Isaac," Liam explained.

"Yes but I am not in anyway equating. The imagery of smoke rising straight to the sky is interpreted as God's reception of and satisfactions in the elder's prayers, just like in the example of Abraham," Meggie said.

"The elders were men who were *libwoben* (older men who were clean from sins). In Kiptarbei's viewpoint, they were not less and not significantly different from the Christian Old Testament teachings. If there were great distress in the Tugen land associated with crime or family calamities, they would ask God, 'we have suffered so much, and we did not kill the son of God.'

"The women designed and developed *kimwoche* (a prayer gazebo) in sacred spots where paths crossed, in varied locations within the community, which served as a local gathering place where neighbors met for worship and prayer. The older women would advise on the type of birch tree branches to be used in its creation. The design shapes were mostly oval and square."

"How does it compare with a standard American gazebo?" Liam asked, pulling up a picture from his phone.

"A little different. The framework is constructed from wood with a solid foundation made to withstand the elements," Meggie said. They built the gazebo walls with mud; a mixture of clay, cow dung, and hay bound together with water and then decorated with paint from various colored soils. The ultimate decoration was with a bright yellow *lobot* fruit. It was a wonder of beauty."

"Meggie, don't you see that both George and Kiptarbei missed the point?" Liam said as he drew Meggie's attention. "The concept of God is that of a higher power, a supernatural being."

"I know that such a power is also associated with good. The divine attributes include wisdom, purity, and love," Meggie said.

"Both of them ought to have attempted to apply those attributes to their lives, that's what's important. There are universal ethical principles that are practiced by most people, such as treating others as you would like to be treated, helping the poor or those in need," Liam explained what he thought George and Kiptarbei should have done.

"I don't disagree with you. At some point, each of my grandfathers committed to a specific worldview and aspired to live by its principles and practices. However, people use religion and some cultural practices for other detrimental reasons."

Meggie appreciated Liam's thoughtful perspective. She found him to be rational. He respected evidence, particularly if it didn't support his views. She was becoming aware of the bond of intellectual chemistry.

CHAPTER 8

Africa: Truth or Fiction?

THE SHUTTLE PARKED AT FLAGSTAFF'S Amtrak station.

Liam looked at Meggie. "That was fast. Your story distracted me."

"You look lost in your own thoughts," Meggie inquired.

Meggie's reflections on her family story raised many questions with Liam, but her narrative stopped when they arrived in Flagstaff.

"Is everyone awake?" Liam asked, raising his voice to check on Ryan, Lai, and Isabel.

"The ride was too smooth. It knocked us all out," Ryan said sleepily.

"The next shuttle should be here within twenty minutes," Liam said.

The drive to Williams was shorter. They were at the hotel's front desk at the Kaibab National Forest within thirty minutes. Because Liam's family often took their out-of-state guests to the Grand Canyon, people at the hotel knew Liam. The receptionist handed him five keys for their assigned rooms, and the hotel porter grabbed their luggage and motioned them to follow him to their respective rooms.

The group agreed to take thirty minutes to refresh themselves before exploring a little before dinner.

Liam booked five king-sized rooms on the third floor, facing each other. The hotel had adopted a consistent standard décor. The rooms were designed in grays, black, and white to create a luxurious, modern feel. A statement chandelier dangled over each bed, amping up the lavish feel of the room. The carpet featured a black and gray abstract design. Meggie immediately noticed the taupe silk velvet upholstered headboard that matched the bed skirt and the white bed linens. The furniture in the room was minimal, just enough to serve essential functions; a mixture of old ornamental pieces and modern pieces meticulously chosen to enhance the sparkle in the room. The uncluttered room was serene and sophisticated.

As an Arizona native, Liam wanted to provide his guests with a relaxed place to stay and dine. About a mile from the hotel was a restaurant with a global vibe, with comfort and healthy food options, and alcohol. "Good evening, sir, and welcome," the restaurant attendant reached out to Liam who was leading the group.

"I made dinner reservation for five at seven this evening under the name Liam Barsy."

"Yes, Mr. Barsy. Please be seated in the waiting area. We'll be with you shortly."

"Thank you. We'll have drinks while we're waiting." Liam said.

"I'd prefer an outside table," Lai said, "if it's possible."

"Fantastic idea. It's Fall here in Arizona, and the weather is cooler. We have to take advantage of it," Ryan said.

"Would you like to take one of those tables?" The hostess asked, pointing to a group of tables on the patio. "I can seat you there right away."

"Sure, that's great. Thank you," Liam said.

The hostess distributed the menus. "Are you ready to order your drinks now?"

"Yes," Liam said. "I'll have a light beer, Corona," he chuckled. "We have a long day tomorrow."

"A Corona for me, too," Ryan said. Meggie ordered tea, Isabel white wine, and Lai a Coke.

A few minutes later, a waiter distributed the drinks. "Are you ready to order?"

The group continued to eat, drink, and chat as they waited for their meals to arrive. Liam handed Meggie some Grand Canyon brochures.

"The Grand Canyon has so many wonderful things to explore. Unfortunately, we don't have enough time to see them all. Check these out. Let me know what catches your eye," Liam said.

"Okay," Meggie said as she took the brochures and distributed them to their colleagues.

"Meggie, tell me about my buddy Willy. Have you talked to him lately? We touch base once or twice a month and it has been a while since I talked to him. I have been more preoccupied with school work lately" Ryan asked.

"Not lately, no. I've been busy, but we text occasionally. Willy is doing well," Meggie said as she glanced at Liam at the other side of the table.

Isabel seemed preoccupied with Liam. Is Isabel flirting with Liam? How long has she known Liam? Meggie wondered.

Meanwhile, Ryan focused on Meggie with long-lasting and intense eye contact as they talked. He had developed some genuine feelings for her, particularly after the incident on the basketball court, but did she reciprocate those feelings?

Lai enjoyed observing the unfolding drama. It was better than reality TV; he thought because he was in it. "I don't know about you guys, but I'm tired. I can walk back to the hotel if you still want to stay, no pressure," Lai excused himself, standing up.

"I'll go with you," Meggie volunteered.

"We're a unit. We'll go together. Let me settle the bill," Liam said.

They left the restaurant and headed back to the hotel.

"Can I talk to you for a minute?" Liam asked Meggie, placing a hand on her arm as the rest of the group went to their respective rooms.

"How can I help you?" Meggie asked.

"The story, I'm dying to hear the rest," he said, smiling almost bashfully.

"You're not tired?" Meggie asked.

"I won't get any sleep wondering what happened next," Liam said.

"Okay. Come on in," Meggie smiled and invited him to her room. They settled in and Meggie continued the narration.

Kiptarbei detested the new cultural changes brought by the mission and the British settlers because they didn't make sense to him. He had known George from young a young age. They lived in the same neighborhood before George moved to the mission station.

During one of George's evangelical visits to the village, he ran into Jerono. She was eighteen and lived next to George's family's homestead. She wanted nothing to do with the mission.

"*Changei*," George greeted Jerono.

"Hello," she responded almost defiantly, her shoulders back, chest out, chin high as she looked directly at George.

George looked at her, impressed with her confidence. "It's been ages since I saw you," he said. "You have grown to be a beautiful woman." He extended his hand to greet her.

Jerono extended her hand toward him, "You are a big man, too," she said and smiled.

He was two years older than Jerono.

"How are your people?" he asked.

"They're okay," she responded, looking straight into his eyes. "I have to go. I'll be in trouble if people see us together." She looked left, right, and left again to ensure that no one was looking, then locked her eyes onto his without saying a word.

George and Jerono were close at a very young age before he moved to the mission. This meeting was their first encounter in the thirteen years since his departure.

After a very long silence, Jerono asked, "Why did you leave?"

"I'm a born-again Christian now. I live a different life, that which pleases the Lord," he replied.

George was interrupted by a voice from behind, "*Bakulei*, go back to where you came from," a male figure said. "We don't need you here. You left, and we are doing fine without you." He moved swiftly and pulled Jerono away from George.

Jerono's eyes never left George's as Kiptarbei dragged her away. George saw her blink, and tears rolled down her cheek.

"Kiptarbei, Kiptarbei, what are you doing?" George asked.

In normal circumstances, George and Kiptarbei would be like brothers, not by blood but through a rite of passage, an age-set bond initiation ceremony. But, because of George's conversion, that was not the case. Kiptarbei was referring to

George as *Bakulei* (a reference to same age-set colleagues or someone in the same rite-of-passage event) as a reminder of what could have happened if he had not left.

Kiptarbei and Jerono's parents brought them up in an exclusively Tugen traditional culture. Their families stayed away from the new British settlers and the Christian lifestyle. However, they had to abide by the movement restrictions and tax laws established by the new order.

Kiptarbei turned to Jerono when they were some distance away from George.

"You should never get close to George and the AIM agents, you hear me?" he scolded Jerono. "If you do, I will inform your father."

"Leave me alone. May lightning strike you, devil," she looked at him blurting out curses. Her face tightened, and tears streamed down her cheeks.

"Calm down now, Jerono," he said and loosened his posture to calm the situation.

Jerono was livid with rage, shaking incredibly with her hand clenched. "Devil, you want me to keep quiet? May lightning strike you dead!" she repeated. "I will not be silenced by you or your father, got it?" She clenched her teeth. "I am tired of being told what to do."

"You have smitten me from a long time ago, and no one will ever take my woman from me," Kiptarbei said.

"Now, that is a decision made alone in your head," she said. "I am not part of it, yet. Do you have a right to decide for me?" she asked with a disgusted snort.

"I'm telling you the truth," he said.

"You're crazy. Your head's not working." she said. Jerono opened the left palm of her hand and spat on it, stroked it with her right hand and said, "I'm taking an oath never to step in your smelly rondavel as long as I live."

Jerono ran home to her family crying. Kiptarbei followed her path but branched toward his homestead.

Late in the evening after dinner and his routine evening prayers, George wondered what he was going to do as he lay in his bed. It was time, and he felt ready to get married. The meeting that day with Jerono ignited some feelings and longing for her. All his childhood memories with her came rushing back.

He recalled Jerono as an energetic, witty little girl. She was seven, and George was nine then. She knew that George liked her attention compared to the other children. At a young age, Jerono knew how to get her way. She was an outgoing, friendly, and unafraid girl. One particular time as George was telling a riddle to the other kids, Jerono squeezed herself into the center of the group, staged herself close to George, looked at him and stole the show commanding everyone to listen to her riddle. They had all stopped talking and paid attention.

"*Tangoch* (I want to ask if you know)?" she asked.

"*Tiony* (I am ready)," he responded.

"*A buch maba* (What is inverted, but does not pour its contents)?" she asked.

"*Kindekab teta* (a cow's udder)," he responded.

"You got it. I have *Sirwoi*, the white, and *Tuyai*, the black cow. Which one do you want?" she responded with excitement.

"*Sirwoi*," he replied.

Young children used informal learning through storytelling, songs, and riddles. This riddle was a lesson about dimensions. Jerono, in a group, would dominate or completely redirect conversations though she was the youngest.

George came out of his time-traveling trance and drifted back to reality. No way the AIM will allow me to marry someone from the village. He was convinced.

Meanwhile, Jerono's parents saw her running and asked, "What is chasing you?".

"It's the devil."

"The devil?" her mother asked, confused.

"Yes, Kiptarbei," she said.

"Why would you call him the devil?" her mother asked. "Your father is very fond of him."

"Then, perhaps he should marry him. Not me. I despise him. I hate him from the bottom of my heart."

"That is disrespectful. Learn your manners, my girl," her mother said.

"I mean it. I truly despise Kiptarbei. That is the opposite of love. Don't you get it?" she said as she ran away from her mother to the rondavel, she shared with her sisters.

Her heart was racing, and she was so short of breath that her body was shaking violently. She felt enraged and frustrated. She lay face down on her bed, sobbing uncontrollably. She felt suffocated without any outlet for her to express her feelings. Jerono hit the side of the bed with her fist again and again. "Why? Why? Why?" she asked herself over and over.

People of the village would call her a slut if she dared to express her love. Customarily, expressing love through verbalizing feelings, emotions or physical touch openly was deemed immoral. Since she was a young girl, she had loved George, yet he was so far away from her reality. She tried to block it all out, but nothing happened. Love is natural. It is conceived naturally and grows—even in the dark. Just like anything that grows, it needs to be fed, Jerono's love was starved. She felt grumpy, and drained of energy. She was lost in her passion for George, and it felt difficult to move forward without it. How worse can hell be from what I am feeling now, Jerono wondered.

A woman had no powers regarding her own heart. Tugen culture had bestowed all of the power to the clansmen. She ran through the Tugen laws in her head to see if any loopholes provided a chance to fulfill the desires of her heart. Thou shall not disobey your father, brother, and clansmen. Thou shall submit to your elders. Thou shall provide for your family. Thou shall bear children, particularly sons. Jerono felt like these laws had destined her to be a servant for the rest of her life. What if I were free like a bird, and belonged to no one, she thought. She would choose her space in the world and play by her own rules without approval from others.

Jerono felt extremely tired by everything. Her life was a perfect war zone of massacred hopes.

Meanwhile, George returned to his living quarters in the mission station. He worked hard to suppress his foolhardy, overwhelming desire to define and fight for his true love. For a moment, he forgot about the mission as his Tugen warrior roots awakened in his bloodstream. Every muscle tensed. "I just stood frozen and looked at him pull Jerono away from me without doing anything," he muttered to himself. "But does it even matter? The mission won't allow me to get married to a girl from a family of non-believers."

George was still a Tugen by blood. To be a Tugen warrior and a Christian at that time meant constant conflicting emotions. He hated that he could not fight back as a warrior for Jerono. Instead, he had to follow the British settlers' law and the mission rules. He loved Jerono. He hated Kiptarbei. He wanted to embrace Jerono and hold her tight. He wanted to strangle Kiptarbei and see him drift into oblivion. Warring emotions tore him apart.

He entered his rondavel and went straight to bed. As he lay down, he wondered if he would survive the pain. Around midnight when he woke up and realized he had fallen asleep. He jumped out of bed and said out loud, "Forgive me, dear Lord, but when did I give Kiptarbei the power to screw me up like this without a fight?"

George ran out of the rondavel toward Jerono's homestead. He knew there was no one other than Jerono with whom he would rather spend the rest of his life. He wanted to be the only anchor she needed. His worst fear was to lose her.

George felt convinced that Jerono would convert to Christianity and join him in the mission when she realized how much he loved her. Yet, he was ready to sacrifice and abandon his Christian ambitions and return to his Tugen roots if that was the only way to be together with her. George was as wild as an angry lion protecting his territory, focused, fearless, and confident.

As he approached Jerono's rondavel, he noticed a *ngotit* (spear). He walked closer and directed the fire torch that he held on his right hand toward it. The metal blade was shiny and serrated, freshly sharpened at the head. It had a long wooden handle, pinned firmly to the ground.

George gave a strangled growl like that of a desperate killer lion. Then, he screamed so loud, the scream's echo reverberated miles away. Jealousy and hatred overwhelmed him. His passion for fighting for Jerono stirred the deepest, darkest side of him. He felt as though he were exploding. He no longer cared about the possible agonizing consequences ahead.

In the Tugen tradition, clansmen used a spear to mark territory. In situations where there was war, and many men died in battle, those who survived would volunteer to take care of the families of the fallen. A spear in front of the rondavel signaled others never to step foot in that rondavel, for someone else took the woman inside. All the tribe understood and respected the spear, no matter what.

George was filled with rage. Not only was he late, but Tugen cultural practice mocked him. He knew he had no other option but to fight for his dignity. He sprinted toward Kiptarbei's homestead.

He was sweating when he arrived at the homestead. Despair and anger made him tremble violently.

"A coward, hiding under the disguise of a spear," George called Kiptarbei. "*Mongun, Mongun* (come out, come out), you coward. How dare you pretend to know what Jerono wants for her life? Did you even ask her if she loves you? I know she loves me. I saw it; I felt it; and I want to marry her," George shouted into the night.

"Sorry brother. I was ahead of you. It was decided already. Forget it and move on with your life in the mission. Get a wife from the girl's hostels. There are plenty of them there. They've taken almost every girl we know here in the village. Aren't those enough? Get out of my homestead," 'Kiptarbei demanded.

Furious, George kicked Kiptarbei's door open and rushed into his rondavel. Kiptarbei was as angry as a black-necked cobra ready to spray its venom at the approaching George. "Leave my rondavel in peace before one of us dies." he barked at George. "Let's take this outside my rondavel."

George obeyed the direction and stepped out.

The battle was officially on. One of them would eventually lose both the girl and the brotherhood relationship. Three crucial things were at stake: Jerono, the connection of tribal brotherhood, and pride.

And who did Jerono prefer? Would she prefer a man who would sacrifice his pride for her or a man who would fight for her with all his might to win her love? Neither was a recipe for an automatic win.

Without any notice, Kiptarbei thrashed George across the head, initiating one-on-one combat. George moved swiftly and grabbed him as he stabilized his relative position toward George. He tried to get Kiptarbei in a clinch but was off-balance and overpowered. George fought back and lifted Kiptarbei off, pushing him to the ground in a takedown, landing on top of him. George pinned Kiptarbei to the ground. He completely subdued him, assuming greater control over him.

"So, what do you say? Are you going to get the spear out of that rondavel?" George asked.

Kiptarbei tried to escape, but George applied extreme force to his spine by twisting and bending his head into an atypical position. Kiptarbei screamed, "*Aya, aya bakulei* (Okay, okay brother). I will go and get it out. Please stop. Stop, I can't move."

George realized how far he had pushed.

"My God, this is not going to end well," he muttered to himself. He pulled himself away quickly, and pulled Kiptarbei to his feet.

"Kiptarbei, I almost killed you," George said regretfully.

"May lightning strike you. May you never bring forth the next generation," Kiptarbei cursed him bitterly as he stood up and pushed past George into his rondavel.

George walked away from Kiptarbei's rondavel back to the mission station. He had taken less than ten steps when he turned back and tried to reason with Kiptarbei. However, before he could take another step, he felt something excruciatingly painful hit him in the thigh. George fell, screaming in such agony that neighboring homesteaders started running toward the outcry.

Kiptarbei had gone back to the rondavel, retrieved his bow and arrow, and aimed at George's crotch. He missed, and the arrow struck George's thigh instead.

Kiptarbei's father was the first one to arrive. He found George in a fetal position with an arrow sticking out of his upper right thigh. Blood soaked through his pants.

"Thank God, the serrated blade was on the other side of the thigh," Kiptarbei's father said. "Who did something like this?" Kiptarbei's father muttered as he examined the extent of George's injuries.

George's adrenaline wore off, and the pain exploded like dynamite. His heart beat like a blacksmith's anvil. His breathing became irregular. Panic showed in both George and Kiptarbei's father's eyes.

"You did this, didn't you?" Kiptarbei's father asked as he looked at his son, who still had the bow and arrow in his hands. "Does it have the poison?" he asked, quietly and severely.

George heard the conversation through the waves of pain and panicked. He suddenly felt light-headed, and finally passed out.

"This is a bad," Kiptarbei muttered to himself and responded, "Yes."

"Which one?" his father yelled back. "Is it the viper-venom or the dart-poison frog dip?"

"Dart-poison frog dip?" Kiptarbei replied. Just like guns, poisons varied according to the degree of damage they inflicted, Tugens had various arrowheads treated with different poison geared to specific purposes. The most poisonous arrows were meant for war—they were meant to kill. They used others to hunt for food.

"Run, go get it."

Kiptarbei knew what his father meant. His father was a *chekerichon* (a medicine man), and Kiptarbei helped him on many occasions to secure, prepare, and administer herbal medicine for community members. He was skilled and highly regarded.

The position of medicine man was a hereditary occupation passed down to his father by his grandfather. His father was the only one in his family who knew the secrets about the herbs. Kiptarbei was the sole child in his family among eight siblings who received the insight of the craft. From a very young age, his father invited Kiptarbei to select the herbs from the forest, sit by him frequently to learn their names, isolate the necessary ingredients, and prepare them for administration, which was thorough training.

Kiptarbei knew that he needed to run to the nearby stream to search for the deadliest frog on the planet. It was brightly tri-colored, blue, red, and yellow—the most toxic among the species.

Dart-poison frogs are about an inch long with killer toxic skin secretions. They thrive in wet, tropical rain forests. *Kipniwai*, the stream, was densely covered with trees that allowed minimal sunlight at its base. Shade-tolerant herbs and shrubs provided an excellent habitat for these poison arrow frogs—the main ingredient for the community's ammunition.

Just as many Kalenjin are known for their dominance in global track championships over many decades, Kiptarbei was no different. He was slim with thin ankles and calves with long legs and a short torso. He propelled himself like a projectile, running for a mile Kiptarbei reached the stream in about seven minutes. He hunted for these frogs many times. Laser-focused on the frogs, he pictured the patterns on the skin and knew where they hid in the stream. He saw the tiny killer poison monster waiting patiently for its prey. There it was. He was face-to-face with the frog where he had imagined it to be. Its distinctive coloration repelled other animals. Kiptarbei knew that these frogs could hop swiftly away when in danger, but Kiptarbei was fast. He had been taught by his father how to safely handle the poison dart frog. He firmly but gently grabbed one of the frog in his right hand and placed it into an holding container. He raced to get back to the homestead.

Meanwhile, his father was nursing George, who was still unconscious. He made sure he was breathing. He tilted his head slowly, opened his mouth slightly to allow more air to get to his lungs, then kept checking for normal breathing. He moved around George as he talked to himself. He could have been praying or cursing; no one could tell.

"Prepare and bring it quickly," he demanded of his son, who just returned panting from his run.

"Yes, father," Kiptarbei responded respectfully.

Kiptarbei's father counted the seconds, fearful of the shock, necrosis, tetanus, or death that could result from the poison and the spear if there were further delay. The anxiety was playing tricks on his mind. He imagined parts of George's body, dead with feasting maggots, appearing from nowhere. However, when he blinked, George was still lying down, motionless and unconscious.

Kiptarbei was moving fast. He burned the frog to produce ash, and mixed it with already processed herbal extract and dried leaves. Once it was ready, he hurriedly brought the medicine to his father.

"Here it is," Kiptarbei breathlessly handed the concoction to his father. He was pacing around George, sweating profusely. He finally extended his hand and took the medicine from his son.

"Get the operation kit, water, and a piece of cloth from the rondavel. Move quickly," he yelled.

He assessed the wound; the point of entry, and the point of exit. Kiptarbei's father inspected the extent of the serration of the metal blade, the thickness of the poison in the arrow, the type of metal used for edge. He noted the position of the arrow in George's upper thigh, how deeply launched in his flesh it was, and how close it was to his bones. His appraisal took several minutes. As soon as his son arrived with the kit, he was ready and immediately began the operation.

"Wrap that small piece of wood with the cloth you came with. Place it between the upper and lower jaw of his mouth. Be sure to position it securely between the upper and lower teeth." he directed his son.

Slowly and meticulously, without unnecessary movements that would disturb the arrow protruding out of George's thigh, he cut off the blade at the joint with the wood. He cleaned most of the poison from the wood and applied the medicine.

He motioned to Kiptarbei, "Ready? I am pulling out the arrow. Hold him firmly to the ground."

Kiptarbei complied, and his father pulled out the remaining part of the arrow from George's thigh. As soon as the shaft was out, panic and horror replaced relief.

"We are in real trouble," Kiptarbei's father muttered with shock.

The arrow had pulled out a massive amount of dead tissue. The poison had quickly killed the surrounding cells, preventing the blood supply essential for oxygen transport and other nutrients needed for their survival. Often patients succumbed and died in such instances.

Kiptarbei's father cleaned the wound as best as he could and poured the medicinal concoction through it, then wrapped it with a cloth.

"Let's take him to the mission. Quick! Bring the stretcher."

He called for additional help from the neighborhood. Neighbors took George to the AIM mission station dispensary for further treatment.

The following day, George emerged from his coma. Jerono and Kiptarbei stood at the left side of the bed when he first opened his eyes. The nurse was to the right of his bed. checking his injured thigh.

"It's great to see you back. How are you feeling?" the nurse asked as she smiled at George.

"I'm in a hell of pain. What happened?" he asked, in a groggy and muddled voice.

"*Bakulei*, I am sorry for what happened," Kiptarbei said. "Jerono is here. We do not need to fight. She will decide who she wants. I came here to apologize and seek your forgiveness."

George just stared. He was too tired and in too much pain to respond. Tears rolled down to the back of his head as he lay in the dispensary bed. Were they tears of sadness, anger, or remorse? Everyone in the room silently pondered.

After five long minutes, Kiptarbei excused himself and walked out of the dispensary. The nurse followed suit.

Jerono took a chair from the right corner of the room and placed it next to George. She uncovered his hand from under the blanket, and held it. For a long time, they sat without a word. George cried quietly, and moments later, Jerono's tears joined his.

"I want to marry you, Jerono," he said. "I love you so much. Please come with me to the mission," he begged and squeezed her hand.

"You remember mom and dad, yours and mine?" she said.

"Of course I do," he said.

"That's why I can't come with you. I'm the only one old enough to take care of them. I take care of both of them now," Jerono said.

"I can come with you. I will never be happy without you. But AIM will not allow me to marry you if you don't become a Christian," he said.

"I know, I know. Our parents won't convert. I'll never put them through any difficulties. They've lost too much, including children, wealth, and dignity to foreigners. I don't think they could endure the pain or any added turmoil. I love you, too, but we've got to do what we have to do," she said with great sadness, giving his hand a gentle squeeze. "Get well soon, my love. If nothing else, know that I loved you."

Jerono embraced him and then walked away hurriedly before George could say anything.

The torture of loving Jerono was worse than the pain of George's injuries. It drove him crazy and left him hopelessly crying for days. He grieved the loss of the love he couldn't have. It felt like death. The torment and sadness were wounds that no one could heal. He wished he could wake up from this living nightmare.

"Oh God, take this pain away from me, I beg you. Heal my bleeding heart," he prayed to God. "You are near the brokenhearted. Please save my crushed spirit."

For a month, George pushed through his recovery with courage and determination. More than ever he wanted to succeed in the vision of the AIM mission and his education.

When he returned home to the mission George revealed his sinful transgressions to the congregation without reservation. The humiliation and admonishment were nothing in contrast to the pain of his injuries and the heartbreak from which he was recovering.

Later, the Tugen elders took up the event of George's shooting to adjudicate it. Senior elders in the community served as judges for the community, others as judges of the Tugen cultural court. The members of this team gathered evidence and thoroughly investigated the actions of both Kiptarbei and George that contributed to the fight.

According to Kiptarbei, he directed Jerono to get away from George. He also advised George to stay away from the community that he abandoned and urged him to stick to his AIM mission territory. Jerono had complied. Both Kiptarbei and Jerono left George initially standing where they met him. Kiptarbei had not initiated, nor provoked, George after that.

George's retaliation occurred in Kiptarbei's homestead, a trespass violation. George committed an offense when he confronted Kiptarbei in his homestead. Kiptarbei argued that he was defending himself considering the physical harm that George inflicted on him. He believed that if George were to turn back and pursue him after he cursed him, he would have been dead. Kiptarbei shot George with a poisoned arrow to defend himself from further harm.

The elders unanimously agreed that if George had not gone back to Kiptarbei's rondavel out of anger, this incident would not have occurred. In conclusion, George confronted Kiptarbei in his own home without any provocation. In the verdict, Kiptarbei was found not guilty. Instead, George was found guilty of trespass. They ordered him to deliver a doe to Kiptarbei, the fine for his actions. The elders directed them to seek reconciliation.

As George recovered from his injuries, his mother approached Jerono. She figured Jerono was the focus of this conflict, and she hoped to help in the mediation process.

Although Jerono still raged with anger at Kiptarbei's approach to the situation, she was sympathetic to George's mother, who the elders assigned to deliver the fine to Kiptarbei's homestead in George's absence. Jerono volunteered to accompany her to deliver the doe.

"I hope we live in peace and harmony going forward," Jerono said as she handed Kiptarbei the rope that was tied to the doe.

"Settled. This kind of thing will never happen again. It shouldn't have happened in the first place. I regret the consequences my actions caused those I care about," he replied.

Kiptarbei took the goat. Jerono and George's mother left for their homesteads. Jerono exuded confidence and power as she left; Kiptarbei standing with the doe felt embarrassed and defeated.

***

Liam was utterly fascinated. "You look tired, do you want to go to bed?" Liam asked. He noticed Meggie yawning.

"Not yet. I still want to look through all the Grand Canyon information," Meggie said.

"And I want to hear more of the story, please," he said, insisting. Now he thought he must be losing his mind. What did he want from her? Was it the story that interested him, or something else?

"Okay, I still have a little time before I read through the Grand Canyon stuff," Meggie gave in to his request.

"So, you study for trips?" Liam asked teasingly.

"Did you know that the Grand Canyon Railway took off the first time in 1900?" Meggie inquired.

"I didn't know that. Very interesting. But not nearly as interesting as your family

history."

"What about your history with Isabel?" Meggie asked.

"There is no history," Liam said, matter-of-factly.

"Good to know," Meggie responded.

Liam sat gazing at her for a while, wondering why she had asked about Isabel. Could she be jealous? He held her gaze for a long time.

CHAPTER 9

A Surprising Proposal

"I'VE BEEN TELLING YOU MY family's story, but I think love is a fairytale, an incredible, sometimes delusional feeling that you're special to someone," Meggie said. "How do you know you're in love?" she asked as she turned to face him.

Liam got up, stretched his legs, and looked at Meggie before he responded. "You've got to live fully to love. Relationships add zest to your life," Liam said out loud. He was thinking something more visceral. He felt attracted to her. They were sitting three feet from a bed. Why did she ask me about love? He thought to himself. I'd love to have just a kiss from her.

"Meggie," he called out her name in a coarse voice never leaving her sleepy, sexy, and inviting eyes.

Holy shit! I wish he understood what his voice did to me, Meggie thought. She was almost finding it hard to breath in anticipation of what Liam wanted to say. His sudden proximity as he moved closer made things even worse. She could smell the scent of Corona from dinner.

He suddenly leaned back, "I won't deny that I want you, Meggie," Liam said and sheepishly smiled at her, then stood. "I've got to go," he said. Liam realized that he wanted more than just sex from Meggie.

Liam's statement did not surprise Meggie. She appreciated Liam's introducing respect into the romance, if there was one at this time.

"I understand," Meggie said. "Here, take my journal," she handed Liam her iPad. "Use 11223344 to open it," she said.

Liam took the iPad, lingering close to her before he left. "Sleep tight," he said as he closed the door behind him.

"Ciao," Meggie said quietly, minutes after the door was already closed.

Liam got ready for bed. Generally, reading relaxed him. Meggie's journals did the opposite. They made him feel alive. He was determined to read through the rest of her family's story even if it meant staying up all night.

The journal continued. "Five years passed since the fight with Kiptarbei. George was still stationed at Kapropita Mission Station. He recovered fully, learned fast, and gained confidence and trust from AIM. He taught at the mission school and also served as the assistant pastor to the AIM agent. George occasionally delivered sermons on Sundays. However, he was not happy and longed for Jerono. George was still torn by his love for Jerono and his Christian missionary work—he knew he could not have both. After many anguished days, he decided to move on and focus on the mission despite his feelings for Jerono. The strictures of AIM did not allow George to reach out to his family, even though they lived close.

One particular Sunday, George was scheduled to deliver the sermon in church. He prepared to talk about redemption. At ten-thirty that morning, the congregation's leader, the emcee of the day, went to the podium, greeted the congregation, led the assembled in an opening prayer, and introduced the worship team. The congregation sang gospel hymns and offerings were collected. The preacher then delivered the word of God.

"Let us bless brother, George. In the hands of God, he will be used as His holy instrument," the AIM agent prayed and introduced George to the congregation.

George was in the middle of his sermon when he noticed a well-dressed man emerge from the front door of the church. George stopped delivering his sermon to look at him. George couldn't initially recognize him. As the man drew closer, George noticed the man's white and khaki pants, then he recognized Kiptarbei.

What was Kiptarbei doing here, he wondered. Was he finally seeking salvation? George continued his sermon after the awkward pause.

Kiptarbei sat and listened to George preaching, but his mind was on overdrive. Kiptarbei knew that he had unlimited opportunities to get married, but he felt drawn to Jerono's independence and her unique demeanor. She pushed the Tugen cultural norms to the limit and had abundant self-confidence. On many occasions, she took care of her family and performed chores normally done by men.

Kiptarbei refused to be told what to do against his wishes. In this way, he realized he was like Jerono. All of Kiptarbei's endeavors to catch his adversary in any contact or relationship were futile. Eventually, he was sure that George and Jerono never advanced their relationship.

So, Kiptarbei thought—I have an opportunity to win her love and marry her. I can't proceed roughly but must try to win Jerono through diplomacy. Kiptarbei knew he needed to be tactful to protect his interest without exposing his intentions.

Kiptarbei learned from his wise Tugen elders that giving is the master key to successful negotiation. Even better was giving things up for those you cared for most. The foundation of a relationship was reliability, the ability to be there when needed—no matter what. Kiptarbei was convinced that he would need to be ready to give as he approached George and Jerono this time around if he were to succeed.

George felt he had to acknowledge Kiptarbei and interrupted his sermon to say, "Welcome, please feel free and at home. Sit anywhere you feel comfortable." The room was silent.

"Thank you," Kiptarbei said and sat three rows from the front.

Meanwhile, George wondered whether Kiptarbei might have changed his mind and was ready to be a Christian after all. He was optimistic and excited for him. It was three years since their painful encounter.

George concluded his sermon. "God loves each one of you. He is calling you to salvation and helping others in His service," he told the congregation as he directed his gaze to Kiptarbei.

Kiptarbei locked eyes with George. It was as if George were talking to him directly, but he did not budge or blink.

"God bless you," he acknowledged a hand raised by a woman seated in front of Kiptarbei. He continued to persuade the congregation to turn to Jesus Christ for salvation. George summed up his sermon with a prayer.

Everyone streamed out of the church. Kiptarbei sat and watched everyone leave the church.

George could not wait for the last person to walk out. He walked toward Kiptarbei, and sat beside him. For a long time they sat quietly, hunched on the bench beside each other.

"How have you been, brother?" George broke the silence.

"Busy," Kiptarbei replied. "Everything is good. Everyone is okay."

"Great, you look good," George said, nodding his head. The conversation was awkward.

Finally, Kiptarbei spoke. "I am planning to go to Kerio Valley, to the lowlands to find myself a wife. I wish you the very best with Jerono. You love her. She loves you, and I was jealous before. It was obvious that day in the dispensary, and that is why I left. I want you to know that I have never revisited the issue, not even with her. You have my blessings, brother. I want you to be happy. I did a terrible thing last time. It doesn't mean I don't care about you. I do care," he smiled.

George felt a rush of sadness. His eyes were teary as he listened to Kiptarbei's words.

"Why the sadness, George?" he asked with surprise. "I thought you wanted to marry her?"

"Yes, I did, I still do, but I can't marry her," he replied. "Things are complicated. You are better off with her than I am. I cannot marry her if she is not here at the mission with me. She is a stubborn woman. Jerono will not be forced to do what she doesn't want to, particularly by those who impose their values on her. I wish I could get into her head to get her to comprehend how this mission is great for both of us. You have my blessing to marry her. Please, take good care of her." Kiptarbei's pulse raced as he listened to George.

Kiptarbei appeared sad for George. "I hear you, brother," he replied. "Women are something else. They are hard to understand. Do you think she will learn to love me? I mean, the way she loves you?" Kiptarbei asked.

"Absolutely. Treat Jerono right and love her. Do you love her, if I may ask?" George asked, bracing himself to hear Kiptarbei's answer.

"Very much. But I don't know how to show Jerono if she hates me," Kiptarbei said.

"Love is like a seed. Sometimes it lands on a spot full of thorns and weeds or a dry plain desert. There is always a chance for it to grow. It requires much patience. Trust yourself. When despised, love anyway. Nurture delicately and do not rush things. Jerono is not going anywhere. She is full of love and will eventually bloom. You will be her anchor when that time comes," he said.

"Thank you so much, brother," he said and asked, "What about you?"

George stood up and walked to the aisle.

"I will be okay. God has other plans for me," he said. "I am glad that everything has been ironed out. I wish you well. I have been planning to transfer to Eldama Ravine. It might be soon. Please convey my farewell to Jerono."

"You don't plan to see her before you go, do you?" Kiptarbei asked.

"Time might not allow it," George replied.

"Are you sure?"

George nodded solemnly.

Kiptarbei, in his calculating mind, thought it was better that way. George's not seeing Jerono made it easier for him to insert himself and get the ball rolling. He smiled at the thought. He could now take his time to plan well and work on developing a relationship with Jerono on his terms.

That evening, George asked if the mission could transfer him to the Eldama Ravine Mission station. Being so near his family and Jerono was too sad for him. He lost them when he chose to be a Christian. The mission granted his request and transferred him a week later.

Meanwhile, Kiptarbei talked to his father a week after visiting George at the church. It was a beautiful evening—that time when livestock streamed home on their own. The cows were lazily ruminating with their heads down, lying on their chests, self-grooming and chewing their cud. His eyes drifted over the horizon, and the fiery red light of the sun was semi-eclipsed as it sunk over the Tugen hills. Everything was lovely and full of life.

Kiptarbei's father emerged from his rondavel. "Dad, how are you?" Kiptarbei extended his hand to greet him.

"I am good," he responded and offered a hug.

"*Kobot Kiptarbei* (Mother of Kiptarbei, this was the name accorded to mothers after they had their first sons) bring us stools," he called to his wife.

A few minutes later, she brought the men stools.

"Some local brew is left. Can I get you some?"

"Bring it," they responded in unison, looking at each other, and smiling.

She took a step and abruptly looked back at her husband, "Kwombo Kiptarbei," she pointed at one of the cows, "That cow is sick. She is not eating well and no longer has any milk."

"I will check and give her something later," he said and shifted to face his son. Kiptarbei went back into the rondavel.

"I want to get married," Kiptarbei blurted out without any warning. His father was surprised, and his eyes lit up.

"It's about time! I was almost afraid that it would never happen," he said, smiling with excitement.

"Where does the bride come from?" his father asked.

"Kapchepkoros," Kiptarbei said.

"This is problematic," his father muttered, shaking his head.

Kapchepkoros was Jerono's homestead. His father was incredulous after Kiptarbei's previous near-cataclysmic event involving a daughter of Kapchepkoros. He stood and paced in contemplation. Moments later, he looked straight at his son.

"I'm not sure if the community elders will want to hear about it. What were you thinking? Did you forget what happened with George?" he asked.

"No worries, father, I made peace with him last Sunday. I visited him at his church, and he gave me his blessing to pursue Jerono. He is my brother. Brotherhood and respect mean much to him," Kiptarbei responded.

"Truly?" his father asked to confirm.

"Definitely. George is moving to Eldama Ravine next week. He isn't coming back. We had a long talk. I sought his forgiveness, and he was gracious. He hasn't seen Jerono since that day in the hospital," Kiptarbei said.

His father sighed with relief. His wife brought them two cups of local brew.

"This tastes good. Where did you get it?" Kiptarbei asked.

"I brewed it myself. I'm preparing to brew more. You can work with me if you want to learn how to do it," Kiptarbei's father replied.

"I'd love to," Kiptarbei said.

"So, does she know?" his father asked, getting back to Jerono.

"No, I haven't seen her since we saw George in the hospital," Kiptarbei said.

"This is ludicrous. Jerono hates you, and you know it. She will not accept coming here to live with you," Kiptarbei's father said.

"I love her. I'll do whatever it takes to marry her. Actually, I came here to inform you so that we can prepare for the next step in the process," Kiptarbei said, matter-of-factly.

"As you wish, son. I'll convene the clansmen and women to deliberate your proposal," his father said.

"How soon can we make that happen?" Kiptarbei asked. He was not a patient man where Jerono was concerned.

"She isn't going anywhere, son. I'll arrange it as soon as I can."

"Make it happen fast," Kiptarbei said with excitement.

"Okay, okay. But first, we need to perform a background check on Jerono. I'll work with your mother to get that done," his father said, smiling at his son's eagerness to be married.

"Perfect, who should we send to Kapchepkoros to convey my intentions to have Jerono for my bride?" Kiptarbei asked.

"I'd rather go myself. After the last fiasco, there will be lots of explaining to do. I'll let you know how it went when I come back," his father replied.

They chatted a while longer before Kiptarbei left for his homestead.

Before George left for Eldama Ravine, he was packing his few belongings when an idea crossed his mind. He looked over at a Bible a visiting evangelist gave him a while back. George thought how wonderful it would be if Jerono at some point accepted Jesus Christ as her savior. He wondered if God's intentions for Jerono's connections were something other than marriage.

George felt that God was revealing himself to him at that time. His role in Jerono's life was to introduce her to God, and God would take care of the rest from there. George felt a huge load lifted off his shoulders. Godly, platonic love replaced the physical attraction he had for Jerono. He was relieved. He rushed out in a hurry to deliver the Bible to Jerono at her homestead and bid her goodbye.

George found Jerono relaxing outside their rondavel, talking to her siblings. She stood up to meet him.

"Hi," she extended her hand to greet him.

"Hi," he replied and offered his hand for a handshake.

"It's been a long time since we last met," she said.

"True. How are you doing? Okay, I hope."

"Yes, I'm doing well. And so are my parents," she said.

He offered her the Bible and announced, "I'm leaving for the Eldama Ravine mission tomorrow. Please, take this Bible."

"Thank you," Jerono said. "I appreciate the gift."

"When you get time, learn how to read. The Bible is all about the love of God. He wants us to love each other like the way He loves us," he said.

"You know that I can't read or write?" she asked quizzically.

"You'll learn, I have no doubt about that," he said. "Jerono, do things to others that you expect them to do for you. Have love as a compass for all your deeds toward others and everything will be okay," he said.

"Thank you, George, for everything. I'm sorry it didn't work out for us," she said with a hint of sadness in her eyes.

"I didn't come here to preach to you," he said.

"And you're not," she responded.

They were quiet for a moment, and it felt awkward. Neither had anything to add to the conversation.

"Goodbye, Jerono," he said, walking away from her.

"Goodbye, George," she said as she waved to him.

He took a few steps, stopped, and looked back at her. "Kiptarbei came to see me on Sunday. He still loves you. He realizes that you don't feel the same, but he loves you, nonetheless. It's natural, you know. Sometimes, you can't help it. He can't. Please give him a chance. He's a good man," he said, his voice choked with emotion as he walked away.

"Did he tell you to come and convey the information to me?" she asked.

"Absolutely not," he said, stopping again. "Kiptarbei isn't aware that I came to see you. Let's keep it that way." he said as he continued walking away.

George ensured that he was as far away from Jerono as possible. Her charm was lethal; the spell she cast left his soul and spirit in bondage. That terrified George. He had to run for his life. "Run George, run," he said out loud as he hurried out of Jerono's homestead.

Jerono started to panic. What just happened? By nature, she was not a worrier, but she wanted to get married—like other girls her age. The problem was the pool of eligible men in the community—the witty, intelligent, and tough. She needed a man who could complement her strong character. As of a few minutes ago, there were two. She had kept an eye on them and knew they were still eligible bachelors. At that moment, she realized that one was now totally out of the game. The one left was arrogant, and they had no chemistry. However, he was the only card left in her deck.

Culturally, the man proposed to a woman through her family. It was illogical and wildly unreasonable for a girl to ask a man to marry her. It was an impossible proposition to even think about it. The best way was to develop a relationship, she thought. Kiptarbei already liked her. Now, she decided to get to know him. The day after George's visit, Jerono visited Kiptarbei.

Jerono knew that he was always home around the evening when the homestead livestock returned. As she predicted, he was home when she arrived. Kiptarbei, greatly surprised, noticed her arrival from afar and walked toward her.

"It has to rain today because you set foot in my rondavel," he said teasingly. Jerono had cursed him and promised never to set foot in his house during his fight with George.

"I think it will," she said and laughed. Jerono was a grown, confident woman. "Your livestock looks great."

"I've been busy. What about you?"

"Same. Busy. I wanted to talk to you," Jerono said.

"Okay. Let's go to the rondavel. It doesn't smell as you might think," Kiptarbei said.

"Kiptarbei, let me apologize for cursing you when we were together with George. I was wrong. I seek your forgiveness," she said. Jerono reflected. I have to give up something to gain some leverage,. Jerono knew—especially after George's visit—that Kiptarbei had feelings for her, and she realized that she could use that to her advantage.

"Please, come in," he walked her into the rondavel. Kiptarbei offered her a stool and positioned one of the seats opposite hers.

"Thank you," she said as she sat down.

"What would you like to drink? *Mursiik* (sour milk) or *kipketinik* (local brew)?"

"What do you think?" she asked, teasingly.

"Of course, the local brew," he responded.

Kiptarbei stepped aside to pour two cups.

Just then, Jerono struggled with some unstoppable force that was daring her to do the unthinkable. Something that, as far as she knew, had never been done in the existence of Tugen culture. She was trying to breathe in and out to calm down, but an overpowering ringing voice in her brain kept saying, Do it! Do it! Do it!

Kiptarbei approached her and noticed that her demeanor changed. "What's going on?" he asked. "Are you getting sick?"

Jerono stood up and stared intensely and directly at him. She was sweating profusely. "Kiptarbei, will you marry me?" she blurted out the words before she could talk herself out of saying them.

Kiptarbei dropped the cups to the ground in horror and looked at her with shock. Her proposal was unexpected. He was not prepared with any response. In Tugen culture, a man asked permission from the bride's father, and if he gave it then he proposed to the woman. A woman would never propose to a man. That was very wrong and rooted Kiptarbei to the spot. He had never heard of a woman proposing to a man before. He was not sure how to react.

The brew spilled everywhere. That saved the situation for that moment. Jerono hurriedly stepped out of the rondavel for some air. To her, the spill was nothing close to the historical event that occurred. She walked a few feet from the rondavel and sat on a stone facing the setting sun. She was scared about what might happen next. For the first time in her life, she completely lost control.

However, she also felt empowered. The proposal may have gone up in smoke, but it felt good to have done it. Jerono had proposed, not the other way around.

Moments later, Kiptarbei emerged from the rondavel and walked toward her. He sat on another stone a little further from her.

"What was that?" he asked softly, still processing this reversal of romantic roles.

"I just asked you to marry me. Is that too much to ask? You can say 'no,' that's okay," she said. She wondered if she were genuinely ruining the whole proposal. There were no guarantees.

"You're avoiding my question. You know what I'm asking," Kiptarbei said angrily.

"Kiptarbei, do you know how it feels to wait for a man to ask when I can ask for myself? It isn't a hard question to ask, is it? The answer is simple, 'yes' or 'no,'" she said, starting to feel exasperated.

"So, what do we do now?" he asked, confused.

"Answer the question," Jerono said, stubbornly.

"It's not that simple. Did you tell anyone about this?" Kiptarbei asked, looking almost ashamed.

"No, only you," she said.

"Can we at least drink and not talk about what just happened?" he pleaded with her. "Allow me time to digest. No discussion about this with anyone, is that agreeable to you?" It was not a straight yes from Kiptarbei, but he wanted to be in the game.

"Absolutely, does this mean 'yes'?" she asked.

"As I said, it's not simple," he said.

"I have my request, too," she said.

Kiptarbei was afraid. He could not predict anything from Jerono, especially now. He had a lot to learn about her.

"What?" he asked.

"I want to get to know you better before we get married. I also want to participate in the planning and negotiations, all of it," Jerono said.

"Is that all?" he asked.

"Yes," she said, wondering if he were going to agree with her or turn her down altogether.

"I can do that. I still don't know how, but we should probably keep this to ourselves for now," Kiptarbei said. "I was in the process of proposing to you," he said. "The proper cultural way."

"I figured. George said good things about you," she said.

"Damn him!" he muttered. "He couldn't keep his mouth shut." Then, he smiled.

"Considering the perception of the community, I'd like to see you more without feeling the pressure of being labeled as a whore," she said. "I don't care about what anyone says if you're okay with it."

"Whoa! Whoa! Whoa! Slow down. You already pushed the limits tonight. Now, you are definitely breaking every custom in the book. Jerono, are you crazy?" he asked, laughing and feeling exhausted. "This one, in particular, I kind of like it. Let's make it happen. Who could refuse such an offer?" he said teasingly.

"How do you suggest we approach the situation?" she asked.

He smiled and said, "Let us reverse the roles. With your permission. I will pursue you persistently. I will make as much time as possible for us to get to know each other well."

"Kiptarbei, this relationship will only succeed if we work together as equal partners," she said, becoming more serious.

"I will keep that proposition in mind," he said. Kiptarbei wondered how he would bring all this to fruition, considering that the rules and regulations governing the culture. However, at the moment, compromise was acceptable to him.

"I better go home soon; people will notice my absence and start looking. No one knows where I am," she said.

"Thank you for coming. I am the happiest man on earth. I hope you learn to love me, Jerono because I do love you," he said.

"I hope so," she said, taking a long look at him before turning to run home.

It turned out alright for both. Jerono and Kiptarbei opened up to each other, and that was the beginning of a good relationship.

Liam finished reading the first part of the story, utterly fascinated. He wanted to ask Meggie some questions. He hesitated at first, given the time, but hit send on a text to Meggie.

"Ask." Meggie texted back.

"Are you going to bed now?" He wondered why he was texting her so late at night. What was he thinking? He started panicking. Maybe he was close to crossing a line.

"Not yet. Still looking at all the Grand Canyon information."

"May I call? Please."

"Yes." Her phone rang almost immediately.

"I have a lot of questions," Liam said. "This particular section has a lot of intriguing Tugen cultural customs."

"We can talk more about it over breakfast tomorrow, if you'd like," Meggie suggested.

"Great plan. Let's do that. Is 7 a.m. okay with you?" Liam asked.

"You're taking this too seriously," she said.

"Yes, I love it," he said, but he actually meant I love you. "The others will join us at 8:30. We'll finish before then," he said providing a rationale for them to spend time alone.

"Okay, will do. Goodnight Liam." She hung up.

Liam stood for a while, holding the phone to his ear before he let go of the silence on the other side.

CHAPTER 10

Rite of Passage

LIAM WAS AT THE RESTAURANT fifteen minutes before seven. Meggie walked in at seven. He stood and pulled a chair out for her.

After polite good mornings, Liam asked Meggie to tell him more about the rite of passage.

"The rite of passage is a very interesting concept,", Meggie's eyes lit up as she narrated the rest of the story.

"Twelve years passed since Kiptarbei's rite of passage. The rite of passage is an event occurring at adolescence involving a six-to-eight-month intensive boot camp. It has three major outcomes; family and community role training, age-set recognition—how you got along with your peer group—and graduation from childhood to manhood or warrior status.

"The community expected each new generation to understand and follow the Tugen societal organizational structures and systems. The bootcamp offered an opportunity to teach everything from lineage to ancestral geographical locations to proper relations and customs in marriages.

"Coaches, former graduates from the same ceremony, and community elders conducted the training. The curriculum covered essential aspects of life's journey: conflict resolution techniques within the family, community, and beyond; the responsibilities of husbands and fathers; homestead, family, and community security; leadership at home and in the community; and weapon design and development."

"Did the bootcamp assure the smooth running of the tribe?" Liam guessed.

"Right," Meggie responded. "The bootcamp prepares each generation to take on the responsibilities for the next," she added.

"Each group chooses a symbol—much like football teams do. There's a mascot for the team, and this mascot is the symbol or representative for the team. Over time, the group uses these distinctive significant symbols as a way to represent particular kinship relations," she replied.

"The symbols are sorted mostly by descent and gender to ensure evolution and diversity within communities from one generation to the next. Locating your ancestor using this system is as reliable as today's genealogy websites. More importantly, the system offers a solid strategy to ensure security for the family. Additionally, the accumulated resources like wealth, experienced medicine men and women would stay within the kinship through generations."

"So, this system approach to wealth, information, and training was passed through the family lineage?" Liam asked

"Correct," Meggie responded.

"Fascinating. Do you have a totem?" Liam asked.

"Yes. I am a frog," she chuckled.

"The dart-poison frog? How many have you maimed?" he teased.

"Oh, no. No. Just a frog. A kind, harmless frog," she replied.

"Oh, yeah," he could not picture her as a poisonous frog, but in his mind, he lasciviously thought of her sticking her tongue out and darting it back and forth. He knew he had to pay attention and stop letting his mind distract him with such erotic visons.

"Anyway, in regard to age-set, most of the Kalenjin sub-tribes (Keiyo, Endorois, Kipsigis, Marakwet, Nandi, Pokot, Terik, Tugen, and Sabaot) shared the same first names in a similar sequence. The names repeated every so many years.".

"Does age-set mean people of the same birth date?" Liam asked.

"An age-set is a category of people of about the same age. They would have a particular group name with a unique totem. They maintain close ties—a kind of brotherhood—for life. A specific age-set group will advance together from young adults, to elders, to old age," Meggie explained.

Meggie continued with the narration.

"The women had a corresponding cyclical age-set similar to those of the men.

Apart from age-sets, Tugen people have specific interrelated families with common ancestry known as clans. Tugen people are related by blood and symbolized by totem animals represented by clan-totems.

The Kalenjin tribe is a small population of people, which gets even smaller within the sub-tribes mentioned earlier. The Tugen developed a sophisticated kin-classification criterion and outlined specific marriage-system policies and processes to govern its people. In regards to marriage, it ensured that people did not marry blood relations, and provided checks on hereditary anomalies such as disabilities, mental illnesses, character, and curses, among many other characteristics."

"I get all that but curses, how did that happen?" Liam asked.

"People who lived in some particular areas beyond river barriers believed that such families were haunted by frequent deaths as a result of a curse," she said.

"As doctors, we know that couldn't be true," Liam squinted his eyes indicating that he couldn't buy into the concept of curses.

"Tell that to my Grandpa Kiptarbei," she replied.

"Shhhhhh...not a word," he replied, teasingly.

"Since the rite of passage took place concurrently for both women and men, the community held a combined community celebration. Many bachelors and bachelorettes attended these events. Those unsuccessful in securing partners over the years also attended."

"Why?" Liam asked.

"People attended this celebration in hopes of romance. Young children were not welcome. Kiptarbei always wondered whether he could have married earlier, but Jerono was one year short of attending the ceremony when he graduated from his coming of age bootcamp.

"During this ceremony, the young men dressed in brightly colored loincloths wrapped around their torsos, and they wore beaded jewelry on their heads, necks, and wrists. Individuals would put more effort into their attire to make themselves more appealing and attractive to potential mates. They dressed diversely depending on their age-set and clan. The additional personal touch was a must if one wanted to stand out from the rest and be noticed.

"Women felt the same need for careful dressing. Their necklaces, earrings, bracelets, and pendants were even more colorful than those worn by the men. Bachelorettes wore the most elaborate pieces. They stood out from the crowd with their elegant, heavy jewelry. The design and type of dress differentiated the women as maidens, women who were newly married but without children, mothers, and grandmothers. At a glance, people could tell which women were potential partners. There was no confusion, which made things easy for the men to hunt without mistakenly hitting on the wrong target.

"Tugen people did not sugarcoat flirtation."

"Whoa! Stop right there. What does that mean?" Liam asked, curious.

"Hahaha," Meggie laughed. "The men made obvious sexual signals and requests."

Amused, Liam said, "Like, can I go to bed with you, if you are available tonight?"

"Oh, no. Not like that. Like, I am attracted to you. I want to marry you, is that okay with you? Something like that. Simple and straightforward, not complicated," Meggie was fumbling and blushing at the same time.

The conversation was exciting to Liam. "That simple?" he said, still amused.

"Their advances were either accepted or declined bluntly. No confusion this way. Simply, take it or leave it. Consent was a big deal, and everyone respected that. During these events, marriage proposals and casual hookups were both up for grabs.

"Socialization started with a feast. The meal consisted of beef and roasted goat as the main dishes, with side dishes of starches and vegetables, dairy products, and alcohol to drink. The entertainment began late in the evening and went on into the early morning.

"The evening was a time meant for romance, with a lot of singing and dancing. The sequence of steps and movements included the red-clad jumping dance. Everyone stood in a circle and sang while warrior after warrior moved to the center and jumped as high as he could. The rest of the men bent over and clapped their hands while their feet stayed on the ground.

"When grandpa Kiptarbei narrated the events of that day, he said, 'I wanted Jerono for a wife someday, but she was not there during my rite of passage.'"

"I told him that was sad, and I felt disappointed. Grandpa Kiptarbei smiled, which confused me. He explained with a twinkle in his eyes, 'There were many other beautiful women that night, I couldn't resist the competitive, sensual spirit at the event.'"

'I got the optimal prize that night: I got laid. Not a word to your grandma,' Grandpa Kiptarbei said."

"I like your grandpa already. I want to meet him," Liam said, jokingly. They both laughed and Maggie resumed the narration.

"Now, that you understand some of the complexity of our clan's relationships, I'll continue with the story about how my grandparents got together."

The week following, Kiptarbei's marriage proposal announcement to his father, Kwombo Kiptarbei, Kiptarbei's father, visited Jerono's homestead. He was unaware of his son's encounter with Jerono in his rondavel and their discussions.

Kwombo Kiptarbei and Jerono's father were close friends until Kiptarbei and George's fight happened. Their relationship was never the same after that—not that they fought, but a great tension existed between them. Something had changed. However, Kiptarbei's father knew what was required.

As with many institutions, Tugen marriage has detailed procedures that the couple needed to follow. Kiptarbei initiated the first step in the process, the preliminary visit of the father of the groom to the bride's father. This exclusively father-to-father meeting happens at the bride's' homestead.

Homesteads had small gazebos with a thatched roof about sixty-five feet from the main rondavel. The gazebos were special places where fathers conducted serious business, such as discussions of marriages, resolution of disputes, and other planning, and development talks. They were also entertainment centers where activities with friends often occurred.

On this occasion, Kiptarbei's father stood at the gazebo wearing a fur hat with two feathers facing his left. He placed his ceremonial stick strategically at the gazebo's entrance. He was nervous but did his best to hide it. He knew this was not going to be easy, but there was no way to prepare for such an event. Just as he was contemplating his next move, he heard a child call for Jerono's father.

"Papa, someone's standing at the gazebo," she said.

"I'm coming." He emerged from the rondavel and stared at the gazebo. Kiptarbei's father's choice of hat, positioning of the feathers, and placement of the ceremonial stick signaled the initial stage of marriage-proposal discussions.

"Who brought you to this homestead today?" Jerono's father asked.

"Kiptarbei," he responded. He was nervous as hell, and shaky. Rivulets of sweat streamed down his face. "My son wants to marry your daughter.".

"He wants who?" Jerono's father asked. He had several girls at a marriageable age.

"Jerono," Kiptarbei's father replied.

"I thought Jerono closed that door five-years ago?" Jerono's father said quizzically.

"I did too. Clearly, it wasn't," Kiptarbei's father responded.

"I'm surprised. Jerono was so angry the last time she was with Kiptarbei. She swore never to set foot in his rondavel. Does she know?" he asked.

"No, unfortunately not."

"I see. I'll speak with Jerono and arrange for another meeting, but only if her response is positive." The initial meeting required no exchange of gifts. Jerono's parents did not invite Kiptarbei's father inside the rondavel at this stage. Then, the two fathers parted ways.

A short while later, Jerono was about to enter the rondavel when she overheard her parents discussing Kiptarbei. She was surprised and quietly took a step back to eavesdrop. She knew that her interactions with Kiptarbei remained unknown to both sets of parents. Jerono was going to act as though nothing had happened since the fight.

"That was Kiptarbei's father," he told his wife.

"I heard that he had a sick cow recently. Was he here about that?" she asked.

"Oh, no. It was about a marriage proposal to Jerono," he said, relaying the surprising news to his wife.

"My, my. I don't know how that will go," Jerono's mother said. She was contemplating how she was going to have the conversation with her daughter, considering how much Jerono loathed Kiptarbei.

Jerono stepped into the rondavel as her mother was about to respond.

"I will marry him," Jerono said.

"Her parents looked at her in shock.

"I will marry Kiptarbei, but he will need to wait for a little while until I am ready," she repeated. "I thought he would never ask to marry me." It was a trial-and-error situation, and she could only wait and see what would happen. She hoped it would turn out alright.

Her mother's eyelids opened wide, her eyes full of surprise. She looked at her daughter with wonderment. She always wanted Kiptarbei for her daughter. Unfortunately, it was not her place to make that choice. The choice was Jerono's to make. No one could take that away from her. Jerono's father was also surprised but pleased.

"We'll move forward in preparation for the next step in the process when you are ready. I'll convey your message to Kwombo Kiptarbei," he said and walked out of the rondavel.

Later that evening, Kiptarbei's father received the good news and went to visit his son.

"We're going for the initial official engagement negotiations, but Jerono would like us to wait until she's ready." Kiptarbei's father was beaming nonetheless as he extended his arms for a tight hug with his son. They were both elated.

"I can do that," Kiptarbei said.

"Since when did the bride dictate when she gets married? I thought the man provided some leadership," his father scoffed.

"Dad, a little more time is nothing compared to the many hoops I've already jumped through to win Jerono's affection. I can wait," Kiptarbei replied—even if I don't want to, he thought.

CHAPTER 11

The Courtship and the Wedding

MEGGIE CONTINUED HER NARRATION AS their breakfast got cold. Both were so into the story that the food was almost superfluous.

Ever since the encounter with Jerono, Kiptarbei was elated by the access and opportunity to pursue her officially. He wanted to make the pursuit worthwhile. For a week, Kiptarbei did not do anything. However, Kiptarbei thought, I'm glad she has accepted me, but Jerono has never noticed what I could offer her as an adult.

"Why is he going through all the worry since she has proposed?" Liam asked.

"Funny, you asked the same question I did," Meggie replied. "Grandpa Kiptarbei thought, like a customary Tugen warrior, that Jerono was simply going to accept everything he said. He had to go through the rituals of the courtship as much for his standing in the community as for the marriage itself. Yet, he also wanted the marriage to be based on her respect for him and for all these reasons he was determined to follow the rituals of the community despite their unorthodox agreement that she initiated. He couldn't understand why Jerono was such a difficult woman. He was also afraid that Jerono would reveal something in the open that would cause him embarrassment from the community."

"Your grandpa was in trouble. The stakes must have been very high," Liam commented.

"Sure, he needed to be ready for anything." Meggie went on.

The chance to impress her on his own merits presented itself, and he had to make the most out of it. That was very important to him. He took time to groom himself, and he looked stunning. He walked out of his rondavel to pay a visit to Jerono as handsome as he had ever been.

Now, he would visit his bride-to-be. Jerono was in her family's homestead garden. She was preparing the soil for planting three types of traditional vegetable seeds: black nightshade, African spider plant, and cherry tomato seeds.

"Your vegetable garden is exquisite. It reflects the looks of the one tending it," Kiptarbei said. Jerono stood up from her planting when she heard a male voice at the entrance of the garden.

Jerono raised her head and looked up. Kiptarbei looked very handsome. She wondered why she had not noticed him in that way before. He was desirable. His words charmed her, and she was beginning to feel more receptive to his advances.

"You love gardening, Jerono. You've fed most of this community over the years," he complimented her work. Kiptarbei couldn't help but admire her. Whatever gardening responsibilities took, it requires hard work, creativity and graftmanship. She had it all, and it showed.

"True. This is the place where I feel I am at my best. I enjoy working here," she said.

"The garden thrives because of your nurturing abilities. Your garden reflects the type of care the plants receive from you."

"Thank you," she replied, accepting Kiptarbei's compliments graciously.

"May I be of help?" he asked.

"Are you sure?" she asked because Kiptarbei was dressed up in fancy clothing—not what one would wear for gardening.

"I had no choice, you know. Do you like it?"

"I noticed you alright," she replied with a laugh.

"Let me have the hoe," he said as he extended his right hand.

She handed Kiptarbei the hoe and wiped beads of sweat from her face.

"If it's okay with you, I'll till the soil and create even rows with a narrow hill of soil," he suggested.

"Sure," Jerono responded. "I'll follow you with manure and the seeds."

Kiptarbei understood that he had to build his relationship with Jerono on reciprocal trust and respect. He needed to take every available opening to learn about her and build that knowledge into understanding her. It was important for him to find qualities that he liked in Jerono and instill within himself these qualities that attracted her. His goal was not necessarily to change who he was, but to be open to adapting. Jerono challenged him. Patience and determination would be essential, he thought.

Together, they finished the gardening tasks, then ate a lunch Jerono prepared. About five hours later, Kiptarbei left. "This was a good day. Thank you for wanting to have me as your husband," he said with sincerity.

"You're always welcome," she responded with earnestness.

Six months passed, and Kiptarbei and Jerono continued to get along well. He pursued her as he had promised. They were very cautious not to draw any negative attention from the community. Kiptarbei was a respected member of the community. The elders were fond of him, and he wanted to keep it that way. He was going to play this game covertly. Though Jerono desired to bring some changes to the Tugen cultural customs that she considered less than desirable, she also enjoyed the respect and the trust that the matriarch of the community gave her. One had to be considered above reproach to earn this precious position. She wanted to be prudent.

Kiptarbei was certain that Jerono would come around soon and end the delay. She didn't. Kiptarbei was getting tired of waiting and was ready to make the next move. He was going to show his marriage intentions to Jerono in the Tugen customary way, and he convinced himself that the proposal was going to happen soon.

Jerono's mother was preparing to milk the cow around four o'clock one afternoon when she noticed an armored Tugen warrior standing at the gate. He wore a traditional Tugen red-brown robe and stood at attention, upright and imposing. In his left hand, he held a club and in the right was a spear.

The homestead gate was near the rondavel door that opened to the front yard. Next to it was the livestock den. The rondavel area was fenced all around. Kiptarbei thought he was strong enough to win the fight against Jerono's delays. He knew that Jerono had her reputation to lose if she did not accept him; besides his ego was involved, and he thought she was trying to play him.

"So, their standoff was a game in which all were equally competitive," Liam said.

Meggie nodded.

In Tugen culture, a suitor should stand at attention at the bride's gate and wait until she walked toward him and removed the armor. No one else was allowed to notice him, not even to let the bride know that a suitor was at the gate waiting. About two hours passed before Jerono saw Kiptarbei at the gate. She smiled. Wow! He is going to go through the whole process of Tugen customs, she thought.

Jerono was expected to bring her suitor to the rondavel, keep his armor in a secure place, feed him, and show him his resting place for the night. Kiptarbei submitted to all her directions without uttering a word. He went to sleep, wondering what her verdict would be in the morning.

The next day, Jerono left before dawn to start her chores. Kiptarbei met with her parents to learn if Jerono was interested in him as her husband and willing to get married. He learned he would have to wait; she was not ready yet! He was disappointed. He was not sure how Jerono would drag out this step because she had more leverage. A man could not force his way until the bride-to-be was onboard. The problem was that there was no direct contact. He could not negotiate on his behalf.

It was Liam's turn to shake his head. He was lost and asked "What was her reason for putting off the wedding? What did she expect to gain? Why was she playing with him?"

"In Tugen customary practices, women make few decisions. However, marriage was one of the areas where women could decide. Jerono wanted not just to be part of the decision making, but to be the final decision maker. Grandpa Kiptarbei was afraid of losing respect if it were known that Jerono was the decision maker. The saying was, 'that woman is sitting on that man's head' and that was bad," Meggie explained.

Kiptarbei was disappointed; however, he loved her and had invested too much to cave in. And, of course, he was stubborn, too.

A month later, he tried again, once more arriving at Jerono's gate in his armor. Her parents were already waiting outside. They looked distraught as if they were about to deliver news of a newly departed loved one.

"Son, we love you so much, you know that," Jerono's mother said. She was trying to speak a painful truth, which was becoming obvious to Kiptarbei. He wondered whether Jerono realized how much pain she was putting her parents through.

"Yes, I do mama," he replied.

"Sometimes, things don't go exactly the way we would like them to be. I hope in the long run, Jerono will see the light and things will work out for…" She was interrupted by Jerono's father, who was vehemently upset with their daughter.

"Son, let's cut this game short. You've tried your best. I can't lie to you that Jerono may change her mind. She is so stubborn. If you wish to close the door permanently for her, I'll understand," he said. He had seen Jerono re-enter the house and knew that she was eavesdropping. "She wants you to wait still. She isn't ready for marriage yet."

Just as Jerono's mother turned to leave, Jerono appeared from the rondavel door holding Kiptarbei's armor, a symbol of her acceptance. Kiptarbei was elated.

"Papa, I accept Kiptarbei, and I will marry him," she said, without looking at Kiptarbei.

"Thank you, my child. We don't want to prolong this thing," her father said. He was happy to end this episode. He was aware of his daughter's unconventional approach to life and was worried that it might get her in trouble. Kiptarbei was pleased. He was ready for the next step in the process.

The engagement occurred on a Saturday giving her enough time to get a maid of honor and select the people to be present at the Kapkoimet's family gazebo. About seventeen people, emissaries from both the groom's and bride's sides of the families, sat opposite each other around a U-shaped seating arrangement. The groom's family arrived first.

Kiptarbei's family waited two hours before the host family joined them. The groom sat beside his best man. Two facilitating representatives from each side of the family acted like family attorneys. Every communication and deliberation went through them.

"Hello, everyone," the bride's facilitator started the event greeting the group.

"We are good," the families responded in unison.

"Call Jerono from this homestead," he said.

Jerono and her maid of honor approached the gazebo. "Jerono, your visitors have come. Do you receive them?" he asked.

"Yes," she answered.

"We want to know from you if it is okay for us to proceed with today's engagement negotiations?"

"Yes, please proceed," she responded. "Thank you, everyone," she said and walked away with her best friend since the bride traditionally was not part of marital negotiations.

"This is the time for us to know each other well. I will start by introducing my people," the first negotiator said.

The introductions were critical components of the engagement ceremony, beginning with a discussion of the clans' animal totems down to age-sets and marriages along the lineage. The negotiations were like elaborate administrative procedures with a thorough, detailed reconstruction of early kinship and clanship through a structured system that revealed the required information. Questions asked ranged from queries about clanship, kinship, deaths in the families, witchcraft practices, diseases, separations, unethical behavioral practices, physical disabilities, and more. One could not live a questionable life and survive the ceremony. The introductions took almost two hours.

After long deliberations, the negotiators agreed upon everything. If anything, ethically or morally questionable proved true in any lineage within the matrilineal or patrilineal descent, the negotiators would dissolve the engagement. The litigators would ask the couple to explore other opportunities.

The second item on the agenda was the dowry—gifts as a token of appreciation from the groom's family. The dowry served as security for the bride in case of disagreement, abuse, abandonment, or death, and she were left to take care of any children on her own. More importantly, this dowry provided a solid foundation and support for the beginning of a new family homestead. After another hour of deliberations, the parties reached a consensus on the dowry. The culmination of these discussions ushered in the beginning of celebrations. Food, mostly meat, cornmeal, fermented milk, and beer was in abundance. The two families began mingling and chatting though this celebration was short because it was not yet a marriage event.

After the ceremony, Jerono realized that all the water in the rondavel was consumed and rushed to the stream to fetch more. Just as she pressed the container into the stream to position it for the water to flow into, she heard a whistle from the other side of the stream. She looked up.

"I thought you would never come to fetch the water," Kiptarbei said. "I've been waiting to see you away from the crowd."

"What are you doing here?" she asked. Her eyes were wide open with surprise. The groom and bride were not supposed to meet until the family officially delivered her to the groom's homestead, in two to three weeks from then.

Liam interrupted. "Why do they need that much more time?"

"The groom's family needs to prepare for the bride-to-be's coming. It's a big deal, and the receiving home should ensure that she will be well taken care of," she replied, before continuing the story.

"I cannot wait any longer. I want to ask if we can just sneak out tonight and live together. I have waited for too long, and even one day longer will kill me," he argued.

"Let me assume that you don't mean that," she said.

"Why not? I mean every word."

"No, no, no. We must do it the right way. Every step of the way," she said and started to ignore him. She continued to fill the container with water.

"So stubborn," he muttered and sulked away.

Jerono wasn't going to be compromised. She was not surprised by Kiptarbei's impatience. Always trying to create shortcuts to get his way, she thought. These were his customs and regulations. She was willing to play by the rules, particularly those to Kiptarbei's advantage.

A week later, Jerono was starting up the wood-cooking stove in the rondavel when she heard someone call from outside.

"Jerono, your visitors are calling you," her mother said.

"Who are the visitors?" Jerono asked.

"Kiptarbei, *cheplakwa* (a young girl who takes care of toddlers), and *mestewon* (a herd's boy)," her mother responded.

Jerono smiled. Kiptarbei did not waste any time, she thought. Despite his hormones wanting to consummate the marriage early, he felt good and respected because he was working hard the right way for Jerono.

"Does dad know about the visitors?" she asked her mother.

Jerono knew that she should refuse to meet the groom until her father promised a gift, usually one or two livestock of his choosing. Many brides-to-be employed the tactic of not going to meet the suitor until he promised her exactly what she wanted such as material things in the homestead, such as cows, goats, sheep, crop harvests, among others.

Jerono wanted to sit down face-to-face with her father and negotiate what she deserved. After all, she was a full-time employee of the homestead and contributed to the property and their home, and had done so for most of her life.

"Dad, Kiptarbei, and his entourage are outside. I need to go and meet them," she said.

Her father smiled widely. "I am proud of you, Jerono, and will miss you. Whatever you need, let me know," he said.

"May I take that cow you've already assigned me?"

"Definitely, and also two doe goats accompanied by a buck," he said. "You are bold and respectful," he smiled at his daughter.

"Thank you, father," she responded.

"I would give you more if I could. I wish you happiness in your new home," he said. Tugen people did not customarily hug, instead Jerono bent to lower her forehead and her father touched and blessed her.

Jerono smiled and stepped out of her home and stood by Kiptarbei. Her father followed suit, joined by her elder brother, Chebuigut. As per tradition, her father and brother blessed her by touching her forehead as she bent forward toward them. They did the same to Kiptarbei. The bride and the groom exchanged special bracelets, which sealed the betrothal. Each of them wore the other's bracelet on their wrists.

The bride still could not leave her father's home after this. The custom was that after another day or two, Kiptarbei's family would send a child under the age of ten to Jerono's home to communicate the details of the move.

"Why small kids, specifically?" Liam asked.

"I asked my grandpa Kiptarbei about this custom. He said, 'Kids are sent because kids are straightforward. You cannot negotiate with them. They deliver the messages, period. Girls were more trusted and more often used in this process than boys because they were difficult to be blackmailed or manipulated.'" Meggie went on.

As Jerono and her family headed back toward their rondavel, the young girl called to them from behind. They turned and saw that Kiptarbei and the herd's boy were nowhere around.

"The move-in is tomorrow," the girl said. They all broke into laughter.

"Okay," Jerono's father said.

The groom and his family expected Jerono at the groom's home at noon. She wore a specific bell ornament to signal her arrival from far. Kiptarbei and his best man staged themselves at their family gazebo as soon as they heard the signal. They invited elders, clansmen, and neighbors to receive the bride.

As soon as Jerono arrived, she stood by Kiptarbei. His best friend also had his wife beside him. Kiptarbei and Jerono stood side by side, followed closely by Kipyarbei's best friend, and his wife. They walked to Kiptarbei's rondavel for two tasks. Jerono's task was to be given away and for the elders to bless them both. They exchanged another set of bracelets, held a knife together, and cut cornmeal from a plate.

Each took a bite of the cornmeal and drank fermented milk from the same cup, first Kiptarbei and then Jerono. The ceremony where the bride and the groom exchanged vows was intimate. Jerono took on the clan's name, Talai, with a frog as the animal totem from then on. No one ever called her by her maiden name again. As soon as the ceremony was over, they joined the rest of the party. Kiptarbei and Talai were officially married.

Meggie took a breath, followed by a sip of orange juice.

"What would happen if someone called her by the maiden name," Liam asked.

"That would be disrespectful. It was a taboo to call a married woman by her maiden name. It still is. I cannot call my mother by that name," Meggie said.

"Where did George disappear to from the story?" Liam asked

"That's next," Meggie promised.

CHAPTER 12

One Christian Wedding

George settled in at the Eldama Ravine mission station serving the church and working with its youth ministries. He helped the women in the church leadership and established an alternative girls' program with a curriculum comparable to the traditional rite of passage that integrated leadership and the Christian worldview. The program was intended to better prepare the girls for their roles as wives and mothers, and especially for being stewards of a Christian family and Christians in the community at large.

George was getting far beyond marrying age, at least according to the church. All of his generation were married; some already had teenage kids. However, when he finally decided he would like to marry, he did not have a woman to marry. Besides, he needed to seek permission from the AIM mission to get married. George scheduled a meeting with the mission agent to discuss the matter.

George and the agent met at the church office at ten o'clock one morning. "I'm impressed by your work, George; soon, you will be able to take over this station," the agent said.

George looked at him and felt a sense of accomplishment. "I'm glad you feel that way. I'm simply doing my job," he replied humbly.

"What can I do for you?" the agent asked.

"I'd like to get married, but I haven't been able to find a bride here in Eldama Ravine," he answered.

Since Christians were not allowed to marry non-believers from the villages, most saved girls were taken to live in hostels operated by the church. They attended school and learned Christian teachings. The hostel at Eldama Ravine did not have marriage-eligible girls at that time.

"I see your dilemma. We need to visit the girls' hostels within the Kalenjin region. We can find a Christian bride for you who," the agent smiled. "I'll arrange for a motorcar from the Kabarnet British Administration District Headquarters. They'll accompany us and provide security. Let's prepare to journey this Thursday. We can start from the nearest hostel, with the Kessup girls," he said.

George wondered if the agent ever considered the concept of love, as it applied to the Tugens. The conversation was like discussing a cow that needed the company of a bull. Feelings and emotions did not seem to be of any consideration.

"Thank you," he said and walked out of the office.

The agent inquired at the AIM girls' hostels in Baringo, Kessup, and Kabsabet. None of the girl's hostels within Baringo had maidens ready for marriage. However, several qualified bridal candidates were in Kessup and Kapsabet, according to the agent.

"There are no Tugen maidens ready for marriage," the agent informed George.

George knew that many Tugen girls were in the village, but they would not be suitable for him because they were not Christian.

"Okay," George looked at the agent without any expression.

"The possibilities available currently are two Elkeyos from Kessup and one Marakwet from Kapsabet," he said. "Are you okay with someone outside your Tugen sub-tribe?" he asked.

"What choice do I have?" George asked, already feeling deflated.

"Fine. We'll leave tomorrow before daybreak."

"Okay," George said and walked away.

At this point, George was willing to move on with his life and do what made sense. He was limited to available women. He was now going to travel far, meet someone he had never seen before, get to know her in a day, and somehow convince her to marry him. In the future, he would possibly learn to love her. It sounded insane—even for him as he thought about it. The Christian AIM community had completely taken over his life. He had no power over anything—including his future wife. AIM prescribed everything. He kept wondering what his life would have been like if he had not decided to become a Christian. Then, he immediately asked God for forgiveness for his unclean thoughts.

The journey to the Kessup girls' hostel started early the next day. George, the AIM agent, Corporal Peter from the Kabarnet British Administration District Headquarters, and the driver embarked on a day's journey. They arrived at the hostel after a fourteen-hour drive and settled in the visitors quarters. They were served dinner soon after they arrived. Then, everyone retired to bed after their exhausting day.

The next morning, the Kessup AIM agent introduced George to two young girls—Ester and Sarah. Both were beautiful. Sarah was shy while Ester was outgoing. The girls ate breakfast with George. He was nervous at first, but Ester made it easier by asking questions about Eldama Ravine's AIM's mission. They chatted for a while, then Sarah excused herself and left the room. George later understood that Sarah escorted her friend Ester to meet with him.

"So, what do you do in Eldama Ravine Mission?" Ester asked.

"I teach and preach," he said. "What about you?"

"I'm a student right now. We're learning to read, write, and do arithmetic. I'm also learning the word of God," she said.

Ester was seventeen. Many Tugen children did not go to school for formal western education. They learned their way of life from their Tugen cultural systems. In those days, the girls were educated to expand the Christian families. As Christian women, they married exclusively Christian men—a sure way of developing Christian communities within the Tugen sub-tribes.

George asked Ester, "Do you like school and living in the hostel?"

"I have no choice," Ester replied. "I like school, but there is no option to stay with my family and commute from home. One day, I hope to help my people. I'm always sad because I miss my family," she said.

"I understand," he said.

"Frankly, I came here to ask for your hand in marriage," he said, matter-of-factly.

"I know. I'm ready to get out of this hostel," Ester said.

"I'm a Tugen, and you're an Elgeyo. Are you okay with that?" George asked. The major differences within these two Kalenjin sub-tribes were their dialects and the regions where they lived.

"Yes," she said.

They talked for another two hours before the agent returned.

"Please, George, may I talk to you?" the agent asked.

"Absolutely," he turned to Ester and thanked her. She walked out of the room.

"How did it go?" he asked.

"Ester has accepted my offer of marriage," he said. He was happy but also anxious. After so much time, things were now moving fast. "So, what's next?" George asked.

"Tomorrow, we'll visit Ester's family," the agent replied. "Brother Chemose of AIM Kessup will help arrange formal family permission for you to marry her. Ester's father disowned her after she was saved and moved to the hostel. They may not care much about giving her up for marriage. However, we still need to go through the process respectfully," he said.

"Of course." George understood this all too well because of his situation with Jerono. "I brought the blankets and some money. I hope my tokens of appreciation will be accepted."

"We'll need to take Ester with us. Her home isn't far from here. If everything goes as planned, you should be able to wed at Sunday morning service. The mission is ready to execute a small wedding ceremony as soon as possible."

"I'm ready," George smiled.

Everything went smoothly and quickly. Ester's parents accepted the gifts and granted her permission to marry George. They declined to attend the wedding but blessed her marriage. For the Sunday morning service, Ester wore a white gown provided by the mission, and George wore a white shirt, black pants, and a blazer. He did not have a tie; the AIM mission donated all of his wedding outfit. By the end of the service that Sunday, George was married to Ester.

CHAPTER 13

The Pebble

ISABEL, LAI, AND RYAN STRAGGLED into the eating area. After sleepy good mornings and piling plates with breakfast, Ryan looked at Meggie and Liam with their empty plates. "Hey, were you guys here all night?" he asked.

"No, we got here a bit earlier to make some decisions about which sights to see," Liam said.

"And, what did you decide?" Isabel asked in a hostile voice.

"We didn't come to any conclusions," Liam said. "What do the rest of you think?"

"There's incredible richness of natural resources here," Lai said.

"Let's try this. Everyone, make a list of things you want to see, in priority order of how much you want to see them," Liam said. "Lai, you'll be in charge of tallying the results, and then we'll figure out the proximity of the sights and plan out our schedule for today," Liam explained.

They spent about fifteen minutes on this exercise. Lai took the results and after making some calculations announced the sights that they would visit. "Okay, Ryan, your turn. Looking at the map, figure out the order we need to take to get in as may of these sites as possible," Liam ordered.

"We'll run the following plays," Ryan announced.

Liam went over to Meggie and softly said, "I can't wait to continue learning about your family. I have this compulsion to know more. We'll figure out a time for the two of us to get together," he said.

In the free moments they had together before the group set out for the Grand Canyon, Meggie gave Liam some background information.

Over time, beginning in the early parts of the 20th century, more British settlers advanced into the Tugen interior. Some worked within the British protectorate administration; others were traders, and a chunk took over a vast area of land and settled as farmers. However, certain groups of the native Tugens were particularly protective of their territory and way of life and attacked caravans of foreigners who crossed their path. They were angered by the threats and warnings of the mighty power that would reign them in if they did not submit to the new laws of the land, the settler's laws.

Kiptarbei was among the generation especially upset at the colonial authorities. Before their arrival, typical internal conflicts and other political bickering occurred in Tugen just as in any other community. However, colonial rule offered challenges that stemmed from disagreements over the control of the spread of infectious diseases, management of drought, livestock raid invasions, among other issues addressed through the internal community organizational structure.

By contrast, the elders among the native Tugens exercised control through seniority and performance. Kiptarbei earned his position in the leadership of the community through exceeding performance expectations. He demonstrated exceptional moral and ethical behavior in all family, clan, and community transactions and relationships. He was considered the go-to person. Native Tugens recognized Kiptarbei as an expert authority in everything to do with Tugen culture; members of the community sought his counsel. He solved serious problems and answered questions from the Tugen population.

Tugen people had rules and regulations that governed their community, stored within the brain trust of the elders. However, the British labeled the native cultural practices *barbaric*. Kiptarbei and other Tugen natives often found themselves on the wrong side of the law. As the youngest senior elder of the community, Kiptarbei witnessed the devastations of his parent's generation and their growing powerlessness against the authoritative British rule.

The settlers lacked respect for the native Tugen culture. They viewed the Tugen community as backward and naïve. Kiptarbei and Talai found the settlers' perspective ludicrous because they both understood the Tugen culture and community norms. Tugens had functioning institutional structures. The settler's perspective of education was learning to read, write, and do some math.

Tugens approached education differently. In their formal education, unlike their setup where learners attended formal schooling in educational institutions, the Tugens' education was within the family, neighborhood community groups, and distinct tribal organizations. In Talai's perspective, just because the administration did not call them seminars, workshops, vocational education, or secondary or primary education did not mean that no one taught them. Talai's resistance to the mission was not necessarily because Christianity was not a good thing. She did not understand why anything cultural was not respected.

Talai cherished the lifelong learning approach of Tugen education that progressed with graduations through scheduled stages from birth to death. Learning and instruction were through oral interactions and practical activities. She was a teacher to her siblings. Her mom and the community were her teachers. She observed what was demonstrated, then participated in and practiced what she had learned until she was ready to execute it on her own. In Tugen culture, one learned by doing.

Since some training was role-based, gender-specific education was prevalent. Extracurricular educational events included storytelling by grandparents, that included folklore, mythology, riddles, and songs.

With time, many Tugen people saw through the settlers' masquerades and grew angered at how these British customs upended their whole society. Under pressure, the Tugen community abandoned the concept of accumulating economic surpluses for themselves through trade restrictions that gave way to free trade. Kiptarbei became one of the elders who saw some opportunities from the colonial rule through these changes. At the same time, he was aware of the exploitations of the Tugen people's vulnerabilities. He was more interested in persuading his community to take advantage of openings that resulted in economic gains.

Kiptarbei convinced his fellow Tugens that they could still enjoy their cultural practices, access schools, medical centers, and jobs without practicing the Christian religion. He encouraged them to send their children to school. Due to limited land resources and movement restrictions, cattle keeping—long a stable occupation for the community—was no longer viable. Kiptarbei encouraged villagers to pursue agriculture and raise small, domesticated livestock, that supplied critical commodities such as eggs, milk, meat, and leather for homestead needs.

Kiptarbei realized that things were never static. His life was a testament to never-ending changes. Changes came in many forms. Whichever way they came, Kiptarbei knew his decisions were critical to the outcomes. He was tired of despair and achieved a mindset of success and progress. He believed that limitations and constraints were temporary and that the community could vanquish their problems with steadfast grit in small everyday and significant long-term pursuits. He assured his community that nothing that could stop them from accomplishing their dreams. Kiptarbei convinced them to think differently, sometimes out of the box. He dared them to be the first to explore new things.

Two years passed since Kiptarbei and Talai's marriage. When Kiptarbei arrived home from a visit to his neighbor's homestead, where he had gone to assist with fencing, Talai was lying on the bed, crying. She looked at him and forced a smile through the tears. "Jepkemoi's mother just left. I informed her that I felt sick the other day. She decided to pay a visit today. I am pregnant," she said.

"Are you sure?" Kiptarbei said with his mouth wide open, surprised. For their whole marriage, they tried for a child without success. At one point, Talai thought she might be barren, but Kiptarbei persuaded her to be patient. He rushed to hug his wife. They agreed that today was their best day, and anticipated many more with their addition to the family.

In those days, culturally trained Tugen midwives assisted women during pregnancy, labor, delivery, and after the birth of the babies. To date, midwives deliver more than two-thirds of infants across the globe. However, today more midwives have additional training.

Talai was more comfortable consulting with a midwife than visiting the dispensary for her prenatal care needs. She heard from other mothers in the village who had their care at the dispensary shocking stories about treatment of Tugen women at the Christian dispensaries—from name-calling to inhumane treatment of delivering mothers. One particular story gave Talai the chills. A young girl had fornicated and conceived. The nurse commanded her to slow down her labor. The nurse positioned her in a lithotomy position,. on her back, her hips and knees flexed, and her legs spread and raised above her hips. The nurse then walked to her desk at the corner of the room, watched as the girl as she complained, cried, and screamed. The girl eventually died due to childbirth complications, simply because the medical staff saw her as a sinner.

Talai knew that risks existed during childbirth regardless of who was directing it. However, Talai decided to work with the community midwife, someone she related to. Talai had observed the individualized prenatal, birth, and postpartum care that experienced midwives provided in the homes of the mothers, and she loved it. With the presence of the missionaries, the local midwifery skills advanced with training programs offered through the dispensaries. At the end of the training, the midwives received basic childbirth toolkits. Overall, safety and hygiene improved tremendously.

Talai had a successful delivery at full-term. Elizabeth Jepyator was born at home, surrounded by loved ones. She was given the name Jepyator meaning "to open the way." Her parents wanted better things in life for her and others that would come after her. She was called Elizabeth because the British required her to have an English first name to fit well in society.

At Elizabeth's birth, the British-designed education system was seven years of primary, six years of secondary, and three years of university, accomplished abroad. The opportunities were extremely competitive and expensive. Elizabeth was fortunate to attend the public primary school near their homestead. Near meant seven miles from school. She had few school supplies. What she had was a pencil only sharpened when the pencil lead was beneath the wooden encasement to make it last longer; several ruled pages; one squared thirty-two-page exercise book; and a school uniform (dark blue dress, and yellow blouse beneath). Food was limited, but no one ate all the time. Elizabeth did not notice many of these issues then, because that was how everyone in the community lived.

Although she came from Kiptarbei's family, she was a daughter of the Kasoiyo village. The mothers, fathers, brothers, and sisters from the village raised her. She was counseled by many and would seek counsel from anyone with whom she was comfortable. She knew that everyone was watching out for her best interests, and she needed to be on her best behavior at all times.

Elizabeth lacked many material things in her homestead; however, the love, the critical component, was abundant, as were appreciation and respect, from the community at large. Elizabeth's mental wellbeing and the virtues of hope and perseverance came from the positive effect of the love of her family and community.

Elizabeth was not always the top student, but she was consistently among the best ten throughout her primary education. She did well in her certificate of primary education (CPE) and enrolled in the Kapropita Girls' High School, where she maintained a high level of performance. Again, she was not the smartest in her class, but she was the most determined and had an ample amount of true grit. She pursued anything she wanted with passion, no matter what it took to get it.

In her third year of high school, Elizabeth enrolled in many extracurricular activities. She was good at athletics and represented her school in sporting events. During the training for the interschool competitions, a pebble landed on her neck during a lecture. Someone just awakened a sleeping tiger.

She was seated in the front row. She turned, irritated, ready to confront the stone thrower. She focused her eyes angrily, looking for the culprit.

"Who just threw a pebble at my neck?" she asked.

Everyone was dead quiet. "Who?" she asked again.

Most of the interschool competitions were held in Kabarnet Boys High School to the north of Kapropita, half a mile away. The pebble incident occurred during one of the joint-training activities, with boys were present

The athletic coach echoed Elizabeth's question. "Who threw the pebble at Elizabeth's neck?" Everyone was afraid to move or make any noise. Corporal punishment was on everyone's mind. "Did anyone see who did it?"

No one budged. The coach apologized to Elizabeth and warned the students about the consequences of such behavior.

On the day of the Rift Valley inter-high school athletic competition, the coach showed confidence in Elizabeth's performance. "So, are you ready to win?" he asked her.

"I'm confident in my training," Elizabeth replied.

Elizabeth trained for the 1,500-meter track race. The coach programmed her training to include race-pack track runs, thousands of squats, overhead presses, deep belly breaths, and other lung-enhancing activities. Her training goals were to improve her running form and faster step cadence, which improved as she trained harder.

"I'm prepared to win. Yes, I'm in it to win," Elizabeth said.

"Go get it. We'll all be rooting for you," the coach said with an encouraging smile.

Elizabeth was among thirty-two competitors in the 1,500-meter race, about a mile. As she waited at the starting line, she focused on what her coach told her. "It isn't about how you start but how you finish," a message of comfort in case she messed up her start. However, she wanted to start well because that would give her an even better opportunity to win.

Elizabeth looked nervous, and this was obvious to her fans and coach. Nevertheless, she positioned herself at the end of the inner lane of the start line. She was among the first to stand on the curved line. Each of the athletes was precisely placed to run the same distance of 1,500-meters or more than 1,640-yards.

As soon as the buzzer sounded, she looked down and leaned slightly forward. She made her first stride, swung her arms forward and backward, and relaxed her body in a straight motion. She ran a smart race applying every tactic learned. Just 200-meters from the finish line, she was in the fourth position and wondered if she were going to win the race. With tremendous pressure from the cheering crowd calling her name, Elizabeth pushed extra hard, crushing everyone to gain the first position. Her supporters erupted in cheers. She raised her fist to the receptive crowd. She was elated.

A boy about her age came toward her as she was exiting the field. "You ran fast; that was a good performance."

"Thank you," she replied and proceeded to walk away.

"I'm Edwin," he said as he kept pace with her and extended his hand to greet her. "I wanted to apologize."

"Why?" she asked.

"For the pebble that hit your neck. It was me," Edwin admitted.

"Why didn't you say something then, coward." Elizabeth scolded him.

"I wanted to apologize then, but I didn't want to get in trouble with the coach," he said. "I'm sorry."

"Why did you do it?" she asked.

"I was aiming at a friend of mine behind you. He ducked, and the pebble hit you, instead."

"I've cooled down since then." Elizabeth said and kept on walking away from the field.

"Elizabeth, believe me, or not, you will be the mother of my children one day," he said.

She stopped abruptly, and Edwin stopped too, looking her in the eye.

Before Edwin uttered another word, she said, "You're not serious, are you?"

"I'm not kidding," he said.

"Not gonna happen, I'm sorry," she said.

"Can we be friends, at least?" he asked, trying to match her stride.

"I don't even know you. How can we be friends?" she asked.

"By getting to know me, and letting me get to know you, for a start," Edwin replied.

Letters were the only means of communicating such matters at the time, apart from face-to-face meetings. "Here, take this," he handed her a folded piece of paper.

She opened the paper, looked at it, and smiled. "So, how did you know my name?" she asked.

"You're my favorite athlete, and I'm one of your many fans. That's how I know you."

"Where do you come from?" she asked.

"Baringo, you?" he said.

"Baringo," she responded.

"Settled, we come from the same district," he said, teasingly. *Lembusin* was a tagline used to brand a particular community in Eldama Ravine. Elizabeth laughed out loud.

"Bragging isn't a crime, is it?" he laughed.

"No. But bragging about material items is absurd," Elizabeth said.

"Agreed," he said.

"I must admit that the *Lembus* branding worked; people there still believe that they have it all. I'll visit there one day to see for myself," she said.

"No worries. That will be your home one day. I believe that," he said.

"You are so full of yourself," Elizabeth retorted as she ran off with the folded piece of paper in her hand.

One week later, Elizabeth received her first letter from Edwin. He had figured out her address. She had not given it to him. However, she replied. They enjoyed a friendly exchange of letters. Elizabeth and Edwin focused on building a relationship. She quickly realized that Edwin was a Christian. Yet, he was like any other Tugen warrior in his mannerisms but treated her as a sister. She liked that because she wanted to pursue other endeavors before she committed to marriage. Elizabeth did not come from a Christian background herself and made that clear, but that did not discourage Edwin from pursuing the relationship.

During their last year of secondary education, Kabarnet and Kapropita high schools closed their schools on the same date. Many people were in Kabarnet town that day. Elizabeth walked toward the shuttle that took her home when she spotted Edwin with three other people standing beside him. She went to meet them.

Edwin moved toward her and extended his hand to greet her, "Hello, Elizabeth," he said. "Meet my parents and my sister."

"Hello," she greeted Edwin then moved to his father, mother, and sister, consecutively.

As she greeted them, Edwin introduced them. "George, my father; Ester, my mother; and Lea, my sister."

"Edwin is a little bit discrete on personal matters. Are you his girlfriend?" his father asked.

"We're friends," she said, smiling.

"Pleasure to meet you," Lea said, grinning.

Edwin closely monitored Elizabeth's reactions. He wondered what his father would say if he knew that Elizabeth was not a Christian.

"Where do you come from, Elizabeth?" George asked.

"Just near Kapropita, Kasoyo village," she said.

"Which family in Kasoyo?"

"Kataribe," she said.

His father's mouth fell open with disbelief. He covered it immediately with his hand. His eyes were wide open in awe. How is this possible, he asked himself.

"Do you know her family?" Edwin asked with curiosity, surprised by his father's behavior.

"Not really. Many people have similar names. I used to know someone by that name. I doubt we are referring to the same person," he said and immediately changed the subject. "Do you go to Kapropita Girl's High School?" George asked.

"Yes," she responded.

"Good school. Work hard, and you'll do very well," George said.

"Bye, Elizabeth," Edwin said.

"Bye," she said.

They parted, and each of them returned to their families for the holidays.

The town was packed, and Elizabeth's shuttle inched through the traffic. She saw a flier taped to the front about a three-day Christian youth conference seminar at Eldama Ravine. She was not a Christian, but Elizabeth was sure that Edwin would be there. She was nineteen, and Edwin was twenty. She wrote down the details of the conference on a piece of paper and kept it in her pocket.

Because her family were not Christians, she had to think of a way to convince her parents about her intent to travel to Eldama Ravine for the conference, in two weeks. Elizabeth disliked lying to her parents. However, if they found out the truth, she was sure that they would not approve. My best friend from school lives there so I'll visit her. If I visit her, even if it is for a few hours or minutes in the four days, the whole thing will not be a lie, she thought.

CHAPTER 14

The Waterfall

Elizabeth arrived late in the evening in Eldama Ravine exactly two weeks from when she spotted the flier. Elizabeth took the few belongings that she had brought with her and headed to the conference, which was already underway.

A woman standing at the door ushered her into the dining hall. Everyone was seated as the regional youth pastor delivered the opening sermon. The youth attendant directed her to a seat near the entrance to minimize any disturbance. She sat and listened. The pastor introduced the lead youth coordinator for the seminar, Edwin. Elizabeth was not surprised; it was his message that surprised her. He asserted that those who failed to believe in God would receive eternal punishment, and those who believed would be rewarded with eternal life in Heaven. He also advised the youth congregation not to be yoked with unbelievers whose ways were wicked.

"Wickedness and righteousness don't mix. It's like day and night or light and darkness. If you get yoked with ungodly people, sin will happen. Never, and I mean never be a partner to impiety. It will be your expedited route to the Prince of Darkness, Gehenna. I would choose heaven if I were you," he said in closing.

Elizabeth was horrified. She stood, looked at him, and quietly walked out. The room was packed with more than 300 people from all around Baringo.

Edwin noticed her. He was confused. He thanked everyone for coming and walked out the side door. Elizabeth was seated outside the main door, contemplating what to do next. As soon as she saw him, she sobbed.

"Elizabeth, hello," he greeted her.

"How could you do this to me?" she said.

"What did I do? I'm so glad you came," he said.

She cursed him. "I'm wicked, and you're righteous," she mumbled. "Because I haven't adopted your Christian way of life, I'm a wreck, a wicked person headed straight to hell. Why did you want to be my friend?" she asked.

"Elizabeth, the two of us are distinct. In our Christian community, we all believe the same thing. We interpret it differently depending on our various organized groups. You have a particular view, and that's okay with me. I wouldn't impose my Christian beliefs on you. What I said there was true for what we believe. You have different beliefs. I want to understand yours so that I can get to know you better. I will do the same so that you will know me, too. None of us is right or wrong. We're just different, and that's okay," he said.

"So, you don't see me as evil?" she asked.

"No. Not at all. You're Elizabeth, my friend," he said. "I'm distinct from my father, George."

"How so?" she asked.

"My job is to live a life that attracts others to my beliefs. If I live by the fruits of the spirit, I show others what it's like to live a Christian life..."

"...and that is?"

"Love, peace, patience, kindness, goodness, faithfulness, gentleness, and self-control," he said. "I won't deny that it can be challenging sometimes. We're imperfect human beings living in a flawed world."

"That's practical," she said. "But how are you different from your father," she asked.

"He strongly measures other's beliefs with his deep-rooted Christian teachings. I'm not saying he's wrong. Christian belief has served as a moral compass his whole life. Guidelines for what is right and wrong, moral and immoral, sin and righteousness are outlined in the scriptures. His reasoning is based entirely on this belief. I see things differently. I let my light shine in my little world for others to see. If they like what they see and would like to follow Christ, then I support them through the journey. I don't judge. I like you the way you are, and that's the truth."

"I'm glad to hear you say that, Edwin. When I heard you speak, you scared the bejesus out of me," she said.

"Let's get you settled. I'm very excited to see you, Elizabeth. I'm so glad you came."

To her surprise, she enjoyed the conference. The guest speakers were motivational. Elizabeth met new people she would not have encountered otherwise. The conference environment provided an atmosphere for genuine conversations that allowed for deep connections. She met with strangers who encouraged her through thoughtful dialogue and fair-minded discussions.

The majority of the conference attendees confessed to being Christians. They all believed that Jesus was the Son of God and that their sins were forgiven by salvation through the death of Jesus Christ. However, there were variations in the ways they practiced the faith.

In one of the Bible studies that Elizabeth attended, she discovered that some Christians believed that Jesus was the only way to heaven. Others made an informed personal decision to follow Christ, but they acknowledged that other people's beliefs were likewise authentic. Their beliefs depended on how that individual perceived the world, which in turn depended on how and where they were raised, where they originated, and with what cultural and religious influence they grew up.

The most interesting discussions occurred during episodes of cognitive dissonance among the group. Elizabeth learned that everyone has a worldview, but that view sometimes differed from what others believed. She realized that her family engrained in her strong, deeply cherished Tugen cultural beliefs. Some of these beliefs contradicted Christian values and ideas.

During the conference, she had to listen to and tolerate opinions or behaviors, even those not permissive toward her own. In the end, what mattered to her was learning about the different worldviews, and the moral principles that she could choose to guide her life.

Edwin immersed himself in the coordination of the conference. Not until the last day of the conference was he able to check in with Elizabeth. He went to see her during breakfast.

"I'm sorry I've neglected you. The details of the conference have kept me quite busy. I had no time to see you, but I wanted to see you immediately," Edwin said.

"No problem. I've enjoyed the experience. I'm glad I came," Elizabeth said.

"I want to show you something, if you're free this morning," he said.

"What?" she asked.

"You'll see," he said, smiling. "I'm heading for a conference wrap-up meeting. I'll pick you up at 10:00 outside the dining hall."

"Sounds good, see you then."

Elizabeth was waiting outside the conference center when Edwin approached carrying a backpack.

"Follow me," he said.

"Lead the way."

They walked outside the main gate, where a shuttle awaited them. Edwin opened the door and ushered her in.

He introduced her to the shuttle driver, a friend of of, and told him to take them to the Chemasusu Forest.

"Where are we going?" Elizabeth asked curiously.

"Patience, my dear. You'll see," he replied.

They stopped midway to Torongo. They got out of the shuttle and hiked through a footpath into the forest—the trees formed a dense canopy and though it was daylight, the thickness of the trees prevented any light coming through. Elizabeth breathed in the air in this unique ecosystem.

"Follow me," Edwin said. "Elizabeth, this is the Chemasusu Forest. It is one of my favorite spots."

"A forest? This place is different; why did you want us to come here?" she asked.

Edwin held her hand as he motioned her to stop just a few steps from where they had started the hike. "Close your eyes and just listen," he requested.

She gave him a questioning look.

"Close your eyes. Take a deep breath and stay silent," Edwin said.

It was peaceful. The air was fresh. The wind blew the scent of wildflowers toward them, providing extra perfume that combined with an earthen, damp scent from nearby bushes. Leaves rustled, birds sang, and insects hummed—all in a meticulously assembled melody. Heavenly, she thought to herself. Elizabeth opened her eyes and smiled.

"I get it," she said. "This place is beautiful."

He led the way through a narrow flat path for about ten minutes and then down a slight slope.

"Edwin, is there a waterfall down there?" she asked.

Before Edwin could answer, she emerged from the path to a spectacular sight—a waterfall gushed water from a cave into a natural quartzite colored pool. He pointed to a spot where he wanted them to settle.

"Let's sit over there," he motioned.

Elizabeth looked at the waterfall and asked, "Why don't we go down there?"

"Are you sure?"

"Yes, though I don't know how to swim. That place looks stunning. I want to see it close and touch it," she said.

"Let's go," he said.

They climbed down. Edwin enjoyed every moment. He was impressed by Elizabeth's adventurous attitude.

When she got to the pool, Elizabeth stopped and appreciated the view of a natural pool with a waterfall. From his backpack, Edwin removed a wrap, (*leso*), with bold print designs in bright red and white colors. On it were the words *moyo wa subira haufanyi ghera* (a patient heart is never in haste) written in black.

He spread out the *leso* and placed two Cokes, two bananas, sandwiches, and cupcakes on it.

Elizabeth turned to ask a question and found Edwin further away from her. He was not very visible but looked busy.

"What are you up to?" she asked.

"Setting up a place for us."

Elizabeth was impressed by Edwin's efforts. She immediately noticed the words on the wrapper and smiled, but she did not want Edwin to notice her reaction.

"I hope you're hungry. There's plenty of food here."

"I see you planned this well. Thank you."

"I'm glad you like it. This is a special place for me. I escape here when I want to be alone."

"Why would you want to be alone?" Elizabeth asked.

"To pray, read the Bible, or just study for school."

Elizabeth nodded and sat beside him.

They were together in the most beautiful place, enjoying the sounds of nature as they ate the food.

"What do you want to pursue for your advanced level of secondary education? What are your school choices?" Edwin asked.

"I want to go back to Kapropita Girls. My second and third choices respectively are Alliance and St. Mary's school in Yala. What about you?"

"Kabarnet, Mangu, and Kapsabet. I chose math, physics, and chemistry (MPC). What subject areas did you choose?"

"Wow, mad people's combination (MPC)," she laughed. This was a nickname for people who managed a combination of math, physics, and chemistry. The community regarded them as highly intellectual, ultra smart people. Elizabeth was impressed. "You're confident. That's great! I chose math, chemistry, and biology."

"That's impressive, too," he said and laughed.

"I know why you're laughing," Elizabeth said. She thought that Edwin did not want to say the nickname for her subject combination because of its connotations.

"What?" Edwin asked.

"Cabbage?" she inquired.

"No. Cabbage is for chemistry, biology, and geography," Edwin said.

"I guess I will never know why," Elizabeth responded.

They ate, walked around, and came back to their spot to eat again, while talking and getting to know each other. Edwin was attracted to Elizabeth. He struggled to keep himself together. He was starting to question his decision to go out alone with her. He wanted to get close to her and show her affection, but he knew better than to pursue sinful lust and immoral habits. A kiss, hug, and hand-holding were the direct thresholds to premarital intimacy. "Oh God, come to my mercy right now," he prayed quietly.

As he pleaded with God, Elizabeth made a move. She threw away the cupcake she had in her hand and kissed him—just a smooch.

He panicked. "Why did you do that?" he asked, flustered. Edwin stood up and hurriedly ran toward the pool below the waterfall.

Elizabeth smiled to herself. I am the temptation, the devil, but he did not fight it off, she thought. He waited until it was all done before he ran away. She followed him.

"I'm sorry. I couldn't hold back. It won't happen again. I respect your beliefs," Elizabeth said.

"What are your expectations of me now that you know about my beliefs?" he asked, scared of what her response would be. He did not want to lose her; yet, he wanted to continue his commitments as a Christian.

"Frankly, you're scared of having sex before marriage. I'm scared of getting pregnant before I finish school. Our common enemy is sex," she said.

"True," he said.

"The idea of no touching, kissing, and holding hands sounds practical to me. Culturally, such things are abominable too, but you have to agree that it felt like heaven, don't you?" she asked.

He smiled, "The devil comes to us with delightful things."

"So, I'm the devil masked as a friend?"

"That's not what I meant, and you know it," he said.

"What did you mean?" Elizabeth asked, defensively.

"I like you a lot, Elizabeth. I feel a lot of things right now. I want sinful things. Thinking about it is sinful. You make me feel, think, and want to do all these things. I can't stop thinking about you," he said.

Elizabeth looked at him. He was genuinely distraught. He was crying.

"May I hug you, please, as a friend. I mean no harm," she requested.

He opened his arms to her, and they hugged each other tightly. Each of them understood the dilemma and was willing to give and take in order to be happy. Something special happened that day.

"I feel much better," he said.

"Me too. We better get back," Elizabeth said.

"Agreed," he said.

They cleaned up and headed back to the main road where the driver was waiting for them. They were back at the conference in time for dinner.

CHAPTER 15

Thermodynamics

Elizabeth returned to Kapropita High School, and Edwin entered Mangu High School for their A-levels. The schools were 120-miles apart.

In Kenya, the educational system is seven years of elementary, four-years of ordinary secondary, two-years of advanced secondary school, and three-year of university. The system is Kenya, was based on the British model of education.

Edwin continued his ministry service at Mangu as the chairman of the school's Christian Union, a church similar to the Baptists in the United States. The Evangelical Christian student group fostered students evangelizing to fellow students. The group was governed and led by the student body.

Meanwhile the relationship between Elizabeth and Edwin was physically distant but very close through an exchange of letters. However, Elizabeth avoided crossing the line or placing Edwin in an uncomfortable situation even though she could have. Many modern things available or done today existed long ago. They might have looked a little different. Elizabeth did not want to write steamy, sexy love letters. The difference was the efficiency and speed of the correspondence. In their time, it took weeks or even months to communicate. Elizabeth still wanted to be sensitive and respect Edwin's beliefs.

One evening when Edwin was home during the holidays in the last year of his secondary education, the family ate dinner together. They celebrated with an after-dinner fellowship. Ester, his mother, cleared the Bibles and songbooks from the table.

"Edwin, I have a favor to ask," George said as he handed Edwin a letter.

Edwin took the letter from Kapropita AIC church addressed to George and read aloud. "We are pleased to invite you to our local church Sunday service…" he skipped over some parts. "It is our honor to invite you to minister on how to shine bright for Christ. We look forward to your response."

"What do you think?" his father asked. "Could you take on this challenge and minister to this youth group? Of course, I will clear this with the pastor at Kapropita Church."

"I'm in," Edwin responded without hesitation. Edwin was not thinking about the sermon.

"You better prepare; it's the Sunday after next."

"Why don't you want to go, dad?" he asked.

"You are a shining light for Christ, my son. I'm proud of you. That's why," George replied.

Edwin was almost teary. "Thank you for your confidence in me. I won't let you down. I'm going to spend the whole weekend in Kabarnet for that event." In his room, Edwin gathered all his thoughts for the sermon. He was ready for a bigger audience, and he did not need much preparation. Edwin wrote a letter to Elizabeth and invited her to the service.

Two weeks later, Edwin arrived in Kabarnet. He booked a room for two days at Lelian B lodging. He spent time preparing for the sermon, which went well. Everyone enjoyed the sermon and wanted him back for their youth ministry at the end of the year. He promised to come back then.

Elizabeth showed up and remained in her seat as everyone streamed out of the church. He walked toward her and stood a row in front-facing her. "Good morning," he greeted her.

"Good morning," she responded.

"Thanks for coming," he said.

"It's my pleasure. I enjoyed it," Elizabeth said warmly.

"Let's get out of here. Where should we go? You know this place better than I do," Edwin said. Elizabeth was born and raised near Kabarnet.

"Follow me," Elizabeth said. She led them to her favorite restaurant, a buffet serving traditional Kalenjin food with a modern twist. "This restaurant is the go-to spot for those who appreciate Tugen cuisine and delicacies. I think you'll like it, or at least, I hope so," she added.

"Ha! Elizabeth, you nailed it," Edwin exclaimed, looking around at the restaurant's atmosphere —the music, artwork, and lighting, which all set the stage for comfort. It was a perfect setting for romantic conversation, he thought.

"Reserve your compliments until you taste the food." She was happy that Edwin had appreciated her efforts.

"Good afternoon, and welcome to Baigaa ('Feed the Home') restaurant," a waiter said. "Feel free to sit where you're comfortable. A beautiful veranda is out that door if you want to dine outside," the waiter explained.

Elizabeth approached the cashier, and Edwin said, "The lunch is on me." Drinks were on a separate table from the food. Most notable was signature Tugen smoked and fermented milk and chai. They were more interested in the food, so they quickly walked past the drinks to survey the food table.

"Edwin, if you could only eat one type of food from all these choices, which one would it be?" Elizabeth asked as they looked over the options.

He looked at the white and brown cake-like product made from boiled water and white corn flour and another from millet flour. "This is my father's favorite. I'll pass on it, though."

"This is my favorite," Elizabeth pointed to the black nightingale vegetables with milk cream. "My mother is an expert in growing this vegetable. She's the major supplier of the town. My father remembers how he courted her in her black nightingale vegetable garden."

They passed by the African spider plant vegetables with milk cream and roast beef.

After a pause, Edwin announced, "I would choose goat meat."

"Why?' Elizabeth asked.

"Nutrition-wise, it's leaner than beef, and I love the taste of it," Edwin said.

"I'd pass the stew with sliced meat, but the *pilau*—made of rice, fried meat seasoned with Indian spice, looks good. I would go for the pilau," Elizabeth said.

"This is another good one," Edwin said pointing at the chapati—unleavened whole-meal bread cooked on a griddle and put some on his plate.

"I'm with you on that one. It's a special delicacy in our home. We cook it in special occasions," Elizabeth said, adding some to her plate. "After all, being together is a special occasion." Then, they bypassed the sweetened deep-fried doughnut dough and spicy fried meat-filled squares at the end of the table.

Elizabeth looked at Edwin and asked, "Where do you want to sit? You're the guest."

He leaned close to her and whispered, "Somewhere private."

"Let's go outside, toward the left side of the veranda," she suggested.

They walked toward the corner of the veranda where visibility from the rest of the restaurant was limited. "Best choice," she said.

While Edwin got them drinks, Elizabeth returned to the buffet table to fill a plate with every brown food item.

Edwin stood behind Elizabeth's seat and pushed her chair in for her.

"That all looks delicious," Edwin said.

"Your sermon was encouraging. You are good with that stuff," Elizabeth broke the silence after they had eaten a few bites.

"I don't want to talk about the sermon," Edwin said. "I want to get to know you, Elizabeth."

"What do you want to know about me that you don't know already?" she asked.

"What is one thing that makes you happy anytime?" Edwin asked.

"I love to read," she said, "but I typically read romance novels."

"I do, too," Edwin admitted.

Tears of laughter rolled down Elizabeth's face. "Isn't that sin?"

"I'm not perfect. I'm just a boy who does what other boys do at my age. I have to read in private; otherwise, I'll be judged," he said. "These romance books are not permitted in school libraries. So, where do you get them?" he asked.

"I use all my pocket money to buy them from the rich girls from the city after they've finished reading, them" she said. "In romance novels, I get to meet great fictional, handsome men. Some are respectful, loving, and kind. Others are villains who scare me about relationships," she admitted.

"Have you ever met one like me?" he asked teasingly.

"Yes, right from the cover page," she looked up to meet his eyes. "You are standing close to the girl about to kiss her, just at sunset," she said.

"What happens inside the book?" he asked.

"You meet the girl," she stopped and looked at him.

"Then?" he asked.

"She gets to know you and falls in love in the process. However, before she can enjoy the relationship, the rollercoaster begins," she said.

"It must be the rivals and her friends," Edwin guessed. "I hope I don't give in to the temptation," he said.

"No, it is about your friends. You have to fight them to get her attention. A fierce conflict arises between the two of you that creates an enormous tension in the relationship," she said, but Edwin interrupted.

"I will fight for her with my life," he said. Edwin's emotions were wrapped up in the story. It was as if Elizabeth's love story scenario was the real one between him and Elizabeth. Edwin looked at her and said, "This is the real thing. No matter where the testing waters will emerge, I will always stand by you." Edwin gazed at Elizabeth. Elizabeth reciprocated. She saw that he was opening his heart to her, to show her all that he was. He extended his hand and held both of Elizabeth's.

"Nowadays, I consider you when I want to make choices," he said, his eyes still locked on hers. "I ask myself, what would Elizabeth say or think? I think about you before I fall asleep, and first thing when I wake up in the morning. I often refer to you more than the members of my family. I understand and like the differences in the way we approach our lives. Every time I think of my future, it's difficult to imagine not having you in it. You have challenged my way of thinking and made me a better person. You are my best friend on the planet. I love you, Elizabeth," he said.

Elizabeth became dewy eyed. She took a deep breath, exhaled, and said, "I love you, too, Edwin, very much."

Edwin stood and walked to Elizabeth, held her tightly. She sobbed into his chest. The walls between them were crumbling.

"The food will get cold," Elizabeth said, laughing as she wiped the tears from her cheeks.

"I'm so happy," Edwin said as he released her.

They returned to their seats and continued with their meal in silence for a while, each one absorbing the enormity what just happened.

"Your family is Christian, mine is cultural. What do you think our home will look like when we have them together for dinner?" Elizabeth asked to break the silence.

"Good question. My father will volunteer to bless the food," Edwin, said, "or he'll bow down and pray for his own food."

Elizabeth responded, "My mother is sensitive and respects others' perspectives. My dad, on the other side, will dig in without any thought. He doesn't care whatsoever. He strongly believes that all people are entitled to their own ideas and that no one should be forced to do anything they don't want to," she said.

"Are you saying he won't pray with others if there is a request?" Edwin asked.

"Yes, he'll do whatever. Just warning you so that you don't get surprised," she said.

"As I said, I'll still stand by you, no matter what," Edwin said and Elizabeth blushed.

"Even if you father disowns you because you want to marry a sinner?" she asked to test him.

"My life without you in it will be meaningless. Anything that stands between us is not worth it. I promise to love you till death do us part. Nothing else will ever separate me from you."

They continued their conversation about their families, their future dreams, mistakes they made in life, and the differences in their spiritual and cultural lives.

"Do you know, we've been here for three and a half hours already?" she said as she looked at her watch.

"I'm having a great time. I don't mind staying here with you for eternity," Edwin gazed at her with lovestruck eyes.

"It's getting late. I have to go. I came here with an unresolved chemistry question that is giving me problems. May I show you?" Elizabeth asked.

"Absolutely. Why don't we go to the hotel lobby? There's more room on the table there. It's close to here," he said.

"That would be great, thank you Edwin."

They left the restaurant and walked to the hotel. When they arrived, all the seats in the lobby were occupied, and they ended up in Edwin's room. "I'll leave the door open. Please have a seat," Edwin said.

"Okay, let me grab my textbook and the question that's perplexing me," she said.

Elizabeth promised Edwin that she would not be a problem in their relationship, and she was going to keep her promise. She was not going to act seductively toward him. She vowed to restrain herself and do whatever it took to ensure that Edwin was successful in his Christian values. She trusted herself and encouraged Edwin's relationship with God. She did not want to lead him into temptation. She was willing to hold off her own needs for the moment as the relationship developed.

"There's only one chair. Let me pull it close to the bed so that you can sit on the chair, and I'll sit on the side of the bed." Edwin pulled the table toward the side of the front door. Elizabeth faced the open door while Edwin sat on the bed.

As Elizabeth opened the text, he asked, "What's it about?"

"Thermodynamics," she replied.

"Oh, the relation between heat and other forms of energy," he said. Edwin's brain was already fried, imagining how he would give her the best sex ever—even though he had never experienced sex with a partner before. He looked at her, wanting to partake in her beauty.

"That's it?" she asked.

"No, a lot happens." he paused, speaking very slowly.

"Like what?" she asked

He moved closer to her, closed the text, and responded with another question, "What is the key principle of thermodynamics?"

Elizabeth loved how she felt. "Tell me, that's why I'm here. It's the area that might cause me to fail in the subject," she said.

Edwin moved again, about arm's distance away—enough to inhale her scent. Elizabeth could feel that.

Elizabeth felt Edwin's presence more intensely. It was irresistible.

Edwin motioned her out of the chair. They both sat on the bed. He continued to hold her with a look of desire. Edwin was no longer paying attention. His overwhelming attraction overtook him. Elizabeth was everything he imagined. She fulfilled his dreams. Nothing was preventing his thoughts and actions.

He touched her at the back of her neck as he moved and whispered into her ear, "The heat generated is proportional to the work done," he said. His voice was smooth and husky.

Feeling his breath hot against her neck, Elizabeth looked up at him. "Are you still referring to chemistry? I mean, the problem that I need solved?" she asked.

He came out of his trance suddenly and said, "Yes. Yes, where were we?"

Elizabeth pointed to the problem. Edwin read through the problem and took her step-by-step through the problem to the solution. He requested that she work through a similar problem following the steps he showed her, and Elizabeth did it correctly.

"You're a great teacher," Elizabeth complimented him. "I understand it completely now."

"Thank you."

Elizabeth stood and packed up her bag, then gazed at him. "I know what you meant," she said softly.

"What do you mean?" he asked.

"The heat generated is proportional to the work done," she said in a sultry and alluring nature that left Edwin defenseless.

Edwin panicked and found himself closing the door instead of ushering her out.

"We're in trouble," he said as he kissed her hard.

She kissed him back just as hard. "Oh God," she groaned after a few minutes as she tried to catch her breath. "If this is hell, it feels incredible. What should we do?" she asked in bliss as she kissed him again.

"I don't know," Edwin replied, breathing hard.

"What do you do when faced with such temptation?" she asked.

Before he replied, Elizabeth kissed him even harder. She took his tongue deep into her mouth, afraid that he might end her pleasure. She dug in and made him lose his mind. Nothing she had read about French kissing came close to the pleasure of the real thing.

Neither of them remembered what happened after the kiss. When Elizabeth and Edwin woke up, the bed looked like a war zone. The sheets were tangled, pillows were strewn across the room, and there was blood everywhere.

"What happened?" Edwin asked in horror.

"I was a virgin," Elizabeth replied.

"Did I hurt you that badly?"

"No, I didn't feel anything then, but it hurts pretty bad right now," she replied.

"This was my first time, too," Edwin replied, looking at her lovingly.

"Seriously?" she asked.

"Yes," he said. Edwin then expressed his prowess, gently pulling her hand toward his crotch. "I'm game if you are," he lustfully said as he faced Elizabeth with confidence.

"Oh, no. I'm not asking for more. Get away from me." Elizabeth said, afraid that Edwin wanted to have sex with her again.

Elizabeth got out of the bed, grabbed her clothes, and went to the bathroom. She cleaned herself and came out dressed. Edwin was still in a miasma—reveling in everything that happened.

"Edwin, I have to go. Goodbye," Elizabeth said as she abruptly left the room.

"Elizabeth, wait. Please, wait!" Edwin begged, rising from the bed to follow her. She took off in such a hurry that by the time he freed himself from the mess of sheets and got to the door to look down the hall, she was gone.

The hotel experience was the last encounter Edwin and Elizabeth had together. He tried to contact Elizabeth later without success. His letters went unanswered, and inquiries through acquaintances were futile. Elizabeth was determined to keep her distance.

They returned to their respective schools for the last term, focusing on A-level examination preparations.

Although some commonly assume that women invest more deeply into relationships than men, Edwin opened his heart to Elizabeth. He compromised his beliefs to have a chance with her and did everything possible to win her back, but he failed. He decided to step back from his Christian union responsibilities to fully concentrate on his coming examinations. Edwin thought Elizabeth treated him cruelly by instituting a permanent timeout without any communication of terms or explanation of her feelings. He felt in limbo about what he needed to do next.

He walked toward his dorm after his last physics class when his roommate approached him with a letter.

"Hey, Edwin. I have a letter for you."

"Where from?" he asked.

"How should I know?" his roommate responded with a shrug.

Edwin looked at the handwriting on the envelope. He saw the distinctive way Elizabeth wrote and knew it was from her. He took it and sprinted to his room, leaving his roommate behind. Edwin felt overwhelmed with intense anxiety. He entered the room, shaking and utterly confused. He gazed at the unopened letter and wondered if it were the formal severance of the relationship. He experienced a rapid heartbeat and had chest pains and shortness of breath. For a moment, he thought he was going to die.

"Breathe, breathe," he muttered to himself in a low voice. Edwin sat on his bed and took a moment to calm down. After he relaxed, he took the letter and opened it. In a brief moment of distress, Edwin gained some perspective and slowly came to terms with his loss of Elizabeth. Over the past few months, he grieved and channeled his energy into something meaningful and purposeful, his career path. He knew that it was time to take the unfortunate and devastating situation of his life and put it into a better future.

The letter contained only one sentence. "Meet me at Baigaa on Saturday, December 8th at 11:00 a.m."—in two weeks, he thought. The letter left Edwin in great suspense. Nonetheless, he was relieved. Questions flooded his mind. At least, he would finally have the opportunity to ask for answers in person.

Edwin was surprised that he still felt the same way about Elizabeth. However, he had learned the hard way that no one has control over a relationship, except for both parties in it. He knew that he could not control what happened to him, but he could control how he reacted to it. Love was different. He could not control how he felt. It was overwhelming and all-consuming for him. It affected his mind and physical being. How can I build a strong mind to protect my heart? Edwin lay on his bed, staring at the ceiling and thinking hard.

As a Christian, he aspired to live by example, to demonstrate by deeds what love looked like. Patience, kindness, and respect are all aspects of love. He could not demand what Elizabeth did not have. They were not dancing to the same song. His father and some of his close friends' time and time again informed him that women were complicated, that there was no need to try to figure them out because that was impossible. Here he was, trying to speculate who Elizabeth was and what she wanted. Pathetic, he thought to himself. I cannot manipulate her to love me, nor can I restrain my love for her. Each one of us is a distinct soul. If there is love between us, it will honor who we are and live through our differences. I have all the patience and time. That is all I can promise. He finally drifted off to sleep.

CHAPTER 16

Reveal

When Edwin arrived at the designated restaurant, Elizabeth was already seated with a cup of tea. "Hi," Edwin extended his hand to greet her.

"Hi," she responded.

He sat in the chair opposite her. Meanwhile, he focused on her, trying to read her face for clues. There were none. Her eyes were alert, staring into space. He was trying to figure out what he did wrong but couldn't figure it out.

"It has been quite some time. What happened?" he asked. He turned and looked away from her as he posed the question.

"About what?" she asked, trying to deflect the question.

"Seriously! Elizabeth! The letters, messages? Did you not receive them? Are you saying that?" Edwin's emotional rage had him seeing red.

The waiter interrupted suddenly and saved the situation.

"Hello, can I get you something?" she asked, looking at Edwin and Elizabeth.

"Yes, I would like to have some chai and *mandazi.*[2]

---

[2] *Mandazi is* a sweet deep-fried doughnut-like pastry.

"I'll have a *mandazi*, too" Elizabeth said.

"I'll be back shortly," the waiter said.

Elizabeth looked at Edwin and tried to redirect the conversation.

"How were your exams? The exam period was challenging for me. I'm not sure how my performance was. I hope that at least I meet the minimum university entry requirements," she said, her voice verging on monotone.

"I'm not sure either. I'm hoping for the best, too." He was not in the mood to go along with the way Elizabeth was dancing around something this important. I want to know why you did what you did. You hurt me so badly, Elizabeth. How do you expect me to react or move on if I don't know what I did wrong?" he asked.

"I'm pregnant," she blurted the words out impatiently.

"What?" he asked, shocked. The message came abruptly. It happened so fast he had no time to think. He looked at Elizabeth in awe.

Elizabeth paid attention to every detail of his reaction, and he was aware of that.

"Yes," she said calmly.

"How long have you known?"

"Just before I went back to school."

"Oh my God," he exclaimed, looking at her intensely. 'Why didn't you tell me?"

Again they were interrupted by the waiter. "Here you are, a *mandazi* for you, chai and a *mandazi* for you," the waiter placed the items in front of them and left.

Edwin was focused somewhere else. He took the distraction as an opportunity to gather his thoughts and compose himself. Things instantly become complicated.

"I didn't want to ruin your life, and I'm not planning to do that now. You're a Christian, and your family will be devastated."

"Who else knows about this?" he asked.

"Just you and my nurse friend at the dispensary near our homestead," she said.

"How far along are you?"

"Fourteen weeks. I'm showing somewhat now. People don't expect it and haven't suspected yet. I wanted you to focus on your exams and not worry about it. Today, I needed to let you know that you will be a father. I'm planning to tell my parents as soon as I get home. I'll see what happens from there," she said calmly. Elizabeth was faking it. She was scared and was taking things one hour at a time. She had no clue about what was going to happen.

Edwin's reaction was unexpected. He was calm and receptive. He was feeling a variety of emotions at the same time; fear, joy, anxiety, and worry.

"I didn't expect this. To tell you the truth, I'm happy for us. I want to do the right thing. I want to take responsibility." Edwin said.

"How?" Elizabeth asked. "You just completed school, and you have no money."

"Not true. I was offered a job yesterday at Makatiat Ltd. Bakery."

Tears flowed down Elizabeth's cheeks. She did not expect what just happened. "You'll be here?" she asked with disbelief.

"Remember what I promised. I'm a man of my word," he said.

"Yes, I do remember. You said you will always stand by me, no matter what."

"We'll figure out college and other things, but I believe that we'll be able to still go to college and take care of our family," he assured her.

"I have a position as an assistant accountant at Makatiat during the break while I wait to enter college," he said. "Elizabeth, I have no money or inheritance, but I am hardworking and determined. Marry me, please?" Edwin asked.

"Are you sure? What about your parents?"

"They have their own lives. I have mine. I make my own choices and am accountable for my actions. I made my mind up to marry you long ago when I first laid eyes on you in that field, and I meant every word I said. My decision is because I truly love you—not just because of the baby," he said.

"Yes. I will marry you," Elizabeth said.

"Elizabeth, let me be the one to break the news to your parents. I will take the heat off you if they don't receive the news well. You did your time to shield me through my examinations. Now it's my turn to do the same for you," he said.

Elizabeth was relieved. She had underestimated Edwin. He was willing to put her first in his life.

"What about your faith?" she asked.

"The God I serve has abundant, steadfast love for me that never ceases. His mercies are never-ending, and He renews them every morning. He promised that in Lamentations 3:22," he said. "I trust him. He will forgive and provide a way for us. He promised that He would not tempt us beyond what we can bear. I have faith in him that he will provide strength to get us through these rough times."

They talked for a long time. Eventually, Edwin and Elizabeth headed to Elizabeth's homestead. Edwin had never been there, nor had he met her parents. They were outside the homestead relaxing.

"Where have you been, Elizabeth?" her mother asked.

"With my friend, Edwin," she said and introduced him.

"Welcome, Edwin," her mother said. "I was getting your dad to come to the house for supper. Please join us."

She left to get the food ready. Kiptarbei stood and echoed his wife's welcome. "Let's follow her. She gets testy if I don't follow her orders," Kiptarbei said. Everyone laughed and went inside.

Kiptarbei and Talai, formerly known as Jerono, had upgraded their homestead. It was about twenty acres of land with a stand-alone one-room wooden squared house with a cement floor, which served as the kitchen. Talai, as the leader of the community women's group, was among the first to use the clean-cooking energy solutions in place of the open fire. She had a concrete plastered built-in three burner fireplace made of a mixture of clay, grass, water, and other organic materials found within the homestead.

Talai prepared her meals early in the day and kept them warm for when everyone was ready to eat. She was excited about Elizabeth's visitor.

Talai decided on every meal's menu. She served her meals on the plates in her kitchen and delivered them to her guests on the dining table. That day's supper was ugali with African spider plant with cream and sliced beef stew.

"Let me assist, mom," Elizabeth said.

Opposite the kitchen was the main house used for entertainment and sleeping. It was a wooden cabin-style home with three rooms. The main door opened to the center room used as the family sitting room. The two other rooms on opposite sides were the master bedroom and Elizabeth's bedroom. Outside, they had another structure—the bathroom.

Kiptarbei ushered Edwin into the living room. "Please sit down and make yourself comfortable."

"Thank you," Edwin responded as he walked to the left corner of the room and sat on the chair. The room was small, with a closed wooden cupboard with multiple drawers used to store dishes. They used this cabinet for storage. At the center of the room was a simple long rectangular table, the height of a standard dining table with five wooden chairs. A blue kerosene lantern, which sat in the middle of the table, was burning brightly.

Elizabeth entered the room and brought glasses to the table, then took two plastic jugs to the kitchen. Her mother entered after her with two plates of food in her hands. She placed one in front of her husband and the other in front of Edwin.

"Elizabeth, can you get the other two plates, please," she called out as she placed spoons in the food she had just brought.

"This looks wonderful. Do you have water with you? I wanted to wash my hands. I love to eat with my hands," Kiptarbei said. Culturally, men did not enter the kitchen. It was the territory of mothers and their daughters. Although Talai was a women's leader and at times didn't conform to some practices, she wanted her husband to be respected in the community. This time, Kiptarbei had to wait to be served.

"Yes, outside," Talai said as she pointed out the door.

"Edwin, let's wash our hands," Elizabeth said, and they walked out.

"I'm scared," she confessed to Edwin as they washed their hands.

"I am, too, but we'll be fine. Together, me and you, we can overcome anything," he assured her. "I'm not a man who runs away from rough roads, not when the ultimate reward is to wake up to your beautiful face every morning."

Elizabeth brought the food, two jugs of water, and fermented milk to the table. Her mother went back to get the tea that she already made and stored in a six-glass thermos flask.

"Let us proceed," Talai motioned for everyone to start the feast.

"Why don't we let the visitor pray for the meal; he is a Christian," Elizabeth said.

"Edwin, please. We don't mind," Kiptarbei said.

"Let's bow our heads and pray," Edwin said as all of them closed their eyes. "May you bless this meal and this family in Jesus' name." He made it short and precise.

It was quiet for a moment as everyone dug into the food, then Kiptarbei broke the silence.

"Who are your family in Eldama Ravine, Edwin?"

"My father is a pastor for AIM in Eldama Ravine," he replied.

"George?" Kiptarbei asked in wonder.

"Do you know my father?" Edwin asked.

Meanwhile, Talai was shocked. She dropped her spoon to the floor and was looking at Edwin with eyes and mouth in frozen, stunned surprise.

"This is unreal," Talai said.

"Do you know Edwin's father, George?" Elizabeth asked.

The situation was getting bizarre. Kiptarbei pushed his food to the center of the table and stood up.

"I need some air," he said as he walked out of the room.

"What's going on?" Edwin and Elizabeth asked in unison.

"I'll come back. Let me check on Kiptarbei." Talai pushed her food aside and followed her husband.

Outside, they looked at each other with shock. Kiptarbei gazed at his wife with tears in his eyes. The news about his childhood friend and rival was overwhelming. "How can this be possible?" he asked. "Do you think George has any idea? The son does not. *Bakulei*, my dear brother, wonders never cease," he said softly.

"Yes, I agree," Talai said, and she guided her husband back to the table.

"Edwin, remember when I met your family and mentioned my father's name?" Elizabeth looked at Edwin as she asked the question. "There was the same reaction, but your father brushed it off."

"George is my *bakulei*. We have a long history. I'm not sure where to start or how much you want to know," he said.

"Everything!" Elizabeth proclaimed.

"Alright," Kiptarbei nodded.

They ate as Kiptarbei told the whole story. He did not hide anything but emphasized how competitive they were, at the same time stressing how they loved and sacrificed for each other. Elizabeth and Edwin were mesmerized by the whole story.

Everyone was touched and happy. However, Edwin wondered how long the bliss would last when they shared the latest chapter. He wondered whether this might be the wrong time to bring it up.

They finished the food, and Elizabeth took the dishes back to the kitchen while her mother served the tea. She was nervous about her own situation and had decided that it was not the right time to tell her parents. She was planning to ask

Edwin to step out of the room as soon as she got back from the kitchen. She sat and turned to whisper to Edwin, but he was facing her father.

"I wanted to ask for permission to marry your daughter. I've known her since secondary school, about five years to date," he said. "She's pregnant, and I want to take care of my family."

There was a long silence except for the sound of birds chattering at a distance. It was a beautiful night with a clear sky with brilliant stars unaware of the turmoil of earth.

"I'm so sorry we didn't do things correctly as expected. Having a baby wasn't part of the plan, but it happened, and I want the best for my family. I just got a job at Makatiat Ltd. and planned to take Elizabeth with me, if it's okay with you," he said.

"You are pregnant?" Elizabeth's mother looked at her daughter in astonishment.

"Yes, mama. Three-and-a-half months," she said. "I was afraid to get everyone worried because of school."

Her father had looked down with his hand over his forehead, concealing his eyes. He slowly raised his face to look at his daughter. "You could have told us because I would have loved you regardless. I still do," her father said.

No one was drinking the tea by that time. Edwin stood. "I don't have to have an answer today," Edwin stood and offered Elizabeth's father a handshake.

Edwin's show of confidence reassured Kiptarbei. "It's okay, son," Kiptarbei said. Edwin was overwhelmed by the grace Kiptarbei granted him by calling him "son."

"Thank you so much for your hospitality. I'm so sorry for all of this. I love your daughter and promise to do whatever it takes to take care of her," he said.

"May I go with him tonight, please?" she requested her parents' permission to go with Edwin.

"No, you will stay here," Talai said. Kiptarbei went to Talai and put a calming hand on her shoulder.

"I know you are upset, but they need to be together right now. Please, let Elizabeth go," he implored his wife. "There is nothing we can do right now but support them." Edwin and Elizabeth left the homestead soon after and went to Edwin's hotel.

One week later, Edwin had rented a two-room house. One room served as the kitchen and living room, and the other was the bedroom. He intended to live with Elizabeth while he worked at Makatiat. Her parents were supportive and understanding. Edwin informed them that he was leaving for Eldama Ravine to break the news to his parents and arrange for a formal engagement to Elizabeth.

When he arrived at Eldama Ravine, George's parents were happy to see him. They wanted to know about his new job and other Christian activities he was involved with in Kabarnet.

"Dad, I need to talk to you in private," Edwin requested.

"What about?" George asked.

Edwin was already walking out as his dad was talking. He followed him outside. They walked to a spot where they had had many important conversations over the years and sat down.

"What's wrong?" George asked him, suddenly worried.

"I know that you have very strong convictions about faith. You walk the talk and are willing to suffer and persevere for what you believe. I want you to know that I admire and respect that," Edwin began.

"I know that son, and I respect your convictions, too. Cut to the chase, what's going on?"

"Elizabeth is pregnant with my child. I have asked her to marry me," he said.

"What have you done?" George was horrified. "You know I am a minister and a role model in the church. What will people think?"

George raised Edwin and his sister in a Christian home. Christian principles and values were the cornerstones of his family. George stood and walked away from his son. He was in agony—the pain of betrayal burned him. He fell on his knees, crossed his arms on his chest, and looked upward to the sky.

"Oh God, I have done everything you asked of me, left my family to follow you. How do I face my congregation now?" He prayed in deep sorrow as if someone in the family had just died. After this prayer, he lowered his head and looked down like a defeated man.

At that moment, Edwin realized the impact of his actions on his parents. He had been too consumed by his situation with Elizabeth that he blocked out thinking about consequences and focused on resolutions instead. He held his breath, engrossed in every reaction from his father. He had disappointed him, the youth group he ministered to, the church, and God. The consequences of his actions had not registered until then. Oh, my God, he thought. Then, it became clear to him how devastating his poor choices would be for others. In haste, he had focused on Elizabeth's emotions and neglected thinking about the other side. He was in a deep dilemma.

His father stood, raised his head, and looked at him.

"This will kill your mother," George said. "Did you think about that?"

Edwin looked down. His shoulders sagged. He was ashamed of his actions and empathetic toward his father. He was worried about his parent's reputations more than his, particularly his mother's whom he loved very much.

"Edwin," his mother called from behind him. She had been listening to them all along.

Everyone was quiet, contemplating what would happen next.

"Elizabeth is pregnant?" she asked.

"Yes, fourteen weeks."

Ester went to her husband and held his drooping shoulders. He was still kneeling.

"It's not as bad as you think. It could have been worse," Ester said to him.

"What do you mean, it could have been worse?" George looked at his wife in confusion.

"Think about it. If it were someone coming to tell us that Edwin got an accident and died," she said.

George was stunned.

"We've been in a worse situation than this. Have you forgotten? We can get through this," she said. Ester was doing everything possible to deescalate the situation. "Get it together, men. No one is going to die. I wish I could get through to your heads," she said.

"Don't be worried about me. Our son needs us more than he ever has had before. Close your eyes," she directed her husband. "Do you remember the *Footprints in the Sand* poem?" she asked him.

"Yes," he replied as he closed his eyes.

"Relax, George," she said in a low, soothing voice. She located the stiff, tightened muscles on her husband's shoulder blades. She squeezed and released repeatedly. "During your times of trials and suffering, when you see only one set of footprints, it was then that I carried you," she said as she stopped the massage and walked around to face him. "Think about it; what would Jesus do?" Ester asked him.

George stood and looked directly into his wife's eyes. "Thank you. Thank you so much," he said and hugged her tightly.

Edwin observed the scene between his parents with wonder.

His father was astounded by the grace his wife showed. He was worried about her, but he wondered if he was the one who needed grace. Do I know what grace is all about? he thought to himself. God looks out for us and expects the same of us. "I am glad I have you," he whispered to his wife, holding her close.

"Me too. I love you," Ester said.

Edwin did not completely disclose who Elizabeth was. He was admiring his parents' courage and the love they had for each other. He had messed up very badly, and they supported each other to get through this initial stage of the situation. With the knowledge that the future was going to be challenging, they were at peace with their joint decision.

"Elizabeth is the daughter of your *bakulei*, Kiptarbei," Edwin looked at his father.

George released his wife from the embrace and smiled. "I didn't want to believe it the last time you told us, but I strongly suspected it could be so. How could that be possible, that's what I asked myself," George said.

"I know the whole story. Does mom know?" Edwin asked his father.

"What story?" Ester asked, curious.

"Not much. It was very painful. I omitted a lot," he said.

Ester was not happy. Her brain was rapidly re-positioning itself for verbal combat. Why was I left in the dark? She wondered, was he hiding a tainted past? At the same time, she was very instrumental in the church as the conflict-resolution expert. During many family misunderstandings that she was privileged to counsel, she never thought that such a conflict would occur in her home, let alone with her. But she decided not to judge George. She wanted to listen to the facts. She readied her mind to swiftly reason through challenging encounters.

George motioned for his wife to sit beside him as he narrated the whole saga. Edwin occasionally interrupted to explain how he reacted the first time he heard about it when Kiptarbei and Talai narrated the story over dinner. It was obvious that George loved Elizabeth's parents, and they, too, loved George very much. The story fascinated but troubled Ester. At the back of her mind she was bothered that she was the second choice for her husband. She wondered if he still had unresolved feelings for Talai. Ester convinced herself that now was not the moment to worry about it. She saw the new life as a celebration of a new beginning.

"Mom and Dad," Edwin called out to get the attention of his parents. "I'm so sorry for the mess I've caused. I've pursued forgiveness from Elizabeth's parents, and I want to make this situation right. I want to expedite the engagement and marry Elizabeth, soon," he said.

"How soon?" George asked.

"As soon as possible," Edwin said. "Can we make it in three weeks or so?"

"Nothing is impossible, with God," George said.

"Let's get to work, then," Ester said as she led her family back to the house.

CHAPTER 17

The Deadly Accident

LIAM AND MEGGIE WERE SETTLED downstairs in the breakfast room when Ryan arrived in the morning. He went directly to their table.

"Good morning, Meggie," Ryan said.

"Good morning, Ryan."

"May I join you?" Ryan directed the question to Liam.

"Yes, of course," he said. Ryan got a chair and sat opposite Meggie.

"Did you sleep well?" Ryan asked.

"The pillow was terrific. I feel fresh and ready for the day," Meggie said. "What about you?"

"The room was clean, but the Wi-Fi was down. Thank God for that, because I needed sleep," Ryan said and laughed.

"Have you been to the Grand Canyon before?" Meggie asked.

"Yes, this is the third time I've come here," Ryan responded, interrupted by the arrival of Isabel.

"How's breakfast?" Isabel asked.

"Great." Meggie thought that the buffet was consistent with other breakfast buffets at restaurants in Kenya. The only real difference was in the thick pancakes. She was used to flapjack-type pancakes, thin and round. "Check out this hot breakfast on my plate. Tastes awesome too," Meggie replied.

"Liam, you're already done with breakfast? When did you wake up?" Isabel asked. Liam noticed that Isabel was annoyed from the way she asked the question.

"As the saying goes, the early bird gets the worm—only in this case, I got hot bacon from the oven," he teased. Isabel was not impressed. She noticed how often he was together with Meggie.

Liam and Isabel were childhood friends, and it never occurred to Isabel that anyone could take away Liam's attention while she was around. On this trip, from the shuttle ride to the dinner and now breakfast, Liam and Meggie were together all the time.

Lai was late for breakfast. He emerged from his room just as his colleagues were on their way out, heading to the first event of the day.

"How come you're so late?" Meggie asked.

"Sleeping. I thought we agreed on the time. 8:30 a.m., right?"

"Yes, I was just teasing you. No worries," Meggie said, "but you will not have enough time to take breakfast."

"No problem. I don't care much about breakfast anyway," Lai said.

"You missed out. The breakfast was really good," Liam said.

"Oh yeah," Lai started to say more, but Isabel hurried over to Liam, grabbed his hand, and pulled him out to the hotel lobby.

"Come on; we're going to be late for the Arizona gunfight," Isabel said.

"I've seen it so many times. Today will be my sixth," Liam said, feeling exhausted from sleep deprivation. He had stayed up late reading Meggie's story and woke up early to hear more of it.

At the gunfight, Isabel and Liam sat together, two rows below Lai, Ryan, and Meggie.

The Cataract Creek Gang performed in the outdoor theater—a drama of a Western town gunfight in the street. The costumes were detailed replicas of authentic Old West era clothing. The story was about a robbery investigation involving four cowboys. An argument and squabbling occurred that included a lot of comedy. Then, the gunfight broke out.

"They're hot! Look at him with that exposed six-pack and horse harness on his shoulder," Meggie said, chuckling as she eyed the handsome, muscular actors.

"Wait until you see me ride that horse; you'll pass out!" Lai commented, jokingly. He had become a close friend to Meggie. There was no romantic relationship between them, but Lai like to flirt, which Meggie found amusing.

"Do you ride horses?" Meggie said, turning to face Lai.

"Anything for love, baby," Lai replied, laughing. They walked toward the early morning vintage- railway express tour.

They caught the 9:30 train from Williams and arrived at the Southern Rim of Grand Canyon National Park at mid-day. Liam reserved the observation dome of the vintage train, a glass-enclosed, refurbished passenger car located at the front of the upper level of the train. The panoramic view of the surrounding scenery was breathtaking.

Everything inside the car was luxurious. At the front was a bar and comfortably plush seats. Their reserved seats were under the dome with a luxury design that provided access to the open-air rear platform. The breeze and the opportunities to look out for elk, mountain lions, and other wildlife and fauna in the park were magnificent. The snack bar with coffee, gourmet pastries, and juice was in the center of the car.

Liam ushered Isabel, Lai, Ryan, and Meggie to their seats. Lai happily went to serve himself breakfast, which he missed because he woke up late.

Isabel reserved a sofa that seated two for herself and Liam. Two sofas faced each other around a gleamingly polished coffee table. Another two armchairs were around the circle to close the gaps. Meggie sat on one of the armchairs while Lai and Ryan sat on the sofa opposite Isabel and Liam. Isabel's intensions were obvious and Liam felt awkward.

"I'm starving," Liam said as he placed his snack on the coffee table and sat beside Isabel.

"Didn't you just have breakfast?" Isabel asked Liam. Liam looked at Meggie. She looked back at him and stood.

"I'll get some coffee," Meggie said as she left for the snack bar.

"What have you been up to? You don't look like you slept well," Lai inquired. He was very adept in reading situations. Liam was uncomfortable and wanted to loosen the tension. Ryan was watching as things unfolded.

"Had some work I had to finish. I'll be fine after the caffeine kicks in," Liam responded, taking a sip of the strong coffee he just poured for himself.

"Would anyone like a drink?" Meggie asked the group as she placed her coffee on the table. "I don't mind getting some."

"I'm good. Thanks for asking," Lai said.

"Me too, thanks, Meggie," Ryan said. "Come and sit by me," he said.

"That's unfair," Lai responded. "You want me to move?" he asked, teasing. "No worries, guys. I'm not moving anywhere. We should be enjoying the train ride." With Lai's invitation to enjoy the train ride, everyone ostensibly focused on the scenery—the high desert, pines, and the glimpses of wildlife. However, the currents of sexual tension remained in play.

"Look right there," Lai pointed to something at the top of a tree. Everyone moved closer to Lai.

"I don't see anything," Ryan said.

"Look closely," Lai said.

"I see it!" Meggie said excitedly, pointing.

"A small cat," Lai said.

"Deadly cat," Isabel said.

"True. If you have an encounter, maintain eye contact. Stand still, speak firmly, and throw something. It will move away," Lai counseled.

Meggie chuckled. "Not the king of the African jungle. You see it up close, and you are dead."

"Do these animals roam freely about, as we hear that they do?" Lai asked, laughing. It reminded him of myths he had heard about wild animals in other parts of the world.

"How do we tell the truth from the myths?" Liam asked.

"Simple," Ryan replied. "Wait for the truth to come out," he joked. Everyone laughed.

Meggie posed a question to foster the group conversation. "We are all the same, true or false?"

"Is that a philosophical or literal question?" Isabel asked Meggie.

"That answered your question, right there," Lai responded, chuckling.

"How?" Isabel asked.

"We're all unique. If we were the same, we would all have responded in unison either true or false." Everyone laughed.

"Agreed," Liam said. "No matter what people think, we're unique."

"That's right. We have to embrace that special thing that makes us different first before we can stand out from the crowd," Meggie added to support Liam's insight. "So, what makes you unique?" Meggie turned to Lai.

"Good question. Mm…Look at me," he said facing Meggie. "I'm a typical Asian man with black hair and have consumed tons of ramen noodles over my lifetime," he said with more laughter from the group.

Ryan suggested, "Look around. Each of us comes in different shapes and sizes," there was more laughter when Isabel interrupted.

"False," she said as everyone turned to look at her.

"What do you mean?" Liam asked.

"Do you realize that I'm the only one who has answered the question correctly?" Isabel said. "The question requires only one word, true or false. Meggie didn't ask for you to give any reasons." They laughed at Isabel's joked.

"I know you're joking, but Lai's issues about myths brings up a major point. Many people define Africa by myths. It's sad because perception becomes a reality for others," Meggie said.

"Myths are everywhere. People think that everyone in America is rich," Isabel countered.

"Everyone has the power to believe whatever they want without any constraints. However, we also can control how we reason." Meggie summarized her argument. "Lai, if you were to believe that wild animals freely roam as you heard without checking out the truth, you would look ignorant," Meggie said.

"True, it's difficult to know the truth nowadays with the constant flood of information constantly bombarding us," Isabel commented.

Everyone was enjoying the stimulating conversations as the train passed through the magnificence of the Grand Canyon. the train's crew of musicians and park rangers interrupted their conversations when they entered their car to share historical knowledge and experiences of the wild west. Two hours later, they arrived at the South Rim of Grand Canyon National Park and headed toward the Grand Canyon Visitor's Center.

"I need to use the restroom first," Isabel said, looking at Liam. All through the train trip, Isabel was acting jealous, and the group started to notice. Liam looked stressed considering the presence of Meggie. He had come to like Meggie. Liam and Isabel were not romantically involved in Liam's perspective. Their parents were neighbors and close family friends since their children were born, and their relationship was that of a brother and sister since then—at least that was Liam's feeling.

At their first stop near the Mather Point, Meggie noticed Isabel's familiarity with Liam and kept her distance. She purposely interacted more with Lai and Ryan. Mather Point already had a sizable crowd, as it was the Grand Canyon's most popular site for pictures.

"Watching the sunrise or the sunset must be spectacular from here," Ryan said.

"There are stunning views from the South and North Rims, too," Isabel responded.

"Which has the best views?" Lai asked

"It depends on the eyes of the beholder, I think," Isabel said. "Liam, which one do you think has the best views?"

"I enjoyed the desert view most because of its high elevation. I climbed to the top a few years ago. Those 360-degree panoramic views were to die for. I saw the sights on one of those clear days with perfect visibility. We saw miles of Grand Canyon wonders," Liam mused.

After they got off the train, they walked the South Rim trail starting from the short distance to the west, then east to Yavapai point. At some point, the group split up; Lai, Liam, and Isabel walked in front while Ryan and Meggie were behind them. Since it was their first visit to the Grand Canyon it took Ryan and Meggie some time to take in the scenery, and snap pictures along the way.

"I'm tired. Can we take a break?" Meggie asked Ryan.

"Of course, I could use one, too," Ryan said.

The two chatted as time passed. Meggie wore a beautiful navy blue and white summer dress—just the right length to protect her thighs from the burning sun. Ryan felt drawn to Meggie. He appreciated her athletic form and noticed her exposed long sexy legs

"My friends in Kenya tell me you're a great person," Ryan said. "They implied you were different than the people we're used to here?"

"How so? Meggie asked. "An easygoing, non-complicated type of woman?"

Ryan chuckled. "Not really, just different," he said.

"I also heard good things about you. Our friends think highly of you," she said. They sat down on a bench and chatted for a while, stopping every few moments to admire the impressive views.

Ryan wanted to know more about her. He made a great effort to stay close to her. Meanwhile, Meggie appreciated Ryan's mannerisms. Their conversation was mutually enjoyable; nothing felt forced but only connected and relaxed.

Meggie learned that Ryan had a girlfriend. Their relationship was a rollercoaster of emotions, with many intense highs and lows, and had been like that for a very long time.

Liam was surprised to find Meggie and Ryan seated together after the one-hour walk.

"Have you guys been here all along?" he asked.

Meggie stood and exclaimed, "Sorry about that. I didn't notice the time go."

After a late lunch, they returned to the Grand Canyon and two hours later were in Williams, where each one of them returned to their hotel rooms for some rest. Around 8:00 p.m., Meggie realized that she had Ryan's camera with her, and went to his room to return it. Liam noticed.

Meggie knocked on his door, and Ryan let her in and left the door slightly open.

"I was just returning your camera, you forgot it," Meggie said.

"Thanks, Meggie. I don't need it tonight. Thanks anyway," Ryan said. "Hey, I have an idea," Ryan said, rushing on, "What if I take a picture with you, and I send it to my girlfriend?" he said mischievously. "Maybe she'll be so jealous she'll break up with me."

Meggie was caught off-guard. "Why would you want to do such a thing?"

"Maybe I've come to like you, and I want to get rid of her," he said, joking.

"That would be the dumbest idea I've ever heard." Meggie said, knowing that Ryan was teasing.

Liam was going to his room when he overheard the conversation between Meggie and Ryan in Ryan's room. He became curious. Don't act like a jealous boy, he thought to himself as he stepped away. The conversation became more audible. It drew Liam's attention, and he slowed down.

"I'm serious. I'll do whatever it takes to make this happen. Even if it means losing her," Ryan said, moving closer to her. "Baby, I mean every word I say," he smiled. Hearing this made Liam feel fierce pangs of jealousy.

"You're not serious. This isn't fair to her, and you know it," Meggie said,. Liam could see a bit, but not clearly from the opening in the door.

"I get to determine that," Ryan said. "My girlfriend isn't here, and she'll never know about it," he said,.

Ryan took the camera and pulled Meggie toward him.

"No, Ryan. Please don't do this," Meggie said, struggling away from Ryan as Liam opened the door.

Liam was jealous, but knew that he had no control over anyone. Curiosity was killing him. He wondered what was going on in Ryan's room. He decided to go in. Meggie's last sentence got his blood boiling.

"Respect what the lady has told you, Ryan," Liam said.

Ryan was angry. "Do you think I'm a rapist or something?" Ryan asked, insulted and upset.

"I don't know what to think. But I know that 'no' means 'no,'" Liam said.

Ryan was enraged. "What do you think I want to do to her? Huh?"

Meggie was shocked by what was happening.

"Hey! Hey!" Meggie yelled, wanting to explain what just happened, but the men were not listening. Their voices were rising, and Lai, hearing the noises, entered Ryan's room.

No one was listening to anyone else, and frustrations soon led to a fight. Liam and Ryan were fighting for nothing. Meggie was shocked by Liam's behavior. Why would he believe such a thing was happening?

Liam punched Ryan's nose. Ryan tried to step back, but Liam was too fast, and Ryan was too late to defend himself.

The punch landed on the bridge of Ryan's nose. Furious, Ryan punched back. Meggie was dumbfounded and tried to defuse the situation.

"What the hell is going on?" Lai asked as he tried to stand between Ryan and Liam.

"Ask him," Ryan said as he pointed at Liam, lunging over Lai to try to get in another punch.

"I can't believe the two of you. What's wrong with you? I have to get out of here," Meggie said with disgust as she stormed out of Ryan's room.

"Liam, what happened?" Lai asked Liam. He couldn't imagine what would make Ryan and Liam go after each other this way.

"I came in, and Meggie was begging Ryan to stop," Liam said.

"Stop doing what?" Lai asked.

"Stop trying to take a picture with her that I wanted to send to my girlfriend," Ryan spat out angrily.

"Wait, what? A picture? That's it?" Liam couldn't believe what Ryan was saying. "I'm so sorry, man. I thought she was saying 'no' to something else," Liam said, his body relaxing out of the tension of the fighting mode as he shook his head and sat down on the edge of the bed.

"Do you seriously think I'd do such a thing?" Ryan asked, looking at Liam with disappointment and frustration in his eyes.

"I'm so sorry, Ryan. I heard her say 'no,' and my brain thought the worst. I definitely jumped to conclusions" Liam said. The men were quiet for a minute, as the ridiculousness of the situation and their embarrassment settled over them.

"Did someone call the police? I could've been killed. You put my life in danger, Liam," Ryan said.

"I'm sorry. Please forgive me. I don't know what came over me," Liam said. "I am bitterly disappointed in myself for the way I reacted."

"Let's discuss this over beer," Lai suggested, trying to make sure the mess was smoothed over. "Clean up and meet me downstairs. No women!" Lai said, forcing a laugh to lighten the mood.

Meanwhile, Meggie was furious, with the men and with herself. She had exposed herself to drama. Before coming to America, Meggie was a drama-free person. The tension in her friends was due to romantic relationships that she avoided. Relationships, for her, had a direct correlation to unnecessary drama. To be successful in love, you had to love fiercely to sustain a relationship and be exposed enough to show your true self and emotions. The fight was proof of her notion about drama.

It was 9:00 in the evening in Williams, Arizona and 6:00 in the morning in Kenya. I have to call Linda; she's not awake yet, but I don't care, Meggie thought and dialed Linda's number.

"Hello," Linda responded, sleepily.

"I'm in trouble," Meggie said.

"Meggie?" Linda called out to confirm that she was the one on the phone.

"Yes, Linda, I'm in trouble," she said again.

"What did you do?" Linda asked.

"It's not what I did. People are fighting over me. I'm very embarrassed," Meggie confided.

"What? That doesn't make sense," Linda said.

"Remember the name, Ryan?" Meggie asked.

"Willy's friend from America?" Linda asked.

"Right. Ryan and another colleague were involved in a fight," Meggie explained.

"What about? How do you come in the picture?" Linda asked.

"I've been spending a lot of time with Liam, the guy who picked me from the airport when I arrived here. He organized a trip to the Grand Canyon with several of our friends. I was in Ryan's room chatting when Liam overheard our conversation. He assumed that Ryan wanted to force me into something. Instead, he forced himself into the situation and beat the crap out of Ryan," Meggie summed up the issue.

"Oh, my God," Linda exclaimed. "Are the police involved?" she asked.

"No. Thank God," Meggie responded and sighed.

"Do you have a relationship with Liam?" Linda asked, wondering.

"No, I don't. He's just a friend and so is Ryan," Meggie said.

"Obviously, Liam is jealous," Linda hinted.

"We spend time together in discussion. I've explained Tugen culture and family. That's it," Meggie said as if she were asked to defend herself.

"I totally understand. Do you like him?" Linda asked.

"There is nothing to hate about him, if that's what you mean," Meggie said.

"So, you love him," Linda quizzed her further.

"We're not romantically involved. He's just a friend," Meggie confirmed.

"Then, you have nothing to worry about. Just tell them to sort their issues out because they are friends to you," Linda recommended. She was not convinced about the friendship story with Liam. That was for another day, Linda thought—not six in the morning.

"Just like that?" Meggie questioned.

"Yep. Just like that. Unless you want to tell Liam that you love him and apologize to Ryan for what Liam did out of jealousy," Linda said, teasingly.

Meggie laughed for the first time in a while. "You're crazy. I won't do that because that's not true."

"I think you love the guy. But then again, what do I know," Linda said.

"Thank you so much for listening to my troubles. Go back to sleep now," Meggie said.

"You too. Sleep tight. It will do you good," Linda said and hung up.

The final day at the Grand Canyon was quiet. Meggie pointedly avoided Liam and Ryan, mostly spending time with Lai. Isabel remained unaware of the incident, but she was still hanging closely to Liam.

The four of them sat in the same spots as they originally had on the shuttle on their trip back to Phoenix. Liam was desperate to make amends.

"I spoiled the whole trip, didn't I," Liam said in a dejected voice as they settled at the back of the shuttle to Phoenix.

"Yes, you did," Meggie said bluntly. "Why?"

"I felt overcome with jealousy, I guess," Liam said, frankly.

Stunned, Meggie looked at him with wide eyes but with a stern look on her face. "Jealous about what? I'm not in a relationship with you," Meggie said perplexed.

"I know. Not yet, anyway," Liam said. "I'm sorry I was such a dickhead. I was extremely frustrated because I didn't get to spend much time with you, and then when I heard you saying 'no,' I snapped. Can we start over?" he asked, a pleading note in his voice.

"Grandpa George always insisted that at times like this we should recite the verse from Matthew 18:21-22 from the Bible," Meggie said. "This happened every time someone was hurt, disappointed, or betrayed by those in the family."

"What does it say?" Liam asked.

"According to the King James version of the Bible, 'Then Peter came to Him and said, 'Lord, how often shall my brother sin against me, and I forgive him? Up to seven times?' Jesus said to him, 'I do not say to you, up to seven times, but up to seventy times seven.'"'

Liam took out his cell phone and used it to calculate the total. "539," he said.

"538 left," Meggie said, jokingly.

"Your family has more grace than any I've come across," he commented. Liam thought that Meggie's family was a close-knit one. "You have an incredible bond with your ancestry, and it's not only with your immediate family. You know and respect your cultural roots. I see in you a great connection to the past and assume you'll pass it all to the future generation."

"What about you, Liam?" Meggie asked.

"The more I talk to you, the more determined I am to learn more about my own heritage. I feel like a tree without roots," he said.

Liam paused, "The journal with your family's story was fascinating."

Meggie smiled softly. "I'm glad you found it so interesting. Now, I want to know more about you, Liam? Where were you born?" she asked, redirecting the conversation to focus on Liam. The tension caused by the fight dissipated as they talked.

He thought for a moment and laughed. "I was born just after sunrise October 23, in Chandler General Hospital, in Chandler, Arizona, on what my parents told me was a beautiful morning, My father was in the delivery room, 'helping my mother get me out,' as my father likes to say."

"Your father was in the delivery room?" Meggie asked in a surprised tone.

"Oh yes! He even cut the cord."

"Fascinating. Culturally, Tugen men wait for the good news of birth from afar. I'm not sure if the rationale is something to do with avoiding trauma associated with childbirth or if it's just an excuse for less participation in the whole process. I've never asked that because anything to do with reproduction is taboo in my culture. I would love my husband to be with me during that special moment, if and when it ever happens," she said.

"You bet I'll be there," he said and laughed out loud. "Just kidding," Liam said, watching Meggie frown.

"Keep dreaming," she said.

"I was born in a mission hospital. My parents named me Jepchumba after the coming of the Europeans," Meggie said. "Our middle names are determined according to a variety of factors, including the time of birth, events, past ancestors, place of birth, situation of the birth, to name a few. The last name is always the family name, just like here. Our first names are English." she said and asked, "What's the story of your family?"

"My father started his career in a law firm before he opened his own legal practice. My mother, as I told you, is a self-employed architect. What about your parents?"

"Based on reading my family's story, you already know a lot about my parents, Edwin and Elizabeth, by now. I'm the child conceived before their final year of high school.

"So, how did they manage college with you?" he asked.

"My parents performed very well in school. Each secured a scholarship package that covered most of the required expenses. They hired a nanny to take care of me while they attended college. Their programs led to solid well-paying jobs. They did very well after they graduated and transitioned to their present professions."

"So, your mother was brought up in the Tugen culture, and your dad was raised as a Christian. How did that dynamic influence your childhood?"

"There was never a dull moment in our house. Their world views were total opposites. They agreed on a few things but were like oil and water most of the time. I remember a conversation they had about how they were going to approach my wedding when I grew up. Grandpa Kiptarbei envisioned a cultural scenario where scotch would be poured into the soil to appease our ancestors. He strongly believed that a long-lasting marriage has everything to do with respecting sacred cultural norms. My father believes that Grandpa George would vehemently oppose such a thing because in his perspective, you can't worship other idols besides God."

"So, what'll happen?" he asked.

"Over the years, they've realized that it's okay to be different, that there can be disagreement on issues and still have a great relationship, that there is no right or wrong—sometimes just different opinions. In regards to my wedding, if I actually get married to begin with, I'll make both of their wishes come true. The most important thing is to create happy memories of the day," she said.

"I couldn't agree more. I have a similar experience but a different situation with my parents. My mom is a political liberal, and my father is a staunch conservative. Their views are the opposite. Our dinners usually began with a five-minute daily catch-up. After that came political topics that sparked opposing arguments between the two of them. Each put forth their clashing viewpoints. They love each other very much because of, and despite, their differences," he said.

"It's ironic. In some families like yours and mine, people thrive on heated, controversial debates," Meggie said.

"I guess it keeps our family's mealtime discussions interesting," Liam said

"Agreed. But I think it's better to discuss what you're eating at the time rather than politics or religion. Don't you think?" Meggie asked.

"Not in our current situation unfortunately. Maybe in the next generation," Liam said and looked at Meggie. "You and me," Meggie blushed.

"Say what?" Meggie asked

"Liam laughed. "Yours and mine," he rephrased. Meggie thought it was not funny and Liam was making a subtle move.

CHAPTER 18

Tugen Culture

MEGGIE TOOK LIAM SHOPPING TO prepare a typical Kenyan meal for him. They both enjoyed the variety of dishes.

"You're a hell of a cook," he complimented, and added more champagne to both their glasses. "Shit, I forgot to wash my hands. The bottle is all sticky now," he said as he placed it on the table.

Without thinking, Meggie extended her right hand and grabbed Liam's hand to inspect the mess.

"This is where I feel most like my real self, too," she said gazing at his messy hands. "It's letting loose and feeling happy. I'm happy, Liam. Thank you," she said and raised her face to look at him. Her hand remained in the same position.

"You're welcome, Meggie," he said, his eyes fixed on hers.

"It's funny, because joy and happiness unleash something in me. I think and do things that I would never do otherwise," she said and noticed that Liam was laughing. "What's funny?" she asked.

"Isn't that kinda how it works with liquid courage?" he asked.

"Not at all! It's the kind of effect that unleashes a real solution to Pythagorean theorem puzzle," she said.

"You sound kinda crazy right now, Meggie. I mean whatever you said doesn't make any sense," he said.

"Love. Love will unleash itself without notice. It is tender and…" Meggie's laughter interrupted Liam's train of thought.

"What do you know about love?" she asked. "I'll tell you something. A guy told me once that he couldn't sleep thinking about me, so I gave him two allergy pills with antihistamine chlorphenamine. He said I was the goddess of love. I've never fallen in love. How does one even know?" she asked, eager to hear his reply.

"Love is free. When you work too hard to love or be loved, it isn't it. When you make mistakes or fail at something, and it's still there, unjudging and unconditional, then you know you've found it. I hope you see it when the time comes," he said as he looked away from her. Meggie noticed how he suddenly lost focus on the conversation and was drifting away. He tried to focus, but he couldn't. Meggie's smooth skin and curves aroused him, but her gleaming, sexy eyes sent Liam over the edge. He sensed that he might do something that would get him in trouble.

"Do you mind if we continue this conversation outside on the patio?" he requested.

"No, actually, I could use some fresh air," Meggie said. She too was having her own issues. She was perspiring though the room's temperature was set to seventy degrees. She added more champagne to Liam's glass and then hers. Both were still quite sober, and they were aware of it. Most of their time had been spent having great conversation. Liam was drawn to Meggie's ability to hold her own in conversation that was engaging and romantic. Meggie led the way to the patio.

"Have you ever fallen in love?" she asked as they settled in seats next to each other. This time, their shoulders touched. Unconsciously, Meggie moved her seat closer to his. Their shoulders brushed each other. He looked at her as she put her drink on the table. She looked incredible.

"It's magical out here, isn't it?" He tried to get the discussion away from sexual areas. It was getting dangerous. His attraction to Meggie was driving him crazy.

"So, have you ever fallen in love?" Meggie couldn't let it go.

"I've watched my parents. Seeing them over the years, I've concluded that love is deep," he replied Although he was physically attracted to Meggie at that time, Liam understood the broader aspect of a long-lasting relationship.

"Not just a surface feeling," she added.

"Yeah. The chemistry is important, don't get me wrong. But, without patience and kindness the couple is in for a rocky relationship. Of course, you need to add forgiveness, trust, and understanding. After that there's the ultimate responsibility of fostering happiness for yourself and your partner, or there will be no sustained love," he said. Meggie was also drawn by Liam's perspective toward relationships.

"Liam, I think you've gotten it. My grandparents are feisty and often butt heads, but their chemistry is evident. My parents display all that is love, based on your description. The reason I have no boyfriend is because of them. I keep looking for a man like my father. He loves my mom and me very much." She was teary. "And now, the idea of it scares the crap out of me because I don't think I'll ever find it, or if I'll know it when I find it."

"I'm scared of relationships, too. There's no litmus test to know if you're in love. We're both single because we're both scared," Liam summed up their predicament.

"Maybe you can find me a romance, Liam," Meggie said. In her mind at that moment, Liam seemed to perfectly fit everything she imagined in a suitable man.

Liam laughed. "Or you find me the perfect one."

Liam leaned over to Meggie. He no longer could resist the pull of attraction to her. "Baby," he called her, his voice low and husky voice as he sat closer. "Have you ever tasted Chinese food?" he asked as he touched her face with both of his messy, sticky hands and wiped the tears from her cheeks. She laughed through her tears. He looked at her with tenderness in his eyes. "It's sweet, sour, bitter, hot, and salty; an excellent balance of everything," he said.

"That's what I'm talking about. The sour, bitter, and hot," Meggie said. "The scary part I'm afraid of disappointment, betrayal, and breakups." She knew that was an understatement considering the giant waves of emotion rapidly rising beyond her control.

"Don't you worry about the hot. I hear it's like a pleasurable pressure cooker explosion that leads to a relaxed, brainless state of peace," he said, laughing. Nothing made sense anymore. He was feeling things he had never felt with anyone. His body and emotions did not want to cooperate with his intentions of not crossing any lines. Screw it, he thought as he decided to push the envelope. He could deal with consequences later.

In haste, Liam took her hand and motioned her out of her seat. He looked at her desperately. She did not fight but followed his lead as he walked her gently inside to her bedroom. It was like being possessed by a supernatural power that could not be explained or controlled. Neither of them could help themselves. Just next to her bed, Meggie put her arms around Liam. He didn't resist. Liam understood what Meggie was asking without saying a word. He leaned his face close and tilted his lips toward hers. She expressed the same desire as Liam. He held her tight.

"I love you," Liam said. He was past the threshold of fear. Liam was acting on what he felt, a genuine love for Meggie. He had never experienced anything like it. He wanted her so much that if he didn't say it, he was going to regret not doing so for the rest of his life.

"I love you too," Meggie said in a soft whisper. He gazed at her and held her so tightly, as though he were afraid she was going to get away if she got loose. He kissed her again, this time with passion, and she kissed him back. Liam then lifted Meggie off the ground and laid her on the bed. Meggie stared at Liam, her eyes begging him to continue. Liam took off his shirt to feed her wanting eyes on what he had to offer. He knew what she wanted and slowly offered it to her. He approached her on the bed and kissed her while gently pulling off her dress down her shoulders, exposing her breasts. "I've never done this before; I'm afraid," she said.

"Me neither. Everything will be alright," he said. He was scared too. His relationships always ended because he was too busy. He was conscious of making mistakes that many of his friend had made, which led to their settling for unplanned relationships.

Then, the loud ringing from Liam's cell phone broke the spell.

He wanted to ignore it, but Meggie was already up and off the bed. She stood on the opposite side of the bed, and adjusted her dress to coverup her exposed flesh. Liam took the phone from his pocket.

"I don't recognize the number," Liam contemplated if he should take it.

"Please," she persuaded him. "It could be important."

"Hello, this is Liam," he replied as he walked to Meggie's balcony and closed the door behind him.

CHAPTER 19

The Accident

A MOMENT LATER, A VISIBLY DISTRESSED Liam returned from the balcony. "My uncle is waiting for me upstairs. He says it's urgent. I hate to spoil the moment, but I've got to go," he said.

"Is there a problem?" she asked.

"Don't know yet," he looked at Meggie, and for an instant and debated calling his uncle back to say he couldn't meet him. But he reluctantly forced himself to leave her. "Meggie, I'm afraid I have to go. My uncle wouldn't be here if it weren't important," he said as he walked to the door.

"Wait, don't forget your gift!" she said, rushing over to him.

"I'm sure this won't take long. I'm not finished with you, yet," Liam said as he grinned suggestively.

"Take your gift, since you're headed to your apartment," she insisted.

"Yes, ma'am. I'll be back." He grabbed the gift and hurried out the door, casting one last lingering look at Meggie.

A few minutes after Liam's departure, Meggie was still surprised by how fast things had moved. More shocking was her lack of self-discipline. Had she really fallen in love with Liam? She didn't know him that well, and they came from very different backgrounds. Being in love with Liam was not remotely possible, she rationalized. I am wasting my time, Meggie thought as she switched on the TV to catch up with news on CNN.

The CNN news anchor interrupted his presentation with breaking news. According to correspondents from the field, Senator Grant Barsy Finley of Arizona died when his campaign plane crashed as it approached the San Carlos Apache Airport in Globe, Arizona. Mr. Finley, a sixty-two-year-old conservative Republican, served Arizona for six years in the U.S. Senate. He was seeking his second term and was in a fierce fight with Kathlyn Dobson, a Democrat, in the upcoming mid-term elections. Also killed were the senator's wife, father, the closest members of his five-member staff, and the charter's two pilots. Thirteen people perished when the plane went down at 9:00 p.m. Central time.

Meggie let out a small yelp. Her stomach felt heavy. Her mouth was wide open with shock. "Oh my God!" she exclaimed. Liam's father was a senator? And, he was dead? She was stunned. She realized how little she knew about Liam. Did he know? The phone call...her mind was racing, trying to fit the pieces together. The phone call must have concerned Senator Finley's accident, she thought. She sprinted upstairs to talk to Liam, but he was gone.

The news continued to pour in. The senator was under enormous pressure due to the countrywide women's equality movements. His campaign suffered from the negative effects of countless protests, marches, and organizations for different liberal causes. What was different from the past was the diversity, from grandmothers through the youngest generation, as partners in the goal of fighting for equal rights.

More importantly, many men realized that women had equal value and deserved equal treatment. Grandfathers, fathers, husbands, and brothers joined their female counterparts in the streets. The message was the same. Respect women and treat them equally. Kathlyn was crushing Senator Finley in the polls, and he was under pressure to turn things around. His campaign schedule was hectic. Some speculated that his pilot's fatigue might have contributed to the tragic accident.

The phone rang, and Meggie picked it right away. "I am so sorry, Liam, where are you? I tried to catch up with you earlier on, but you already left," she fumbled her words as she cried out loud, confused.

"Meggie, it's Ryan. So, you heard already? Have you seen Liam?" he asked.

"I was with him when his uncle called him with an urgent message. I didn't know that his father was a senator," she said.

"I can understand. Liam never talks about it, and his father doesn't use his middle name often," he said.

"I was going to text him," she said.

"Why don't I come over?" Ryan said and hung up before Meggie could respond.

Meanwhile, new information emerged about the two passengers in the plane who had escaped with their lives. One was gravely injured and was whisked by Angel MedFlight Airjet to Phoenix for advanced medical care. The other escaped with minor bruises to her leg. In an interview with a news correspondent, she recounted how the pilot announced to the passengers that he was going for a crash landing, and everyone needed to prepare. She thought he meant an especially rocky landing. It never dawned on her that it would be an actual crash.

"Panic was everywhere around me. People leaned forward and covered their heads with their hands. All safety instructions went out the window," she explained, in a daze. She recalled the smell of screeching tires and the boom of a loud crash. As soon as she opened her eyes and realized she was alive, she released her belt and moved toward the exit. She was still disoriented, and a paramedic advised the interviewer release her for a medical checkup.

The doorbell rang and interrupted Meggie's focus on the news report.

"Come in," she said absent-mindedly and invited Ryan into the living room.

"I'm so sorry for Liam. He's lost his family," he said.

"Yes, it's so sad," she broke down in his arms. "He must be devastated," she said through tears.

"I've tried to call him. I have no idea where he is right now," Ryan said.

"Do you know where the San Carlos Apache Airport is? He could be there," she suggested.

"I doubt it. Even if Liam's family is still trapped over there, there must be heavy security. We wouldn't be allowed to get close because of his father's prominence," Ryan responded as he held Meggie tightly against his chest, stroking her back with his right hand. "Globe is about ninety miles from here, too far to go by car. Let's wait a few minutes to see what happens. Then, we can decide what to do next."

Upstairs Liam met his uncle, Jackson, who asked Liam to accompany him to his car. in He ushered Liam inside his spacious white Chevy Silverado truck. He wanted to break the news before he started the car.

Jackson looked at him and said, "Liam, your dad, mom, and grandpa are in Globe." Liam interrupted as he smiled,

"Dad told me about it in a phone call this morning. I think he's going crazy with this tight campaign schedule."

His uncle took a deep, shaky breath and tried to swallow the lump in his throat before struggling to get out the worst of it. "His charter plane malfunctioned as they approached the San Carlos Apache Airport. It was a very hard crash landing. Your dad, mom, and grandpa didn't make it out of the plane alive. They're gone, Liam. Right now, it makes no sense. This tragedy is heartbreaking to all of us."

Liam looked at Jackson with disbelief. He heard what his uncle said, but it felt as if he had said it to someone else, and about someone else's family. Maybe it was a joke. He waited for a punch line, but he knew his uncle would not joke about something like that.

Jackson waited for any reaction in silence for a few minutes before continuing.

"The paramedic on the scene informed me that the three of them died instantly, along with the pilots and several members of your father's staff. Liam, the memories we have of them will always stay with us. And, I promise I'll always be here for you—no matter what. You're not alone." His uncle started sobbing, and Liam leaned toward him, fell into his uncles' arms, and let out an agonizing wail.

"Oh God," Jackson exclaimed, and moved closer to the passenger seat to tighten his embrace. "I'm so, so sorry," he told Liam, both of them in tears.

After a short while, Liam sat up straight in his seat. His face was red and blotchy and his eyes bloodshot. His voice cracked as he tried to speak. "So, what do we do now?" he asked.

"I haven't figured that out yet. I saw it on the news and got a call from the paramedic immediately after that. Then, I got in my car and came to see you," he responded.

Liam's head felt compressed like a pressure cooker, and he wanted to scream but could not. Instead, he felt helpless and stunned. He wondered if the whole scenario were real or just a bad dream that would fade away. He kept looking at his phone, waiting for his father to call because he often called more than twice a day. He expected a call before he went to bed. Liam suddenly felt exhausted, and as though he no longer had control of his own life.

His uncle started the car suddenly, which brought Liam out of his deep thoughts. "We're going home," Jackson said.

Liam was quiet, but tears ran down his cheeks in steady streams.

A message alert pinged on his phone. *Where are you?* the text read. It was Meggie. He realized he never mentioned his father's position to her. He was too tired and shocked to reply. Even the simple task of writing back felt as daunting as climbing Mt. Kilimanjaro. He didn't have the strength left for it. He ignored Meggie's text. The current situation wiped out every blissful moment they shared earlier.

When they reached his family home, his uncle's truck stopped at the gate. "Open the gate, Liam." Liam was in deep thought, and his uncle had to call him a second time. Unlike many families who move from place to place over time, this was the only home Liam knew. His parents purchased their "forever home" just before his birth and had lived there since.

The steel electric-sliding gate opened to a beautiful, contemporary mansion. Liam's parents had lived on a piece of paradise in the South Mountains of Phoenix with a breathtaking view of the city, sunrises and sunsets, and the surrounding mountains. You could see across the entire valley from every corner of the home, yet Liam could not see it on this day. His north, south, east and west was his family, and they were gone. The panoramic view that often looked stunning was empty; he could not see as well without them.

Liam entered the house, with his uncle walking behind him coming into a grand foyer with a soaring decorated ceiling. As they continued through the house, the sophisticated furnishings looked much darker to him, even with the lights on. His mother's absence spread everywhere. The house felt empty. Liam imagined shadows of his mom and dad, not just them but everything connected to them that he had ever known, their laughter, their love—all gone. The emptiness was overwhelming.

He walked past Jackson. Opposite the kitchen were glass walls that allowed the long space to expand to the outside; 1,500 square feet of patio with a resort-like ambience. His father added the patio to the house when Liam was a teenager. Now, he poignantly remembered the days he and his father spent together, renovating. The more Liam remembered, the more his agony deepened. Now, Liam stared blankly at the waterfall.

"Not again," Liam rushed toward the living room coffee table. "Mom forgot her phone; she does this all the time. I always try to remind her," he said as if he expected her to walk in through the door. His uncle approached him from behind and tapped him gently on his shoulder.

"Liam, she isn't coming back. I wish it were a dream, but it's not. We'll get through this together." Jackson guided him to the seat, beside the table. Liam covered his face with his hands and wept.

"Death often happens unexpectedly and requires a lot of strength for survivors to live through it. It's important for us to celebrate the time we spent with them, and remember the memories they've left with us," Liam's uncle said as he also sobbed while stroking Liam's back.

The doorbell interrupted them. Liam opened it with the remote. His father's communications director was there. He expressed his condolences and then requested that the family issue a press release. With the help of his uncle, they drafted a simple statement. Half an hour later, the news released an alert from the senator's office. According to the newscaster, the senator's only son and the family's sole survivor—because he was not aboard the aircraft—appealed for privacy to allow him to mourn the loss of his family.

Meanwhile, when Meggie saw the press statement in the news, she wondered whether she was also supposed to honor Liam's request for privacy. Her messages to Liam went unanswered. She felt devastated by the tragedy because she could only wait.

Ryan looked around and noticed all the food left out in the dining room and the kitchen.

He walked toward the kitchen. "Let me help with this," Ryan offered.

"There's plenty of food. I'm sure it's still good. Please have some," Meggie said.

"I just ate. Thanks for the offer," Ryan replied. "It looks and smells great. I'll take a raincheck."

Meggie felt like a zombie as she packed the food and stored it in the refrigerator. Ryan did his best to clean up the kitchen. "I've got to go now," he said. "I just wanted to see if you were okay." Meggie thanked him. "I'll call you later," Ryan said, giving her a hug before leaving.

A message alert popped up on her phone as she wiped the last part of the counter. Unfortunately, it was not Liam as she had hoped. It was an inquiry from Sally who wanted to know the status of Meggie's part of their group project. Sally's part of the assignment depended on Meggie's information. Sally wanted to complete her tasks and be ready for the meetup with the members of the Falcons' team at the library the next morning.

"Oh, crap!" Meggie muttered out loud. The events of the day had distracted her so much that she forgot to complete her assignment. Since it was so late, she decided to go to sleep and wake up early to complete her assigned team task. An hour passed without any signs of sleep. Frustrated, she woke up and decided to tackle her class obligation instead of tossing and turning.

Liam's parents' accident reminded her that life was unpredictable. No one had control of it except God, as her Grandpa George always reminded them. "Be thankful and celebrate every breath because it is through grace that you are alive," he said.

The next day, Meggie decided to find out more about Liam. She ached to see him and provide support. She approached a student worker at the residence hall reception desk. "A friend of mine lost his parents in a plane crash, and I wanted his contact information. I need to see him," Meggie said.

"I'm sorry to hear that. Are you a family member?" the student worker asked.

"No, I'm just a friend, a good friend," Meggie responded.

"I'm sorry. I can't provide you with that information unless you're an authorized family member," the student worker responded.

"Why?" Meggie asked.

"The disclosure of any student's personally identifiable information is protected by university policies and the Family Educational Rights and Privacy Act (FERPA) laws. Names, addresses, birthdates, and other important personal data are confidential information and require a higher level of protection against unauthorized disclosures," the student worker clarified.

Ryan approached them. "Meggie, is everything okay?" he asked.

"Not at all. I wanted to see Liam, but I can't get his contact information. Only authorized family members can access his contact information," she said.

"I know where he lives. I've been there many times. When do you want to go?" he asked. "I can take you there whenever you want to go."

"What about right now? Are you available?" she inquired pleadingly.

"Yes, let's take my car," he offered. Ryan drove a sophisticated Lexus LC sports car. He always bragged that he was more athletic than the performance of his car.

Thirty minutes later, they arrived at Liam's home.

"The security here are incredible," Ryan said. "His dad was not only a U.S. senator but the party whip. Since he served directly under the minority leader, he had round-the-clock protection of the U.S. Capitol Police both in Washington, D.C. and back in Arizona." With the death of Liam's parents, security measures were tightened to ensure protection and privacy to the family at their home.

"Now what?" Ryan asked Meggie when they noticed the security barrier.

"I'm not sure. Let me check with security and see if we're allowed to visit," Meggie suggested.

Ryan drove slowly close to the security barrier and stopped the car about thirty-feet away. As an officer approached, he immediately turned off the ignition, rolled his window down, and placed his hands on the steering wheel in plain view of the officer. He was calm to avoid any probable cause for his car to be searched for suspicious behavior.

"Good morning, sir. How are you this morning?" Ryan greeted the officer.

"Great, thank you. May I see your identification?" the officer requested.

"Sure, it's in my wallet," Ryan responded.

"Get it out, please," the officer said. He reviewed Ryan's driver's license and handed it back to him.

"Are you family?" the officer inquired, a bit suspiciously.

"No, we're Liam's classmates from the university," Ryan responded.

"The family requested privacy at this time. They're not receiving visitors except close family; however, you can leave a note with us. We'll be happy to pass it on to the family," the officer said as he handed Ryan a paper and pen.

Ryan passed on the paper to Meggie. "We won't be able to see him now, but we can leave a message. I'm sure Liam will get back to us when he's ready."

Meggie turned to Ryan and asked, "Do you think it's appropriate to leave a message if he's requesting privacy? Maybe we should leave. We'll let him know that we came when the time is more appropriate. He needs this time to be with his loved ones. We aren't family," she said. "Anyway, we need to get back to the Falcons' project discussion as soon as possible." Ryan handed the paper and pen back to the officer and thanked him before driving back to campus.

A few minutes before ten o'clock that morning, Ryan and Meggie were at the library and met with the rest of the team. Sally took the lead. "Let's get to work." None of the other team members knew about Liam's loss since he had not disclosed his father's name or status to them.

"Ready to rock," Lai responded as the rest of the team directed their attention to Sally.

"In my view, the center of major global issues and challenges is poverty. As a complex-multidimensional phenomenon, each of us in our diverse professions can relate to it." Sally said.

"Let's outline the expectations of the project first. Each one of us then can select an item in the outline to discuss. This ensures accountability," Leon explained.

After devising an outline, the group turned to the substance of their presentation. "Poverty is characterized differently depending on who you ask. How should we define poverty for this assignment?" Meggie asked.

"According to the World Bank, their participatory-poverty assessment (PPA) used the views of the poor to define what poverty meant to them," Ryan said and offered a probable definition from this report.

Lai objected, "The definition does not include psychological aspects that impact the physical lack of goods."

"For example," Meggie explained, "I've witnessed kids who refused to go to school because their parents were too poor to buy them decent clothes to go to school in."

Ryan added, "I've seen the same. Fathers feel ashamed standing in front of their children when they cannot provide for them. Some run away because they don't know what else to do."

"Why can't they get some help from somewhere? There are many avenues here in the United States, I don't know about the rest of the world," Sally paused, awaiting a response.

"Sally, if that were the case, everyone would be okay here in America. In fact, a third of the U.S population is living under or near the poverty line," Ryan argued.

"The truth is," Lai broke the silence. "When you're poor, you have no say. It's like your existence is there to serve the rich. You feel inferior all the time."

"And due to lack of voice, power, and independence, poor people are subjected to rudeness, humiliation, and inhumane treatment," Ryan concluded.

Lai supported Ryan's input and said, "To add to Ryan's description, many have lost their social norms and cultural identity."

"What do you mean by that?" Leon asked.

"My grandfather tells me that it used to be easy to become engaged and get married. Now, even marriage is all commercialized. It's almost impossible to go through the ceremonies because of the expenses required. Poor people are humiliated if they cannot afford to dress or offer gifts to the level of societal standards," Meggie clarified.

"Are you saying that they then can't participate in their community's lifestyle? There's always community support, isn't that right?" Leon questioned.

"When people lack basic needs, reciprocation of gifts and participation in community events become an issue. They become alienated and stay away from participating in traditional ceremonies," Ryan explained.

"Right. If I were poor and Lai invited me to his wedding, let's say it's a traditional wedding where cultural customs are practiced. I would need to buy clothes, and they aren't made of cheap sheepskins as they used to be. I will feel humiliated and undignified if I can't afford new clothes or have substandard clothes and a cheaper wedding gift than everyone else's, I may toughen up the first time, but eventually I'd stop going altogether or not participate with any important social networks," Meggie explained to Leon.

"In many ways, the absence of basic infrastructure is also a major problem," Sally added. "In rural areas that get flooded, for example, the villages are cut off from medical help during monsoon seasons."

"True to your point, Sally, I have seen firsthand, how lack of infrastructure is a major issue, particularly in remote rural areas where roads, means of transportation, water, schools, and health facilities are completely nonexistent," Lai said.

"Great point, Lai. Now let's focus on project expectations to help us stay on course," Sally redirected the conversation.

Ryan volunteered to read the social policy assignment, the Global Policy Brief and Group Presentation Competition. "Prepare a four-page policy for one of the board members and policy decision-makers of the World Bank Executive Forum. The team is working on a mission to eradicate chronic problems on the planet. The statement should be non-technical. More importantly, it should be relevant to the board member and the media. Chose a region most affected by the issue and identify the most affected group, the key risk factors, the social and economic development issues, and then provide a cost-effective way of dealing with the issues. Provide recommendations for priority steps to be taken and the rationale for the choice of these recommendations. The policy brief should be concise, well-argued, data-driven, and evidence-based. Begin with a summary paragraph that abstracts the policy brief, and lays out the most pertinent information required for action." Ryan let out a sigh of relief. "That was quite a mouthful."

"I like Sally's suggestion of poverty as the chronic problem. What if we approach it using Meggie's vision of providing security and focus on the family? You educate the family so that they can make informed decisions. Then, you need to look at how to provide access to health care so they stay strong. After that, we examine how to open up opportunities so that they can thrive and prosper. The objective is to empower them to participate in shaping their own destiny and for generations to come. These are some of the critical elements in the complex multidimensional nature of poverty that we should address" Lai suggested.

"How would that work?" Leon asked.

"Eradicate poverty by ensuring full security through health care, education, literacy, peace, prosperity, and governmental authority," Lai clarified. "Encapsulating this into a cost-effective policy will be challenging."

"How will we convince anyone about the cost of this plan?" Leon asked.

"Who said eradicating poverty was cheap?" Ryan said chuckling.

"There has to be a way to do it with a palatable balance sheet," Sally said thoughtfully.

"If the economist thinks it's possible, let's give it a try," Leon said.

"Okay, we know the assignment's expectations, and we've identified our issue, great progress. Who's taking notes?" Sally inquired.

"I will," Lai volunteered.

"Fantastic. Thanks, Lai. I think some of us have done some preliminary research, but since we now have more details on the project, we need to assign action items and plan to meet again as we put the policy brief together," Sally suggested.

"Agreed," Meggie seconded. "Let me define the problem," she offered.

"I'll work with Meggie to provide the scope of the problem," Ryan volunteered.

"Who are the stakeholders?" Sally asked. "I mean, who is affected by this issue? Seniors, children, men, women?"

"Let me tackle that. What region are we considering? A continent or a country? A county or a village?" Leon asked.

"Africa is the most affected by poverty according to World Bank data. I think we should go with Africa," Lai suggested.

"I second that," Ryan said.

"Okay, Meggie and I can look at current policy approaches and propose some options for our project," Sally suggested.

"What's our timeline?" Ryan asked.

"We need a week with Sally to review your information and complete ours," Meggie said.

"A week will be enough for us. Leon and Lai, does that work for you?" Ryan asked.

"I think so," Lai responded.

"Let's post our completed tasks by next Friday," Leon affirmed the timeline.

"Then, next Friday, Sally and I will have the proposed draft policies ready for discussion," Meggie said. "I suggest we use Google.docs since we can write, edit, and collaborate easily. I'll take care of that and direct you to the address."

"I just sent you all an invite for another meeting in two weeks to review our policy brief. Great work, team! Meeting adjourned," Sally thanked and released everyone.

As Meggie left the library, she felt inspired. Many people in her homeland of Kenya were not as fortunate as she was. Many families had no chance at a life like hers. Considering that more than 1.3 billion people globally live in poverty, something must be done, and I can help in this something. What if I have power through education? My role is to plant a seed. With water, sunshine, and good soil, this tiny seed may one day grow to transformational possibilities for a promising future. Meggie's mind flooded with optimistic visions of a more vibrant future for the people living in poverty.

Eventually, she refocused on her assignment. After a thorough review of the project requirements, she located quality information from the library and credible online sources. Meggie was thankful to have the project to work on to take her mind off of her sadness about Liam and his tragedy.

CHAPTER 20

The Family as a Cell

MEGGIE WAS BACK IN HER apartment. Hearing her alarm clock, she automatically shut it off. Damn! I just fell asleep. How is it already five in the morning? Meggie jumped to her feet realizing that she had work to do on her part of the group project. I have no choice but to get my body revved up. Nothing will accomplish that better than a cold shower; she convinced herself as adrenaline coursed through her body. She headed to the shower yelling some pro-wrestling smack talk as the cold water assaulted her, awakening her.

Ten-minutes later, she walked out of her apartment feeling fresh and alert on one of the first winter days in Phoenix. A cold air mass from Canada dropped the temperature to 39 degrees. She walked with focus, seeking protection from the chilling cold. She noticed Liam's car in the parking lot. The cold, the focus on the assignment, everything else ceased to exist for her.

Liam came back! I have to see him. A rush of excitement consumed her. Meggie decided to hurry and check up on him in his apartment. As she approached the door, she knocked softly and waited. Liam always responded swiftly.

Uncharacteristically, there was no immediate answer. She noticed that Liam's front door was unlocked. She turned the knob and opened the door. Surprisingly, it opened. As she entered, she immediately noticed an extra pair of shoes in the entryway—shoes that definitely did not belong to Liam. Then, she heard noises coming from the bedroom—erotic, moaning sounds of pleasure. Meggie moved away from the sound in a panicked rush, making the floor creak. The noises stopped instantly. Meggie swore under her breath, unsure of what to do next. A woman rushed out from the bedroom, her pants still unbuttoned and a yellow blouse in her left hand.

Meggie stood still, frozen as she watched the half-naked woman in front of her. "It's not what you think," Isabel said, flushed and embarrassed. "I was just on my way out."

"Oh, no. No. I intruded without notice. You have nothing to worry about. I'm out of here," Meggie said as she turned to leave.

Liam's face displayed panic and profound shock. Despair and disbelief were all over his face. He was speechless for almost a whole minute as he covered his nakedness. He finally recovered his voice and said to both women, "Please, don't leave." Liam, looking like a stranded fish out of water, said, "This was a big mistake. I never imagined I'd be in a situation like this. And, I have no clue what I'm supposed to do. I didn't plan it for sure," Liam said.

"No one plans for this kind of stuff, let alone predicting what they are capable of. Do you have a relationship with Meggie? I never asked," Isabel questioned.

"What? Do I have a relationship with Meggie? Good question," Liam pondered the question. As if he just woken from a dream, Liam looked for signs that he was having a real experience and not just a bad dream. He pinched his right hand for a reality check. "God, I'm not dreaming."

"Yes, that's right. You're not dreaming. Are you in a relationship with Meggie?" Isabel asked a second time.

"Maybe you can tell me if I am. I look forward to being around Meggie. I long for moments when I can be alone, so I can replay everything that's happened between us and think about everything that has yet to happen. I care about how I say stuff when I'm with her. I agonize over how best to respond to every message and conversation. Her hugs feel electrically charged. Our chemistry is real, and sometimes I have a hard time letting her go," he said with his eyes shut tightly. At this point, Meggie gave Liam a sad look, sighed heavily, and left the apartment.

Isabel walked toward Liam and embraced him tightly. "Liam, you need time for yourself. Be safe and take care," she said and left. It was clear to Isabel that Liam never loved her. They had grown up together but their relationship never blossomed into anything more than a brother-sister relationship—well, until today. Isabel always hoped that one day she and Liam would be a couple.

Back in her apartment, Meggie cried herself to sleep. She knew what she saw, but she pondered Liam's words about his relationship with her. He had never articulated these thoughts to her. She awoke to a ringing doorbell. Liam was standing on her doorstep. She ushered him in without a word. Liam stepped in and sat in a dining chair. His eyes were bloody red. He looked as if he had been run over by a truck, and Meggie was more sympathetic than angry at that moment.

"Can I get you some coffee?" she asked gently.

"I haven't had any food since I left here. I'm starving," Liam said.

She rushed to warm up some of the leftovers from their last meal and handed Liam a plate filled with food. She also set out a glass of water.

Liam looked at her with sorrow. "It isn't what it looked like," he said. Liam noticed Meggie was crying too. "I've made a terrible mess, haven't I?" he asked. "I seem to specialize in creating disasters," Liam explained.

Meggie responded, "Well, we're just friends who happen to be close. We've never discussed an exclusive relationship between us. However, I didn't expect to feel sick after walking in on you with Isabel. The emotional pain and grief were unbearable. I can only imagine the pain you must be going through, losing your parents. I'm so sorry for your loss," Meggie said. "How long have you known Isabel?"

"Isabel has been in my life as long as I can remember. She lived next door, and my parents and hers knew each other before we were both born. I'm five years-older than she is, and I remember when her parents brought her home from the hospital as a newborn. I was excited and eager to take care of her as my younger sister. We had a deep friendship over the years but were never intimate. She was more like a sister than anything else. Today was a stupid emotional mistake," he said. "That's not an excuse, but I'm a mess right now."

"Liam, you have a lifetime to figure that out. There are no obligations here. You're not married to anyone. Right now, you need time to grieve. You're going through tough times. My Grandpa George always directed me to this verse in the Bible, Isaiah 41:10: 'Do not fear, for I am with you; do not be dismayed, for I am your God. I will strengthen you and help you; I will uphold you with my righteous right hand.'"

"I don't deserve your kindness after what I've done to you," he said weakly.

Meggie juggled all the mixed messages in her brain. She recalled her parents' message that love cannot be owned nor taken away. One can only give love. The choice is twofold—receive and reciprocate or not. It isn't love if your actions stem from pity, loyalty, duty, or fear of losing the other person. You've got to love someone enough to let them go without displaying any negative emotions, or bear the consequences of dealing with the drama associated with it. The collateral damage was not worth the risk. She contemplated her next step, took a deep breath and let her infatuation with Liam go. She thought, it's good that I got to know this part of Liam before our relationship went too far.

Although she was hurt badly too, part of her needed to display strength. Liam had messed up badly but had lost all his family, too, and that was worse than her loss of faith in him over Isabel. At least, Meggie tried to convince herself of this.

Meggie told him, "No worries. Right now, I'm here to support you in any way I can," she said. Even saying that was painful to her. She was hurting. She remembered her grandparents, what they had gone through and how they carried on with resilience and grace, and she hoped that everything would be all right. Meggie now had to listen to Liam.

"My dad will be laid in state in the Arizona Capital on Thursday. The observance will open with a private ceremony inside the Rotunda. After that, the public will be invited to pay their respect from 12:00 to 9:00 p.m. On Friday, a memorial service for my dad, mom, and grandpa will be at 10:00 at the South Mountain Baptist Church. Dignitaries and others who worked with my dad will give tributes. I'm giving the eulogy. Please come," he begged.

"Of course, I'll be there. Now, please eat. Food is very vital to you right now. You need the strength to fulfill the tasks and duties before you."

"Thank you. I appreciate your kindness." Liam ate, but eating anything was difficult, and certainly not how Meggie had planned for him to eat this special meal.

Finally, before Liam left her apartment, Meggie reminded him of God's steadfast love that never ceases with mercies that never run out. Everything that she had learned from her father, and Grandpa George, came alive. She reminded Liam, in God's eyes, we are not perfect. We make mistakes all the time, but He renews his mercies every morning so that we can hope for a better day.

All the local channels aired the funeral procession of the official motorcade, which transported Senator Grant to the Rotunda. With all the commotion and rhetoric of the election, Liam was surprised at how much the people of the state loved his dad. Liam was too consumed with his career to recognize how much he missed out on his dad's work. Liam once told Meggie that his father preferred to let Liam map his path without his father influencing his career.

Two hours before the public observance, the military honor guard brought Liam, his uncle, Isabel's parents, and Isabel to the Rotunda. Liam's uncle supported him as he passed by his father's casket. Liam's shoulders sagged, and his normal gait slowed. His grief was evident in his bent posture. He looked broken. Liam wept over his father's casket until Jackson motioned him out of the Rotunda.

Liam requested privacy during the family's part of the service. Cameras were not allowed. Isabel's father, a close friend of Senator Grant, delivered the benediction. Many others testified about how the senator helped them.

The next day, the motorcade arrived at South Mountain Baptist Church. The military team retrieved the casket and placed it inside the main room of the church. Liam's mother and grandfather's caskets were already there. In his sermon, the pastor referred to Senator Grant as, "A man of faith who loved the people he served with his whole heart." When the time came for Liam to eulogize his father, he shared a different perspective on who his father was in addition to his personal relationship with his father.

"I don't know much about my father's political life apart from a few glimpses. Nor do I know the details of my mother's interior design business or my grandpa's endeavors. They exposed me to only the little they wanted me to know. However, I was their number one priority. They all loved me unconditionally. I trusted each one of them, and they were always there for me. They allowed me to make mistakes without judgment. Likewise, they punished me when I went astray. My father, in particular, made me face the same legal and family consequences as any other kid. He made me understand consequences and taught me to be accountable for my mistakes. I hated broccoli, and I still do, but to his last day, he still put it on my plate, and I had to finish every agonizing piece of it. I don't know what lies ahead for me, but I believe that they will be watching over me for as many days to come as I have. Rest in peace, dad, mom, and grandpa. Until we meet again."

Meggie was among the first to leave the church because she was near the door. Isabel approached her as Meggie walked toward the parking lot to her car.

"Hello, Meggie. How have you been?" she said coolly as she extended her hand.

"It's a sad day, it must be very difficult for Liam," Meggie said.

"That's right. It's been very difficult for us, too. We're very close to Liam's family," Isabel said.

"It must be. Liam told me about that. I'm sorry for your loss," she said, genuinely.

"Did Liam tell you about our relationship?" she asked. "You're fighting a losing battle with me if you continue to pursue him. I've worked on this relationship for a long time, and I intend to get what I want. Back off. I mean that, or else," Isabel threatened.

"I'm not pursuing him. But you might be working too hard on the floor, dancing on your own in the dark. Are you sure he is in sync with you?" Meggie asked.

"Bitch, how dare you? How dare you? How long have you known him? A few months? Just keep away, I'm warning you," Isabel began to raise her voice, and Meggie interrupted.

"I came here for an education, not for Liam. He is not and never will be a prize for me to fight for. But, let us assume that I care for him; I can't fight with you to get him to love me. It has to come from him. I'm not sure if anyone can coerce love out of someone. It was a pleasure knowing you. He's all yours, and I'm sincerely sorry for the loss of Liam's family," she said, turning her back to Isabel and walking away.

What was that all about? Meggie asked herself as she opened her car door. She was shaken but determined. It is time to refocus on important things, Meggie told herself. The sideshows and drama associated with this Liam situation are distracting me from my main mission here in the United States.

Liam's uncle interrupted her thoughts. "Meggie, I have a note for you from Liam," he said as he extended an envelope to her. Meggie read the message—an invitation to the family residence that evening. She reflected on the confrontation with Isabel and decided that she would decline.

"I'm sorry, there's a meetup for my college group this evening that's very important. Let me reply to Liam through the card," she said as she removed a pen from her handbag and wrote, "Liam, thank you for the invitation. I know how much this means to you. I regret to inform you that I'm unable to be present due to a school commitment that I have to attend. Thank you for extending this invitation to me. Sincerely, Meggie."

That evening, Meggie met with Sally to work on their part of the project. She and the other Falcons finally knew about Liam's relationship to their state's senator. "How was the senator's family funeral service?" Sally asked as she joined Meggie at the dining table.

"It was sad. Many people said positive things about the family. Although there was nothing anyone could do or say to take away the pain of Liam's loss, at least, he got to know many people cared for him, and his family," Meggie responded.

"I wasn't able to come, but my prayers are with him and his family," Sally said.

"He needs lots of prayers—for sure," Meggie replied. "I was just winding up my preliminary research. Your arrival was perfect timing," Meggie explained, hoping to immerse herself in her project so as not to think about Liam.

"What have you got so far?" Sally inquired.

Before the meeting, Meggie actively researched ways to best present the introduction to the policy brief. She knew the emphasis would be on the family unit, the unifying structure of the continent. Meggie explained to Sally, "I think that the continent will succeed if every family has a place at the table. Picture Africa as a cell. A cell is composed of unique parts with a specific set of complex functions. The family unit is the nucleus. The family unit drives the success of the continent and associated nations. In essence, we can imply that the family unit is in charge of almost everything that occurs within the continent.

"The cell membrane represents the parents, guardians, and other major stakeholders directly responsible for the family. They are supposed to control what comes in and out of the family. They are the custodians and first responders for anything that comes to the family, which includes keeping the home secure, accessing and disseminating information, and providing for the health and economic wellbeing of their unit.

"The cell wall represents the continent, and all the countries, with their governing systems. It provides structure and support, and more importantly, it keeps the family safe and secure at all times. Security encompasses all aspects of a good standard of living and allows each of the members to pursue their happiness. The family unit's strength depends on it being a functional loving and caring heathy family. To achieve that requires a lifelong journey of equipping and empowering them to develop knowledge and skills to enhance their well-being. A peaceful home life is a result of a heathy family and a healthy family fosters prosperity. Prosperous family units have strong bonds that unite a powerful continent. Invest in families to achieve a strong continent."

Sally read out her findings. "I have four main statistics related to poverty. First: Out of eight billion people worldwide, about a billion are chronically undernourished. Ninety-eight percent of these undernourished people live in developing countries. Every sixty seconds, a child dies from a condition caused by poverty. A billion people globally live on under a dollar a day. Almost half of these people are from Sub-Saharan Africa. To be specific, a third of African people live in extreme poverty. Third: three-quarters of the world's poorest population depend on agriculture, and 99 percent of Sub-Saharan African people are farming families. Almost everyone on the continent is poor. Fourth: three in ten people globally lack access to readily available water. Six in ten lack proper safe sanitation. Every sixty seconds, a child dies of diarrhea in Sub-Saharan Africa."

Meggie was laughing hard as Sally presented her evidence. Sally was confused by her reaction.

"What's so funny?" she asked.

"Did you also know that in Sub-Saharan Africa, in every sixty seconds a minute pass? This is trending on Twitter right now as we speak." Meggie joked as she continued to laugh.

"Okay, okay. I know it sounds like I'm painting a very bleak image of the continent."

"I didn't say that, but yes, you are. I understand how it might look, because of the data out there. I come from there, and I don't see the picture as dire as painted by the statistics you quoted," Meggie replied tactfully.

"So, how would you tell the story?" Sally asked.

"From my research, I discovered that despite the presence of some conflicts in some regions within Sub-Saharan Africa, this geographic area shows continuous geographical containment—stopping the expansion of foreign powers and developing regional autonomy and democracy. As a result, deaths have significantly decreased," Meggie said as Sally sat there a bit befuddled.

"Security is enhanced throughout Africa, and conflict caused by community wars (either those intertribal or caused by outsiders) are constrained to limited geographical regions. Africa is a huge continent, and the majority of people in Africa live in peace," Meggie said.

"Got it," Sally said and Meggie continued. "Economic growth of the area has consistently improved. The World Bank expects the growth rate for the area to be steady at about 4 percent in the coming years. In 1961, the gross domestic product (GDP) grew from 60 billion to the current estimated two trillion. From 1970 to date, primary school enrollment has steadily increased from about 54 to 98 percent. The increase in education indicates increased literacy.

"In my view," Meggie continued, "not everyone needs to reach the highest level of education. However, it is important to receive training for people in society to contribute and earn a decent living. Accessibility of technology and information is an additional key to unlock the potential for many. Locating, evaluating, and effectively using information are basic necessities. Life expectancy was forty-years of age in the sixties and has gone up to sixty-years of age currently.

"And in the field of health, Sub-Saharan Africa has great opportunity to improve through preventative initiatives that increase the quality of health care services and products. The unemployment rate is still a bummer at about 8 percent, which especially affects young people—the foundation of the continent. The high unemployment rate is the major policy issue in my opinion. A reduction in unemployment would boost confidence, and more importantly, contribute to the continent's development."

"What does confidence have to do with unemployment?" Sally asked.

"Confidence affects one's life every day. I made a bold decision to spend money and come all the way to get my education here in the United States?"

"Why?" Sally asked.

"The investment is worthwhile. The return is worth the risk." Meggie said.

"I get it. Confidence is the driving force for the continent's economy. Job security is linked to investor decision-making, another major factor, especially considering the young workforce of the continent," Sally added.

"Not quite. To be able to advance and sustain Africa's global leadership and competitive position in innovation, technology, and economic prowess, a world-class skilled and talented workforce is critical. That's the confidence I am talking about," Meggie said

After Meggie outlined her overview, Sally noted, "Wow. This sharply contrasts with what I found. I have a problem with your approach. I don't see the intensity of the issue. No one will be convinced of the need for immediate action," Sally argued.

"I think your approach is reactionary, and will only lead to attempts at short-term policy fixes," Meggie countered.

"So, tell me, how will anyone be convinced to take action if things are improving and everything looks to be moving positively?" Sally asked.

"I hear what you're saying. However, I see a larger issue that requires a multidimensional solution, covering both short and long-term problems. The story I just told you is evidence that many are working tirelessly toward a better future. The progress is marred by too much focus on exaggerated negative narratives. This negative view shifts discussions toward the development of reactive policies to remedy problems instead of expending energy to prevent the occurrence of emergencies," Meggie explained the rationale for her approach.

"I'm not convinced yet, because every data point I've indicated shows Sub-Saharan Africa is distressed in every aspect of development."

"We both know that numbers sometimes lie, Sally. I've always questioned the validity and reliability of some of the data available," Meggie said.

"Why?" Sally inquired.

"The idea of poverty is subjective, depending on the region of the world you come from. The questions asked to determine socio-economic status sometimes don't make sense. For instance, what one owns, the cultural operations of communities, and many other aspects vary across the world."

"For example, I live in a small village in Kenya, and I don't own a TV. You live here in Phoenix and you own a TV. Does it imply that I am poor?" Meggie asked.

"Yes, it does here in America," Sally responded.

"My grandfather did not have a TV but had lots of livestock and many hectares of land. However, he wasn't poor because he didn't own a TV," Meggie said.

Sally gave her a quizzical look. "But you understand to provide comparative data, that you need to ask questions that produce consistent results," Sally said. "I can't provide different questionnaires to people from Chandler, Gilbert, Tolleson, Tucson, or here in Phoenix. Yes, some parts of the sample will be from rural areas, or affluent or struggling communities."

"Correct. But, again, when you scale your data-collection measurements, would you equate someone with a TV or a boat as poor in America and compare that to someone in Sub-Saharan Africa?" Meggie asked.

"Why not? I don't see a problem there, if you leave out the boat," Sally responded.

"Exactly. As soon as you want to leave out the boat, that tells you something. The major problem is insufficient official demographic data-collection systems. I'm not sure there's a deep enough understanding of Sub-Saharan

Africa to determine an ideal sampling and authentic survey instruments. Sometimes, the problems are limits of accuracy, timeliness, and availability of data.

"Quality data depend on skilled personnel employing appropriate instruments. Constant changes also require dynamic data updated constantly. Politicians base too many policies on extremely outdated poverty data. Real-time dynamic data is optimal so that information is obtained as it happens. Everyone in Africa is working toward that, part of the reason I'm passionate about this project. It's dear to my heart," Meggie said.

"I understand. Remember, this project is just an assignment. It's not the real thing," Sally said as she smiled. Meggie understood what Sally said. However, Meggie knew that it was going to be challenging to change perceptions about Africa. She thought—helping people view Africa in a positive light is my long-term goal.

Sally was impressed by Maggie's passion for her people and continent. However, Sally was anxious to see whether others in the class would be convinced by the presentation as Meggie refined it.

CHAPTER 21

DNA

In a period of months, everything changed for Liam. The funeral helped him process some of the emotions from the loss of his family. However, the absence of his family took a heavy toll on him, especially since he kept much of his feelings bottled up, which disrupted his physical health and his ability to think clearly. On occasion, emotions he never experienced before triggered other feelings, and he had no clue about how to deal with them. He felt little motivation for continuing his education. Thinking about tasks related to his college assignments overwhelmed him. Liam considered taking time off to recover.

A month earlier, Liam's uncle Jackson discussed with Liam what Liam's next steps might entail. Liam met with the family attorney to go through his parents' will. His parents and grandfather left him everything. However, now a mountain of deeds, titles, insurance policies, financial accounts, and other records were in Liam's custody. The attorney offered his personal administrator to initiate death benefits, and assist with the payment of bills related to the legalities of death.

After a long day with the attorney, Liam was about to go to bed when he remembered the gift that Meggie gave him before his world turned upside down. The gift was in his apartment, but he was at his parent's house. Seeing the gift can wait until tomorrow, he initially thought. On second thought, he decided to drive by the apartment to get it. As he opened the door to his apartment, he remembered the horrible mess that happened the last time he was there. The encounter with Isabel was in the past. Liam thought, such negative energy is the last thing I need right now. He motivated himself to think positively.

He spotted Meggie's gift in front of him, on the coffee table. He sat down and unwrapped it. It was a DNA test kit from Ancestry.com.

Ever since Liam told Meggie about the mystery of his grandfather's adoption, he realized that she wanted to support his dream of finding his roots. She seemed fascinated by stories of people who traced their genealogy through the current advanced technology. In some reality TV programs, ordinary people, as well as celebrities, succeeded in locating family members, authenticating family stories, tracing medical conditions, and determining inheritance and family ownerships along with other, often surprising, outcomes.

Many of the people in these stories used Ancestry.com. All Liam needed to do to create his account was to activate the test. Meggie wrapped the gift with printout instructions on how to collect the sample, and a summary of what he could expect from the results.

He smiled to himself thinking that Meggie's gift was truly as exceptional as she was. As he stared at the gift, he wondered if he had any mysterious family connections. He perused the instructions. He starred at the box for a few minutes and acknowledged what his parents always told him about meaningful gifts. "It was not the gift, but the thought that counts." He realized that Meggie knew how much finding out about his family meant to him, and she made it happen.

A small card dropped as he returned the package to the coffee table. He opened it and read: "You have lived life with a missing part of your ancestry. I hope this gift helps you to write a new chapter. Best wishes, Meggie."

A few seconds later, he texted Meggie: "I apologize for the delay. Thank you very much for the much-needed thoughtfulness. You could not have chosen a more perfect and timelier gift. The effort and energy you spent on this are highly appreciated. It made today very special for me. Thank you."

Meggie immediately responded that she was glad he liked it.

Liam reviewed the documentation further and realized that the subscription had a start and an end date. To take full advantage of the kit, he had to use it immediately. He needed to discover links to his family and other generations, especially since the death of his parents.

Liam thought further about dropping out of school for the time being. He decided to defer his education to a future date when he was ready to participate more fully. He planned to take a leave of absence from his medical practice, as well. Unlike the university, that required a phone call to hold and reschedule his return, his job as a doctor required a smooth transition. Fortunately, the other doctors were aware of his tragedy and everyone were willing to cover for him as he took time for himself. His patients understood Liam's circumstances, and wished him well.

Shortly after he talked to the hospital to confirm approval of his leave of absence, he called Meggie. Liam wanted to discuss the decisions he made about school, work, and his intentions to take advantage of the gift she gave him.

"Liam, how are you doing?" she asked.

"I've had better days. Thanks for asking," Liam said in a sad voice.

"I'm with the Falcons in Ryan's apartment. We're finalizing our policy brief."

"Good for you. I wanted to let you know again that I appreciate your gift. I've dropped out of the program for now and took a leave of absence from work. I need some time to figure things out," Liam said.

"I'm sorry to hear that. I hope everything goes well," Meggie said.

"I want to see you. Are you free tomorrow?" Liam asked.

"No, we have class and will be working on an assignment after that."

Liam was determined to have some time with Meggie. Throughout his time of sorrow, Liam completely opened up to Meggie and shared his joys and sadness. He felt his relationship with her was in-sync. She had been a real friend, a good listener who walked back into his life when everyone he loved perished. Meggie was more than a friend; he was kidding himself to think of her as just a friend.

Since the dinner before his parent's accident, Liam thought about her often. His emotions toward her were intact. He recalled how alive he felt when he was with her. They had been seeing each other often, and he remembered telling her that he loved her. He didn't remember her response. Liam knew that after the Isabel incident, he had to build up their relationship all over again. He wanted to do it right this time around.

Eight o'clock in the evening the next day, Meggie heard a knock on her door. She did not expect anyone. When she opened the door, Liam stood there, gazing at her.

"Liam, I told you I wasn't available today," she said, smiling.

"I know, but I wanted to see you," he said as he stepped into her apartment.

"Have a seat," she motioned him toward the sofa and sat opposite him on her lounge chair. "I'm sorry that you had to drop out. We all miss you in class," she said.

"I appreciate that, but I need to take my mind off stuff, and I'm excited to search for my unknown relatives. Thanks to you, I'm newly motivated," he said passionately.

"Good for you, Liam. Are you doing it on your own or hiring a genealogist?" Meggie inquired.

"I never even thought of getting. I should look into hiring a genealogist. Meggie, you're a genius," he said, looking at her tenderly. "A genealogist will make it a lot easier," he said.

Meggie searched on her computer. "There's an Association of Professional Genealogists here in Phoenix with a list of registered consultants. At least, using one of their consultants, you will be assured of professional standards of the organization," Meggie said as she continued to search.

Liam moved closer to examine what was on her screen. "There's so many. How do I know who I need?" he asked.

"I'll help you focus on research specialists. I also think you should create a family tree in Ancestry.com based on the members of the family you already know—to start the process."

"Great idea. I'll start from there tomorrow and contact a specialist. I submitted the DNA sample yesterday. The results will be back in four-to-six weeks," he said.

Meggie put her laptop back on the coffee table. She looked up, and Liam was staring at her intensely.

"Meggie, I'm ready to be in a relationship with you," he said solemnly.

Meggie laughed, surprised.

"Why are you laughing?" he asked. "I'm completely serious."

"Don't get me wrong; I feel the same way. However, we haven't known each other long, and I don't know much about you. I learned more from the public forum than I did directly from you," she lamented.

"I know. Things happened so fast and messed up how I wanted things to go," he said.

"How do you know when you're ready for a relationship?" Meggie asked.

"Good question," he pondered for a while. "I haven't previously been interested in relationships. But our connection feels different. It's frightening to think of losing you," he said.

"I understand what you mean. The situation with you and Isabel in your apartment was unbearable. I'm terrified of losing you, too," she admitted, to Liam and herself.

Liam moved closer to Meggie and held her hands tightly. He fixed his eyes on hers and kissed her, gently and said, "as I told you that day, I love you even more now," in said in his husky voice.

Meggie stood and walked to the sink for a glass of water. She wasn't thirsty but wanted to cool off her emotions. "I love you, just as I said last time. My heart is pounding with joy telling me to trust, but my head is scared—begging me to run," she said.

"You and I know that we love each other because we have told this to each other, correct?" Meggie asked.

"Correct," he replied. He was ecstatic to discover that they both had feelings for each other but he worried if that were enough for Meggie.

"A relationship needs to be built on a solid foundation—just like a house," Meggie responded. "A fragile relationship built on sand will not withstand the test of time. I'm more afraid of losing our friendship because of a hasty decision. I have yet to learn how to let you know when I'm pissed off. Right now, I care more about feeling good all the time with you than having difficult conversations that might result in outcomes I don't like.

"What I am trying to say is that I'm not ready to commit yet, but would love to get to know you more. In a committed relationship, I should be able to put your interests before my own, and I can't promise that right now. I need to be ready to share myself with you. That's what a relationship means to me," she said.

"I'm afraid to lose you to someone else, Meggie," he pleaded with her.

"Liam, I would rather take the time to know you and work through challenges together. I haven't had that experience with you. I don't want us to break up because we don't know how to resolve our conflicts," she said.

"What if one of us moves on while that's happening?" he asked.

"It will be sad. But then, it wasn't meant to be," Meggie said.

Liam had doubts, but he conceded. "Okay, if that's what you think will work, I'm willing to try things your way."

"Trust is one of the most important things to me," Meggie explained. "I've learned many new and unexpected things about you during the past weeks. Time is vital for us to have a deeper understanding of each other."

Meggie wondered what Liam's expectations were of her family and her because their backgrounds seemed so different. How will my family react to him? Once more, she realized that having the time to learn more about Liam and he about her was crucial. She had strong feelings for Liam but was unsure if Liam were the right one for her. She thought about him most of the time but was still scared. This relationship thing was too complicated, and she was too new in this game. She wanted to give it a try if Liam were in. Whatever happened going forward, she knew that she should be prepared to take the consequences if Liam decided to move forward with someone else. Isabel was right there in her mind, and she remembered the hostility of her last encounter with Isabel.

Liam sighed. "I still have a lot going on related to my family's deaths. I also need to consult with a genealogy expert to begin the other process," he said.

"Know that I'm here for you if you need anything. I'm also looking forward to our future," Meggie said, smiling.

"Thanks," Liam said, squeezing her hand as he stood and left. The visit with Meggie hadn't gone quite how he had hoped, but he felt encouraged about their future. Now, he needed to work on learning about his family.

Meanwhile, Isabel stepped up her game. She was tired of being patient. Liam's slow pace of action indicated that it was time she made her position known. Since the funeral, she had sent Liam flirty, friendly text messages and made frequent surprise visits to his family home. Liam planned to disclose his relationship with Meggie to her, but it did not work as well as he thought it would. He tried to think of the best way to tell Isabel that he only wanted to be with Meggie.

As Liam reflected, he realized that Meggie was straightforward and honest in her expectations with him. She knew she wanted to build a strong relationship founded on trust and self-respect. She had not closed the door but left it wide open for him to pursue her. It was a privilege, and he intended to take full advantage of the opportunity. His only problem was Isabel. He did not remember any time he had been in love with Isabel. He always felt sick when she flirted with him. So, why does she still follow me around? How do I make her understand that I don't love her and will never love her? Liam thought about it long before he drifted off to sleep that night.

Liam made an appointment with a genealogy researcher, Meera Ramesh, the next day. Her expertise included ancestry traces, descendant research, and record searches. The DNA analysis was out of her scope of practice, but she could track down services for DNA testing and interpret the results.

At their first meeting, Liam provided copies of the birth, death and marriage certificates. Liam thought that he had met most of his relatives and always wondered about the other family—that of his adopted grandfather—who he didn't know. Where were they? What did they look like? The only clue was in the letter left when the mother dropped his grandfather at the doorsteps of the couple who became the baby's adopted parents.

Numerous versions of stories circulated within the family that grandpa's mother was African-American. Some claimed she was a Native-American girl who got pregnant by an American boy. Her parents did not want anything to do with the child. She eventually decided to hide the pregnancy from everyone and eventually gave it up at the doorsteps of a generous family. The other version was that she was an American girl who got pregnant with an African-American or Native American boy whose parents vehemently objected. In all the stories, no one ever heard from her again. Everything after that night was a mystery. Liam explained the story and handed Meera a copy of the letter.

Meera acknowledged the complexity of the assignment and outlined the next steps in the process. She would develop a research plan and follow it to the libraries, courthouses, archives, cemeteries, and other places to obtain authentic information. Next, she explained that she would analyze whatever information she found to confirm or disprove findings. After that, she would prepare a report and share these findings with Liam.

Four weeks later, Meera called Liam with a preliminary report. The paper trail had run out at the point of Liam's grandfather's adoption. Liam received his DNA results from Ancestry.com and brought them to Meera.

"You're a doctor, but how much do you know about the test?" she asked.

"Assume I'm not a doctor. I want to understand how it works," he replied.

"Three tests are commonly used: the autosomal DNA test, the mitochondrial DNA (mtDNA) test, and the Y-DNA test," Meera explained.

"I know that the autosomal DNA test involves the first twenty-two chromosomes except those that contribute to gender," he said.

"Correct. The genealogical test specifically determines how closely one is related to someone else. Considering that a quarter of one's DNA is from each of the grandparents, one-eighth from the great-grandparents, one-sixteenth from great-great-grandparents and so on, this test is only useful for newer generations," she said.

"How new?" Liam asked.

"About four-to-five generations," she responded. "This test can provide clues, particularly if you don't have any information on your ancestors. It can provide an estimate of the level of ethnicity or the region of one's ancestors over a period of a few hundred years."

"Impressive," he said, radiating with excitement.

Meera continued. "The mtDNA is found inside the mitochondrion of the cell. You already know that" she said and smiled. "The key to this test is that the mtDNA remains almost the same through sixty or more generations, but it's transmitted only through the maternal line. This test determines how closely you're related to a group of people sharing a common ancestor. The challenge with this test is that some of the relations could be extremely distant," she explained.

"Finally, we have the Y-DNA test. I presume you already know that it exclusively shows the paternal line since females do not have the Y-chromosome, which also undergoes minimal changes over time through generations. With these results, one can determine close relations with people of the same surname and groups of people in one or more regions. It's mainly used to confirm relations and locate relatives," she said.

"This is fascinating. Let's get to it," Liam said excitedly.

"Liam, I'd like to go through the results and do some further research to report back more accurately. I need some time to work on it. Unfortunately, I can't open that envelope today with you. I have to do it on my own, spend some time in libraries and archives, and make lots of calls to verify the information. I'll call you soon," she promised.

Liam was disappointed but wanted to let Meera do whatever she needed so that he could get the most thorough results possible. He stood up and shook Meera's hand before heading home.

A week later, Meera called Liam to share a complete report of his ancestral roots. Meera handed him a folder.

"Liam, you already know your relatives to the point of the adoption of your grandfather. We'll look at the missing parts of your ancestry after that," Meera said as she narrowed the scope of her reporting.

"Got it," Liam said, shifting impatiently in his seat.

"I have your DNA results, but I also found your grandfather's DNA test results from the National DNA databank. That's where we'll focus our discussions today." She opened the portfolio and went through historical documents and other information that he already knew. Then, she stopped at the page that was titled "Admixture Test."

"What does all this mean?" he asked.

"The data provides an estimate of regions and people who have some connections to your grandfather. After a variety of tests, you can see from the pie chart that 73 percent of your DNA is from Europe, and 27 percent is from Africa."

"Whoa!" he exclaimed.

"Okay, 41 percent of my DNA is from Ireland, Scotland, and Wales; 25 percent from Southeast Africa; 21 percent from Great Britain; 7 percent from Scandinavia; 4 percent from North Africa; and 4 percent from Western Europe," he read. He looked at Meera in surprise.

Meera opened the next page of the portfolio.

"Now, we dig deeper. The results said 29 percent of your grandfather's DNA comes from Africa. The next level provides additional details that included Southeast and North Africa. Look at your grandfather's DNA range from Southeast Africa, as little as 7 percent and as much as 36 percent of his DNA match the ancestry of the population who lived there and who still live there."

"So, I have relatives in Africa?" he asked.

"Yes. Turn to the next page."

Liam realized that, although his parents and grandfather were gone, these discoveries would help him move on with life. As he thought deeply about his departed family, tears ran down his face. Meera handed him tissue.

"I'm sorry, Meera. I lost my family recently. I'll be okay in a minute," he said.

"I'm sorry to hear that. Going through this family genetics must be difficult for you," Meera said. "Should we stop for a moment?" she asked.

"No, please, I'm dying to know what's next," he said with a smile through the tears. Meera turned the page.

"To achieve ethnicity estimates, data of DNA markers are all brought to Google Earth, mapped, and correlated. Some of the DNA data have information that includes names, places of birth, residence, and other details. In rare cases, it includes tribe and clan. Over the years, people migrated or traveled beyond their borders. Others married within the same region. In such cases, they may have shared a similar religion or ethnic group," she said.

"You found more than fifty DNA matches for Africa that matched my grandfather?" he asked with amazement.

"Yes. Most of the matches are from a specific region in Kenya, the Great Rift Valley."

"Sh-," he started to exclaim and covered his mouth. Liam moved his chair back in awe.

"There's more," Meera said. "Many family searches on genealogy are on Facebook. These communities are ready to help with genealogical or translation requests from anywhere in the world. I posted your grandfather's results on Facebook, and guess what? I found four people from the region who share a distant connection with your grandfather."

"Can I have their names?" Liam asked.

"I contacted all of them. Three of my attempts were unsuccessful, but one was a success. A kind man shared extensive information about his family with me," she said, turning the page and pointing to a photograph. "Meet your cousin, Kipng' eno Barsiran."

Liam was elated. "That last name sounds familiar," he said. "I've got to go. Thank you very much, Meera." He stood up and held the portfolio close to his heart. "I think I can figure out the rest. You'll be paid in full this afternoon," he said and dashed out of Meera's office. His mind focused on Meggie as he left the office.

CHAPTER 22

Silence Speaks Louder

THE FIRST FALCON TO ARRIVE in class was Sally Cohen. She wore a Sally Ride astronaut costume and looked ready for lift-off. Unlike the specialized parts of the spacesuit, she wore a white zip-front jumpsuit with a replica NASA patch. Her white helmet had a push-button retractable visor oxygen vent, a communication receiver, and a boom microphone. Her gloves were white with wrist toggles. She wore white boot covers over her shoes. Each of her accessories had the NASA logo and the U.S.A flag patch.

"Woah, that's awesome," a member of the Hawks' team yelled out. Everyone in the room turned to the door.

Then, Lai Li entered the room in a conservative, practical Hakka traditional attire: a daju shan, a plain-collared shirt with wide sleeves fastened near the collarbone with no pockets, and blue cotton very straight tailored trousers. His wore a bamboo hat surrounded by embroidery standing about three inches high around it. His footwear was simple—light martial-arts shoes with matching socks. Lai's arrival also drew the attention of his classmates.

"Was this planned? How come I didn't get the memo?" a member of the Owls asked jokingly.

"Ask Sally," Lai said with a laugh.

In a short while, a group entered the room with Leon Pameres and Meggie Jepchumba.

Leon was in a semi-formal Scottish attire. His knee-length kilt was a white, red, and black plaid kilt pleated at the back and tightly fitted to his waist with a black belt and kilt pins. He had a white shirt under a black argyle jacket with three-dimensional overlapping motifs. He topped this with additional colorful accessories, including a brown leather sporran pouch that matched his outfit, a white kilt hose socks with tartan flashes that matched his kilt, and traditional shining black Gillie Brogue shoes. He crowned his look with a Scottish bonnet hat. All he lacked was bagpipes.

Meggie entered the class at the same time. She wore her hair short as usual but dyed it slightly brown from her usual black. She wore a beautiful ornamental tiara made from colorful beads. Her silver-tone oversized hoop earrings made a bold statement. On her neck, she wore her signature tribal coiled golden choker necklace with a sun pendant dangling from a small loop in the middle with a matching bracelet on her right wrist. Meggie added the four theme-colored black, red, green, and white Kenyan bracelets on her left wrist. Both of her upper arms had plain white beaded bracelets. Her dress was a sleeveless brown leather-like texture embroidered with varied colored beads and cowry shells. Two cowry shell embroidered long strip loops fit over each shoulder. She wore the sash only on special Tugen occasions. She wore ankle-length golden, brown and black beaded gladiator sandals on rubber soles.

Odette stopped at the door to soak in the colorful display from the Falcons.

"Should I have come in dressed in my Halloween costume?" she asked the Falcons.

"No, this was just a team thing," Sally said.

"Next time, everyone may want to dress up. Your costumes are fantastic," Professor Dyer said as she walked to the podium.

Ryan was last to enter the room. He had gone over the top as Batman. He wanted to inspire everyone with his fair-and-square, strict code of justice. He started with a molded foam mask and continued with a deluxe dark black polyester jumpsuit. The padding broadened Ryan's shoulders and the sleeves decorated with foam spikes emphasized his natural athletic power. Ryan wore foam boot tops fastened to each foot. A gold utility belt encircled his waist. He covered his head with a black hood fastened to his neck. He emulated the authority and strength of Batman.

"Let me take a picture of the class today," Odette requested as she took her phone out from her bag.

"Now, back to business. Today is the big day. Each team will present its proposal. I've booked this room for an additional two hours. We'll have a drawing to determine the order of presentations," Odette said.

The Owls went first. Their policy brief focused on the issue of relevance and reliability of health information in developing countries. They found the problem with the relevance and reliability of health information stemmed from inadequate, inefficient data collection and analysis. Because of inadequate controls and staff-training problems, the errors increased along with either misinterpretation or a poor understanding of the results, archaic IT equipment, and the worst—weak leadership—among other things.

Meggie was frustrated because the Owls portrayed people who were helpless, and for whom nothing could be done except to start all over from the beginning stages. She wondered if this were the case in other world-stage forums.

Meggie realized that many people have preconceived myths about developing countries. Too often, people see the individuals in these countries as extremely backward in technology, and view the country's inhabitants as uneducated, poor, and living solely in the rural areas. Developed nations in the west spend most of their money to help these countries through foreign aid. Another part of this myth is that almost everyone is corrupt. These perceptions seemed so wrong to Meggie. She worried—how could anyone demystify these deeply rooted untruths.

"I'd like to question your approach to the presentation on the magnitude of the problem," Meggie argued. "Your presentation doesn't provide a trend of observed achievements, even if these achievements are small. The approach you described doesn't provide what worked and what didn't. You've painted the worst-case scenario, and this scenario will lead to a reactionary policy train, just as it does in real-life situations," Meggie explained.

"Let them finish their presentation. We'll debate when they're done," Odette directed.

The Owls concluded with policy options that included the role of the government in training and skill development; and assuring access, availability, and connectivity to the rest of the world. After the presentation, open forum discussions affirmed Meggie's assertion that unfair negotiations occur at high intergovernmental levels. In Meggie's assessment of the discussions, she saw a supposition of people in the developing world who wanted things from the others without working for them. She focused on making notes to react to later.

Sally then presented on behalf of the Falcons. "Sub-Saharan Africa lies south of the Sahara. Africa is a continent, not a single country—as you all know."

The rest of the teams responded with laughter. "People make a continent, and the family is its core. A secure family is the basis of security in the area. Security includes being healthy, educated, and informed. Security derives from being peaceful and prosperous. The facts indicate that although Sub-Saharan Africa doesn't have one of the best economies of the world right now, it's part of the fastest-growing continent. The majority of its young population is literate, and working hard to make a difference. Many on the continent use whatever resources are available. Such necessities lead to outstanding innovations within the continent.

"However, Sub-Saharan Africa also has immense unexplored potential. Connecting families to systems, information, and resources will unlock that potential. Take, for instance, M-Pesa, the cell phone-based money transfer and financing services. It allows users to deposit, withdraw, transfer money, and pay for goods and services easily with a mobile device. Its simplicity and efficiency allow everyone to use it regardless of level of education, from the city of Nairobi to the remotest parts of Maasai land, to the vast wheat famers of the Rift Valley and coffee farmers of the Central Province. You can pay wages, bills, or transfer money instantly. This is one example among many of innovations already in place, with more to come.

"I differ with the image that Sally portrayed of Sub-Saharan Africa," a member of the Hawks' team reacted. "An ongoing myth about Africa rising contends that their sustainable economies are founded on the development of viable large-scale industries, not just agriculture and livestock. Wars, illiteracy, and extreme poverty plague Sub-Saharan Africa. Convince me otherwise. You're implying policies requiring immense investment instead of foreign aid. How do you expect them to pay it back?"

"We told you so," Leon whispered to Meggie. "You can't convince anyone with this approach. Not with what is already widely accepted about Sub-Saharan Africa."

"And what is that?" Meggie questioned, bristling at Leon's comments.

Their conversation was distracted by another reaction, this time from a member of the Eagles' team.

"I find the Falcons' policy brief over the top. It would have been different if this were Europe, America, or Japan. Those regions meet the basic needs of their populations already. More than 50 percent of Sub-Saharan Africa's population doesn't even have their most basic needs covered. They're helpless and depend solely on the west and others. Haven't y'all seen ads for or contributed to charities decrying the devastating state of African children? Worst of all, there is no, and I mean nada, access to modern technology. Where are you supposed to start building systems, data collection, and libraries of information, and so on? Thus, that policy brief is a non-starter," he concluded.

Meggie was getting angrier and more frustrated by the direction of the discussion. Finally, she reached the end of her fuse. "Why do you focus on the most unpleasant situations to illustrate your point? I don't dispute that there are such miserable situations, but parading these isolated situations to put the continent in a disadvantaged position and push it to the side of the negotiating table is getting old," Meggie exploded.

"Meggie, don't take it personally. It's just an assignment. Take it easy," an Owls' member spoke.

Meggie felt overcome with frustrations and anger. After years of hearing this narrative about her home continent, she wasn't surprised by the attitudes her classmates held, but she reached the point where her need to provide a constant defense of her home touched the wrong nerve.

She often spent time debunking myths about Africa. Thoughts about the level of myths and untruths about Africa rushed through her mind. She remembered one occasion where she was asked if her grandparents lived in tree houses without doors because they couldn't afford doors. Another colleague with a Ph.D. once talked ignorantly about the country of Africa. Then, in the most personal and hurtful inquiry, someone asked her if she had been tested for Ebola and HIV/AIDS. Wasn't this some kind of profiling?

Meggie was on a one-woman crusade to get the truth across to her classmates and the larger world. She was exhausted. No one was listening. She felt as if she were drowning with her eyes wide open in front of a huge audience and screaming for help, but no one could hear her. The more she thought about it, the angrier she became.

Her breathing became heavy, as if she were suffocating. She made tiny sobbing sounds. Tears streamed down her face. The Falcons turned to look at her, surprised. Without noticing their astonished faces, Meggie stood and pushed her laptop and books off the table. They hit the ground with a loud bang. Everyone stared at her. The room was quiet. Someone tried to say something but Odette gave a signal to be quiet.

In that quiet moment, everyone finally understood how important the conversation was to Meggie. The pain and frustration she had felt for so long was evident on her face. She was no different than any of her colleagues, but through the discussion, there seemed to be a blatant bias and immediate dismissal of her ideas. All eyes were on her. Meggie looked at the class. Then, she picked up her belongings from the floor and left the classroom. Odette watched her leave and then directed the rest of the class to complete their presentations.

Although Meggie had a strong personality, she felt overwhelmed by the incident. She wondered whether her thinking was rational. Maybe Liam can help me figure this out, she thought. She rushed toward her apartment. If anyone could help her get past the horror of the presentation, it was Liam. She was a mess and finally decided to go to one of the conference rooms in the library to cool down before she went in search of Liam.

Meanwhile, the teams completed their presentations and returned back to their routine.

An hour passed and Meggie cooled down. Nevertheless, she was exhausted. She simply wanted to complete her education, then go back to Kenya and work.

Unbeknownst to Meggie, Lai secretly recorded a video of the classroom scene as it unfolded. He thought it presented a rare occasion that required special attention. He empathized with Meggie. He titled the video "Demystifying African Myths." He streamed it on YouTube, and posted it on Twitter and Facebook. It went viral almost immediately. There was Meggie, in full Tugen gear, defiant in defense of her homeland. Within three hours, it had more than 358,000 views on YouTube and 224,000 on Twitter.

The Falcons regrouped in the evening to check on Meggie. Her door was locked, and it took several rings of the doorbell and loud knocks on her door before she responded. She was surprised to see her teammates outside her door. "May we come in, please," Sally pleaded.

"Yes, please. Come in. Make yourselves comfortable."

Meggie was still in her Tugen attire. She ushered them in and rushed to the bedroom to change. A few minutes later, she joined them in the living room.

"So, how are you feeling, Meggie?" Lai asked.

"Like shit! I have a throbbing headache and am still recovering from some sedatives I took to help me cope. Blame them in case you notice any strange behavior from me," Meggie said.

"We submitted our project. Everything will be okay on that front," Ryan said.

"How did it go after my outburst? It wasn't intentional. I apologize for embarrassment that I may have caused," Meggie said.

"I have a confession to make," Lai said as he looked directly at Meggie.

"To the team or me?" Meggie wasn't sure what Lai meant.

"To you, Meggie. I recorded our presentation and posted the entire episode on the internet. It went viral," Lai said.

Meggie was shocked.

Ryan checked his cell phone, "372,000 views on YouTube as we speak."

"242,000 on Twitter," Leon added.

Meggie's stress intensified. Too much had happened within a short time.

"Meggie, I want to explain why I posted the video. I felt you had a very important message that needed attention. No one in the class understood how strongly you believed in the propositions you put forth. To the class, it was just another assignment. To you, it was an opportunity to plant a seed for social change," Lai said.

"You must be going through a lot of emotions right now. I learned something from today's class. We were talking too much about preconceived notions about Africa; however, the point you wanted to convey got lost in the noise. Your silence finally got us to pay attention to what was important," Ryan said.

"We're here because we all have your back," Lai said.

"What am I going to do now?" Meggie asked.

"About what?" Lai asked.

"The viral video."

"Nothing. Enjoy the fame," Ryan said jokingly.

"Seriously, you'll have those who support you and some haters, too" Sally said.

"Many people around the globe are rooting for you, and we are, too," Leon explained.

"Thank you so much for coming, I appreciate your support," Meggie said, touched by their concern, as she bid the Falcons goodbye. Since she had not fully recovered from the sleeping medication, she returned to bed.

Early the next day, the front-desk student worker in her apartment awoke Meggie. She told her that a host of people were outside and wanted to interview her. Satellite trucks, news cameras, and associated crews from local news agencies gathered outside the building.

As she thought about her next move, the doorbell rang. It was Odette. The university leadership contacted her to show their support for Meggie. Meggie opened the door and embraced her tightly. She desperately needed a shoulder to lean on, and Dr. Dyer appeared at the right time.

"Take it easy, Meggie. Everything will be okay," Odette consoled Meggie who was in tears. "Everything will be alright. I want you to prepare. The press is waiting outside for information about the viral video." As they approached the door and the onslaught of microphones and cameras, Odette whispered, "Do it as if it were the only chance you'll ever get."

"Will do," Meggie responded confidently with a smile.

Dr. Dyer stood behind her as Meggie read a brief press release that she prepared with Odette's help. "I thank Dr. Dyer for providing an environment that allows students to share competing ideas passionately with their classmates without fear. Yesterday, I learned a lesson that involved rigorous debate regarding a brief policy assignment. Ingrained untrue myths about Sub-Saharan Africa are out there. These myths detrimentally impact vital policies that significantly affect people's lives—not only in Sub-Saharan Africa. Poverty is a malignant cancer that uncontrollably destroys many vulnerable lives, and myths deter opportunities to address the underlying issues.

"I strongly believe that every family has a basic need to feel secure. A family that is healthy, educated, informed, peaceful, and prosperous is secure. A secure family is better-equipped to contribute to society. An equal opportunity to negotiate at the table is part of that. Thank you." Dr. Dyer pulled her out of the media frenzy as soon as she finished speaking.

CHAPTER 23

A New Beginning

THE PAST TWENTY-FOUR HOURS EXHAUSTED Meggie. The ups and downs of her relationship with Liam left her feeling wiped out. The feisty assignment discussions challenged her, but Liam's betrayal took her over the edge, and traumatized her. The sight of Liam kissing Isabel felt like someone had sliced her heart with a surgeon's blade. After the public statement, she took another sleeping aid. Sleep was the only way she could shut down her painful reality. She woke up at two in the morning. Meggie felt alone in a foreign land. She stared at the ceiling for a long time until she decided to call Linda in Kenya.

"Hey, Meggie. What's up?" Linda asked as she looked at her watch. It was noon. "Aren't you supposed to be asleep over there?"

"Yes, I just woke up. I don't know where to begin."

"Are you okay?" Linda asked. Meggie did not sound like herself.

"Yes. No. I mean, there's trouble in paradise. Everything's been going downhill in the past twenty-four hours," Meggie said.

"What did you do this time?" Linda asked. "Are you in jail?" Linda asked.

"Oh no. Not that. I messed up my team's major project presentation and saw Liam kiss another woman," she said.

"I thought you didn't want to commit? Did that change?" Linda asked, confused.

Meggie hesitated, then changed the conversation to the project to get away from the relationship discussion. "Do you know how it is hard to explain to people what happens in Kenya? It's like we live on another planet. No one knows what goes on over here. Almost everyone sees disease, famine, poverty and everything bad," Meggie said.

"So what?" Linda asked.

"It doesn't bother you?" Meggie asked. Linda's perspective was different. She was not exposed to the situation as Meggie was. For her, she couldn't see what the problem was. People can think whatever they want; it didn't matter to her. Anyhow, she was living in Kenya, and the western world was very far away.

"Nothing I can do about it. Why should I? Anyway, you're smart, and you'll sort that out. I'm more interested in learning about the Casanova. He doesn't deserve you. Why are you even still with him?" Linda was becoming animated on the phone. The last time she had talked to Meggie, Liam had messed up with a woman.

"Liam isn't like that," Meggie defended him.

"Once a liar, always a liar. Don't you get it?" Linda asked.

"Liam was remorseful the first time, and we reconciled. He was going through a tough time due to his family passing," Meggie said.

"How sad," Linda paused. It was quiet for a moment. "Do you love him?" she finally asked.

"I think I do," Meggie said.

"You think you do? Meggie, you have to make up your mind," Linda said.

"I know," she said.

"Ultimately, you've got to take responsibility and make the choice. Get over your fear of commitment," she said. Linda had come to know Meggie very well.

"I know, I know," Meggie said.

"No one's perfect. But again, not everyone cheats," Linda said.

"Yes. I can't imagine cheating on someone. I'm in, all the way, and I expect the same," Meggie said.

"No one forced Liam to cheat on you. He did it, and the sad part is that he chose to do so," Linda said.

"I think I may have contributed to the situation. He wanted me to commit, and I told him that we needed to know each other more before we rushed to commitment," Meggie explained.

"Are you trying to justify his actions now? You know what? It'll happen again and again. No one causes someone to cheat on another," Linda said.

Meggie sighed. "I'm stupid," she said.

"Yes, stupid," Linda responded, joking. "You're not stupid. Liam is the stupid one. You did nothing wrong except love him," Linda reassured her friend. "Meggie, Liam doesn't deserve you. Get rid of him, now."

They were on the phone for a long time and finally hung up. The discussion with Linda refocused Meggie's attention on what was most important. She was almost ready to move on with her life without Liam. It wasn't going to be easy to forget him, but she was determined to put her hopes and dreams about their relationship behind her.

With that resolution, she had more energy. She took a long bath and got ready for the day. Meggie was on her way to SSU mall when she saw Liam with a friend of his chatting. He immediately turned towards her with excitement as soon as he spotted her approaching. Meggie was still raw with jealousy from the previous kissing scene she had witnessed the previous day.

"So much has happened since I last saw you, you've been busy," Liam said with excitement.

"Same to you. You've been more busy that I," she said with sarcasm.

Liam noticed immediately that there was something wrong going on. He had come to know her very well.

"Have I wronged you, Meggie?" He asked.

"Hi, Meggie," they were interrupted by Isabel.

Meggie turned to look at Isabel, then Liam.

"I'm dying to know why you want to ran away from me?" Liam asked.

"I saw you with Isabel, at the library after the class presentation." Liam listened without interruption. "You just chatted and left. But, later on as I was going to the apartment, I saw you were making out in the lobby entrance to the apartment. I wasn't ready for any more drama, and I didn't want to hear any more excuses," Meggie said as Liam started cursing. Isabel was watching as it unfolded. She could see that Lian was getting angry with every passing second.

"I am so stupid." He hissed at Isabel, resentful. "So stupid of me. You must have planned it all," he said as he wandered around. "What do you mean?" Meggie asked confused

"She must have seen you at the library, because she called me to meet her there. I told Isabel many times that we would never be more than friends. Yet she kept pulling these stupid tricks. I remember, in the lobby, Isabel came to me so fast and kissed me before I knew what was happening. I didn't kiss her back. Isabel, are you trying to destroy my life?" Liam asked. He turned back and faced Meggie. "I'm so sorry you had to see that."

Liam turned back to face Isabel, "our friendship is toxic, I want out,"

"Anyway, this relationship wasn't fulfilling my needs anymore, so much for waiting for that long." she said with anger.

"I am sorry if I gave you the wrong impression," Liam said as Isabel walked passed him without looking back.

They stood quite for almost a minute without a word, just soacking in what had just happened.

"I am sorry if I gave you the wrong impression too, it was not my intension," Liam said as he moved closer to Meggie.

Liam held Meggie's hand excited, "please come with me, I have news to share with you about my ancestry,"

"Where to," she asked.

"Follow me," Liam said as she took her to his residence.

He ushered Meggie to the living room and warmed some leftover food he had the previous evening since it was lunchtime.

"I hope you don't mind leftovers," he said as he opened the folder next to Meggie. "This folder is the key to my passed. Thanks to you.

Liam explained to her that his great grandfather was a Brit with African roots. He visited the region and fell in love with a Kalenjin woman in Nandi. They had a boy, and the father took him to England as an infant after his two-year tour. He grew up, traveled broadly, and attended Harvard University for his graduate studies. While there, he had a one-night stand with a nun at the same university and got her pregnant. The letter my grandparents received with the baby in the basket was from the nun, the mother of my grandfather.

"How did you learn all this?" Meggie asked.

"Thanks to your Ancestry DNA gift," he said. "Look how accurate it is. They traced the DNA to one of my cousins by the name Kipng'eno Barsirian. My middle name, which my mother insisted that I should have, is Barsy."

"Amazing, this is one in a million, Liam," Meggie said.

"You're saying your great grandfather was a Brits Kalenjin?" she asked and laughed.

"Yes. That is, if Ancestry is telling the truth," he said.

"You're a Kale—the short name for the Kalenjin tribe.

"I'm not a vegetable," Liam brushed her shoulder jokingly.

"This is serious stuff. What are you going to do about it?" Meggie asked.

"I'm excited to learn more about all of my background. For the moment, I know that it's possible for us to have a relationship with both of us bringing our own cultures to the table. Ironically, we now learn that we may have originated from the same place. That's magical," Liam said.

He took a deep breath. "I want to spend eternity with you, Meggie. When you're ready," he said and gave her a quick peck on her check. They finished their food and he cleared the table.

"Meggie, we've been through hard times, and you've been my rock through it all," he said gazing at her. Meggie put down her glass of wine and leaned gently toward him. Liam took her in his arms. She kissed him. Liam reciprocated, gently at first and with increasing passion.

"I've fallen in love with you, too, but I'm scared to take the leap," Meggie said as she came up for air. Then, she kissed him again. Liam held her tightly.

"I've fallen in love with you, and I'm never going to let you go again," Liam told her. She motioned him to stand and guided him to the guest room. Liam stopped her before she could open the door.

"I'll do what you want, you know that?" he asked her. She nodded in agreement. "That is only if you want to," Liam wanted her to be sure. He pulled her back.

She had known what she wanted all along; this time, she dared herself to go all the way. She wanted him very much. The more Liam hesitated, the more Meggie felt her desire for him increase.

He hesitated a little. Liam was sure that if they went into that room, their lives would never be the same. Their lovemaking was going to be a life-changing experience.

"Come on, please," she begged as she leaned toward him. Her insides were inflamed with passion. Meggie touched him and her touch sent delightful shivers through Liam's body. "Kiss me," she begged.

"Not yet." Liam took command and lifted Meggie off her feet. He gently laid her on top of the bed.

"Should we close the door?" Meggie asked.

"No one is here, just you and me," he said with a smile as he hurriedly stepped back, took off his shirt and undid his belt buckle. Meggie watched, breath catching in her throat. Her first sight of Liam's body made her feel a tantalizing ripple of deep excitement. He had broad shoulders, hard muscles, and a taut, narrow waistline. She moaned for what was below his waistline. He was like a sentinel on parade. Liam, now completely nude, reached over to Meggie, impatiently pulling off her peach-colored dress, then reached around and undid the snaps on her bra, taking time with her nipples. With a smoothness, he lifted off and looked at her beautiful shape. She moaned and let out a sharp cry as he took her to a place, she had never been. It was a new beginning for both of them.

"I've decided that I want to have a relationship with you, if your offer is still open," Meggie said as they took her luggage to Liam's car the next day.

He kissed her in response, signifying his agreement to their relationship. Then, he reluctantly took her back to her apartment. Just as they were pulling up in front of Meggie's apartment, Meggie's cell phone rang interrupting them. The caller invited Meggie to a leadership summit in Washington, D.C. The audience was 200 African youth representing the fifty-four nations of the African continent. They would gather in Washington, D.C., to be inspired and in turn inspire those in their communities for the next generation of leaders and entrepreneurs. Her viral video had encouraged many. The attendees wanted to hear from her, and they asked for her to be one of the featured speakers at the closing of the summit in two weeks. Meggie explained the call to Liam, who was excited for her.

"I'll be there with the audience rooting for you in D.C.," he said, touching her cheek and looking into the eyes of the woman he loved.

CHAPTER 24

A Secure Africa

MEGGIE TRAVELED TO THE SUMMIT with Liam. Her highly anticipated speech did not disappoint. Meggie strode to the podium and adjusted the microphone. She paused, looked intently at the audience for about ten seconds, then picked up the mic and approached the audience. In a strong voice she said:

"Once upon a time, there were two boys, George and Kiptarbei. Both were born to ordinary families in a remote village in the Great Rift Valley in Kenya. They spoke the Tugen tribal language. They kept livestock and cultivated sorghum and millet for their subsistence. Then, British settlers and the missionaries came, and their lives diverged. George became a Christian, and Kiptarbei kept the Tugen cultural practices. Their lifestyles became incompatible. They clashed and parted ways. George ended up going to school, pastored a church, married, and had two children, Edwin and Lea. Kiptabei never went to a formal school but received his education, in the Tugen informal way. He became an elder in the society, married, and had one daughter, Elizabeth. At the time when both Kiptarbei and George had kids, the western settlers' culture and the Tugen traditional culture assimilated and every child was expected to

attend school. Kiptarbei and George crossed paths later again with the marriage of their children, Edwin and Elizabeth. Edwin and Elizabeth lived different lives than their parents."

She paused, then returned the microphone to the stand. She waved to the audience and said, *"Hello, everyone. Thank you for inviting me. My name is Meggie Jepchumba. I'm the daughter of Edwin and Elizabeth, and I'm going to speak to you today about us—you, me, and our home. This is a story about daughters and sons of Africa."*

Everyone stood and applauded her.

She approached the audience. *"You are about 200, I was told. Add me and the number increases to 201,"* she paused. *"The story we are told is that one in every two of us will die of HIV/AIDS. If we go by that statistic, half of us right here are sick. I have a question for you,"* she raised her voice. *"Who should tell the story about us?"*

She pointed the microphone to the audience. Multiple audible responses included "us," or "we should." She turned the microphone to herself and again asked, *"Who is telling the story about us now?"* She turned back the microphone to the audience for a few inaudible murmurs from the audience, then silence. She went back to the podium and replaced the microphone in the holder.

In a somber voice, she said, *"It's not me, nor is it you. It's pop culture, cable TV, and every online social media outlet imaginable. They've branded the African continent in ways that aren't pretty. We're called simple, primitive, unsophisticated savage, war-torn, famine-prone, disease-infested, lawless, vile, dark, and the list goes on. These outsiders paint with a broad brush. Breaking news frequently describes the worst experiences in general terms. The worst is what sticks—it doesn't matter whether what's said is true or false. You know why? The uglier the story, the more traction and followers. Many cite Africa as an example of a continent that lags behind the rest of the world. We, the sons and daughters of Africa, have the real story to tell. The true story deserves to be told by those who live it. We must become the experts at our own story.*

Do you know what that story is?" Meggie asked the audience. *"I do. Africa has great abundance in its natural resources. It is inhabited by the most beautiful, generous people, with incredible cultural diversity. The African continent has fifty-four independent counties. Each country has varied tribes, which speak unique languages. Every tribe has distinctive characteristics, values, traditions, music, style, cuisine, and architecture, among many other aspects. Some experts estimate that Africa has about 3,000 distinct ethnic groups that speak about 2,000 unique languages.*

African people are the most genetically diverse compared with any other continent. We could add, exotic, hard-working, and resilient. I get goosebumps when I think of Africa and her people. My DNA runs deep with African roots, and I am proud to be an African. I am proud of my continent, my ancestry, my brothers and sisters throughout the world. Damn Proud!" The applause was thunderous. Meggie tapped a sensitive nerve and the audience was fired up.

"Like any other continent, Africa has come a long way. Every generation is stronger than the one before because of the foundation laid by those who came before them. My grandparents, George and Kiptarbei, survived despite great obstacles, because of their grit and resilience. My mom and dad were steadfast and worked hard, and here I am, standing in front of you carrying forth their legacy. I am here because my family is an example of many that make up the fabric of our motherland. I am fortunate because my family is secure and by that, I mean healthy, educated, and informed. Security in a family derives from being peaceful and prosperous and is sustained when that society is powerful."

Meggie invited the audience to follow her thought process. She posed a 'what if' question in a somber voice. *"What if dreams came true? What would my life be then? Where would I be?"* She paused and looked to the audience to affirm what she believed. *"Dreams are magical. Those thoughts, images, and emotions that pass through your mind during sleep or with our eyes wide open are truly miraculous. Keep them alive. Look to the past and your everyday heroes. Each one of them had the courage and self-discipline to make their dreams into reality. Your dreams and ambitions sometimes may defy the understanding of the current generations. Right now, your presence here is a testimony of your extraordinary vision—a magical African continent, which is a different world to wake up to, one that is secure, healthy, educated, informed, peaceful, prosperous, and powerful.*

By the way, it already started a while back; from M-Pesa, the money app, to iCow, the communication tool, to Ashifi Gogo that fights counterfeit drugs, to safeMotos, a safety app, and Tupuca, the home delivery app. The list is endless. These are examples of the work of young sons and daughters of Africa. Each of their extraordinary inventions or innovations started with a great dreamer. And all of you are great dreamers. What you already do is testimony to that. You show courage and resilience. You have the strength and passion for keeping your dreams alive, which is solid evidence that you have no illusions about your dreams. You are fully awake, fired up, and already working on fulfilling your dreams to break the cycle of generational issues across the globe.

Each one of you is special because you have the power to dream big. Some of you may not even know it, but you have that capacity. Use that ability. Many will underestimate your intelligence and wisdom. What they do not know is that you have already owned the responsibilities of the future, and you are not looking back. Isn't that why you are all here?" Meggie asked the audience.

The current generation may sometimes be afraid of change. They tell you to accept the things they cannot change, that your ideas are over your heads, and you've said 'enough is enough.' The train just left the station, and those who are not riding along will be left behind because change is inevitable. The time is now. This change is not a request but a demand.

You demand a secure home, a continent that is conscious about creating the abundance that leaves plenty for everyone. You will realize that this dream, is not just a pipe dream. We, the sons and daughters of Africa, will work hard until everyone survives. All of us together must work toward building homes where parents, guardians, and communities have sufficient resources and support to focus on raising children in an environment of love and understanding, while in peace.

You have come to realize that you are the generation that Africa has been waiting for to make the changes that you wish to see. The wait has come to an end because staying stuck in a world that is not of your dreams is not an option.

You are not naïve enough to think that challenges will not come your way. You are aware of some who have already dismissed you for your lack of experience and judgment. They are unaware that you already see what is wrong and are no longer going to wait for change that is not coming.

Many great people along the way will honor your course and lend a helping hand to support your goals. Cherish their wisdom. Remember their wise words, particularly when you are going through obstacles that cast a shadow of fear and doubt on your journey. Listen keenly when you can, use knowledge or information from them to confidently make the best decisions possible.

At times, you will face cowards who only comprehend the language of strength and the threat of force. Do not fall for their conniving tactics. Let them wake up to a better tomorrow. By then, they will need to catch up to survive in the new order of peace and prosperity with different rules of engagement.

In today's world, be it in schools, communities, institutions, organizations, local and national governments, there exist bullies, partisanship, manipulations, and misrepresentations, among other issues. Many of you may have experienced these roadblocks already in one way or another. Occasionally, you may have a big brother or sister, a friend, a teacher, or a neighbor with the courage to stand up for you. In some cases, the powerful undermine and discredit anything that challenges their perspective by branding your message as a false narrative so that no one will believe you. Some will be desperate enough to threaten you with underhanded tactics to discourage you from moving forward with your vision. Don't be surprised if a time comes when you have to buckle up tightly with the courage to go it alone. Do not lose focus. Instead, bring all the passion, determination, patience, resilience, and power you have to get the job done.

Teamwork and collaboration will be critical. Your generation's diverse culture, professions, knowledge, and skills will be essential in understanding and addressing both current and emergent issues.

You might be surprised by how much good prevails in the world. For those distressed and consumed by darkness, use light as your weapon of choice. Remember, you will face assaults by people using every trick imaginable to corrupt you—to turn you rotten like they are. You can detect their sorry asses before they know it and call them out on their lies and misrepresentations. I would urge you to always choose light.

When I look around, I see in all of you what I see in me. We're sick and tired of outsourcing our story. If you feel the same way, let's treat our responses with the urgency and the passion they deserve. I believe with all my heart that if the sons and daughters of Africa hold fast to their dreams, every family will be secure. I believe we can make everyone healthy, educated, and informed. I believe that our motherland, Africa, will be peaceful and prosperous because we can sustain a powerful society. Thank you, and God bless each one of you." Meggie concluded her speech and received a standing ovation.

CPSIA information can be obtained
at www.ICGtesting.com
Printed in the USA
FSHW011952291020
75392FS